Three powerful tycoons!

*ee thrilling, sexy romances from three
favourite Mills & Boon authors!*

In November 2008 Mills & Boon bring
you two classic collections, each
featuring three favourite romances
by our bestselling authors…

IN THE GREEK'S BED

The Greek Tycoon's Wife
by Kim Lawrence
The Greek Millionaire's Marriage
by Sara Wood
The Greek Surgeon by Margaret Barke

TO CLAIM HIS MISTRESS

Mistress at a Price by Sara Craven
Mother and Mistress by Kay Thorpe
His Mistress's Secret by Alison Frase

In the Greek's Bed

THE GREEK TYCOON'S WIFE
by
Kim Lawrence

THE GREEK MILLIONAIRE'S MARRIAGE
by
Sara Wood

THE GREEK SURGEON
by
Margaret Barker

 MILLS & BOON®
Pure reading pleasure™

*Harlequin Mills & Boon Limited,
Eton House, 18-24 Paradise Road, Richmond, Surrey TW9 1SR*

IN THE GREEK'S BED

ISBN: 978 0 263 86136 5

05-1108

*Printed and bound in Spain
by Litografia Rosés S.A., Barcelona*

THE GREEK TYCOON'S WIFE

by

Kim Lawrence

MILLS & BOON
100 YEARS
of pure reading pleasure

100 Reasons to Celebrate

We invite you to join us in celebrating
Mills & Boon's centenary. Gerald Mills and
Charles Boon founded Mills & Boon Limited
in 1908 and opened offices in London's Covent
Garden. Since then, Mills & Boon has become
a hallmark for romantic fiction, recognised
around the world.

We're proud of our 100 years of publishing
excellence, which wouldn't have been achieved
without the loyalty and enthusiasm of our
authors and readers.

Thank you!

Each month throughout the year there will
be something new and exciting to mark the
centenary, so watch for your favourite authors,
captivating new stories, special limited
edition collections…and more!

Kim Lawrence lives on a farm in rural Anglesey. She runs two miles daily and finds this an excellent opportunity to unwind and seek inspiration for her writing! It also helps her keep up with her husband, two active sons, and the various stray animals which have adopted them. Always a fanatical consumer of fiction, she is now equally enthusiastic about writing. She loves a happy ending!!

Don't miss Kim Lawrence's exciting new novel, *Desert Prince, Defiant Virgin*, available this month from Mills & Boon® Modern™.

CHAPTER ONE

ONLY the privileged few ever got to see the top floor of the towering glass edifice that was the Lakis Building, and entry to the boardroom was even more exclusive. It therefore came as something of a shock to the élite few gathered there when the big double doors crashed open in the middle of a board meeting.

Nikos Lakis, silver shards of annoyance filtering into his dark almond-shaped eyes, opened his mouth to deliver a devastating reprimand, then closed it again as the identity of the intruder was revealed.

The attractive redhead strode into the room and planted her hands on her curvy hips just as Nikos's breathless PA appeared behind her. The younger woman rolled her eyes and shrugged apologetically towards her boss before retreating post-haste.

'Well!' There was a long dramatic pause, timed to perfection, before Caitlin Lakis delivered her punchline.

It was worth the build-up.

'Is it true, Nik? Are you actually planning to marry *that* woman? Have you lost your mind...?'

Caitlin didn't actually expect her stepson to defend his actions or lack of them to her. In her experience Greek men in general were not prone to explaining themselves and the Lakis men in particular.

The individual these scathing accusations were aimed at appeared to be the only person around the long table who was not excruciatingly embarrassed by the attack. During the pulsating pause that followed his stepmother's heated harangue Nikos sat there calmly rotating the pen he held between his long brown fingers.

'If nobody has any objections…?'

The suited figures he addressed showed no inclination to object, most would sooner have leapt from the twentieth-floor plate-glass window that revealed the city below than disagree with him. Two years earlier they had been reluctantly prepared to accept his presence just because of who his father was, most had not thought he would last long.

Now the respect they gave him was based on the fact they knew he delivered the goods. The playboy had turned out to have a brain like a steel trap and nerves to match. He gave his all and expected those around him to do no less.

'Then I think that's it for today. Thank you, gentlemen.'

The board members got to their feet with alacrity.

'How is Father?'

'Your father is fine. Don't change the subject,' Caitlin retorted. 'I'm waiting.'

Nikos appeared more amused than dismayed by this stern pronouncement as, one dark brow raised, his glance slid significantly towards the men who were hurriedly gathering their belongings.

Though she looked irritated, Caitlin managed to restrain herself until the door closed behind the last of the board members; she even responded politely to several stilted enquiries after her health.

A flicker of amusement slid into Nikos's silver-shot eyes as he watched her efforts to contain her frustration. The woman who had married his father some eighteen years earlier had many virtues, but patience wasn't one of them. Though he conceded Caitlin had been patient enough when it had come to gaining the trust of her suspicious stepsons.

He could recall the exact moment she had won him over. He still couldn't decide if her display of ignorance and panic when faced with a table groaning with antique silver and priceless porcelain had been genuine or just for his benefit.

'It doesn't really matter what fork you use,' he'd explained. 'Just act like you know what you're doing and people will think they've got it wrong.'

For a full sixty seconds Caitlin had stared at the twelve-year-old before shaking her head and exclaiming, 'That could have been your father talking.'

Nikos had felt a warm glow at her words.

'You must be thinking of Dimitri.' Dimitri the favoured eldest, was being groomed to take over from his father.

'Dimitri looks like Spyros,' Caitlin conceded. 'But you…' she tapped her head '…think like him…'

Now the owner of her own successful fashion business, Caitlin, an extremely attractive forty-five, didn't look so very much different as she had done back then.

'Right, they've gone,' she said briskly the moment the big double doors closed. 'Though I think it's a bit late for discretion. Since I got to Athens that's all I've been hearing…*when is the wedding?*' She gave a snort. 'You can't tell me you're in love with Livia Nikolaidis.'

'What's love?'

Caitlin rolled her eyes and clicked her tongue at this blatant piece of provocation. 'So you've had a couple of bad experiences…who hasn't?' she snapped unsympathetically. 'So kindly spare me the weary cynicism and stop avoiding the issue, Nik.'

Nikos accepted the reprimand with a rueful grin.

Caitlin might be his stepmother, but she was female and her stern expression briefly softened perceptively.

Even as she tartly observed, 'You should smile more,' she privately conceded he maybe didn't have that much time or reason to smile since the responsibilities of the entire Lakis empire had fallen on his shoulders. No matter how broad those shoulders might be—in Nikos's case, enough for two average men.

'I'm not in love with Livia,' he admitted calmly.

Being in love with Livia might have been an obstacle to their successful union, because if he'd been in love he wouldn't have been able to see that though Livia was beautiful and accomplished she was also extremely selfish and terminally vain. This way he had no unreasonable expectations of her that might later disappoint him. And Livia, being a product of a background very similar to his own, would not make unreasonable demands on him and his time.

Caitlin gave a deep sigh of relief. 'Then it's not true, you haven't been seeing her...'

'Did I say that? Many women fantasise about marrying a rich man...'

'My, you do have a high opinion of my sex.'

Nikos acknowledged his stepmother's dig with a shrug. 'I can only speak from my own experience.'

'Which is wide and varied...' Despite the disapproval in her tone Caitlin didn't find it particularly surprising that her stepson had gained this jaundiced perspective of women. From the moment he hit puberty girls *and* women had been drawn to him like a magnet and he was selling himself short if he thought his wealth was the only thing they were after.

'The reality of marriage to the man who is responsible for the day to day running of the Lakis business is something which many women couldn't handle.'

'I did,' Caitlin reminded him. The severity of her expression softened. 'With a little help from my friends.'

'You are an exceptional woman. Livia is not exceptional, but she is born to the life. I think Livia and I might suit very well.'

Caitlin stared at him, horrified; it seemed there was nothing more humourless or stupid than a reformed playboy. *'Oh, my God...!'*

'I take it you don't like Livia,' Nikos observed, smiling in an indulgent manner his stepmother found extremely provocative.

'My liking her has nothing whatever to do with it.'

Nikos raised one eloquent winged brow.

'Well, maybe a bit,' his stepmother conceded, thinking of the perfectly groomed brunette with the calculating smile and the hard eyes. As she worriedly scanned her handsome stepson's face her antagonism slipped away, leaving an expression of deep concern. 'Nik, darling, she's all wrong for you. You *can't* marry her.'

'That's true, I can't—not while I'm already married.'

His stepmother fell gracefully off her chair.

'Wow, what a rock!' Sadie breathed, catching hold of her friend's small hand before she could hide it beneath the table. She blinked as the diamond, which seemed almost too heavy for the younger girl's finger, caught the light. 'It's gorgeous,' she said enviously. 'Though I have to admit,' she mused, lifting her eyes to Katie's slightly flushed face, 'I'd have thought you'd have gone for something a little less…'

'Flashy…?' Katie responded without thinking. She frowned to hear the wistful edge in her voice. There was just no pleasing some people, she chided herself irritably.

'Less…conventional,' Sadie contradicted tactfully. 'Something to go with your charity-shop bargains. It's so unfair, I spend more on clothes in a week than you do in a year and look at me!' she invited gloomily. 'Maybe if I didn't eat for a month clothes would look like that on me…' With an envious sigh she examined her friend's tall, effortlessly slender figure. 'No, that wouldn't work—I'd end up with even smaller boobs than I already have!'

She eyed the younger girl's well-defined bosom with good-natured resentment and then philosophically bit into the last cream cake on the plate.

Katie's thoughts drifted as she sat looking at her finger, thinking a little wistfully of the ruby ring set with seed pearls she'd seen in the window of a small antique shop.

The one Tom had seemed to quite like until he had got a look at the modest price tag; then he had dismissed it as a pretty trifle not worthy of consideration.

'You pay for quality,' he explained patiently as they left the shop empty-handed. 'What a peculiar girl you are,' he added with a perplexed expression on his open, good-looking face. 'Tell most girls price is no object and they'd head for the most expensive jewellers in town. I'm not a mean man, sweetheart.'

'I know that. In fact you're *too* generous, Tom.' A frown pleated Katie's broad, smooth forehead. Tom just wasn't able to accept the fact that she would have been just as happy with an inexpensive token as the extravagant gifts he showered her with.

'Well, once we're married you'll have to get used to it,' Tom announced. 'You're a beautiful woman, you deserve beautiful things, and I,' he told her firmly, 'am going to make sure you get them. Whether you like it or not,' he added with a determined grin.

'But all I want is you, Tom,' she told him earnestly.

Tom looked startled and then pleased as he drew her to his side. '*Really…?*'

'Of course really.' Katie was uneasily aware that she sounded like someone trying to convince herself. 'I guess I'm just not a very…demonstrative person,' she admitted regretfully.

'I've told you I don't mind waiting,' he told her quietly. 'I admire your principles, darling.'

Principles or just a low sex drive…?

Katie ignored the vexatious voice in her head and reminded herself how incredibly lucky she was to have discovered such a sensitive, understanding man who loved her to distraction.

But not so much distraction that he can't keep his hands off you… Katie muttered to herself.

With extra warmth she pressed a soft kiss to Tom's lips.

After all, why would you want to be with a man who would be unable to restrain his base animal urges…? The sarcastic voice in her head just had to have the last word.

'Tom really liked this one,' she told her friend.

'That figures.' Sadie bit her lip and looked apologetic. 'Sorry, love, but you have to admit he does operate on a strict "if you've got it, flaunt it" policy.'

Katie sighed. 'I know, but he means well, Sadie, and he really is the *kindest* man I've ever met,' she told the older girl earnestly.

And dull as ditch water! 'So it's official now.'

For six months Tom Percival had pursued Katie with single-minded determination.

Sadie balanced her chin on her steepled fingers. 'So how did he take it when you told him?'

Katie took a sip of her tea; her grimace wasn't because the liquid was hot. 'Well, actually…' she began, avoiding eye contact.

Sadie gasped. 'You *did* tell him…?'

Katie's shoulders hunched defensively as Sadie's shocked response reinforced her guilt. 'He was so happy and I was waiting for the right moment.' It sounded a pathetically lame excuse even to her own ears.

Sadie groaned so loudly that half the people in the tea shop turned around to look at them. 'When would be a better time—at the altar?' she croaked, gazing at the younger woman incredulously. 'Listen, I'd be the first to agree that what happened before he came along is none of his business, a girl's skeletons are her affair, but you're still *married*, love. That does sort of make it relevant.'

'I know…I know!' Katie closed her eyes and twisted her fingers. 'I just don't *feel* married. I was *going* to tell him…I *will* tell him, but I might as well wait now until I hear back from Harvey.'

'Harvey's the lawyer who brokered the marriage deal?' Katie nodded.

'He sounds a bit shady to me.'

Hearing the very proper and fairly prim Harvey Reynolds, QC described this way made Katie smile; she felt she had to defend his good name.

'Well, he isn't, he's one of the top criminal lawyers in the country. I've known him since I was a little girl.' She caught her full lower lip between her teeth and gnawed gently on the soft pink flesh. 'I can't see that there will be any problem getting a quickie divorce…?'

Sadie's eyebrows lifted to a satirical angle. 'I'm probably not the best person to be asking about amicable divorces,' she responded drily.

'It's not like it was a real marriage or anything.' Surely that made a difference.

'Have you *really* not seen him since the ceremony?'

Katie shook her head, she wasn't surprised at the incredulity in her friend's voice. Who wouldn't be shocked about someone marrying a total stranger? Heck, she was herself. Sometimes it seemed to her as if it had happened to someone else.

'No, not for seven years. My only link is Harvey. It always was.' The assistance of her mother's patient, but ultimately unsuccessful admirer had only been forthcoming when Katie had convinced him that she would go ahead with her plan with or without his help.

'If you're thinking about recruiting someone whose visa is running out and wants to stay in the country, forget it,' Harvey had told her in the plush surrounding of his City chambers. 'Unless, that is, you *want* to expose yourself to criminal prosecution.' He pushed his metal-framed half-moon glasses up his thin nose and looked at her severely.

'I hadn't thought of that,' Katie admitted with wide-eyed dismay.

'Seems to me you haven't thought much at all.'

'If you're going to try and stop me…'

'If I thought I had any chance of succeeding I would,'

the legal brain admitted with engaging candour. 'For your mother's sake I want to make sure you think this thing through properly—if such a thing is possible?'

'She was very fond of you too.'

Poor Harvey; there had only ever been one man for her mother and she had given up everything to be with him. Katie had wondered whether she'd ever find a love like that—one that didn't think of consequences, one that lasted for ever. She wasn't actually sure she wanted to. The idea of falling victim to such a blind, relentless passion was actually rather scary.

'You do appreciate that it's very unlikely that the sort of man who would marry you for a one-off payment would be satisfied with that?'

'How do you mean?'

'I mean there's a strong possibility that a man like that would have questionable scruples. He'd be back for more,' Harvey explained bluntly. 'And then there's the question of making yourself vulnerable to blackmail.'

'But there won't be any money, I'm giving the rest away.' Katie couldn't help but think that dealing with hardened criminals had made Harvey a little overly suspicious.

'That's another thing—is it really wise to give up your *entire* inheritance too?'

'Non-negotiable,' Kate interrupted abruptly.

'In that case—' the lawyer sighed '—how do you feel about raising the amount you'd pay the groom?'

'By how much?'

Harvey told her and she gasped. 'You've got to be kidding…?'

'It might seem a lot, well, actually it is a lot,' he conceded. 'But in the long run I really think this is your safest bet. As it happens I know of a person who needs an injection of cash and for reasons I can't go into he prefers not to approach the usual sources…'

'Five hundred thousand pounds is quite a big injection,' she began doubtfully.

'True, but the capital left over would still be more than enough to provide a very generous income for the Grahams, and there would be no question of this man ever demanding anything else of you or troubling you in any way. I'd personally guarantee that.'

'Why does this man need so much money?' she asked bluntly.

'I'm really not at liberty to discuss that, the choice is yours. All I can say is that I will *personally* guarantee this person's integrity.'

Even if this man was shady, what were her alternatives? She could advertise in a personal column but, Harvey was right, what sort of weirdos would respond to an ad for a husband?

'All right, then.'

'Excellent. All I have to do now is persuade N...him...'

'Persuade *him*...?'

'Don't worry, dear, I'm sure he'll come around,' Harvey soothed.

He had come around and up until now Katie had had no reason to regret her decision.

'So this man you married, he could be anywhere, doing anything...he might even be dead. Oh, that would be convenient.'

Her friend's joking words jolted Katie back to the present. *'Sadie!'*

Sadie grinned sheepishly. 'Well, it would. I'm just being practical.'

'I want to divorce the man, not put out a contract on him!'

Sadie normally respected the younger girl's reserve but at that moment her curiosity got the better of her. 'So all you know about this man is his name?'

Katie had never elaborated beyond saying that marriage

had been the only way she'd been able to inherit the money from her Greek grandfather's estate. Which begged the question why was Katie flat broke these days?

Katie nodded. 'Nikos Lakis.' She found herself strangely reluctant to say the name.

'Is he Greek?'

'I assumed so.'

'Nikos Lakis…mmm. Did he look as sexy as he sounds?' Sadie giggled huskily. 'Or was he short, fat and balding?'

'I can't remember,' Kate replied shortly. She wasn't quite sure why she lied. Many of her memories of that day were hazy, but not the face of the man she had stood beside and exchanged solemn vows with.

She didn't know what she'd been expecting but it hadn't been Nikos Lakis.

Harvey, watching her face anxiously as the tall Greek had arrived, must have seen the spasm of shock that had passed over her features.

'I suppose there is a little resemblance to your brother,' he murmured, intuitively sensing the source of her distress. 'I should have said…'

Katie shook her head. 'He's not really like him.'

She wasn't just saying this to make Harvey feel better. Peter's face had been extremely attractive, but stood next to this man he would have been invisible. Her twin hadn't possessed the sheer physical presence that this stranger had in abundance.

As the stranger she was about to marry inclined his dark head in acknowledgement of Harvey and turned his attention briefly to her, Katie saw there was none of Peter's petulance in this austerely beautiful face, nor any of the warmth. In fact, she saw as he came closer that he wasn't anything like her twin at all.

This man was ice.

Seven years later she was helpless to control the little shudder that slipped down her spine or the nervous flutter in her tummy as she visualised those silver-shot midnight-dark eyes fringed by decadently dark lashes set in an otherwise starkly uncompromising bronzed face.

Even if he hadn't been an attention-grabbing six feet five of solid bone and muscle and moved with the natural grace of a top-class athlete, who could forget those eyes…? She hadn't. They'd even featured in some disturbingly erotic dreams that had disrupted her sleep over the years.

'*He's alive.*'

Sadie raised her eyebrows at her friend's emphatic tone.

'Actually I've never seen anybody quite *so* alive.' His vitality had been like an electric current. His brief touch had made her skin tingle and she'd been relieved he hadn't prolonged the contact more than absolutely necessary.

'I thought you couldn't remember what he looked like.' Sadie watched the distant, almost dreamy expression cross the younger woman's face.

'I can't, it was just an impression,' Katie replied a little quickly, too stubborn to admit even to herself the impact her bought bridegroom had made on her.

'Quite a coincidence you both being Greek.'

Katie's soft lips firmed and her eyes filled with scorn. 'I'm *half* Greek.'

It was a half that showed in the contours of her oval face with its proud, high forehead, straight classical nose, delicately sculpted lips and long, swan-like neck. It was also a half she was always ready to deny. The half that had heartlessly cast off the daughter who had offended their precious family honour.

Not even after her husband had died and she'd been left to bring up two young children on the small salary she'd earned working part-time as a legal secretary had Katie's mother tried to contact her family who had rejected her on her wedding day.

Katie and her twin had been brought up with very little

knowledge of their mother's culture, which suited Katie fine. She had no time for people who could punish a woman for falling in love outside her class and culture. No, as far as she was concerned she was all British.

CHAPTER TWO

KEPT late by an unexpected emergency at work, Katie rang Tom to arrange to go directly to the hotel where they were having dinner. She dashed home, fed the cat, a particularly evil-tempered ginger tom called Alexander, and got changed in record time. As she emerged from the taxi nothing about her demeanour hinted at the breathless haste with which she'd got ready.

High heels crunching on the gravel, Katie hurried across the forecourt unable to dismiss the nagging feeling she had forgotten something. Walking into the brightly lit foyer, she smoothed down her freshly washed hair, which she hadn't had the time to blow-dry properly; it fell river-straight almost to her waist, gleaming like the finest spun silk under the bright lights, which picked out the rich chestnut highlights in the deep glossy brown strands.

Tom was waiting. His face lit up as she appeared and his obvious pleasure made Katie glad she had decided to wear the dress Sadie had given her with a plea for her to make use of it.

Tom kissed her hard on the mouth, which was surprising; he was normally quite undemonstrative in public. 'You look beautiful!' he said huskily as they drew apart.

'You sound surprised…' Her teasing hid a secret worry. Was it entirely normal to be thinking about whether you'd remembered to unlock the cat flap while you were being passionately kissed by the man you were going to marry? 'It must be the dress.' Though he never openly criticised the way she dressed, Katie knew he would have liked her to dress up more.

'I didn't even notice the dress,' Tom replied huskily.

'Well, there's not a lot to notice, is there?' she responded, glancing uncertainly down at the midnight-blue slip dress that clung to the soft curves of her body a little too lovingly for her comfort. 'You don't think it's a bit... *obvious*?'

The appeal made Tom throw back his head and laugh. 'You couldn't look anything but cool and classy if you tried, and I'm the luckiest man in the world.'

He might not think so soon.

Katie took a deep breath. There was never going to be a good time to tell him this, so now, she reasoned, was as good a time as any other.

'Tom, there's something I need to tell you,' she told him urgently.

A flicker of impatience crossed her fiancé's boyishly handsome features. 'We'll talk about it later, sweetheart,' he said, grabbing her hand. 'We're late as it is, and Nikos isn't used to people keeping him waiting.'

The name was so unexpected it hit her like a blow, snatching the air from her lungs and the thoughts from her head. There was a loud whooshing noise in her ears and it took several heart-thudding seconds before the room stopped spinning.

'*Nikos...?*' she faltered. 'That's a pretty unusual name.'

'Not in Greece.'

No way could fate be that cruel. 'He's Greek...?' she asked with extreme casualness.

Tom nodded. 'That's right. We were at Oxford University at the same time, though Nik dropped out before he graduated.'

'That doesn't sound like someone you'd know...' Katie gulped hoarsely. Dropping out equated with someone being reckless, someone who might at a push get into debt, someone who might resolve the problem by... *Stop this*, she told herself sternly, *you're getting paranoid*.

'You mean I'm a boring old stick.' Tom pouted, exploiting his boyish charm for all it was worth.

'You're not old…' Katie protested, subduing a flicker of irritation. 'Or boring,' she added hastily. 'You're solid and responsible.'

'That makes me feel a hell of a lot better,' Tom responded, his charm fading abruptly.

Conscious she had hurt his feelings, Katie tried to soothe his injured pride.

'Women don't actually want to marry exciting men,' Katie told him, believing it. 'They're too unreliable.' She stopped, unhappily aware that she was only making matters worse.

To her relief Tom recovered his humour and laughed loudly.

'No, they just want to make mad passionate love to them,' he suggested, thinking she looked especially adorable flushed and confused.

'Some women might, but not me,' Katie insisted firmly. 'Men like that are vain and shallow and only interested in looking cool,' she sneered.

Tom winced. 'You'll not share that with Nikos will you, sweetheart?'

'I shall hang on his every word like it's inscribed in stone,' she promised dutifully, willing to flatter his friend if it made Tom happy.

'You'll like him.'

Katie couldn't hide her scepticism.

'Women do,' Tom assured her authoritatively. 'Actually you're right, Nik wasn't in my circles of friends; in fact he was a bit of a loner. He used to ride around on this dirty great motor bike…'

Katie nodded. She was beginning to get the picture, and she didn't find it comforting. Someone reckless, who liked danger…her imagination had no problem at all picturing

Nikos Lakis in motor-bike leathers looking brooding and dangerous.

'I was there when he swerved to avoid a kid that ran out into the road. I didn't do much, but he got it into his head that I'd saved his life.'

Katie listened to his modest pronouncement with a tender smile. 'Which means you probably did.'

'I only did what anyone else would,' Tom insisted with a self-deprecating shrug. 'To be honest I was surprised when he kept in touch after he left. Apparently it caused some almighty family row when he dropped out, but everything's cosy now. His old man had a heart attack and major bypass surgery a couple of years ago and Nik took over the family firm…they're a Greek shipping family, though since the seventies they've diversified dramatically…They're billionaires… Are you all right?' he added, examining her waxily pale face with concern.

Katie took a deep breath and refocused on his anxious face. Relief made her feel quite light-headed. A Greek billionaire's son! She felt like laughing at her irrational fears. Let him be the biggest bore of the century; it no longer mattered.

'Fine.' She lifted her hand briefly to her forehead and felt a light sheen of moisture on her skin. 'Minor blood-sugar dip, I didn't have time for lunch today,' she admitted, making a silent vow to tell Tom the truth before the evening was out.

Tom frowned disapprovingly. 'They take advantage of you at that place.' He squeezed her shoulder. 'Never mind, not long now and you'll be able to hand in your notice.'

'Hand in my notice?' Katie echoed blankly.

Tom laughed. 'You'll be far too busy to work when you're my wife. Of course, if you want to continue with a little charity work…'

Katie could hardly believe what she was hearing—Tom

expected her to quit work when they were married! There was no way!

'You've got a bit more colour in your cheeks now,' he observed, blissfully unaware that it was hostility to her impending retirement that had produced the delicate tinge of creamy rose to her pale honey complexion. 'Come on, love, the sooner we feed you the better.'

'And your friend doesn't like being kept waiting,' Katie couldn't prevent herself from adding drily.

His friend called Nikos.

How stupid she'd been to be spooked by a name. There were most probably hundreds—no, *thousands* of men called Nikos in the world, she told herself as she followed Tom into the dining room.

This isn't happening!

'Here she is, Nikos.' Tom, oblivious to the frozen state of the young woman beside him, proudly pushed her forward. Like a marionette she responded stiffly. 'This is Katie. Didn't I tell you she was totally gorgeous and clever too? Come on, sweetheart, don't be shy…'

Shy? More like paralysed with shock and horror, not to mention being scared witless into the bargain! Oh, God, this meal looked like one she wasn't likely to forget in a hurry!

If the floor had opened up at her feet Katie would have jumped into the black hole rather than live this moment. Even at the best of times she hated it when Tom introduced her to his friends with this sort of fanfare. Maybe there were women out there who could live up to the sort of lavish build-up he gave her, but Katie knew she wasn't one of them.

The dark-suited, long-limbed figure rose with languid, almost feral grace to his feet. 'You did indeed, Tom.'

All thoughts of hallucination vanished. Katie hadn't heard it for seven years, but the deep, cultured voice was exactly as she recalled it. The bitter-chocolate tone with the merest hint of an accent made goose-bumps break out like a rash over her skin and had, she suspected, some worrying connection with her tingly feelings.

Despite her scornful dismissal, the *tingly* feelings continued to make their presence felt.

'Tom's told me so much about you I feel as though we already know each other.'

Unlike her, Tom didn't seem to notice the sinister, sardonic edge in the soft words or see the cold hostility in the other man's remarkable eyes as they roamed casually over her body, lingering longer than was polite on the exposed slopes of her breasts.

Despite the fact disbelief was ricocheting wildly around inside her head, Katie could almost admire his nerve, her own was very near to breaking-point. It wasn't just not knowing how or why he was here—*and that was bad enough!*—it was the not knowing what he was going to do or say next that really terrified her.

Their glances locked, the expression on those finely chiselled features revealed little, but as their eyes briefly touched Katie was left with the definite impression that he was enjoying every second of her discomfiture. It was that discovery that enabled her to hold it together.

Katie welcomed the fortifying flicker of anger; it was something solid and real for her to cling to. The malicious pleasure she'd seen in those dark, unfathomable depths was inexplicable to her. Admittedly buying a husband might make her deserving of the odd sneer and snigger in some ungenerous quarters, but if she'd been doing the buying he'd been bought, which hardly made his position one of superiority...not that you'd know, he looked so damned pleased with himself.

Though that smugness and self-satisfaction might have something to do with the billions he no doubt had in his bank account. *And I gave him money...* When her mind started working again she might be able to figure that one out, but right now she had to swallow a bubble of hysterical laughter; the situation was positively surreal.

'Katie, darling, this is Nikos Lakis.'

Like Tom, he was wearing a dark grey suit; unlike Tom's, it was not cut to disguise a spreading waistline. It was hard to imagine the man standing there indulging himself in the necessary excesses to result in a thickening waistline...everything about him was hard and he exuded an aura that said, 'I'm in control'. She'd not come across many men like that but those she had she hadn't warmed to. They thought the world revolved around them.

Her mind drifted back to the small, stuffy little ante-room of the register office. She recalled the tall, commanding figure so much younger than she'd been expecting who'd strode in displaying an unnerving *presence* and none of the humility she'd expected of a man desperate enough to marry for money. Knowing he'd been born with a solid gold spoon in his distressingly sexy mouth explained the arrogance, but not why a billionaire's son had married for money.

My God, I've been married to a Greek million...no, billionaire for seven years and I didn't even know it. Even the most soapy of daytime soaps wouldn't dare come up with a storyline that far-fetched.

Katie was forced to revise her opinion about control slightly as her wide, shock-glazed eyes slid to the passionate curve of his wide, sensual lips...the light, quivering sensation in her belly intensified. If he did lose control he'd probably do it in a spectacular way. A totally inappropriate mental image of those predatory lips crashing down on her own flashed across her vision...

Katie was just getting on top of her wayward imagination when her nightmare smiled—it wasn't helpful. The smile exuded a sensual menace totally in keeping with her wild imaginings. Her bemused brain sought refuge in irrelevant details like the sculpted curve of his lips and the slashing angle of his high, angular cheekbones. Over the years she'd decided that her imagination had exaggerated the raw sexuality Nikos Lakis exuded—she now knew differently! The man oozed sex appeal from every pore; it was hardly decent.

Katie's obedient lips did the necessary social smiling, but her eyes were another matter; they continued to broadcast horror, confusion and bewilderment.

Tom, cheerfully oblivious to the screaming tension or her reluctance, pulled her farther forward with pride.

'Pleased to meet you, Katherine.' One dark brow quirked. 'It is *Katherine*…?'

She glared…he knew full well it wasn't. Like herself, he had a copy of the marriage certificate that Harvey had locked safely away…*Harvey*! The trusted family friend must have known his identity and he hadn't told her—the duplicity of men was staggering, she thought, wisely skimming over her own forays in that direction of late.

'No, actually it's Katerina.' *Do you, Katerina, take…* She gave her head a little shake to chase away the intrusive memory. 'Only nobody calls me that any more,' she added, anxiety and escalating antipathy making her soft voice terse and sharp.

'That's a pity, it's a beautiful name.'

It was the way he said it, but then a bus timetable would sound dreamy when spoken by that silver tongue. No, not silver—if that deep, velvet-textured drawl had a colour it would be a deep, decadent purple. She gave her head a tiny shake, irritated by the whimsical nature of her thoughts. Purple or puce, a voice like that constituted a very dangerous ability in a male, especially one who looked like this.

If he was as shocked as she had been to discover the identity of his dinner companion he was hiding it well, which meant what? Had he known? Maybe he didn't recognise her? She ditched that possibility before it was even fully formed. Was he here because Harvey had contacted him about the divorce? Or was this one horrible, horrifying coincidence?

Questions she had aplenty, but no obvious answers surfaced in her spinning head.

Oh goodness, why didn't I tell Tom when I had the chance…? She groaned at herself. Now it was too late… he'd hate her, and who could blame him? The fact that this was only happening because she hadn't come clean made it seem as though she was being punished for her cowardice. Perhaps it was appropriate that her retribution had come in the form of a man who possessed the sinful, dangerous beauty of a dark fallen angel.

Lips compressed to keep them from trembling, she shot the tall, dark figure a covert look from under the sweep of her long lashes. What she saw in his lean face was not comforting. *Please, please don't let him say anything until I've had a chance to tell Tom myself.*

That was it! If she could explain to Tom herself…sudden hope surged through her. Maybe it wasn't too late. If she could get this Nikos creature alone and explain how things stood, she could appeal for his temporary silence until she'd had a chance. Their eyes collided; it was a fleeting collision but enough to make her forget about appealing to his better nature. She repressed a shudder—nobody with eyes like that had one!

Of all the men in the world why had she ended up married to this one?

If Nikos Lakis kept quiet about their marriage deal it would be for his own reasons, not out of consideration for her or Tom. Maybe it didn't fit in with his macho image to admit he had married for money, she speculated. Although it seemed to her that Greek men were quite pragmatic about such things. She gritted her teeth; the best she could hope for was that he'd keep silent for his own reasons.

Katie didn't know how her trembling knees managed to

support her weight as her hand was enfolded in a firm grip. Her tummy muscles cramped violently as long, lean brown fingers folded over her own. The contrast of small and large, dark and pale…once again her beleaguered brain was distracted from coping with much more urgent matters like should she beat him to the punchline and tell Tom now herself?

How would she do that exactly…? *Actually, Tom, I've met Nikos before…yes, isn't that a coincidence? I don't know him exactly, we just got married…*

The men were talking, though the words were just a discordant buzz in her ears. Katie found she was sitting but couldn't recall taking her seat. Neither could she recall how the glass found its way into her hand, but it seemed an extremely good idea to make use of it.

With a sigh she replaced the drained glass on the table and as she shook back her hair discovered both men were looking at her.

'Is that such a good idea on an empty stomach, darling?' Tom spoke lightly but his eyes were shooting furious warning messages.

Tom was desperately anxious for her to make a good impression on this man he admired. *If only all Tom had to worry about was me having one too many drinks!* The irony struck her forcibly, and she struggled to control the bubble of hysteria lodged dangerously in her dry throat. Laughing like a hyena might just draw unwanted attention…

'Katie's had a tough day at work.'

Katie's smooth brow wrinkled…again the anxiety to please in Tom's manner. Maybe this wasn't so surprising. Two things impressed Tom, money and power, and this man had both in abundance, and it showed. Tom had money, Tom had power, what he didn't have was the tall Greek's quiet, understated confidence. Confidence that came when you didn't feel the need to prove yourself to anyone.

'You work, Katerina?' The dark winged brows knitted as Nikos Lakis managed to imbue the casual enquiry with amused incredulity.

Katie's eyes narrowed as those black eyes broadcast useless ornament. It seemed as if the antipathy she felt was fully reciprocated.

'When it doesn't interfere with shopping or polishing my nails.'

Tom, who had never heard that particular tone in her soft, pleasing voice before, laughed uncomfortably as though she'd made a joke he didn't quite understand. Nikos didn't laugh; his merciless eyes continued to rake her angry face and then, much to her dismay, his long fingers curled over her left hand, which lay clenched on the table-top.

Without haste he unfurled her tapering fingers one by one. The tip of his thumb grazed the blue-veined inner aspect of her wrist as he turned her hand over, exposing the short, unpolished condition of her nails; his touch also exposed her nerve endings, which came to tingling life.

Katie would have liked to crawl out of her skin.

'Not today,' he remarked softly.

His soft voice did things almost as uncomfortable to her as the light touch. Dabbing her tongue to the tiny beads of sweat across her upper lip, she snatched her hand away.

Breathing hard through her flared nostrils, she lifted her chin. 'I'm an events organiser.' And a flipping good one too, she felt like adding to the patronising prat.

'Impressive,' he drawled, sounding anything but impressed. 'And what does an events organiser do exactly?' he added, making it sound as though as far as he was concerned it couldn't be much.

Tom, sensing the atmosphere for the first time, looked slightly uneasy. 'Katie works for a charity, but she'll be giving up work after the wedding.'

'Ah…the wedding—and when will that be?'

'I can't get Katie to set a date.'

Nikos's lazy glance turned to Katie. '*Really?* You do surprise me.'

He reminded her of some sleek cat playing with a mouse, not because he was particularly hungry, just because it was in his nature to be cruel. The more she saw of this man, the more she saw to dislike. Kate's nostrils flared as her teeth came together in a smile that was as brittle as it was brilliant.

Two could play at this, she thought grimly. If he was going to drop her in it there didn't seem any point prolonging the agony or his pleasure.

It was a dangerous tactic, but Katie felt uncharacteristically reckless, and at least this way she'd know one way or the other.

'And you, Mr Lakis—is there a *Mrs* Lakis?' she enquired sweetly. 'Or any little Lakises?'

Katie held her breath; the silence that followed her question seemed to last for ever. When her lowered gaze lifted she was surprised to see something that might have been admiration in Nikos Lakis's dark, glittering eyes.

'There is only one *Mrs* Lakis in my life, and she's my stepmother, who's very much an active force in my life.' He smiled, not in a snide, snooty, I've-just-stepped-on-something-nasty way—anything but. Katie's jaw dropped as she watched the stern lines of his proudly sculpted face soften as he produced a real, honest-to-goodness grin.

The transformation was nothing short of devastating. Katie only just stopped herself grinning fatuously back.

'So you're not married, then?' she persisted doggedly.

'If Nik had married, Katie, I think we'd have read about it.' Tom laughed. 'The media would have had a field day.'

You don't know the half of it, Katie thought, feeling a tide of guilty colour seep up her neck. She pressed a hand to her hot cheek.

She was disgusted with herself that in her desire to score points against the detestable Nikos Lakis she'd lost track of what was most important. The public humiliation and scandal of having his fiancée revealed as being secretly married to Nikos Lakis would be devastating for Tom and her primary concern had to be protecting him from any fallout.

'Marriage is inevitable if only for the procreation of… how did you put it?…little Lakises. We Greeks are a little old-fashioned about such things.'

'I'd have said cold-blooded.'

Tom began to look seriously disturbed as he laid a warning hand on her shoulder; the pressure made Katie wince. Nikos's eyes followed the other man's gesture, and the permanent line over the bridge of his masterful nose deepened fractionally.

'Shall we order?' Tom said, patting her arm before his hand fell away.

'I'm not hungry.' Katie doubted she could have eaten a scrap even if her future had depended on it, which was no more an absurd scenario than the real one—having her future and Tom's dependent upon the discretion of a man who seemed as capricious as he was overbearing.

'Greeks are not renowned for their cold-bloodedness, Katerina.'

'Oops, was that your ego I stepped on? Oh, but I'm sure they're *spectacular* lovers.' She turned the voltage of her insincere smile up by several watts before allowing it to fade away to grim contempt. 'But pardon me if I happen to think that picking out some poor girl with good child-bearing hips and the right blood lines to produce an heir is *extremely* cold-blooded.'

'Katie!'

Nikos, a smile fixed on his sensual lips, lifted his hand in a soothing gesture to still the other man's appalled protest. 'You are marrying a *romantic*, my friend,' he drawled. 'Someone to whom arranged marriages are anathema.' He scanned her face with derisive eyes. 'Am I right, Katerina?

You would never marry for *anything* but love? Certainly not for anything as base as…security.' His long forefinger seemingly accidentally brushed the diamond nestling on her finger.

His mockery, as corrosive as battery acid, made her long to wipe the smirk off his face. Her hands curled into fists on the table-top.

'In a perfect world everyone would marry for love,' she told him stiffly.

Nikos's mobile lips curled contemptuously. 'So you are a pragmatist after all, which is of course infinitely preferable to a hypocrite.'

At his soft, sibilant words the last remnants of Katie's trepidation were washed away on a violent tide of anger. It was one sneer too many. She lifted her furious sparkling eyes to his lean, dark face—just where did he get off looking down his superior nose at her?

Buying a husband might be a pretty pathetic thing to do, but at least she'd had a damned good excuse, whereas what excuse had Nikos Lakis had? A quick way to get money to fuel his extravagant lifestyle when he'd fallen out of favour with his rich daddy seemed the safest bet. *If anyone is the hypocrite here, it isn't me,* Katie thought scornfully.

Tom, who had the suspicion he was missing something in this rapid exchange, seized on the mention of something he felt he was an expert on. 'Oh, Katie is very practical.'

Nikos looked from the ring on her finger to the diamonds encircling her narrow wrist and smiled. 'That I never doubted. Ah, I hope you don't mind, I ordered champagne,' he said as a wine waiter approached the table.

'Much appreciated, Nik. Isn't it, darling?'

Katie nodded. It pained her deeply to see Tom's unsuspicious pleasure at the empty gesture. Normally an astute man, he couldn't seem to see what was under his nose where Nikos Lakis was concerned. Maybe it was the glamour of his wealth that made Tom blind. As far as she was concerned, the man was a prize creep!

Nikos took the bottle from its bed of ice and personally popped the cork with an expert twist of his long brown fingers and a flick of his strong, supple wrist, but then he would be an expert at drinking champagne and making love to beautiful women, Katie thought sourly, for wasn't that what playboys like him spent their time doing? The irony was that she had probably financed some of that champagne and those women! The realisation only made his attitude all the more hypocritically sanctimonious.

Her chin firmed in determination; they'd had a deal and he'd got his money's worth for precious little effort on his part. She was damned if she was going to let him ruin her life just when it was going where she wanted it with his silent threats, and the first moment she got him alone she was going to tell him so.

The thought of being alone with him made her stomach flip. Katie was surprised to discover that excitement and disgust could sometimes feel much the same thing. Naturally, given the choice she'd never want to be alone with the hateful man, but under the circumstances there wasn't an option.

'To the happy couple.'

Katie, her eyes shining with belligerence, obediently sipped the expensive bubbles, not tasting a thing.

The meal was torture; Nikos's cryptic remarks were so numerous that Katie was sure Tom would catch on. It took all her will-power not to react to his wind-ups. The intrusive chime of Tom's mobile just as they reached the main course was for once something of a welcome break.

He apologised but took the call and spoke for several minutes to someone on the other end. From the way his expression darkened it wasn't hard to tell it was bad news he was hearing.

'I'll be there in about thirty minutes,' he said, before

sliding his phone back into his pocket. 'I'm really sorry, folks.' His apologetic glance slid from Katie to Nikos and back again. 'But I really have to go. That out-of-town development I'm working on has been nothing but trouble from the start. I'd heard there was going to be some sort of demonstration so I arranged for the bulldozers to move in tonight, but it seems the damned eco-warriors beat us to it.

'And,' he added gloomily, 'they're not alone. A local TV station has picked up on it.' Looking grim, he folded his napkin and got to his feet. 'Can you believe it? All this over a scrubby bit of bog land nobody has ever heard of. Now they've come up with rare weed...I ask you, a *weed*!'

Katie, who found she had some sympathy with the local businesses and residents who didn't want the out-of-town development, kept a tactful silence.

'Some people,' he complained darkly, 'can't stand progress.'

'The future, my friend, is green,' Nikos observed.

Tom's laughter suggested he considered his friend's remark a joke. Katie, who wasn't so sure, began to get to her feet.

Tom motioned her to sit down. 'No, sweetheart, you finish your meal—no need for everyone to suffer. Nik will see you home?' He looked enquiringly at the other man, who responded smooth as silk.

'My pleasure.'

Katie's stomach gave a horrid lurch. Only a determination not to give him the satisfaction enabled her to conceal her dismay.

'Thanks, mate.' Tom gave Nikos a thumbs-up signal. 'You two enjoy your meal,' he encouraged, bending down to kiss the top of Katie's head.

'Perhaps I could help,' she said, speaking quickly. 'I know Mark Rogers's mother.' Tom gave a growl at the mention of the leader of the local opposition to his project.

'She's a lovely woman, Tom, and she was saying that it's the scale of the development and the lack of local consultation that has upset Mark and the others. Perhaps if—'

'I appreciate the offer, Katie,' Tom said, unable to hide his impatience. 'But this is business. I'm sure Rogers's mother is a nice woman, but you can't reason with troublemakers like him—they just see it as weakness. I'll ring you in the morning.'

Katie had told herself that that was just the way Tom was and it wasn't something she could do anything about, but on this occasion as she watched his departure part of her wanted to call him back and confront him. *Why are you acting like a prehistoric jerk? Why are you treating me like a brainless ornament?* she wanted to demand.

She'd seen him work perfectly amicably with high-powered female executives. He'd come across as an enlightened new man on the occasions she'd heard him express admiration for females in top jobs. So why, when it came to his own fiancée, did he assume that anything remotely connected with his business was over her head?

Maybe it was his upbringing, she reflected, *or maybe I just look dumb?*

She gave a sigh as he reached the door and, turning back to the table, discovered that Nikos Lakis was watching her.

CHAPTER THREE

'WHAT,' Katie snapped testily, 'are you looking at?' There was entirely too much understanding in those disturbing eyes of Nikos's for her comfort.

'The dynamics of a loving relationship.'

The reply didn't soothe her; she didn't want those cold, clever eyes dissecting her relationship with Tom.

Maybe you're afraid he'll make you see something you don't want to?

Katie turned her attention back to the food on her plate; it was hard to simulate interest in the beautifully prepared meal.

'He's going to ring you...so you've not moved in together...' Nikos regarded her down-bent head speculatively from over the rim of his glass.

'No, we haven't.'

'Shrewd and beautiful?' he drawled admiringly. 'No doubt your tactics have a lot to do with a confirmed bachelor like Tom popping the question. Living together inevitably makes a man less eager to commit to marriage.'

With unwarranted viciousness Katie speared an innocent butter-coated new potato with her fork; it made a poor substitute for what she longed to stab.

'Seeing their beloved first thing in the morning rarely matches up to a man's romantic fantasy,' he observed in a superior, amused tone.

'Like *you'd* know such a lot about romantic fantasy!'

Nikos didn't seem offended by her gibe. 'Oh, I wasn't referring to myself; you're right, I'm no romantic. I don't expect or particularly want perfection in a woman and I was seventeen the last time I put one on a pedestal. Tom on the other hand...' His arched brows rose.

Katie lifted her head from her prolonged contemplation of her food. 'Tom does not put me on a pedestal!' she retorted uneasily. 'That's a disgusting thing to say!' Her nose wrinkled with distaste at the idea.

'Disgusting...?' His broad shoulders lifted. 'An interesting choice of adjective.' His upper lip curled in a cynical sneer. 'I'd have thought that being worshipped was most women's dream.'

'Being *loved* is most women's dream.' *Oh, God, I sound like a starry-eyed teenager...* Her resolve stiffened as she stuck her chin out fully expecting his scorn—why should she be embarrassed by something that she believed? She wasn't going to let some dyed-in-the-wool cynic make her feel self-conscious. After all, you couldn't expect someone like Nikos Lakis to appreciate the difference between being loved for what you were and being loved for what someone wanted you to be.

Their eyes touched; hers were defiant, his were... Katie swallowed; then again maybe Nikos understood more than she thought. Uneasily she observed the subtle shift in his expression as he registered her loaded riposte.

Without saying anything he made her feel she'd just made some remarkably revealing comment.

'Tom *loves* me,' she gritted. 'And he doesn't care how I look in the morning. I suppose *you* look marvellous after a late night,' she snarled.

The instant the words were off her tongue Katie knew they'd been a bad idea. It was like opening the floodgates of her imagination. Unwelcome images of tousled dark hair, slumberous, sexy eyes and hard, olive-toned flesh minus any form of clothing—Nikos Lakis *definitely* slept naked—flashed through her undisciplined mind. She sucked in air through her flared nostrils and then exhaled hard through her parted lips.

Thoughtfully Nikos watched the soft colour mount the smooth contours of her cheeks. 'Actually I've not had any complaints as yet,' he revealed softly.

The colour in her cheeks deepened. 'Amazing what some women will put up with if they think they stand the chance of snagging a rich man,' she grunted contemptuously.

'I bow to your superior experience in such matters.'

It was the closest he'd come yet to an outright accusation of gold-digging. Katie's fork fell from her grasp; she barely registered the noisy clatter of the metal on porcelain.

'I wouldn't kiss a man before he's cleaned his teeth in the morning for any amount of money!' she declared loudly enough to draw the amused attention of several diners close by who heard her forthright words.

For the first time she had the impression her response had perplexed Nikos. His glance slid to the undulations of her heaving bosom before returning to her angry face.

'If you really mean that, I think you've been spending your nights with the wrong sort of man.'

Katie, her attention hopelessly held in thrall by the low, husky throb of his voice, watched as the heavy lids of his exotically slanted eyes dropped lower over his dark glittering gaze.

Elbows planted on the table, he leaned towards her, it seemed to Katie's feverish mind that his closeness had cut them off from the rest of the room. Her senses were teased by the elusive male fragrance he used and the even more elusive but naturally occurring faintly musky male scent rising off his warm skin.

'There is a special sort of pleasure in kissing someone and tasting the scent of your body on their lips...' With each successive syllable his voice dropped lower until it was just a husky purr. The mesmeric drawl sent tiny shivers trickling through her body. 'The intimacy awakens memories of the pleasures of the night before,' he rasped.

The images that filled her brain sent a scalding hot flash

of heat washing over Katie's body, sending her core temperature off the scale. Katie tore her eyes from the dark ones of her tormentor. It would have been a lot less humiliating to pretend that it hadn't happened...that Nikos Lakis *hadn't* turned her into a mindless bundle of lustful longing with a bit of coarse sexual innuendo, but he had.

Forewarned is forearmed, she told herself without any particular conviction—there were some things even she, the eternal optimist, found hard to put a positive slant on.

'Give me fluoride any day,' she gritted stubbornly.

For a moment Nikos looked nonplussed by her response. Then a slow grin spread across his lean face. Katie found her eyes drawn to the brown flesh of his throat as, head back, he laughed. Presumably his skin would be that firm and golden elsewhere?

'And you, Katerina...'

'Me...?' she squeaked, lifting a hand to cover the mortified colour in her cheeks. To be caught drooling was bad enough, but to be caught drooling over Nikos Lakis made her certifiably stupid!

'Am I wrong to think that you feel some sympathy for these little flowers that Tom is going to cover with concrete?' He leaned back in his seat and replaced his almost full wineglass on the table.

She was unable to match his mental agility; the abrupt change of subject escalated Katie's growing mental confusion.

'What?' she asked, playing for time. It was unthinkably disloyal to voice her doubts on the subject to anyone, let alone this man. 'I'm totally behind Tom.'

'Even when you think he's wrong. How loyal.'

'Tom would never do anything illegal.'

'Legally, I'm sure he wouldn't do anything wrong.'

All thoughts of confronting Nikos and reminding him he had to honour his side of their bargain had long since vanished from her head. Katie just knew she'd explode or do something equally socially unacceptable if she spent another moment in this detestable man's company!

'How dare you? I'm not going to sit here and debate my fiancé's morals with someone like you,' she spat in a shaking voice as she rose to her feet. The abrupt but graceful motion sent the soft fabric of her dress hissing softly around her shapely ankles.

'Not a pudding girl, then?' The lazily mocking observation was addressed to her rigid slender back. Nikos spent the next few moments until she disappeared from view admiring the elegant line of her stiff spine and the gentle sway of her softly curved behind. The image, though quite delectable, brought a brooding frown to his face.

It wasn't easy when every cell in her body was agonisingly aware of him, but Katie stubbornly refused to acknowledge the tall figure at her side as she stood in the foyer—nobody else felt similarly inhibited. She had never felt so conspicuous as she did standing next to someone that everyone seemed inclined to goggle at—so much for good old British reserve! For his part Nikos seemed genuinely oblivious to the intense interest he created.

It was only when he cancelled the request for a taxi she'd made to the uniformed figure who arrived all effusive apologies for his absence at the reception desk that Katie could no longer pretend he wasn't there.

'Go away,' she spat. 'Or I'll call Security.' Her fury was fed by the fact the receptionist was automatically obeying him despite her loud protest.

'I'm taking you home; it is what Tom would expect.'

This struck Katie as the height of hypocrisy. 'The same way he'd expect you to insult me every chance you get.' If he thought she was getting in his car with him he was off his head—*or I would be if I did,* she thought, recalling uneasily the strange things that happened to her when she was in close physical proximity to him…

Her delicate feathery brows drew together. Something as shallow and superficial as sexual attraction ought in theory to be easy to control or at least ignore…

'Is that what I've been doing?'

Katie lifted confused eyes to his. 'I don't know what you've been doing,' she revealed shakily. She bit her lower lip and added in a hard, contemptuous voice, 'I should have known you'd be the sort of man who'd drink and drive.'

Katie watched in reluctant fascination as the handsome face above her grew taut and forbidding… *My Lord, he really is formidable,* she thought, unable to tear her gaze free.

'If you were half as observant as you like to think yourself you'd have noticed that, unlike you, I barely had a mouthful of wine,' he announced austerely.

'Are you calling me drunk?' she demanded spikily.

Nikos muttered something inaudible but definitely not English or polite under his breath. 'That at least would be some excuse,' he gritted. 'But I think your unreasonable behaviour is a result of an intractable, obstinate and shrewish disposition, not inebriation.'

'I hate to disillusion you but not agreeing with you is not actually the accepted litmus test for pigheadedness. Just because women fall in with your wishes doesn't mean they actually agree with you, or even think that pearls of wisdom fall from your tongue.' Pausing to catch her breath, she delivered a breathless, snide laugh. 'It just means you've got more money than they have. Privately they probably think you're just as much of a pain as I do.'

Incredulity—maybe people didn't speak to him that way?—metamorphosed into sizzled anger in his dramatic eyes and Katie wondered with a strange sense of objectivity if she might not have gone too far. It was almost as if she had a compulsion to push him, test him to his limits.

'I can only assume,' he replied in a voice with a chill factor straight from Siberia, 'that Tom has been kept in ignorance of this charming aspect of your personality—he never struck me as a stupid man, but then I suppose a beautiful face will make the wisest man foolish,' he concluded cynically.

It wasn't the attack alone that made her eyes open wide in amazement, it was the inference that he thought she had a beautiful face... Her preoccupation with this discovery struck her as unhealthy. She'd never counted vanity as one of her sins...now pride and obstinacy were quite another matter!

'Now be a good girl and let me take you home.'

His patronising drawl fanned the embers of her temper into hot flame. 'Go jump in the lake!' she bawled childishly up at him. As she was tall, Katie wasn't accustomed to being forced to tilt her head back to look a man in the face. She silently seethed with discontent. It wasn't fair, she reflected resentfully, that simply because the gene pool had made him so damned tall he immediately had an unfair advantage in any argument...

'If you are still concerned that I have been drinking, don't be,' he continued sombrely. 'I am very conscious that cars can be a lethal weapon—my elder brother was killed by a drunk driver.'

His frosty manner was not one that invited sympathy; despite this, Katie's attitude tumbled abruptly from extreme hostility to aching pity. Notwithstanding his terse tone, she was convinced that behind that stony façade he was hurting.

She knew of course it was probable that the Peter factor had something to do with her response—up to this point they'd had nothing in common, but now she knew that they'd both lost their brothers in motor accidents. Though the circumstances were very different, she felt, quite illogically, that some tenuous link had sprung up between them—not enough to make them inseparable friends, but maybe it just made him seem a little more human, more fragile. Fragile...? She glanced up at his tough profile and shook her head; maybe that was taking it too far.

It was ironic, considering that she'd been trying to discover a weak spot in his defences all evening, that now she had actually found one all she wanted to do was kiss him better. *Kiss...don't go there, Katie.* But of course she did.

Her active imagination had rapidly progressed beyond the kissing scene; by now things had got a lot further! Katie stopped herself; she was sure Nikos Lakis was the person in the universe *least* likely to need to be kissed better.

'I'm sorry about your brother.' *I suppose I just don't have the killer instinct.*

Nikos's dark, well-defined brows drew together as he watched those extraordinary sapphire-blue eyes fill until they glistened luminously with unshed tears. It struck him as bizarre that someone so hard-nosed and single-minded should have tears to spare for someone she had never even met.

This unexpected display of empathy was totally incompatible with the character of the woman that he had in his mental file marked 'Katerina Forsythe'. Nikos scowled; he didn't want her to be more complex than the two-dimensional character he had imagined. Mostly he considered himself pretty flexible and open to new ideas, but in this instance he was extremely resistant to revision.

'And I'm sure you're an excellent driver,' she added generously. 'But I've no intention—'

His deep, strangely abstracted voice cut softly across her rambling rejection. 'I thought that day I first saw you that you were wearing tinted contact lenses, the colour of your eyes was so...*extreme*. But the colour is real, isn't it?' His expression took on an almost accusing cast as he gazed down into the clear blue of her widely spaced, darkly fringed eyes.

The total unexpectedness of his comment made her blink, or maybe the intensity of his regard had something to do with her need to break the contact? It surprised her that he'd even noticed what colour her eyes were, let alone given the shade any thought.

'Of course it's real.' For some inexplicable reason her heart began to act as if she'd decided to sprint across the lobby.

Nikos cleared his throat and ran a long-fingered hand through his dark glossy hair. 'It is a very unusual colour— almost violet. Did you inherit your colouring from your mother?'

The tight feeling in her chest made her voice sound unusually breathy when she replied. 'No, my mother was very dark. It was Peter who inherited her colouring.' Her expression softened as she thought of Eleri's glossy jet-black hair and golden skin. 'Dad was a blue-eyed, redheaded Scot.'

'*Was?* Is he dead?'

'They both are.'

'So there is just you and…Peter? Or do you have other siblings?'

Katie shook her head. 'No, it was just us two—and Peter, he died.'

'Long ago?'

'Seven years.'

He nodded, but did not comment further on what she'd told him.

Katie wasn't quite sure *why* she had told him. Peter wasn't a subject she discussed with anyone, though sometimes the weight of her secret made her long to share the burden with someone.

'I know my presence disturbs you, Katerina…'

And then some! 'Are you surprised? I wasn't expecting Tom's billionaire friend to turn out to be the penniless man I married seven years ago?'

If Nikos heard the unspoken question in her resentful

observation he chose to ignore it. Katie was starting to get the idea he did that a lot.

'If you put aside your animosity…'

Katie was unable to restrain her incredulous laughter; as if he were the soul of impartial reason! 'I don't think I'm the only person with an animosity issue here, mate.'

'If you stop spitting and snarling for a minute you might recognise that we have things to talk about.' His brows lifted to a quizzical angle. 'Don't you agree?'

Katie opened her mouth and then closed it again; she could hardly deny it. You couldn't really meet up with a man you'd just requested a divorce from and *not* talk.

'Now seems an excellent opportunity,' he continued, his eyes observing the inner struggle very clearly revealed on her expressive face.

Katie swallowed and, without looking directly at him, nodded her consent.

CHAPTER FOUR

FOR someone who'd wanted to talk, Nikos showed precious little inclination to do so once they were in his car—predictably a low-slung luxurious sports car. In Katie's present mood she'd have criticised his driving had the opportunity arisen, but it didn't. He proved to be competent but not dangerously erratic as many men were when placed behind the wheel of a powerful car.

Other than ask directions as they'd left the hotel he had said nothing at all.

She cleared her dry throat, and swallowed; it seemed it was up to her to break the ice. She wondered what to say.

'Why are you here?'

It wasn't exactly slick, but you had to start somewhere.

'When we spoke on the phone Tom could not stop talking about the woman of his dreams. I was naturally curious to see this paragon.'

Sarcastic beast. She eyed him with dislike. 'And that was it?' She gave a sceptical snort. 'I don't believe in coincidences.'

'Neither did I until I opened my mail immediately after speaking to Tom. When I read Harvey's letter relaying your request for a speedy dissolution of our union I realised why the name Katie Forsythe seemed so familiar. Katie... Katerina...I thought I'd check it out. I dropped in on Harvey on my way here and tried to get your address. Being an exemplary example of the legal profession and impervious to bribery, he refused...'

'You didn't try and bribe Harvey!' Katie exclaimed in a scandalised tone.

Nikos spared her a fleeting glance that made her feel

45

ridiculously gauche before he returned his attention to the narrow, ill-lit road. 'It was much simpler and more rewarding to take a look at his laptop when he was called from the office.'

This offhand attitude to such sneaky actions confirmed Katie's first impressions of his character—the man was totally without scruples. Something she would do well to keep in mind in her dealings with him.

'It might interest you to know that Harvey told me he'd personally guarantee your integrity,' she choked, regarding his perfect profile with disgust mingled with unwilling appreciation. There was a lot to appreciate: his jaw was firm without being chunky and, even though it was probably due to generations of inbreeding amongst the ruling classes, a lot of men might have sacrificed a sense of humour—you couldn't count warped—for strong features of such staggeringly perfect dimensions.

If that doesn't shame him, nothing will.

It seemed he was shameless.

'That would explain why he didn't take the most elementary security measures.' Katie looked at him blankly. 'He left the thing turned on when he left the room.'

'God knows where Harvey got the idea that you were some sort of paragon of virtue.'

'I think he received his information on my exemplary character from a prejudiced source.'

'And that would be?'

Nikos's mobile lips twitched at the corners. 'Caitlin.'

A woman, that figured, Katie thought darkly. 'What exactly did you find out when you *illegally* accessed Harvey's computer?' she interrupted uneasily.

The idea of Nikos Lakis knowing chapter and verse the intimate details of her history was not a comfortable thought.

Harvey was the only one other than herself who knew the entire story of Peter's death; the rest of the world thought, as she had until the letter written in that familiar hand had dropped on her doormat the day after his funeral, that her twin's death had been a tragic accident—a young man fond of speed who took a bend too fast on his motor cycle.

For a long time she'd just held the letter, afraid to open it and read words that seemed to come from the grave.

'Sorry, Katie,' she'd read, 'but I just can't bear the guilt.'

Katie had read on in denial, unable to think of her brother so young, so filled with life, being in such despair that he had taken his own life. *It's not possible…I would have known… I should have known…!*

'I thought I'd killed the guy, I should have stopped but I panicked and rode away. The guy lived but he's going to be paralysed for life.'

Katie had cried; she'd cried for a long time. She'd cried for her brother and she'd cried for the man whose life his recklessness had ruined.

'Why didn't you come to me?' she'd yelled at the happy, laughing face beside her own in the framed photo. 'You always come to me!' It was true the twins had always turned to one another for support in times of crisis; they'd always presented a united front against the world.

Very much later Katie had discreetly gone about finding out what she could about the man Peter had left for dead at the roadside. She'd discovered Ian Graham had been a thirty-year-old electrician. He had married his childhood sweetheart and they'd had a ten-month-old baby.

Listening in to conversations at the corner shop in the village where they'd lived had told her he had not come to terms with his disability and his young wife had been at her wits' end. Financially, the gossips had said, they'd been in a bad way; rumours had abounded that they wouldn't be able to keep up with mortgage repayments for much longer.

Katie had vowed that she'd do something to help them, even if it took her the rest of her life, which sounded very grand but the Grahams needed help now, not in twenty years' time.

It was only when she'd remembered the legacies she and Peter had been left by their Greek grandfather on condition they marry that she'd seen a way out. The shocked twins had concluded that this generosity from a grandfather they'd never even received a Christmas card from was the old man's way of controlling the grandchildren he didn't know. She and Peter had joked that they would never marry just to spite the man who through their childhood had always featured as the current villain in their games.

It was amazing really that such a strange series of circumstances had led her to exchange solemn vows with the man beside her.

'Relax, your secrets are safe, there was just your address, which revealed you shared a postcode with Tom. It therefore seemed safe to assume that my wife and Tom's angel were one and the same person.'

Katie released a gusty sigh of relief; he might be scarily perceptive but he wasn't clairvoyant. Fortunately his ability to read her thoughts—or was it her body language?—had its limitations.

'But it didn't occur to you to let me know you were coming.'

'Only momentarily,' he admitted frankly. 'But I quickly realised that your reactions might be less guarded if you had no warning.'

In other words he wanted to see me squirm and I obliged. 'Tell me,' she choked, 'did you deprive many flies of their wings when you were a little boy?'

He seemed unmoved by her withering contempt. 'Tom is my friend; I would not like to see him make an unwise marriage.'

'And marriage to me would be unwise?' Her voice rose a couple of outraged octaves, which made Nikos wince. 'You didn't seem to think so once!'

'I arrived here with an open mind.'

Katie let out a mocking howl. 'Like hell you did! What is it with you? Can't you stand to see people happy?'

'It's only natural that you would be concerned, I am going to be uncooperative about the divorce.'

Katie's eyes widened in alarm as she took an abrupt tumble from her moral high ground. 'You're not, are you?'

He didn't reply to her dismayed whisper, but his enigmatic smile seemed calculated to keep her worried. There was no point demanding a straight answer, she decided; the man seemed determined to make her squirm. He had a sadistic streak a mile wide!

'Actually when I read Harvey's letter it seemed fortuitous timing. I've been thinking of marriage myself.'

Relief flooded through Katie, who slumped back in her seat. 'That's marvellous,' she breathed happily. She supposed with his looks and money there must be any number of women out there willing and eager to overlook his overbearing and egotistical character. 'Who's the lucky girl?'

'You wouldn't know her.'

In other words, we don't move in the same circles...what a prize snob he is, she thought contemptuously.

'Why didn't you tell Tom that you were married?'

Now that was something Katie had asked herself quite a lot recently. None of the answers she'd come up with showed her in a very favourable light. 'It slipped my mind,' she responded flippantly.

He threw her a wry look.

She sighed and lifted her slender shoulders in a gesture of defeat. 'Well, I didn't *feel* married,' she told him crossly. 'And if you must know it's not an incident in my life I feel particularly proud of.'

And if she had told him, she'd have had to tell him why she'd done it, and would do again, and that wasn't an option. Nobody but Harvey knew the truth and she intended for Peter's sake it would stay that way. Her brother had paid the ultimate price for his mistake—with his life.

'I needed that money. It was a means to an end, no more, no less,' she told him coldly. 'And I had hoped that Harvey could organise things so that Tom would never have to know.'

'So your marriage is to be based on lies…excellent foundation.'

Katie flushed angrily at his sarcasm. 'I never lied to Tom. If he had asked me if I was married I would have told him.'

'So, a marriage based on half truths…I congratulate you, a *massive* improvement!'

Katie inhaled sharply. 'God, you're so sharp I'm amazed you don't cut yourself.' *I should be so lucky,* she thought viciously. 'I take it your girlfriend knows you're already married?' she added innocently.

Katie had the pleasure of seeing what appeared in the subdued light to be a faint flush highlight his high cheekbones as his jaw tightened with annoyance.

She folded her arms and smiled. 'I'll take that as a no, shall I?'

'It isn't the same thing at all.'

'*Gosh!*' she gasped, widening her eyes. 'That's so spooky. I must be psychic—I had the strangest feeling you were going to say that.'

His long, lean fingers tightened on the steering wheel. '*Theos!*' he thundered…the flush of anger was no longer in doubt. 'You will not speak to me in this fashion.'

'Do people always do as you say?' Katie wondered, crossing one ankle elegantly over the other.

'Yes!' he bit back.

'That must be boring.'

'Why are you marrying Tom?'

'For the usual reasons people get married.'

'You mean you're pregnant?' He shrugged as Katie gave an outraged gasp. 'So you're not pregnant.'

'Even if I was there is no shame in having a baby outside marriage.'

'My father might not agree with you there,' Nikos inserted drily as he imagined the uproar that would occur if he produced an heir but no wife. 'And,' he continued, his brows drawing together over the bridge of his nose, 'you're not in love with him. That leaves—'

'Who says I'm not in love with Tom?'

His low-pitched, mocking laugh made her prickle with antagonism.

'I can only conclude,' he added, with the air of someone who had cut through the crap and was adding two and two, 'that your nest egg has run out? Mind you, if you have many designer outfits like that one, it's hardly surprising,' he observed, allowing his eyes to briefly skim the silky blue dress and the pleasing contours it covered. 'It is a CJ Malone, isn't it?' Caitlin, he reflected, would have appreciated seeing one of her creations worn by someone who possessed the sort of unlikely proportions designers had in mind when they created outfits.

'Probably.' Katie, who wouldn't have recognised a CJ Malone if she fell over it, replied vaguely. She wasn't about to admit to him that she was wearing a hand-me-down.

'I know a lot of women with expensive tastes, but none of them who wouldn't know if they were wearing a CJ Malone.'

She shrugged. 'I'm bad on names.'

'But good at signing cheques. I suppose once you've married for money once it's easier the second time?' he mused, slowing at an unsigned crossroads.

'Left,' she replied tersely. 'You're pretty handy with the lofty disdain for someone who married for money himself, but then I suppose arranged marriages are in your blood.'

Katie was pleased to see his taut jaw tighten, presumably with anger—she *hoped* with anger. She wasn't quite sure why she wanted to make him angry and, anyway, it was hard to be sure from this angle if she'd succeeded, because his eyes were screened by the sweep of his luxuriant lashes, which cast a shadow across the high plane of his cheekbones. He had the sort of face that was aesthetically pleasing from any angle.

She arranged her own features in an expression of mock sympathy. 'What's wrong, Nikos? Did the idea of getting your hands dirty like the rest of us seem too sordid when Daddy withdrew his support?'

He slid her a look of smouldering dislike before taking the road she had indicated. 'I'm not about to explain myself to you.'

'Ditto,' she added nastily. Of all the men in the world for Harvey to produce for her to marry, why, oh, why had it been this one? Sometimes fate had a very poor sense of humour.

'*Theos!*' he ejaculated raggedly. 'You are the most poisonous female I've ever had the misfortune to encounter!' he gritted. 'It will be well worth the inconvenience to myself to prevent you ruining my friend's life.'

Katie stiffened as an icy shiver slid up her spine. 'What do you mean by that?'

'I think you know exactly what I mean.'

'Pretend just for a moment that I'm not a mind-reader.' She was unable to conceal the fearful quiver in her voice.

'If I thought for one moment you would make Tom happy I would give you this divorce.'

'I will make Tom happy. I love him...' she declared loudly.

A scornful sound vibrated in Nikos's brown throat. 'I watched you together; you do not love Tom,' he announced calmly.

'And you'd know, I suppose?'

'I know how a woman in love acts, and you were not that woman. There was no passion in your eyes when they touched his; you act as if he's your brother,' he sneered scornfully.

'We don't all wear our hearts on our sleeves and there is a lot more to marriage than sex!'

'Both these things are true and I agree that many successful marriages are based on more pragmatic reasons; I have no problem with that, so long as both parties enter into the arrangement with their eyes open.'

'Like us.'

'Unless you are planning on not sharing Tom's bed there are some very obvious differences, but, yes, on your part there are very obviously similarities. However, unlike Tom, I was not madly in love with you,' he ground out sarcastically. 'It is your hypocrisy in pretending you are marrying for some pure and elevated reasons that I despise. The thing you *love* is the idea of being married to someone who can buy you diamonds and keep you in your expensive clothes.'

'How dare you act as if you know me? You may have married me, but you don't know me at all!'

'But we are married and, while we are, Tom is safe from making the worst mistake of his life…'

'And you can't marry your girlfriend.' Surely that consideration had to carry weight with him.

'She will wait.' His faintly startled tone suggested no other possibility had even occurred to him.

For a brief moment Katie allowed herself the indulgence of imagining Nikos Lakis left at the altar, a shattered man. The bride leaving him in this happy vision bore a startling resemblance to herself. As pleasant as this fantasy was, Katie had to think of some way of dealing with Nikos in the real world, and denying him her favours was hardly going to do it…what would?

It was so obvious she didn't know why she hadn't thought of it earlier.

'So maybe you've got a girlfriend who will let you walk over her and wait for you until doomsday, but the press are a different kettle of fish—they don't have so much tolerance for rich playboys.'

Katie sensed his big body tense behind the wheel. '*Meaning…?*'

Katie refused to be put off by the menace in his silky voice. '*Meaning* that some sections of the press would have a field day if they found out a member of the Lakis family had gone through a fake wedding ceremony so he could get the money to maintain his lavish lifestyle.'

Greek billionaire, young and more beautiful than any man had a right to be… Katie didn't know much about such things, but she was betting the press would have files several feet thick on Nikos Lakis and more than a passing interest in his wedding plans past, present or future! Of course she would never actually go to the press, but he didn't have to know that. On this occasion, him thinking she were some avaricious cow definitely worked in her favour. She flickered a cautious glance at his profile…and swallowed; she had *definitely* made her point.

'I can just see the headlines now…' she breathed airily. Even though she was staring fixedly out the window she was aware of the explosive tension in the tall figure beside her. The silence between them lengthened until Katie could no longer bear it; she swivelled in her seat and shot a look at him.

If Nikos's expression was any indication, he was seeing those headlines she'd spoken of too. Katie salved her troubled conscience by reminding herself she would not have had to resort to these sort of tactics if he hadn't played dirty first.

'*You are threatening me?*' he finally asked incredulously.

Kate found his silky shark's smile and soft voice a million times more menacing than a lot of shouting and swearing.

In fact it was so unnerving that had she had any alternative or been any less stubborn she might have retracted there and then.

'Think very carefully before you do that, *yineka mou*.'

Now who was threatening…? 'I am not your *yineka mou*,' she gritted automatically, before adding, 'it's the third house on the left after the telephone kiosk.' She took some comfort from the fact that the street lights in this tree-lined avenue of solid Edwardian houses were fairly bright, and even in subdued light the car Nikos drove was likely to be noticed. He struck her as the practical type of man who would wait until there weren't any witnesses before he strangled her.

The fact that he wanted to strangle her was not in doubt!

'You speak Greek?' Nikos sounded startled.

Katie froze; her response to his sarcastic endearment had been unconscious. 'Just a few words,' she mumbled, thinking of the lullaby her mother had sung to her when she'd been unable to sleep. That and a few endearments were the limit of her vocabulary, though she wished right now that she had a better grasp of her mother tongue.

'When I visit a country,' she told him blandly, 'I make it a rule to know how to ask directions to the loo, order a drink and understand what a man is saying when he makes love to me.'

That's me, the sophisticated woman of the world, well travelled and even more well versed in other things. My God, would he laugh if he knew how far from the truth this was; the only time her passport had come out of mothballs was on a day trip to Calais and as for the other! There could be few twenty-five-year-olds less experienced!

All regretful thoughts of bilingualism and the blank page that was her sex life left her head as they rounded the next tight corner.

'Oh, my goodness…! Stop the car!' she suddenly shrieked urgently.

'There is no need for theatrics, or threats. Be reasonable.

I would be a bad enemy to make and a resourceful woman like you will no doubt find another gullible man with a fat bank balance. But I cannot permit you to marry Tom.'

Katie wasn't listening to these powerful words as she literally bounced in her seat in frustration. 'I said stop the car!' she bellowed, grabbing the steering wheel.

There was a short-lived tussle during which the car slewed violently to the left, barely missing a large beech tree before Nikos, white-faced and cursing, brought the vehicle safely to standstill.

'Are you mad?' he thundered, raking her face with silver-shot blazing eyes. 'You could have killed us.'

Katie, who had been thrown against the door, shook her head to clear the ringing in her ears. 'Well, if you'd done what I said instead of ignoring me…' she retorted, reaching for the door handle.

Long brown fingers came to cover her own.

'You are not going anywhere…'

Katie turned her head impatiently towards him. 'Shut up and phone for the fire brigade—that's my flat over there with smoke pouring out of the damned window.'

'*Theos!*'

CHAPTER FIVE

KATIE didn't wait around to see if Nikos was doing as she requested. She tore open the door, which he no longer barred, and, gathering her long skirts, ran full pelt down the path to the entrance she shared with Sadie.

In between pounding on the door she fumbled in her purse for her key. Before she found it Sadie, dressed in a baggy pair of silk trousers and a low-cut top that made her look like an inmate of a harem, appeared blinking sleepily.

'Where's the fire…?'

Katie had no time to waste on explanations. 'Upstairs.'

Sadie's eyes widened as she appreciated for the first time the urgency in Katie's manner. 'You're serious!' She sniffed the air. 'I can smell smoke.'

Katie barged unceremoniously past her friend. 'That's because my flat's on fire, and Alexander is still in there!' she yelled over her shoulder as she raced up the stairs two at a time.

She ignored Sadie's alarmed cry of 'Katie, you can't go up there…he's just a cat!'

The smell of smoke got stronger as she climbed the stairs, but when she arrived at the top all she could see that was out of the ordinary were a few puffs of pale smoke oozing from the gap under the door of her attic apartment— it wasn't good, but Katie had expected worse. With any luck the fire brigade would arrive before it got out of hand.

For a moment she stood there indecisively, at a loss to know what to do next. What did people do under such circumstances…?

'If in doubt cross your fingers,' she declared unscientifically. Taking a deep breath, she opened the door.

She exhaled noisily with relief as no lethal fireball knocked her over, and she pressed a hand flat against her chest where her thudding heart was trying hard to escape.

Perhaps this is my lucky day after all… she mused. *'Lucky…!'* She rolled her eyes. *Oh my word, I'm turning into one of those irritating people who see a bright side to a calamity, no matter how dire.* 'There's optimism, Katie, and then there's insanity. Your flat is on fire because you forgot to turn off your iron—that's not lucky, it's disastrous.'

The sound of her own voice calmed her nerves and strengthened her resolve. Her flat consisted of an open-plan living-area-cum-kitchen and a small bedroom with *en suite* facilities. Though the main room was filled with an acrid smoke that stung the back of her throat and made her eyes water, Katie could see no more obvious signs of the fire, which seemed to advance her theory that it had started in the bedroom. That was where she had ironed the creases from her dress on the floor rather than be bothered getting out her ironing-board.

'Alex…good puss, nice kitty,' she called, advancing cautiously into the smoke-filled room.

She had barely gone a couple of yards into the room when the visibility became nil. The only thing she could now see was a dull orange coming from underneath her bedroom door; it was the only thing that gave her any sense of orientation in the gloom. It also gave her a deep sense of foreboding…how long would the door contain the flames?

At times like this a well-developed imagination was not helpful.

No good thinking about that, she told herself, *just get on with it. The sooner you find that damned cat, the sooner you can get out.* Despite this stoicism her knees were shaking as she cautiously proceeded.

She stopped every few feet to listen but there was no response to her calls.

Katie didn't know why she had expected him to respond, because Alexander was not a nice kitty, or a good puss, he was a belligerent animal who brought live mice into her bedroom and spat when you tried to show him affection. If he'd been human, doctors would have said he had a personality disorder.

And if I had any sense, she reflected grimly, *I'd leave him to fry!*

'Alex, puss, puss...' Mid coaxing call she walked straight into a solid object—the coffee-table she'd discovered in the garage sale. The impact of solid teak on her vulnerable shin was enough to send her to her knees. She eased her weight from her bruised knee and felt the tangled fabric of her dress rip.

'*Damn!*'

It was while she was on her knees that she realised the smoke was thinner nearer the floor. She decided to continue her search from this position.

She was crawling cautiously along when she heard a deep voice calling her name.

Nikos...well, if he wants to murder me this would be the ideal opportunity, she thought. If ever there was a situation where black humour was appropriate, this was it, she decided, continuing her search, studiously ignoring his increasingly urgent cries.

Her grim smile turned into a cough when she heard a loud sound of impact closely followed by a strong Greek curse. It must, she realised in retrospect, have been the cough that alerted him to her position because moments later she was aware of strong hands sliding underneath her arms and hoisting her off the ground.

'Let me go, you fool!'

'Be still and keep calm. I have you.' He did, in an iron

grip that made escape impossible. 'You are quite safe now,' a deep, soothing voice in her ear informed her.

Katie, who had no desire to be saved, knew instinctively that *safety* was something Nikos Lakis's arms would never offer her. It was the thought of what they might offer that made her start to struggle in earnest. As several of her blows connected the reassuring note in his deep voice began to sound a lot more strained.

She let out a shriek as he stopped trying to gently soothe her when, reverting to character, without so much as a 'by your leave' he threw her resistant body over his shoulder fireman-fashion.

This is a classic case, she told herself, lapsing into exhausted passivity, *of resistance being quite definitely futile.*

Katie was forced to maintain this undignified position until they had reached the hallway when she found herself plonked on the wooden floor, which Sadie had only had stripped and polished before Christmas... *Oh, God, poor Sadie...! And this is all my stupid fault! I'm the tenant from hell!*

She felt cool fingers press against the pulse point at the base of her throat, then a hand, the same one presumably, slid under her chin and began to firmly tilt her head back.

Her watering eyes shot open; embarrassingly it seemed that Nikos had wrongly attributed her sudden inertia to a loss of consciousness. She was ashamed that for a spilt second she had actually considered letting him try to revive her—her curiosity was purely of the scientific variety, of course.

'Will you stop that?' In her head her voice had been strong and defiant, but annoyingly what actually emerged from her dry lips was a weak croak.

'Well, that's a relief, you don't require mouth to mouth,' said the big figure who was straddled over her body as he settled back on his heels.

Though his face and clothes were blackened and soot-stained, he still managed to looked as incredibly handsome as ever, Katie noted despairingly.

'Imagine your relief and quadruple it,' she croaked.

'I did not expect gratitude for saving your life, but civility would have been nice...'

'*Saving my life!*' she squeaked, struggling to sit up. 'My life didn't need saving, I had everything under control until you got all Neanderthal.' Panting and unable to rise, she grabbed onto the first available solid support to provide leverage, which happened to be his thighs, which were clamped either side of her waist.

The iron-hard firmness she encountered made her pause and caused her sensitive stomach muscles to tighten; escape somehow seemed less urgent as her splayed fingers explored a wider area and discovered no give in the bulging contours.

Then she came to herself and was deeply ashamed. It was unforgivable under the circumstances that she'd wasted precious seconds.

'Thanks to you,' she snarled, 'Alexander is probably frying in there,' she informed him, sliding out from between his legs and struggling to her feet. She got to them when, unaccountably, her knees gave way.

Nikos, a startled expression on his face, had also got to his feet, but with considerably more agility and athletic grace than she had. He caught her as she slid to the floor, which cushioned the impact of her contact with the bare wood.

With her head thrust between her knees, Katie batted blindly with her hands connecting only with empty air. It was only after she stopped fighting that he let her up.

'You stupid, *stupid* man!' she quavered, wiping with the back of her hand angry tears that coursed down her filthy face leaving paler tracks in the grime. Nikos, who was kneeling beside her, did not look particularly chastened by

her attack. 'Alexander is still in there.' She gestured towards the door.

Nikos looked grim. 'I heard you. Stay calm—hysteria
will achieve nothing.'

'I am calm!' she bellowed.

'Why on earth didn't you tell me what you were doing
earlier? Surely this was not the time to preserve your image?'

Katie's brow creased in impatient bewilderment—image,
what image? As for staying calm, the part of his recrimi-
nation she did understand was not only unjust, but would,
if she'd been the type given to throwing wobblers, have set
her off again. Katie was rendered speechless—but only
temporarily.

'Like you gave me a chance!' she yelled. Or would have
yelled if she hadn't been coughing so much.

'Katie…oh, Katie! You're all right, thank goodness!' A
sobbing Sadie gasped as she reached the top of the staircase. 'Oh, my, I really should lose a couple of pounds,' she
moaned, clutching her chest. 'I'm signing into that fat farm
next week…'

Nikos was looking with some bewilderment at Sadie,
who was babbling wildly on about the detox therapies guaranteed to shed the pounds.

It seemed likely to Katie he was about to make one of
his nasty sarky remarks.

Katie elbowed him hard, wanting to protect her friend
from his nasty tongue. 'She's terrified, it's her way of coping,' she hissed at him. God, the man had the empathy of
a brick.

Nikos seemed to take her explanation on board. Nodding,
he left her side with a terse instruction to *stay put*!

'Just take some deep breaths.' Katie watched in astonishment as, with a smile of incredible charm and gentle
manner, Nikos bent over Sadie.

The sound of Nikos's voice seemed to calm Sadie, who

nodded and looked up at him gratefully. Katie saw her do a double take and then an appreciative grin spread over her face.

'Are you asthmatic?' Nikos asked.

'No, just fat and unfit.' Sadie laughed shakily. 'I ran all the way from the gate,' she explained. 'I think the fire brigade are coming. I heard them in the distance. Shall I go back and wait for them…?'

'Take Katerina downstairs, and leave the house immediately.'

I suppose, Katie thought numbly, *that people like Nikos come into their own in situations like this—situations that require someone to take charge and make decisions. Not even his worst enemy—which might be me—can accuse Nikos of having a problem with decision-making,* she conceded wryly.

'I'm not going anywhere until Alexander—'

'I will get Alexander and you will leave the building,' Nikos announced in a lordly fashion. 'How old is he?' he asked, advancing towards the door from which smoke was now billowing.

'You can't go in there,' Katie said positively, as convenient as it might be, she couldn't let the rat die for her cat, who might still have a few of his lives left.

'Concentrate.'

Katie was, on the amazing silver flecks in his eyes. She was stressed, exhausted, terrified, and frankly there couldn't be a worse time to admit that you were sexually attracted to a person, and had there been any other conceivable explanation for the way her mind disintegrated and her body came to life around him Katie would have plumped for it.

'How old is he?' Nikos asked as though she hadn't spoken.

The relevance of this escaped Katie, but she recognised she wasn't totally immune to the indefinable something

Nikos possessed that inspired compliance, no matter how silly the question or request.

'Threeish, I think.' That was what the vet had estimated when he'd given the ginger tom his injections. 'I think we'll sedate him next time,' he'd said drily as he'd disinfected the scratches on his arm.

Nikos stopped in his tracks. *'Three!'* he ejaculated, his lips twisting in a grimace of appalled disgust. His chest lifted. 'You left a three-year-old child alone?'

Katie's jaw dropped. He thought…he actually thought she…! Words failed her. God, she'd known he had a low opinion of her, but she hadn't thought it was *this* low!

Sadie, who was supporting Katie, came to her aid. *'Child?'* She looked at the tall Greek as though he'd gone mad. 'Alexander is a cat.'

At her words Nikos, whose body was primed for action, each muscle clenched in anticipation of the task ahead, went quite still. Only his eyes moved; they slid from Katie to Sadie, who nodded, before returning to the original object of his scrutiny.

Katie observed the muscles in his throat move as he swallowed.

'You risked your life for a cat?' There was no discernible inflection in his voice.

'Sorry, I realise it would have suited you much better if I had left a helpless baby alone.'

He gave an impatient frown. 'What are you talking about, suited *my* purposes? I have no hidden agenda.'

'You're right—it's not hidden, it's blatantly obvious. It's so much easier for you to carry on pretending you're doing the dirty to save your friend from making a terrible marriage if I reveal myself to be an avaricious monster with no redeeming characteristics whatsoever. If, however, I turn out *not* to be a heartless bitch you'll look less like the true friend and more like a spiteful, vindictive pig who can't bear to see anyone else happy because he's too emotionally retarded and shallow to form a decent relationship himself!' she concluded breathlessly.

The blank incredulity of his expression gradually metamorphosed into one of smouldering fury. 'Have you *quite* finished?' he enquired with clipped hauteur.

'Actually, no, I haven't,' Katie heard herself grit back belligerently, even though she'd run out of emotional steam.

As the expectant silence lengthened Nikos lifted a satirical eyebrow.

'I didn't risk my life. You said I did,' she reminded him. 'But I didn't,' she ended lamely. Though actually, now that she came to think about it, her actions looked a little different. This no doubt had something to do with the fact she was viewing it without the stimulation provided by gallons of adrenalin pumping through her veins.

'I might have known you wouldn't like animals,' she heard herself grouch pettishly. *Why can't I keep my mouth shut while I'm still ahead?* she wondered in exasperation. What was it about this man that made her say stupid things? When he was around she seemed to be possessed by a need to prove she was even more selfish and superficial than he thought her.

'I like animals—in fact I frequently prefer them to people, especially the crazy, stupid, female type of person.'

Katie, who was normally capable of giving as good as she got, was deeply embarrassed to feel her eyes suddenly fill with tears at this fairly mild—by his standards—insult.

She wasn't the only one to feel uncomfortable. It seemed that quite by accident she'd discovered another of Nikos's weak spots...he looked even more dismayed by her tears than she was.

He cleared his throat. 'I didn't mean...' As he spoke he seemed to notice for the first time the hand he had extended towards her. For a split second he stared at it as if it didn't belong to him, an expression of shock on his dark, lean features. Then his expression became as unrevealing as ever as he lowered it to his side. His chest lifted as he took a deep breath.

'Take Katerina outside and wait for the fire brigade,' he instructed tersely as he turned to Sadie, who silently handed him a torch from her pocket. 'Thank you.'

'I don't need taking anywhere…' Katie's voice rose to a querulous squeak as her comments fell on deaf ears. 'And you can't go back in there.'

'Look on the bright side—if I don't come out you'll be able to marry Tom.'

Katie gave a cry of alarm as he turned and stepped back into her smoke-filled flat. If it hadn't been for Sadie's restraining grip on her arm she would have followed him.

'Don't worry, he's not daft,' Sadie soothed. 'He was only trying to wind you up.' Curiously she searched her friend's face. 'He won't take any silly risks.'

This confidence from someone who had only just met the man seemed wildly misplaced to Katie. 'I am not worried, well, no more than I would be about anyone else. Absolutely not at all,' she said half to herself. 'I just can't believe he had the cheek to accuse me of risking my life. What's he trying to prove?'

'Do you mind if we discuss this outside?' Sadie wondered nervously.

'What? Yes, of course.' With one last look at the door of her flat, which Nikos had closed behind himself, Katie followed her friend down the stairs.

'What did he mean when he said—?'

'I thought you said you heard the fire brigade…' Katie interrupted, craning her head to look up the road for any sign of flashing lights.

'I thought I did,' Sadie replied apologetically.

'When that guy—?'

'Nikos,' Katie supplied distractedly.

'When Nikos said. Good grief...*Nikos*...?' You could almost hear the sound of Sadie's chin hitting her chest as the name clicked. 'You mean he's the one you...'

'I married, yes. I don't know how you can think about that when your house is on fire and it's all my fault. You should be screaming abuse at me.'

'I will if it will make you feel better, but first tell me about that *incredible* man.'

'There's nothing to tell.' Nikos was the one subject Katie wanted to avoid. Although the way things were going it didn't seem likely she would have much choice. Her choices were narrowing in other areas too. Her hopes of concealing the marriage from Tom now seemed hopelessly optimistic. She found that she was no longer thinking in terms of *if*, but *when* her sordid secret would be revealed.

'He turned up tonight—apparently he and Tom went to university together.'

'I don't believe it!' Sadie gasped, clearly startled by Katie's taut explanation. 'What were the odds on that? That must have been a bit awkward for you.'

'Ever so slightly,' Katie agreed drily.

'Has he spilled the dirt to Tom?'

'Not yet, but it's only a matter of time.' For the hundredth time in the past two minutes she glanced tensely over her shoulder towards the house. 'Shouldn't he be out by now?'

'It's only been a couple of minutes, Katie,' Sadie soothed. 'You know, I don't know how much you paid for him, but if it had been common knowledge he was available on the open market I'm betting the price would have been higher,' she joked with a lascivious grin.

'I did not buy him!' Katie denied hotly. 'Well, not like that, it was a business arrangement, nothing more.'

Sadie shrugged pacifically. 'If you say so. Are you sure you two haven't met since the wedding?'

'I don't think I'd have forgotten.' No, an encounter with

Nikos Lakis was something that stayed in a person's memory for ever like…like…eating bad shellfish, she thought sourly.

'Fair enough. It's just that you two don't talk or act like people who have as good as just met…'

Katie never had to respond to this thought-provoking observation because at that exact moment they both heard the unmistakable and very welcome shriek of a siren.

Hands folded against her chest, Katie began to jump up and down. 'They're here!' she yelled, silent tears slipping silently down her face.

Both women watched with relief as the engine drew up outside the house, disgorging several capable-looking uniformed figures. The noise of their arrival had attracted the attention of several neighbours in the tree-lined avenue, who came outdoors to investigate the activity in the normally sedate neighbourhood.

'Have I ever told you about my fireman fantasy?' Sadie caught the tail-end of Katie's incredulous expression and looked sheepish. 'Well, you have Nikos—you can hardly begrudge me a fireman.'

'He's not *my* Nikos,' Katie retorted.

'If you say so, but be a sport, Katie, I'm trying to distract myself and that one—' she pointed '—is absolutely gorgeous…'

Katie was no longer listening; she was busy running towards the fireman who had inspired Sadie's lustful fantasy.

She caught his arm and tried to speak; considering the urgency of the occasion, this seemed a bad time to lose her voice. The fire-fighter, who was probably used to dealing with people gibbering with fear, exuded a calm aura that helped Katie finally get her words out.

'Th-there's a man still in there,' she told him beckoning towards the window on the top floor.

'Has he been in there long?'

Katie swallowed and pulled distractedly at her long hair.

The sooty smell that came from it made her nose wrinkle—
no doubt the rest of her smelt just as terrible and as for
how she looked... *Aah, how shallow am I, thinking about
my lipstick when all this is going on?* 'I don't know...it
seems like a long time.' Her lips trembled and she scrubbed
at her dirty face. 'It's my fault,' she confessed. 'I think I
left my iron on...I knew I'd forgotten something, and now
I've killed N...Nikos and Alexander.'

'There's more than one person?' he queried sharply.

'Alexander is a cat,' Sadie explained for the second time.
'Katie, he'll be fine. He didn't look like an easy man to
kill to me.' Sadie smiled at the fire-fighter. 'I'm the owner,
officer.'

'Hello. Is there any means of access other than the
stairs?'

'There is a fire escape around the side of the house.'

Katie, not placated, shrugged off the comforting arm that
slid around her shoulders. 'I'm a selfish cow, I sent him
back in there for a...' Her lips began to tremble as she
fearfully contemplated the consequences of her actions.

Before she could reveal to the fireman what Nikos had
gone back in for there was an almighty deafening explosion
as her bedroom window exploded. The fireman, his arms
outstretched, shielded the two women as glass from above
showered on the garden below.

'It would be better, ladies, if you waited a little farther
back until the ambulance arrives.'

Katie saw his mouth move, she heard the words, but she
felt as though she were in a black hole; she felt numb.

Sadie nodded, getting a firmer grip on the box containing
family photos and treasures that she had automatically
snatched up before they'd left the house. She urged Katie
backwards while the burly fire-fighter, shouting instructions
to his crew, strode off purposefully.

Katie resisted and Sadie looked with concern as the slim
figure who was standing gazing with horror-filled eyes at

the wicked tongues of orange flames shooting out of the window pushed her away.

'Come on, Katie, we should get out of their way,' Sadie suggested gently. 'Mrs James next door has put the kettle on.'

Katie, her arms wrapped tightly about herself, continued to rock back and forth. Under the layer of grime her skin was paper-white. 'He's dead, isn't he? I mean, if he was in there he has to be, doesn't he? Nobody could survive that.'

Sadie shrugged helplessly. 'I really don't know.' The muffled keening sound that suddenly emerged from Katie's bloodless lips before she choked it back made the hairs on the back of Sadie's neck stand on end.

The next sequence of events occurred with such bewildering speed that Sadie didn't have a chance to do anything but yell a warning to the fire-fighters as her friend, running as if all the fiends of hell were at her heels, suddenly began to pelt towards the door of the house.

Katie was never going to make it there, the two fire-fighters aiming to cut her off were closing fast, but before they had an opportunity to do so she tripped and fell. Though she landed on her knees it was the sharp pain that shot through her ankle as it turned awkwardly that made her cry out.

Just what I need—a sprained ankle, or, the way this day is going, it will probably be broken!

Impatiently brushing the tears of self-pity and impatience from her face, Katie squared her shoulders and, catching her soft lower lip between her teeth, concentrated her efforts on getting to her feet.

So far, so good, she thought as she tentatively took a cautious step; to her relief her ankle hurt but it took her weight. Wincing, she hobbled over to a convenient Japanese flowering cherry tree that was shedding its sweet-smelling blossoms onto the damp grass below and leaned against the trunk.

She gazed towards the house. The fire crew, seeing she was not seriously hurt and no longer capable of dashing headlong into a burning building, had turned their attention elsewhere.

Katie was pondering the compulsion that had been responsible for her stunt—*as if I could do something the firefighters couldn't*—when she finally recognised what the fire crew had turned their attention to. A tall figure was emerging from the smoke.

'Thank God!'

She watched through a teary haze of relief as a couple of paramedics headed purposefully towards Nikos. The incredible noise of a fire scene seemed to recede to a low background buzz and the hurrying figures appeared to slow; only her heart continued to beat fast, so fast she could feel the vibration of each inhalation in her throat. She lifted a hand to her spinning head; each breath she took was an effort.

If I faint now he'll probably accuse me of faking it to steal his moment of triumph. Only she didn't faint, the nervous tension found a more prosaic release.

'I think I'm going to be sick,' she gulped to nobody in particular, before she quietly did just that—not that anyone noticed; they were all crowding around Nikos.

Trust him to turn out to be a hero…it was a part he was born to play, she thought, a wry but relieved smile on her face as she leaned back against the tree trunk.

CHAPTER SIX

THE hero was clearly not comfortable with his moment of fame.

'I am fine.' The cough that followed this impatient pronouncement did not add weight to his claim. Ignoring a recommendation to breathe deeply, Nikos pushed aside the oxygen mask that someone was trying to slip over his head. 'I don't need that!'

'You've inhaled a lot of smoke,' the paramedic explained patiently.

Nikos smiled thinly and resisted the impulse to point out to this well-meaning individual that as the one who'd done the inhaling he didn't need any reminders. After a few moments of fruitless arguing they reached a compromise, of sorts.

'Though it is an unnecessary precaution I will come with you if you give me a few moments to speak to my wife.' Nikos gestured towards the solitary figure on the lawn and immediately regretted it because by no stretch of the imagination did she look in need of comfort. In fact she looked extraordinarily composed. 'I think she's in shock,' he improvised.

Hopefully this would adequately explain away the fact that his *wife* had been able to contain her joy at his miraculous escape. His lips curled in a cynical smile, then he shrugged; at least she wasn't a hypocrite.

'Well, just a few minutes…'

Everyone, Nikos reflected, was a sucker for a couple in love.

Did the professionals think it strange his wife had not been part of his reception committee? That she hadn't dashed to throw her arms about his neck, tears of joy running down her cheeks? Nikos did not ponder the question for long; he rarely worried about how his actions were viewed by strangers. Though the potent image did remain in his mind, not because he was thinking about the impact on others—no, it was the impact on himself that occupied his thoughts.

Smooth arms wrapped around his neck, a soft, pliant body pressed to his, a silky head close to his heart. As he closed the distance between them anyone noticing would have wrongly assumed that the dark bands of colour highlighting the slashing curve of his high cheekbones were a product of the inferno he had just escaped—they'd have been wrong.

This scenario in his head was not a displeasing one, so the primitive response of his body was not, Nikos reasoned, to be wondered at. It was an explanation he was content with, but his reluctance to release this image was less easily rationalised.

Katie levered her back from the tree trunk and pushed a large hank of heavy hair from her face. 'You found me, then…'

Nikos nodded. Her question made him realise that even though she had made no push to attract his attention, some inner radar had located her the moment he'd emerged from the building.

If you ignored the dark film of grime covering his skin and clothes he looked quite remarkably unscathed by his recent brush with death. In fact, he radiated an almost indecent amount of edgy vitality. It occurred to Katie that this was probably the most natural and relaxed she'd seen him. Near-death experiences obviously did for him what a box of chocolates, a soppy romance and a glass of wine did for her.

One corner of his mouth lifted as their eyes touched. Katie felt a flare of indignation—it clearly hadn't even occurred to him that she had been through hell and back during the last few minutes because of his ridiculous macho stunt.

She didn't know if she wanted to hit him or kiss him. Not *literally* kiss him, of course, because that would involve…her stomach took a sharp dive and the flow of her thoughts skidded to an abrupt halt. Her wide eyes were drawn by an invisible but irresistible force to the sensual curve of Nikos's mouth.

She swallowed convulsively, unable to prevent the image forming in her head of that sexy mouth claiming her own, parting her lips, his tongue invading her mouth, tasting…touching.

She shook her head and took a deep, tremulous breath. But it was too late, the chain reaction had already started.

Her eyelids fluttered as a rush of fluid warmth worked its way up swiftly from her shaking knees until her entire body was bathed in the golden glow. She held her breath and willed the flames consuming her to subside.

Katie couldn't deny she had wanted to experience that kiss for real; for several moments she had been consumed by the wanting. Even now her bones ached with the raw desire that had swept through her with the ruthless force of a forest fire.

She was guiltily aware that she had never felt that way anticipating Tom's kiss. She struggled to understand what had happened and more importantly why it was happening. It had to be her hormones; this was some sort of revenge attack because she'd neglected them.

Or maybe this wasn't just hormones—it was conceivable that she was actually suffering from some post-traumatic thing? Her flashbacks just happened to be of something that hadn't happened yet—*yet*! A grammatical error, nothing more, and she for one hated people who banged on about Freudian slips.

The more she considered it, the more she became convinced that the extraordinary things she *was* feeling were a result of the near-death thing. That sort of 'we could have died but didn't, let's go to bed' thing—it apparently happened in war situations all of the time. Her eyes widened in alarm as she realized she'd jumped from kissing to bed!

That was an alarming leap by anyone's standards.

She realised that Nikos was waiting for her to say something.

'You're not dead,' she heard herself blurt out stupidly. Stupid it might be, but it was a far safer option than begging him to kiss her.

'Sorry. I'm a bit singed if that's any help.'

Katie took a deep offended breath. 'Don't be facetious!'

Nikos inclined his head in meek acknowledgement of her censure. 'It's true, look at my eyelashes.'

'I don't want to look at them,' she snapped, turning her head away. In fact looking at any part of him was a bad idea, though unless she wanted to appear extremely odd she had no option. 'This might be a joke to you,' she remonstrated severely, 'but how do you think I'd have felt if I'd had your death on my conscience? Huh, I don't suppose you even thought of that, did you?' The hot, impassioned words tumbled out of her. 'No, of course not, you were too busy being Action Man. Talk about grandstanding!' She gave a disgusted snort.

It was one of life's injustices, she reflected bitterly, that men got to do all the glamorous action things and were then patted on the back and told what marvellous chaps they were. While women, because they were delicate and frail creatures, got to wait at home, look after the babies and go prematurely grey.

If Tom ever wanted to do something rash and life-threatening she was going to go with him. It didn't seem likely her resolve would be put to the test; if anything like that came up Tom would most probably delegate someone else to take care of it—which was the sensible thing to do.

You wouldn't catch Tom rushing into burning buildings for a cat; he would have, quite correctly, left it to a properly qualified person.

Actually, when you thought about it, have-a-go heroes were a bit of a liability.

Katie was disturbed to discover Nikos was looking at her rather too intently. 'You were scared for me?' he said, in the shocked manner of someone who had just made an extraordinary discovery.

She strove to calm her laboured breathing. 'I was… concerned, as I would have been about anyone in the circumstances. Though it seems my fears were groundless. You seem to lead a charmed life,' she observed heavily.

Her resentful gaze had examined most aspects of his person and she could see no obvious signs of injury other than a bloody gash on his temple. Even if he had emerged unscathed she considered his composure after such an incident abnormal. What did it take to shake this man? Demanding to be kissed would most likely do it. It was almost worth putting the theory to the test…*almost*!

'That has been said of me,' Nikos conceded with one of his charming, high-voltage grins. 'I'm touched by your concern, but it is unnecessary, I was in no serious danger.'

Katie had a sudden flashback to that awful moment the window had blown out. The metallic taste of fear was once more strong in her mouth as she again experienced that creeping paralysis of dread.

'Are you all right?'

'What could be wrong?' She was beginning to think that maybe he was one of those peculiar men who indulged in extreme sports, the sort that got a kick from risking life and limb.

'I managed to locate the fire escape,' he went on to explain, 'thanks to Alexander who was sitting at the top of it crying. That is, I'm assuming this is Alexander.' He opened his shirt, revealing a good deal of bare chest in the process, and presented her with a large, dirty cat who, at the prospect of being clutched to his loving owner's bosom, stopped purring like a steam engine and spat furiously before leaping into space and disappearing into some bushes.

Katie began to laugh a little hysterically. 'Oh, that's Alexander, all right, he's one of a kind. I'm surprised he let you carry him.'

'He was not too keen on the idea at first,' Nikos conceded drily. 'But he came around to it in the end.' He rubbed his face and revealed in the process a long, nasty-looking scratch.

'That's a first, Alexander is not a very…*pliable* animal. The vet did say he might be a little less aggressive if I had him done, but I couldn't bring myself to do it.' Nikos's penetrating eyes held an expression that made her wonder if he didn't have a hormone issue of his own? The introduction of this possibility made her lose the plot for a second. It was hard to concentrate when illicit thrills were fizzing through your body.

'Done?' Nikos echoed, looking puzzled.

Katie slowed her breathing and told herself that a man who had just escaped from the jaws of death was not likely to have sex on his mind. She mimed a snipping action with her fingers—an action guaranteed to pour cold water on the flame of the most persistent male lust—and Nikos gave a very predictable male gulp in response.

'I don't want to be responsible for an explosion in the local cat population so I keep him in at night,' she told him matter-of-factly.

From Nikos's glazed expression she had the feeling this was more information than he wanted. Not that he looked *bored*, precisely, *more*… A little shudder snaked its way down her spine. Perhaps she was way off beam, maybe the thoughts of a sizzling kiss were still on her mind. But while they were standing here talking about cats she felt as though there was a silent conversation going on that had nothing to do with words and everything to do with the way his dark eyes were eating her up.

'Don't you think you should do up your shirt? You might catch cold,' she suggested huskily as her eyes returned for the umpteenth time to the expanse of hard-muscled torso. The olive-toned flesh looked silkily smooth and hard and was dusted across the widest part of his broad chest with a fine sprinkling of dark hair that thinned the nearer his waist it got. Her stomach gave a lazy somersault as she followed the directional arrows.

He laid a hand against his firmly muscled midriff. 'Actually I feel quite warm.' For one awful moment Katie though he was going to invite her to feel for herself—an invitation she would *obviously* have rejected? 'How about you?'

Katie dabbed her tongue to the tiny beads of sweat along her upper lip and drew a shaky sigh. This time there was no longer any doubt about the undertones in this innocent enquiry. If she'd felt more herself and less like a lustful stranger Katie would have confronted him about his inappropriate flirting...*flirting*, with its light, frivolous overtones, was actually far too light a term for the erotic verbal games he played.

'I'm fine,' she returned, throwing him a look that dared him to contradict her. 'I'm really sorry about your face.' *Really sorry that it's so damned beautiful,* she thought weakly.

'I'll survive.' He suddenly reached across and pulled a piece of blossom from her hair.

Like a hunted deer being stalked by a wolf, Katie backed up into the tree. Her heart was beating like a war drum as he placed a hand on the smooth trunk above her head. If he leaned any closer their bodies would be touching...the crushing pressure reached the point where her shallow, painful breaths were clearly audible.

'You weren't hurt or anything?' It didn't really matter

what she said, she just had to speak, not only to demon-
strate that he hadn't disturbed or rattled her, but to banish
the erotic images from her head.

It did neither; her weak, wispy voice sounded as though
it came from a great distance away. As for being undis-
turbed, she was clearly insane! It was taking literally all of
her will-power to prevent herself turning her cheek into the
palm that remained close to her face.

'Mr Lakis, I really must insist that you come with us
now. You need to be checked over. Your wife too.' The
paramedic turned to Katie, who tried to gather her wits. 'I
understand from your friend that you too were inside the
building earlier.'

It took Katie several seconds to register what he was
saying and who he was saying it to. 'Oh, yes, but I'm fine.'
Wife, he had definitely said *wife*. Her alarmed blue eyes
flew accusingly to Nikos's face; he returned an insouciant
smile. 'I'm perfectly fine,' she gritted.

The sexual tension might have dissipated, but she sensed
it was still there, waiting beneath the surface to bubble up
given the right conditions... Katie resolved never to permit
that to happen.

Dark eyes gleaming with mockery, Nikos continued to
smile down into her wrathful features. 'Let's allow the doctors to decide that, shall we, *yineka mou*?'

'Your husband's right, it's always best to be on the safe
side, and that was quite a tumble you took. Did you do any
damage?'

'You fell?' Nikos inserted, for all the world as if he actually was a concerned husband.

'She went down like a stone,' the other man confirmed.
'It isn't exactly a good idea to enter a burning building,'
he added, slanting Katie a wry look.

'You went back into the building?'

Bemused by his anger, Katie shook her head. 'No, I
didn't.'

'She fell over before she could get there. That's quite a turn of speed you have there, Mrs Lakis. I wouldn't bet against you in the hundred metres,' he teased.

Nikos, who was regarding her with total incredulity, did not appear to share his amusement.

'I wasn't thinking,' Katie said in a small voice.

'Don't worry about it,' the paramedic advised kindly. 'People rarely do think when they know a loved one is trapped in a burning building. Ask any of the fire crew.'

Katie didn't know where to look—except *not* at Nikos!

'Katerina has always been an impulsive creature, haven't you, *yineka mou*?'

The satiric bite in his voice made Katie wince. She did her best to disguise her limp, but evidently not well enough.

'You've hurt yourself!' the paramedic exclaimed in concern before she'd taken a couple of steps. 'Hey,' he hailed, 'the lady here needs a stretcher.'

Katie laid a restraining hand on his arm. 'Please, no stretcher,' she appealed, shaking her head. 'I'd much prefer to walk and it's nothing serious.'

To her intense annoyance he looked towards Nikos, who presumably gave her request his husbandly seal of approval, because the guy walked away and left them to make their own way to the ambulance.

Unbelievable! If she had been his wife in the real sense of the word, admittedly a scenario about as likely as seeing a herd of flying pigs overhead, but had she been, she would definitely have challenged this outrageous sexist assumption that she needed permission…that she wasn't capable of making her decisions.

Oh, my goodness, wouldn't I just! she thought grimly.

Obeying another of those unwise *impulses*, Katie lifted her head and for a split second her eyes meshed with midnight-dark orbs. It was long enough to reveal Nikos seemed to be really steamed up. This struck Katie as particularly perverse; she was the one who'd been made to feel a total fool. How dared he go around telling everyone she was his wife? As for the image the guy had drawn so vividly of a woman pushed beyond reason by an overriding compulsion to save her man, she had thought she would die from sheer embarrassment!

'Lean on me,' Nikos wanted to throttle the woman, but felt obliged to put aside his natural inclinations and offer his assistance having watched her painfully hobble a few steps while maintaining the pretence every one didn't hurt her like hell.

'I'd prefer to crawl on my hands and knees.'

The air hissed through his clenched teeth as he exhaled. 'As you wish,' he replied stiffly.

He made no concessions to her injury as he strode off, not that Katie wanted or expected any, but the grim smile pinned on her lips got harder and harder to maintain with each step.

'So were you so frightened for me that you were willing to risk your life in a futile attempt to rescue me?' Nikos's dark, sardonic voice observed somewhere above her head.

Katie's spirits, already badly mauled, sank to knee-level. Her worst fears were confirmed. This was exactly what she'd been dreading—he'd thought about her crazy rescue bid and come to the conclusion she'd acted that way because she was nursing some burning passion for him. Maybe he half expected women to fall in love with him? And maybe that expectation was usually justified, an ironic voice in her skull suggested.

Actually, when you thought about it, it was quite funny.

Despite recognising the humorous potential of the situation Katie found herself unable to laugh or even smile. She was, however, seized by a desperate need to establish that she was not one of the worshipping masses.

'It wasn't like that...' She paused and gave a frustrated sigh; how could you explain away why you did something when you didn't know yourself? 'I didn't think...' she revealed lamely.

'That I never doubted,' he incised grimly. 'For the past seven years when I have thought of you at all it has been as a shrewd, hard-headed young woman who, despite an extraordinarily innocent exterior, is capable of bending the rules ruthlessly to get what she wants. In short, a woman well able to take care of herself.'

He exhaled and dragged a hand roughly through his dark hair. 'That is what I expected, you understand? A woman like you should know how to negotiate. But what do I get?' His revolted gaze came to rest on the top of her head, which had she been able to stand upright would have just topped his shoulder. '*You...!*' He shook his head and, with an expression of rampant exasperation, began to list the traits he had discovered her to possess. 'Not only are you opinionated to the point of derangement...' he choked.

Good grief, she thought, lifting her astonished eyes to his furious face. *I needn't have worried—he doesn't think I'm in love with him, he just thinks I'm crazy! Could be he's not far out,* she thought, contemplating the firm contours of his mouth with an expression of dreamy speculation.

'Do not interrupt!' he thundered, holding up his hand. 'You are sentimental and you possess no sense of self-preservation whatever. I am a patient man...' he revealed without a trace of irony.

Too late, Katie clamped her hand over her lips to prevent the gurgle of laughter escaping.

Nikos gave her a thunderous look as he visibly fought to retain control of his extremely volatile temper—only he didn't have a volatile temper. 'I have humoured you too long,' he announced forcefully.

'That's a laugh—' she began. She let out a strangled shriek when without warning he swept her up into his arms and strode off without a single word.

'Put me down this instant!' she hissed. His arms were muscular and extremely strong because, although Katie was slim, she was not a small woman and he barely seemed to register the burden he carried.

'What, and see you stagger along in that ridiculous manner?'

Silently seething and reduced to winding her arms around his neck to anchor herself, Katie allowed herself to be carried to the ambulance with as much dignity as she could muster—what choice did have?

Sadie was waiting at the steps. 'Why did you tell them I had been in the flat?' Katie demanded of her friend in a trembling undertone.

Sadie looked startled at her vehemence and followed them up the stairs. 'Sorry, but they asked.'

Katie felt a wave of remorse. 'Sorry, I didn't mean to take it out on you. That man,' she explained, glaring at Nikos's ear, 'is a manipulative snake.' Even his hair curled perfectly into the nape of his neck.

She held herself rigid while, apparently oblivious to her insult, Nikos deposited her on a seat and straightened with sensible caution considering the limited headroom.

'I wouldn't trust him as far as I could throw him—*less*, in fact!' she declared loudly.

Sadie shot a wary look in Nikos's direction and he in his turn returned her look with a smile of spectacular charm, which much to Katie's disgust had an immediate effect on Sadie. She melted like an ice cream on a warm day.

'A sexy snake.'

Sadie's sly remark earned her an amused grin from Nikos. 'Thank you,' he said, inclining his head. 'And may I say that a true English rose like yourself is much admired in my country?'

Katie shook her head as Sadie blushed. 'What a load of b—'

'Don't spoil it, Katie,' Sadie interrupted, casting her

friend an irritated glance. 'Do go on,' she begged Nikos with a throaty laugh.

Katie glared at her friend indignantly—she was flirting, and flirting pretty well. 'Has anyone ever told you that you're a sucker for a pretty face?'

'Frequently,' Sadie admitted. 'I'd better go,' she added as the ambulance crew began to display impatience to be off. 'Call me later.' She smiled at the paramedic who, after checking that his passengers didn't require anything, had taken a seat at the opposite side of the vehicle.

'I feel terrible leaving you to cope with all of this mess,' Katie fretted.

'You know me, I thrive on challenge,' Sadie replied, cheerily waving goodbye.

'Your friend is very nice.'

'She's just recovering from an extremely messy divorce. So leave her alone, the last thing she needs is some slick operator moving on her,' she warned him grimly.

'I can pass the time of day with a woman without contemplating sleeping with her, you know.'

Katie snorted and Nikos looked amused. 'I have never been in an ambulance before,' he remarked, looking around with interest as the door closed. 'Or even,' he added with a mock growl, 'made love in one.'

'Very funny.' No doubt tonight's events would be regurgitated for the amusement of his glitzy friends—with suitable witty additions—for many weeks to come. 'I suppose *you* ride around in gold-plated limousines.'

'No, as a matter of fact I fly my own helicopter when possible. So do you really think I have a pretty face?' he continued seamlessly.

Talk about anything you say being used in evidence!

'That was a figure of speech.' Actually his was not a pretty face, it was a formidably *beautiful* face. She didn't need to look to see his dark, fallen-angel features or be transfixed by the brooding sensuality of his sexy eyes and mouth—they were etched in her mind.

How, she puzzled, could something as basic as the arrangement of planes and angles of a face make it so...? She struggled for a term adequate to describe it—unforgettable was a term casually bandied about, but in this instance it was fully deserved. Her memory would never be free of the image, she acknowledged, looking down at her hands tightened into fists on her lap.

'If you continue to breathe like that the professionals—' Nikos glanced towards the uniformed figure who had left his seat opposite and was now talking to the driver '—will assume that you need oxygen.'

Katie was disconcerted to discover that his eyes were contemplating the rapid rise and fall of her breasts... actually, disconcerted didn't really cover the things that were happening to her body. Nikos had to have noticed at least one of them as his attention was riveted in one of the areas in question; her breasts felt tense and tender and her nipples were active in a pleasurably painful way.

It had reached the point where she couldn't be sure what shocking surprise her body was going to spring on her next. Even the things coming out of her mouth seemed to be bypassing her brain.

'Why did you tell them I'm you're wife?' she asked in a desperate attempt to divert his attention from her aching, brazen breasts.

'You *are* my wife.'

Her inability to dispute this made Katie scowl. 'Only when it suits you,' she pointed out tartly.

Somehow she doubted Nikos would have been so eager to recognise their relationship if she'd turned up at his place of work declaring to all and sundry that he was her husband! What she couldn't figure was why he'd carelessly gone public, in this admittedly limited way, now. The last thing he struck her as being was a careless man; quite the contrary, she was pretty sure he never did anything without a reason, but what reason?

Possibly his actions were simply designed to wind her up?

For the past seven years he had successfully managed to forget he had a wife so she could strike the possibility that he'd decided she was the perfect bride for him.

No, he was up to something.

'We may have gone through a ceremony and signed on the dotted line, but it takes more than a signature on a piece of paper to make me your wife!' she told him scornfully.

'So, what does it take...?'

Katie shuffled away to lessen the contact of his heavy thigh against her own. The action only increased the worrying air of smug triumph she sensed in him.

'It takes...oh, for goodness' sake, will you stop that?'

'Stop what?'

'Will you stop looking at...you know?'

'No.'

Katie gave a snort of exasperation; the innocent look sat very uncomfortably. 'Well, how would you like it if I kept looking at your...?' Content she'd made her point, and deeply embarrassed into the bargain, she decided it would be expedient to move quickly on.

Nikos, however, seemed in no hurry to do so. 'I think I would find it quite stimulating,' he said.

Taking a deep steadying breath, Katie gritted her teeth and doggedly refused to allow him to distract her. 'It takes...' she began.

'What does it take?' he prompted, his curiosity genuinely aroused by the wistful expression he saw flit across her delicate, fine-boned features.

Katie shook her head; she was not about to expose her idea of an ideal marriage to his cynical scorn.

'Do you think they might let us a share a room at the hospital?'

'I suppose in Greece that passes for a sense of humour?' She gave a disdainful sniff and tried to stop herself coughing. 'Just for the record, I'm not sharing a room with you and I'm not staying in any hospital.'

Nikos shook his head. 'Did nobody ever tell you it's dangerous to tempt fate?'

CHAPTER SEVEN

'MARRIED?' the on-call radiographer, or Clare, as she had introduced herself, glanced towards Nikos. 'Yes, of course you are,' she said, not without a hint of envy. 'Date of birth...?' Katie gave it and the older woman checked the details on the form and nodded. 'Is there any possibility you are pregnant?'

She stood with her pen in her hand waiting for Katie's response. Katie, aware of Nikos's very interested presence beside her, felt her face flush. After a lengthy pause she shook her head and mumbled an indistinct, 'No, there isn't.'

The radiographer obviously misunderstood her hesitation. 'If you've any doubts?'

'I've no doubt at all,' Katie responded firmly. 'I can't possibly be pregnant. I haven't...' she choked.

'Oh, I see...' The radiographer nodded understandingly and shot a speculative look in Nikos's direction. 'So long as you're sure.'

'We have been living apart,' Katie was dismayed to hear him suddenly volunteer glibly. Equally suddenly he picked her hand up from where it lay twisted with its partner on her lap. With a tender smile he raised it to his lips. 'We are only recently reunited.'

His words and the fervent kiss he planted on her open palm managed to hint at a lovers-parted-and-reunited story of epic proportions.

The radiographer was clearly a big fan of a happy ending. 'Oh, isn't that lovely?' she sighed soulfully. 'You just wait here a moment, Mrs Lakis, and I'll be right back.'

The instant she was gone Katie snatched her tingling

88

hand away and wiped it across her lap vigorously, as though she could wipe his touch away.

'Was that charade really necessary?' she enquired icily. It seemed he couldn't resist any opportunity to provoke and embarrass her. Or maybe, she mused scornfully, he just couldn't let the implied slur on his manhood stand. Yeah, that would be right.

'So you're not sleeping with Tom?'

Katie stiffened defensively as his question took her off guard. 'That's none of your business, but if I was,' she added confidently, '*I* certainly wouldn't be stupid enough to get pregnant.'

Though she wasn't as a rule a judgmental person, she had always found it hard to understand how in a day and age when contraception was so readily available people still fell pregnant unintentionally—though the *falling* was part of the self-deception as far as she was concerned; there was nothing accidental about it.

'Maybe, maybe not…people in the grip of passion do not always think logically.'

'*Rubbish.*' One dark brow lifted at her forceful denunciation. 'There's absolutely no excuse for neglecting to take basic precautions.'

Katie frowned to hear herself sound so self-righteous and dogmatic…it was the sort of uncharacteristic response he brought out in her. He said night and she was almost falling over herself to screech day.

An enigmatic half-smile touched the corners of Nikos's wide, passionate mouth as he observed the flare of panic in her eyes.

'So you don't think that the dizzy heights of passion could make a person, could make *you*, forget?' His heavy lids lifted and Katie found herself captured and as helpless as a butterfly caught on a cruel pin by his dark gaze. 'Forget your own name, where you begin and your lover ends…?' he persisted throatily.

His rough velvet voice was describing a situation that was beyond her understanding, but one that held a dangerous appeal. Just listening to his sweetly insidious drawl made her feel hot and cold at the same time, and increased that tight, achy feeling that had been a more or less constant presence low in her belly all night.

The way his knowledgeable eyes were scanning her face made Katie, bitterly ashamed of her body's wanton response, shift uncomfortably in her seat.

'Forget the most basic precautions? Do me a favour,' she scoffed stubbornly.

'You cannot visualise yourself in a situation like that?'

'No!' Katie gritted through clenched teeth as she tried very hard not to allow the images he spoke of to crystallise in her mind. Even though she tried very hard some images filtered through her mental block; they were of limbs entwined, warm brown skin gleaming with sweat, fractured gasps and soft moans. She was hard put not to moan herself.

Nikos was beginning to think that the favour that would most benefit her would come from someone who could wipe that smug look of superiority from her face—his narrowed gaze homed in on the soft contours of her full lips—and why should that person not be him?

The voice of reason in his head immediately provided at least half a dozen legitimate reasons why it should not. Despite this, the idea, however ill advised, lingered on.

'No matter how sophisticated society becomes, mother nature has built in some very efficient safety systems into the human design that will ensure the continuation of the species despite our best attempts to foil her.' In a voice that was all honeyed temptation and earthy suggestion, he expanded his theory into territory Katie found even more uncomfortable, yet despite this she found herself perversely hanging on his every word. 'It is not by accident that we are intoxicated, that sense and reason are suspended in the heat of passion.

'Men,' he proclaimed confidently, 'are programmed to impregnate and woman are programmed to bear children.' He shrugged and studied her shocked face; it seemed to Katie that the silver flecks in his eyes glittered like stars in a night sky. 'You can't fight against basic instincts, *pethu mou.*'

She tried to escape but her restless gaze was repeatedly drawn back to his; a stab of sexual longing so fierce it robbed her of breath lanced through her body.

Katie shook her head. 'You can't talk like that,' she gasped in an agonised whisper. The men she knew didn't casually discuss impregnation in hospital waiting rooms.

'You find my frankness offensive? Such things make you squeamish?'

Offended? She was terrified.

'I am not squeamish. I just don't think this is the appropriate time or place for talking about such things,' she told him repressively. Unfortunately Nikos was not so easily repressed.

'Sex is not a subject for open discussion?'

'Not between people who are virtually strangers.'

'So if I was Tom you would feel comfortable discussing sex.'

Katie took a deep, infuriated breath. 'Tom and I do not discuss sex,' she yelled.

'Mrs Lakis…?'

Katie spun around to find the radiographer standing there.

'We're ready for you now.'

Her ankle was declared a nasty sprain, which they strapped with a stretchy support bandage and advised her to keep elevated. The doctor said he was satisfied that she had not sustained any damage to her lungs, though he did suggest Katie might like to stay in overnight to be observed.

To her relief when she politely but firmly refused the invitation he wasn't too perturbed.

'The doctor should be finished with your husband in a few minutes,' the nice nurse who had attended her promised, showing her to a waiting area.

I can hardly wait.

Katie had caught sight of her reflection in a plate-glass door so wasn't surprised that on the way there she was the focus of a number of curious stares.

Not to put too fine a point on it, she looked scary!

It was hard to tell what the original colour of Sadie's once lovely dress was and there were several rips in the long skirt that revealed more than was decent of her long, grubby legs. Though she'd had the opportunity to wash the worst of the dirt from her face and hands, what she longed for most was to soak in a lovely hot bath until the acrid smoky smell that seemed to have penetrated pore-deep was gone.

'I feel awful for asking, but I don't suppose you've got any change for the phone, have you? I didn't exactly come prepared,' she explained with a rueful glance down at her ruined outfit.

Katie waited until the helpful nurse was out of sight before she headed for the pay phone she'd spotted in the foyer. First she phoned Tom; he wasn't at home and he wasn't answering his cell phone. She was about to leave him a message, but thought better of it…there was nothing he could do and telling him about the fire would only alarm him unnecessarily.

Next she rang Sadie's mobile number.

'I was starting to think they were keeping you in,' Sadie said, sounding tired but pretty upbeat, which in the circumstances said a great deal for her powers of endurance.

Sadie got the bad news over with first.

'Your flat's a write-off. The good news is they managed to contain the fire to the top floor. The rest of the house is all right, barring some smoke damage in the hall and down the stairs. I'm staying with the Jameses next door tonight, they said you're quite welcome to kip down on their sofa. I've got the spare room.'

'Say thanks to them from me, but actually I can't face the journey back.' The hospital was a fifteen-mile trip from the village and she was ready to drop; in fact, remaining upright was difficult. 'I'm just going to get a taxi to the nearest hotel and sleep for a week.'

'Fair enough, see you tomorrow?'

'Definitely,' Katie agreed. 'Sadie…I'm really sorry,' she added in a rush.

'God, we don't even know if it was your fault and I'm the one that didn't get around to refitting the fire alarms after the painters finished last month. Besides, nobody was hurt, that's the main thing, and I'm extremely well-insured,' she added cheerfully. 'So don't beat yourself up about it.'

It wasn't until she'd hung up that Katie realised she had no money for a taxi, hotel room or, for that matter, any more for the phone. *Don't panic, think about this calmly and logically,* she told herself.

So *logically* she had no money, and calmly she had no transport, her head hurt and she was dressed in revealing rags—Katie reckoned she was entitled to panic a little and to feel mildly despondent.

Maybe I should have taken up the offer of a hospital bed, she thought as she stepped into the reception area, a big densely carpeted open space that was divided by banks of greenery and seats—obviously meant to give a welcoming impression. The place, a hive of activity during the daytime, was, barring a few porters and sundry members of staff who were on their way somewhere in a hurry, almost completely deserted at this time of night.

Katie wasn't on her way anywhere. She wrapped her arms across her chest feeling incredibly conspicuous and rather lonely. Her adrenalin levels had dropped and the events of the evening were beginning to catch up on her with a vengeance.

'Here, take this.'

Startled out of her gloomy thoughts by the deep voice, Katie looked at the jacket being offered to her and then warily at the man himself.

He was as dishevelled as she was, his skin and clothes streaked with black, but unlike her he appeared supremely indifferent to the fact. It struck her as deeply unfair that, whereas torn clothes and messy hair made her look like a scarecrow, they lent him an indefinable edge of mystery and danger...mean, moody and macho...nobody was going to overlook him in a crowd!

She was inclined to think that if you stripped this man of his wealth, status and even his clothes he wouldn't lose his infuriating imperious air of command.

Katie raised her eyes with a jerk to his face feeling, and probably looking, as guilty as any nicely brought-up girl would caught in the act of mentally stripping a man—*make a note for future reference: do not think naked around Nikos*—but then no matter how things turned out she wouldn't be around him for very much longer.

This reflection ought to have made her feel upbeat—but somehow a heavy feeling had settled over her.

'You are shivering,' he observed with a frown.

Katie looked again at the jacket; she thought of refusing it and then decided this would be an empty gesture and, besides, she didn't want to risk being arrested for indecent exposure!

'Yes, I am. Thank you.' She slid the jacket over her hunched shoulders, and drew it around herself. It still held the warmth of his body; she found this second-hand warmth disturbingly intimate. 'My dress has a little more ventilation than was intended.'

'I could say I hadn't noticed, but I'd be lying.'

Katie shot him a wary glance but his enigmatic expression was unrevealing—maybe that was just as well.

'Sit?' he suggested, nodding towards a seated area.

Katie shook her head. 'Hospitals at night are strange, don't you think?' Her restless glance took in the big empty area. 'Almost spooky,' she heard herself babble.

'I thought you'd gone.'

Katie didn't tell him that that had been her plan.

'Have you contacted Tom?'

She shook her head. 'I tried to.' Not so very hard, a voice in her head suggested drily. 'He's not picking up, but it sounded as if he was in for an all-night session, didn't it? He could very well be in the middle of sensitive negotiations,' she elaborated, 'so it's probably better I don't bother him.'

'I don't think many men would consider it a *bother* to drop whatever they were doing if their woman had just escaped death.' The contemptuous curl of his upper lip seemed to be a reflection of Nikos's opinion of any man who wouldn't rush to the side of their woman.

Katie was annoyed that she felt impelled to defend her absent fiancé.

'And Tom would!' she began. 'Escaped *death*…' she added, frowning. 'Isn't that a tad over-dramatic?' Her light laughter trailed away as she tried to imagine Tom calling her *his woman* in that way, and if he had she would probably have laughed.

When Nikos used the term it didn't sound funny. It must be the accent—men with exotic, sexy accents could get away with saying things that a native speaker could not. It went without saying that she didn't want anyone to call her *his woman*; it was sort of dated, sexist stuff—the sort of things the man that her grandfather had picked out for her mother would have used.

She concluded that his accent must be responsible for

the shivery sensations she experienced every time he was around.

'Possibly.' He conceded her words with a careless shrug of his broad shoulders. The flimsy nature of his shirt made it difficult not to notice how his taut muscles flexed and bulged through the fine material. 'But nevertheless I think you should let Tom decide that for himself.'

Katie's lips tightened; his persistence, not to mention his perfect musculature, was beginning to annoy her.

'Can't you wait until the morning to tell him what an awful creature he's got mixed up with?' she taunted.

'Actually I was thinking of how I would feel in his place.'

Katie flushed, not enjoying the sensation of being quietly put in her place. 'I suppose that must have taken quite a stretch of your no doubt limited imagination.'

'*Theos!*' Anger lent his dark, taut features a menacing cast.

'And I suppose *you* would walk away from an important business negotiation if your girlfriend needed you. That's *really* likely.' This was the sort of man who put personal relationships way down his list of priorities.

A wave of weakness suddenly hit her; it was so strong she swayed. Nikos, whose simmering anger had left him the moment he'd taken in the white-faced exhaustion in her face, took her by the arm.

'Sit!' he urged strongly. The woman was clearly unfit to take care of herself. He wondered why Tom let her out alone!

Katie complied, reasoning it would be a lot more embarrassing to fall on her face than follow his direction. Pride had its place but you had to know when to swallow it. She sat for a moment with her eyes closed, waiting for the awful weakness to pass. To her relief Nikos let her be.

'I'm a little tired.'

Nikos slanted her a veiled look through half-lowered lids.

'I find it strange that you feel obliged to apologise for be-haviour that needs no apology but not for insults you throw so indiscriminately at me.' He shook his head when she opened her mouth to respond.

'Hush!' he urged, pressing a finger to her parted lips. 'We will not squabble. I am not so unimaginative that I cannot see you are at the end of your tether. As for what I would do, we are not talking about me.'

Not talking, thinking or fantasising about, which was something she really ought to bear in mind! Unconsciously she ran the back of her hand across her lips where he had touched.

'I just thought that Tom isn't going to lose any sleep over what he doesn't know about. Besides,' she added brightly, 'he knows I don't need him to hold my hand every time something goes wrong.'

'You are a tough, independent woman, then?' Nikos asked, sounding amused.

Katie's eyes narrowed. Her want-to-make-something-of-it? look was weak, but strong enough to make her opinion of his condescension known.

'If you're asking if I'm quite capable of taking care of myself, then,' she told him proudly, 'yes, I am. Do you have a problem with that?'

He would prefer his women clingy and needy; that went without saying. The sort that would tell him at frequent intervals how big, strong and marvellous he was, and never, *ever* disagree with him! In short, women who would not upset his theory that the world revolved around him, she concluded scornfully.

'Does Tom?' he fired back smoothly.

Katie waved her tastelessly large diamond ring at him. 'Quite obviously not.'

'Maybe you are more circumspect around him?' he suggested drily.

'Around *Tom* I can relax,' she breathed, closing her eyes

and imagining herself in his undemanding company. With Tom she never felt stressed or under pressure or...*excited*?

Her eyes shot wide open; where did that come from?

'But not around me?'

Katie laughed; she couldn't help herself. It was such a ludicrous idea: relax with Nikos! She could more readily imagine falling asleep on top of an active volcano! But then, she mused as her eyes moved over his tall, elegant figure, he did have something of a volcano's explosive qualities...and he was liable to erupt for no apparent reason.

'Do I look that stupid?' If ever there was an invitation, this was it.

Katie heaved a sigh and squared her shoulders, steeling herself for the inevitable scathing riposte...it didn't come. In fact the strange, tense silence between them stretched on and on...

He had stilled to the point of seeming not to breathe at all as his restless dark eyes got as far as her face and didn't move. An expression she couldn't decipher flickered across his taut face; it was only there for a moment, but this was long enough to unsettle her completely.

'*No.*'

After the build-up she'd been expecting something a bit more—memorable than that.

'You didn't answer my question.' Except with a question—he seemed to be good at that. 'Do you have a problem with strong women?'

Nikos shrugged. 'Strength is not an issue. My relationships with women are rarely competitive either physically or intellectually.'

Katie's contempt increased. In other words he picked them weak, thick and great in bed. *Just as well I'm not after the job because I don't qualify in any of the above.*

'Some women feel there is a need to sacrifice their femininity in order to compete on an equal footing with men;

that is their choice. I just happen not to find them particularly attractive. I admire women that manage to succeed
but do not try to be one of the boys.'

'Are you calling me unfeminine?' she demanded hotly.

'I would hardly categorise you as a high-flyer who is
anxious to compete with men on their own terms.'

Why, the patronising—!

'Are you leaving your job before or after the wedding?'
he wondered with a guileless smile.

Katie caught her breath. You had to hand it to the man—
he could deliver insults with a smile better than anyone she
had ever met.

'I'm not leaving at all. My job may not be high-powered
but I happen to enjoy it,' she told him with frigid dignity.

'Really?' One dark eyebrow lifted. 'Tom led me to believe you could not wait to leave…'

'I haven't told Tom yet,' she interrupted tightly.

'Do you tell Tom *anything*?'

'My relationship with Tom is none of your business.'

'Actually it is very much my business.'

'Only because you're an insufferably, interfering…' Lips
compressed, eyes glittering with suppressed frustration,
Katie bit back the rest of her tirade; this was neither the
time nor place for a slanging match, especially one she was
likely to lose.

'Don't you think Tom is capable of making his own
decisions without you to shove him in the right direction?
Not that you could,' she added quickly. She lifted her chin.
'Tom is his own man!' she declared proudly.

'I'm sure Tom is more than capable of making his own
decisions when he is in possession of all the facts…once
he has them I will be more than happy to abide by his
decision.'

'It's not the facts, it's the way you present them.'

'Then you present them in the manner you feel shows
you in the kindest light; I have no objections. Even if Tom

accepts his wealth has nothing to do with your desire to be his wife.' His expression made it clear he was a lot less gullible. 'That does not alter the fact you are not free to marry him.'

'I could be if you weren't such a stubborn, malicious...' She heaved several steadying breaths; she would not resort to name-calling. 'Why should I marry Tom when apparently I'm already married to a billionaire?'

Nikos, who seemed prepared for her comment, totally misinterpreted her throw-away sarcasm.

'Before the pound signs start flashing before your eyes I will draw to your attention the fact that the pre-nuptial agreement Harvey had me sign works both ways. I've checked, Harvey knows his business, it's watertight. Sorry, but I'm not your golden goose. What's wrong?' he asked as the colour seeped from her skin.

Katie, her eyes bright pools of shimmering anger stared up at him. Incredibly his bafflement seemed genuine...how could anyone possibly insult a person like that and not realise it might offend?

She began to slide his jacket off her shoulders. 'Don't let me keep you,' she said pointedly.

'Don't be foolish,' he retorted impatiently. 'You are cold, I'm not. This is a foolish gesture.'

Katie shrugged and let the jacket slip to the ground. 'Maybe I want to make a foolish gesture.'

'Now you're just being ridiculous,' he gritted, bending to retrieve the garment from the carpeted floor. His colour was heightened when he took his seat; the twist of his sensual lips was overtly contemptuous.

'That's your fault,' she blurted resentfully.

One supremely eloquent dark brow twitched as his expressive eyes swept over her face. 'This I have to hear,' he remarked, throwing the jacket casually across one shoulder. 'You were saying?'

Katie flushed. 'There's no point saying anything because

no matter what I say you'll just twist it,' she announced mutinously.

'In other words your accusations have no foundation.' Before she could protest he replaced his jacket over her shoulders and, keeping a grip on each lapel, jerked her gently towards him. Katie was overpoweringly conscious of his strength; she breathed in his warm male scent and felt uncomfortably giddy.

He bent his head towards her. 'No matter how outrageously unpleasant you become,' he imparted softly, 'I am not leaving you alone.'

'So you'll just call me an avaricious grasping bitch!' To her intense dismay Katie felt her eyes fill with weak tears.

Nikos looked into the swimming blue pools, an expression of genuine surprise stamped across his handsome features. 'I said nothing of the sort!' he ejaculated.

'You accused me of wanting to screw you for some nice fat divorce settlement!' She breathed wrathfully. 'For your information I wouldn't take my bus fare off you,' she added tremulously.

How, she wondered, could you detest someone so much yet find you wanted to lay your head against his chest and cry? Why in the circumstances would anybody in their right mind seek comfort and safety in the arms of their enemy? It was inexplicable and extremely scary, she concluded, staring with a dazed expression at the broad expanse that filled her with the strangest yearning.

As he surveyed her downcast features the harsh lines of Nikos's face softened. 'I did not intend to offend you, Katerina. Let us stop arguing, you're not well.'

'What's this—Greek chivalry?'

He picked up on her scorn but reacted with curiosity, not injured pride. 'You doubt such a thing exists?'

'After meeting you—*yes*!'

Surprisingly her acid retort made him laugh, then as his

appraisal of her weary, strained features continued his expression sobered once more. 'Let's be practical.'

When am I anything else? Katie thought with a spurt of revolt.

'What actually are your plans?'

Did she have any? She shrugged. 'Hopefully I won't be reduced to sleeping on a park bench.'

'What's this—British humour?' Despite her determination to be angry with him, Katie was amused to hear him cleverly use her own format against her. Whatever else was wrong with him, the man did have a quick wit and clever tongue—far too clever, she brooded darkly. A conversation with him had more dips and bends than a roller coaster.

'You doubt such a thing exists?' she quipped.

'What can I say without insulting a person's cultural heritage?'

Katie flushed at the subtle reprimand, then got even more worried when it occurred to her that he might have imagined there were xenophobic overtones in her earlier gibe. She frowned as she tried to recall whether what she had said could be construed that way.

'Have you ever actually met any Greeks other than myself?'

'Yes. As a matter of fact I've lived with one.' She was pleased to see her enigmatic reply disconcert him; if she had been better acquainted with him she would have been even more surprised.

'Does Tom know about this?'

Katie gave him a sunny, composed smile. 'Yes, he does.'

'I suppose this failed relationship explains your antipathy to me.'

'Did I say I had a failed relationship?'

'I naturally assumed as you're not in it any longer...'

'Well, you assumed wrong,' she replied, her eyes locked to his. She hadn't intended to make her reply vague, but

now that she thought about it having Nikos imagine she
had a colourful past did not seem such a bad idea.

'As a matter of fact it was a *beautiful* relationship.' The
taunting tone suddenly died from her voice and her eyes
softened. 'Very beautiful,' she revealed in a tone of deep,
ineffable sadness. 'I doubt if I'll ever have a relationship
quite like it again.' Unless she had a daughter of her own
one day?

'Then your antipathy to me...'

'Is solely due to the fact that you're an offensive, malicious, detestable man.'

In the thunderous silence that followed her pronouncement Katie started to regret being so mean. *I haven't even
asked if he's all right,* she thought, glancing guiltily towards the wound on his forehead. It was barely visible
through the heavy swathe of hair that had fallen across his
forehead.

'I didn't mean to offend you,' she added when he didn't
respond. 'Well, I did, but not— Oh, for heaven's sake,
don't sulk!' she blurted out in frustration. She waited for
the inevitable ice to filter into his expression and wondered
if there was a medical condition that could account for what
her tongue was doing.

'Relax, Katerina,' he advised. 'I'm not offended.'

She gave a sigh of relief. 'Good. What did the doctor
say?'

'My chest is clear.'

Your chest is perfect, Katie thought. 'That's excellent,'
she said gravely.

'And the X-ray of my skull was as it should be. They
insisted on putting a stitch or two in my head,' he admitted
in a casual manner.

'One or two?' Katie echoed doubtfully. 'It looks more
to me...' Without thinking, she reached out to lift the concealing hair from the wound. Before she touched him long

brown fingers curled over her own. A bolt of neat electricity sizzled along her raw nerve endings.

'Will you not take my word?' He gave a humourless smile. He seemed a little tense…but then there was a lot of it about, she thought, swallowing a bubble of hysteria. 'No, of course you won't.'

'I only wanted to see if you're all right.'

Nikos dismissed her concern with a terse shake of his head. 'The amount of stitches is of no consequence.'

He brought her hand down but didn't release it immediately; instead he turned it over and ran his thumb across her open palm.

'You have pretty hands.' He looked as if he was almost as surprised to hear himself say this as she was.

Katie's eyes lingered on his long, tapering fingers. His were strong, expressive hands and her tummy fluttered again.

'Thank you, so do you.'

She sensed some of the tension slip away from him and, though his lips twitched, he didn't respond to her comment.

'You know, I think we can do a little better than that park bench.'

Although the physical contact had disturbed her she felt a twinge of regret when he released her hand. She tried to gather her straying wits. 'What do you mean…?'

'I mean I have a suite at the Hall Hotel.'

He would, of course—staying in anything less than a five-star hotel would obviously be beneath his dignity, and the Hall was the only five-star hotel in the area.

'That's you sorted, then.'

Nikos gave a heavy sigh and looked impatient. '*Theos*, you are hard work,' he observed tersely. 'We're both tired…'

'Which is no excuse to snap.'

A nerve in his lean cheek began to pump. 'So kind of you to remind me of *my* manners.'

'I get the feeling that doesn't happen too often.' *More's the pity,* she thought, sending him a sour look.

He signalled his disapproval of the interruption with the faintest twist of his lips. 'I was about to say that I'm quite willing to take your extreme reluctance to accept my help as read? It will save a lot of time and frayed tempers in the long run. If anyone asks I'll swear you fought me tooth and nail. You hate me, I'm arrogant, you'd prefer to sleep on a park bench…blah…blah…' he drawled.

She shot him a look of intense dislike. 'I know this confirms my boring predictability, but I *would* prefer to sleep on a park bench!' she declared.

'Well done!' he congratulated her. 'The first step in correcting our faults is accepting you have a problem.'

'Once you go away I won't have a problem.' *If you overlook my penniless and homeless condition.* Heavens, what was she going to do if he took her at her word…?

'Don't make a song and dance about this. You can't stay here, you have no money. I, on the other hand, have—'

'Too much money.'

'Some people might think so,' he conceded, 'but actually I was thinking of a spare bed and a taxi which should arrive any moment.'

'*Spare* bed?'

'Sorry if you thought otherwise, but it has been a long day…' he explained apologetically.

Katie blushed fierily at the silky innuendo in his voice. She gathered the jacket and her dignity around herself as best she could.

'You won't know I'm there,' she promised grimly.

Nikos regarded the top of her dark head with a twisted smile. 'That I very much doubt, *agape mou,*' he drawled.

She pretended not to hear the endearment.

CHAPTER EIGHT

KATIE sniffed a few of the luxury bath products provided and, selecting one that had a tang of rosemary, she poured it into the water.

She inhaled deeply, enjoying the scent from the pungent-smelling oil in the steamy air. She gave a deep sigh as she slid slowly into the hot water. It was bliss.

She lost track of time as she lay there, drifting in every sense of the word. The delightful idyll was only spoiled when there was a loud knock on the door.

Katie groaned and slid under the water to block out the noise; fronds of water-darkened hair floated on the surface like exotic petals above her head. When she emerged, wet hair plastered to her face, the knocking was louder and accompanied by a voice. She wiped the moisture from her face with her hand and grimaced.

'Are you all right, Katerina? If you don't answer me I shall be forced to come in!'

He would too.

This was a situation fraught with dangerous possibilities...which no doubt accounted for the dramatic increase in her pulse-rate.

Katie bit her lip and blew a section of frothy suds from her arm, watching as individual bubbles detached themselves and began to float across the room.

'It's locked!' she shouted, hoping he'd go away.

If she hoped he'd go away, why then did she have this image in her head of being joined in the water by a sleekly muscled male body...? Why even as she spoke was she seeing water sliding over powerful shoulders...?

She almost certainly didn't want answers to these questions.

There was a short silence. 'A locked door is not an obstacle to a determined man,' he told her, sounding irritated but a lot more relaxed than he had done before she'd spoken. 'So if you are not unconscious answer me.'

Katie watched the bubble that had travelled the farthest ping on a mirrored surface. 'What do you want?' she called crossly.

'Do you want anything from room service? I'm ordering some supper.'

Her stomach responded to the offer with a hungry growl. 'No.'

'You hardly ate anything at dinner.'

'And whose fault is that…?'

'You ought to have something,' Nikos persisted, choosing to ignore her indignant accusation.

'What are you going to do, force-feed me?' She winced at the sound of her own voice. *God, this is starting to sound more and more like a playground squabble.* One of them had to start acting like a grown-up. 'Actually…Nikos…' she began tentatively. Why was it so hard for her to say his name? 'I wouldn't mind a sandwich? Nikos…?' she called, but there was no response. She shrugged; he obviously hadn't hung around.

Katie sank back down into the scented water but found it impossible to recapture her relaxed mood, so after washing her long hair until it was squeaky clean she climbed out of the roll-top bath. As she reached for a towel she caught a glimpse of herself in a mirror—how could she not? The ceiling was about the only place in the bathroom that didn't have a reflective surface.

She barely registered the fleeting image she had of the tall girl with long, slim legs, flat belly and firm, fairly full breasts with small pouting nipples that stood out darkly against pale honey skin. She picked a large soft towel from the pile on the vanity unit and was about to dry herself when an impulse made her turn and rub some of the condensation from the nearest mirror.

Towel still in her hands, she extended one leg in front of her and pointed her toes, watching the effect of her balletic pose in the mirror. Thoughtfully she replaced her foot on the tiled floor then turned, viewing her body critically from several angles. How, she wondered, would a stranger view this body? Would they notice that her hip bones were too bonily prominent or detect that, viewing from this angle, you could see that her right breast was just fractionally fuller than the left?

She ran her fingers slowly down the damp flat contours of her belly; the sensitised nerves in her abdomen quivered under her touch. She found herself staring into her own eyes...they were darkened, alien, the pupils dilated. She shivered, not from cold because her skin was hot to the touch.

'Oh, my goodness!' she gasped, wiping a shaking hand across her lips, which appeared pinker and fuller than usual—*as if I'd just been kissed. Who am I kidding? It's no stranger's eyes I'm trying to see myself through, but a very specific pair of eyes—inky-dark fathomless eyes.*

It was bad she was thinking about Nikos looking at her naked, but infinitely worse was the inescapable fact she was getting seriously aroused thinking about him doing so!

Shaking with reaction, she covered her shamefully engorged nipples with her crossed arms and stumbled towards the washbasin; gulping, she turned on the cold tap. The cold water she splashed on her face did clear her head but not her deeply troubled thoughts.

I'm about to marry one man and I'm thinking this way about another.

'What does that say about me?' she demanded of the image in the mirror. The fact that she was actually married to the object of her lustful fancies was not, considering the exceptional circumstances, relevant.

Maybe it was time to admit what she had with Tom was not a basis for a lifelong commitment? She shook her head, rejecting the idea. Friendship and respect lasted longer than lust—this inevitably led her thoughts full circle back to Nikos.

'I will not let him do this to me!' she gritted out loud. Only an idiot would want a spectacular burst of showy fireworks when they could have a steady, slow-burning flame. But did she?

Shaking the excess moisture off her face, she took a deep breath and began to rub herself vigorously with a towel. Long before she'd finished her skin was pink and tingling.

When Katie went back through to her bedroom the door to the sitting room shared by the two bedrooms in the large, luxurious suite was open. She couldn't hear any signs of life beyond it, but just in case she tiptoed quietly towards it with the intention of surreptitiously shutting it. She'd feel safer with a visible barrier between them…*but would he, the sly voice in her head wondered…if he knew what you were thinking?*

That was never going to happen!

Pretending she wasn't attracted to him was not going to work any more—actually it never had worked particularly well to begin with—neither could she blame it on the heightened emotions surrounding the fire. The truth was every time she looked at him she was overwhelmed by a mindless hunger with an emphasis on the mindless. Lust was something she could deal with, she told herself without a great deal of conviction.

If only, she thought wistfully as she grasped the door handle, Nikos could be as easily shut out of her thoughts. As part of her new honesty policy she acknowledged it was going to take a lot more than two inches of polished mahogany to accomplish that—*yes, that's going to take a bit of good old-fashioned self-control,* she told herself sternly, *so stop acting as if you don't have any choice about this!*

'There's always a choice!' Katie grimaced to hear the lack of conviction in her voice—*once more with feeling, girl!* 'There's *always* a choice...?'

She frowned and leaned her weight against the door, which, only half closed, had come to an abrupt halt. She grunted softly and gave a shove just as the obstacle revealed itself to be a six-feet-five-in-his-bare-feet obstacle!

Her stomach dipped dramatically as she angled a dismayed look up at his lean, imposing features.

Oh, heavens! Not only could she not get him out of her thoughts, her assumption she could physically shut him out was proving to be optimistic as well!

'Sorry, I didn't see you there.' She smiled tensely as he opened the door fully, and tightened the belt on the calf-length hotel robe. As befitted an up-market hotel, the robe in question was as sumptuously rich as the décor; in fact it was so fluffy and comforting it was hard to tell she had a waist.

Only Katie didn't feel particularly comforted wearing it; it wasn't the provocative nature of this modest get-up that bothered her, but what she was—or rather what she *wasn't*—wearing underneath!

Her glance skimmed over Nikos in what she hoped was a casual way, not likely to be misconstrued as an I-want-to-rip-your-clothes-off sort of way! It revealed that, like herself, he had used the time to bathe, but unlike her he did not have to rely on the robes the hotel supplied. He had changed into casual light-coloured jeans and a polo shirt in a slightly darker silky fabric.

This relaxed version of Nikos was equally devastatingly attractive as the formal one.

'Were you talking to yourself...?'

Katie, lips clamped tight, shook her head vigorously.

One dark brow quirked. 'I thought I heard something.'

'I must have been thinking out loud…'

His lips quivered faintly. 'But not talking to yourself.'

His mockery made her want to hit him, which was not a civilised response, but somehow civilised was hard to achieve around Nikos.

'Sorry if it disturbed you. Goodnight?' she added with more hope than expectation of him taking the hint. He was not big on taking hints.

'You thought I was asleep, perhaps?'

A perfectly innocent question, but something about the gleam in his slightly narrowed eyes made Katie suspect some sort of trap in his seemingly innocuous words.

Nikos had found that many women with expertly applied make-up were almost unrecognisable when seen without it; this was not the case with Katerina. A searching scrutiny of her freshly scrubbed features had revealed a complexion that was flawless, her full, wide lips were a delightful deep pink, the only flaw in fact was the faint bruised bluish shadows beneath her wide-spaced, incredibly blue eyes. Did she not sleep enough? The thought of what she did when she should be sleeping brought a harsh, uncompromising frown to his brow.

'*Asleep?*' she repeated, wary and resentful of the stern look of disapproval he was giving her. 'I hadn't really thought about it.'

'Then I really can't account for it.'

'Account for what?'

Still frowning, Katie turned, her eyes following the direction the sharp tilt of his dark head indicated. She almost groaned out loud when she saw what he was showing her. The large gilt-framed mirror above the queen-sized bed was clearly visible from the other room through the door. It must have given him a perfect view of her approaching the door.

'You looked as if you were trying not to disturb anyone, like a little mouse.'

Katie, recalling the furtive way she'd crept across the room, felt a hot tide of mortification wash over her skin.

'One would be excused,' he continued, 'for thinking you didn't want me to hear you.'

Katie bit her lip; the rat was enjoying her discomfort, she could see it in his eyes. *Just so long as he doesn't find mine equally revealing.* The thought sent a shudder slithering down her spine. She swallowed.

'I said you wouldn't know I was here,' she reminded him.

'So you did. You are so considerate,' he murmured with palpable insincerity. He nudged the door wider with his shoulder and his features hardened. 'Except when you let me think you've passed out in the bath.'

She was startled by the unexpected comment and her eyes flew to his face. 'You didn't think that.' Her scornful smile faded as their eyes locked, her own widened. '*Did you?* But I don't faint…'

A swift mental review of the events in question left her uneasily conscious that her refusal to respond to his calls just might have been interpreted that way by someone who was totally over-cautious.

'It was not such a great leap to make. Consider,' he suggested. 'You are obviously totally exhausted, you have had a traumatic experience…and of course I did not have that one vital piece of information which would have made me realise that my fears were groundless—you don't faint,' he observed with heavy sarcasm.

Katie tossed her head back and gave a combative smile, she'd show him that a totally exhausted—which in her book translated as 'you look like hell'—person was not going to meekly accept his lectures.

'Who do you think you are?'

'Your husband.'

For a moment Katie thought he really could read her

mind until common sense intervened and she reasoned that she must have spoken out loud.

'I take it the traumatic experience you are referring to is you showing up?' Her defiant shrug had a hint of desperation about it; though pitting her wits against Nikos was stimulating in a sticking-your-finger-in-an-electric-socket sort of way, it was also deeply exhausting and Katie felt she was losing momentum. Not to mention her mind.

The problem was she wasn't a naturally aggressive person, *normally*, and she was extremely hampered by the fact she knew she was behaving extremely badly. Nikos, on the other hand, obviously lacked any form of self-awareness; the man had autocratic leanings, which unless someone took him in hand soon would turn him into a fully fledged despot before long.

Nikos released a strangled expletive. 'It had not occurred to me,' he revealed coldly, 'that you would be stupid enough to lock the door.'

If he carries on talking to me as if I'm a silly child caught in misdemeanour I'll… She stopped mid furious thought as her mind produced an image to match his words.

'You mean if it hadn't been locked you'd have come barging in?' she yelped as a remarkably vivid image of Nikos exploding into the bathroom danced across her vision. For some reason her imagination had taken some poetic licence when it came to what he was wearing—*very little*! And as for having him leap energetically into the bath with her—that was a totally unnecessary sequel!

'If you were ill or in need of assistance, yes, I would have, but if you mean do I get my thrills from entering bathrooms uninvited? No, I do not.' Though his facial expression did not alter his abrupt shift of mood was evident in the smouldering gaze that rested on her face. 'If I get invited in…' he gave an expressive shrug '…that changes things.'

'The picture that conjures up makes me queasy.' For all

the wrong reasons, she thought. Jealousy was all she needed!

'I didn't realise that you had such prudish tendencies. Though I should have guessed when you said you and Tom do not talk about sex.'

'I am not a prude,' she denied angrily. Aware that her reaction was a bit OTT, she moderated her voice but couldn't prevent her distaste creeping in. 'I just think what goes on between a man and woman in private should remain that way and should not become the subject of crude jokes.'

'Well, at least you recognise it was a joke. Perhaps some food will help you gain some sense of proportion?'

If he wanted plain talking she'd show him she could do that too! 'And for your information we don't *talk* about sex, we *do* it!' She smiled triumphantly as she flaunted her non-existent sex life under his superior nose.

For a moment Nikos looked startled, then a deep laugh was wrenched from the depths of his throat. 'Thank you for sharing that with me,' he said solemnly.

Katie had never felt so humiliated in her life. She didn't know how she'd allowed herself to be goaded into making such a childish retort.

'Why shouldn't I have a healthy sex life? What's so funny about that?' she demanded.

'You talk about sex with the same swaggering bravado as a boy who has not yet lost his virginity.'

'I am not a boy.'

'Nor a v—'

'You know, I think I am a little hungry,' she cut in brightly.

This attempt to change the subject was so blatant that Nikos smiled. His smile guttered as an incredible thought occurred to him. He shook his head, dismissing it almost instantly; it was amazing what crazy ideas a man could get into his head when he hadn't eaten or slept.

Being an honest man, he couldn't be totally sure if his diminished mental acuity didn't lie at the door of a quite different basic need that was not being met. A basic need that he was conscious of every time he looked at his friend's lover…his own wife.

Nikos frowned. He had all the complications and surprises he needed in his business life; he made sure his personal life was unstressed and uncomplicated. It seemed if he wanted a return to that desirable status quo it would be necessary to remove Katerina Forsythe from his life as soon as possible. Which was the reason he'd come here, but somehow in between rescuing cats from burning buildings and being hospitalised he had been losing track of that detail.

'Fortunately I ordered enough for two in case you changed your mind.'

Katie looked beyond him and saw the glass-topped table set with a tempting array of light refreshments. Her stomach growled softly, reminding her of how little she'd eaten during the past twenty-four hours.

'Oh…' She gave a last wistful look at the spread. 'Actually I think I'm fine after all,' she explained unconvincingly.

'This sudden loss of appetite—is it a case of…cutting off your nose to spite your face? Have I got that right?' he asked innocently.

'Don't be cute!' she accused. 'Your English is a damned sight better than mine and we both know it,' she growled.

'Nobody has ever called me *cute* before. I'm touched.'

She found she couldn't carry on acting as though she were unaware of the malicious mockery in his lean face. 'So must I be…in the head!' She banged a hand against the side of the area in question. 'Just being here makes me certifiable.' Her expansive gesture took in the luxurious surroundings.

'Are you crying?'

Katie heard the wary quiver in his deep voice and re-membered he didn't like women's tears.

'No, but it would serve you right if I was,' she told him, sniffing loudly.

Nikos's expression softened; she talked so tough but looked so vulnerable. The combination affected him strongly.

'It's true I don't like women's tears, but if anyone has reason to weep it is you. You have been very brave...but now you are tired and hungry. Come and eat. Let's call a truce.'

Though she was highly sceptical of his offer of a truce, quite irrationally his unexpected kindness cut through Katie's defences where all his clever taunts had not.

'What's on the sandwiches?' If she persisted in being stubborn, he might jump to the totally wrong conclusion—namely that she was scared to be in the same room as him!

Nikos had the good sense not to act as if he had won. 'Smoked salmon and cream cheese, beef and horseradish and cucumber?'

Katie found it hard not to drool. 'I am hungry.' As if to back up her words her stomach chose that moment to growl again—this time extremely loudly. Her glare dared him to laugh. 'And I hate to see good food go to waste.'

'Indeed,' he agreed, maintaining his gravity. 'Especially just to prove a point.'

'So much for a truce. I knew you couldn't do it!' she crowed.

'It doesn't start until we start eating.'

'Well, if you're going to make the rules up as we go along...'

'I surrender, you win,' he conceded, holding up his hands in mock submission.

'I'm not the one scoring points, I'm hungry.'

Nikos stepped aside to let her pass. 'So am I,' he mur-mured.

Katie took his enigmatic words at face value—she wasn't going somewhere that anybody with an ounce of sense would fear to tread!

Nikos led her to a long cream sofa piled high with plump cushions.

'Elevate your foot,' he suggested, pushing the cushions into a pile one end.

She had sat down at the opposite end before the extent of his inside knowledge struck her. 'How did you know I'm supposed to?'

Nikos slid a hand under her knees and neatly swivelled her round. 'I asked the doctor,' he divulged, placing her feet on the pile of cushions.

Katie's toes curled; she was astounded and indignant. 'And he told you?' So much for patient confidentiality.

'You are my wife.'

'Will you stop saying that?' she begged.

'Even if I do it will not change anything. I doubt the doctor saw any reason not to tell me. Now where is this bandage?'

'In my pocket.'

'It should be on your foot.'

'Well, I couldn't get it on, it's too tight. I tried.'

He held out his hand. 'Let me.'

Katie shook her head. 'Don't be silly.' She scooted her feet up the sofa and tucked them protectively under the hem of her robe.

A nerve began to pulse in his lean cheek. 'My touch offends you?'

'Don't be silly, of course not!' she scoffed.

Telling him what his touch actually did was naturally not an option.

'You are hyperventilating.'

'I am not and there really is no need for a bandage; my ankle feels perfectly fine after the bath.' Her voice rose to a shrill squeak in her frantic efforts to convince him.

'No, it is not, I saw you limping.'

Katie closed her eyes in frustration. 'Go on, have it your way,' she gritted, untucking her leg and stretching it out stiff-kneed.

She could hardly tell him the idea of him placing his hands on her skin for any length of time made her hot with excitement and cold with dread. What if she got turned on? Who was she kidding? There was no *if* about it! Hell, he only had to look at her and she felt emotionally mugged. What if when he touched her she did or said something *really* stupid?

Nikos silently looked at the ankle extended towards him but he made no attempt to touch it or her. The moment stretched on…

He remained motionless so long the muscles in her thigh started to quiver. The silence between them was heavy with tension; finally Katie could bear it no longer.

'Are you going to do this or not?' she demanded peevishly. *Not* would be good.

Nikos rolled up the sleeves of his shirt, revealing the sinewy strength of his forearms. Katie was engulfed by a wave of longing that filled her with despair.

'Then for goodness' sake get it over and done with!' she snapped.

When he did take her ankle between his big hands, they felt cool and capable. His attitude as he gently examined the tender bruised area was detached but sympathetic.

'It is badly swollen and the bruising is coming out.' His dark brows met in a frowning line as he examined her injury with strong, sensitive fingers. 'It looks extremely painful.'

It was, but this wasn't the reason Katie evaded his questioning glance. When she looked at him she saw his fingers touching, stroking areas on her body other than her ankle. The dangerous fantasy fuelled the pulse of inappropriate excitement that throbbed through her.

She took out her self-disgust on her innocent ankle. 'You didn't mention ugly,' she told him with a disconsolate sniff. With a frown she compared the injured ankle with her sound one; it was at least three times the size.

'I'm sure Tom will still love you if you had ankles as thick as tree trunks.'

She supposed it was the thought of Tom's uncritical adoration that brought the thin sneer to his lips. As far as Nikos was concerned she would never be good enough for his friend or him.

'I'm not so sure,' she mused half to herself as her thoughts turned to Tom's love of all things beautiful and perfect.

It was only his way of talking but sometimes, when Tom referred to her as his most precious possession, it made her uncomfortable. Tom liked his possessions in mint condition; if anything fell below the high standards he demanded he got rid of it. He had laughed and called Katie hopelessly sentimental when, after dropping a valuable vase, she hadn't let him throw it away.

'You bought it for me that day we went to an antique fair, and if I turn it like this,' she explained, 'you won't be able to see the crack at all.

'It's not worth anything now. I'll buy you another one.' He looked perplexed when she told him a new one wouldn't be the same.

'No, because then it won't have a flaw,' he replied drily.

Would he buy another wife just as easily when the old one got too worn? Katie was immediately ashamed of the unbidden thought.

'You place a high value on your looks and a low one on yourself.'

The stinging contempt in Nikos's voice brought Katie's attention swinging back to his face. She discovered he was angry. Inexplicably and impressively furious.

'If people can't see beyond your beautiful face and attractive figure, don't you see that that is their problem, not yours?'

Katie blinked in bewilderment at the harsh reproach in his voice. He thought she had a beautiful face…?

'I…' She bit back a cry of pain as his lean fingers tightened painfully around her bruised ankle.

Nikos immediately loosened his grip. 'I'm sorry I hurt you.'

'Not really,' she lied.

He grunted and slid her a look of irritation. Supporting her ankle against his own knee, he proceeded to roll the tubular bandage into a manageable shape.

'I would ask you to tell me if it hurts, but—' he raised his dark head from his task and there was an ironic gleam in his eyes '—I'd be wasting my time, wouldn't I?'

Katie doubted any pain could be worse than that sharp but sweet pleasure of having his fingers brush lightly against her skin.

'Thank you,' she said quietly when the support was back in place.

Nikos finished smoothing invisible wrinkles from the bandage over the curve of her calf and lifted his head; there was a faint flush along his high cheekbones. 'It was hardly brain surgery. Sit there,' he added. 'I'll bring you some food.'

'Oh! I thought I'd just take something to my room.'

One side of his mobile lips dropped. *'Running away?'*

'I can't run.'

'That's true. I don't like to eat alone; stay.'

Not likely. 'All right, I'll stay,' she heard herself reply. 'It seems a strange time of night to be eating.' But then it had been a strange day.

'You eat when you are hungry.'

Katie smiled at this simplistic philosophy; it was very Nikos.

'People have far too many hang-ups about food,' he revealed. 'How's this?' he added, passing her a laden plate.

'If I had any hang-ups about food I'd faint, but it looks great.' Her enthusiasm sounded false and hollow to her own ears; it was the fault of his slow-burning smile, the one that crinkled the corners of his eyes.

'We can pretend we're having a midnight feast, is that not what they do in English schools?'

'Not the one I went to,' Katie replied, thinking of the local comprehensive she had attended. She imagined it was a far cry from the sort of school Nikos had gone to. In fact her life was a far cry from his.

'Were you clever at school?'

'Not particularly,' she replied, suspicious of his interest. 'But I was very popular.' She gave a sudden impish grin that gave him a glimpse of the dry sense of humour that she had not had much opportunity to display in his company. 'But only because I had an extraordinarily handsome twin brother. You'd be amazed at how many girls wanted to come home for tea with me.'

'You were a twin?'

Katie, her mouth full of sandwich, nodded.

'It must have been especially hard for you to lose him,' he mused. Katie didn't reply; talking about Peter was still hard. 'What sort of man was your brother?'

Katie considered the question.

'He was handsome, impetuous, funny...' She stopped and flicked a wry look towards Nikos—best to beat him to the punchline. 'In short he was the exact opposite of me.'

He didn't dispute her assessment. 'You were the sensible twin?'

His perception was spooky; Peter had been the creative, impulsive twin and she had been the practical, grounded one.

'Peter was very special,' she said quietly.

'My brother was older, and we were not particularly

close. It was hard on my father when he died—Dimitri was his favourite.'

It was impossible to tell from his impassive expression whether he had minded this. Katie, seeing him as a little boy trying to gain parental approval, discovered that she had enough indignation for them both.

'He was groomed to take over virtually from birth. When we lost him my father literally almost worked himself to death because he didn't think I could fill my brother's shoes.'

And psychologists wondered why children went off the rails! With fathers around like the insensitive clot Nikos was describing it was a wonder any children ever turned out normal!

'That's so unfair!' she blurted out angrily. She flushed as he shot her a strange look. 'I just hope,' she added stiffly, 'I never make any child of mine feel inadequate,' she declared fiercely.

If Nikos had ever had any inadequacies he had obviously worked through them long ago—it was hard to imagine anyone *more* assured and confident than he was.

'And do you plan on having any children soon?'

Katie sighed. 'Tom doesn't think it would be a good idea to start a family for a few years yet.'

Nikos suspected she was unaware of how wistful she sounded. 'And you?' he probed gently.

'You shouldn't have a baby to fill a gap in your life.'

To Nikos it sounded as though she had told herself this many times before. 'Some people might say that if you are married to the right man you don't have a gap in your life.'

'Of course, but when you love someone it's only natural to want to have children with that person…' She looked at him, listening attentively to what she was saying, and stopped dead. 'I *am* marrying the right man!' He never lost an opportunity to get in a sly dig. *And how,* she wondered, *do I come to be babbling on like an agony aunt about life, love and babies with Nikos Lakis of all people?*

'Did I say otherwise? I was just making a general observation.'

'It didn't sound very general to me.' It was, she decided, her turn to ask the questions. 'This *father* of yours—' she couldn't keep the cold note of disapproval out of her voice '—does he pick out your bride too?' She knew that her mother's experience was not an isolated one, even now in the twenty-first century.

Nikos shook his head. 'My father says he's not giving me the excuse to turn around and say he's to blame when I mess up my marriage. His own marriage to my mother was arranged by their families; it was not a happy union,' he explained unemotionally. 'They virtually lived separate lives; when she died her lover phoned my father to tell him.'

Katie was unable to imagine living like that and what would it be like for the children of such a union?

'Cheer up.' He pressed a finger to the corners of her down-turned lips. 'He found true love the second time.'

His light touch had gone but the tingling sensation persisted. 'Poor true love,' she muttered mutinously.

Nikos looked amused by her venom. 'Oh, she manages to hold her own. You know, my father is not *all* bad. I have to admit in his defence that I did very little to disabuse him of the notion that I had no natural inclination for hard work. I was no angel.'

'Seven years married and now he tells me!'

His slow-burning smile appeared in response to her wry grin. It was almost, she mused, as if there was a connection, a real rapport between them; she froze, panic racing through her veins. *Connection! Rapport! You don't get cosy with the man who's doing his best to stop you marrying the man you love!*

'Listen,' she said with a tight smile that didn't reach her

worried eyes, 'you don't have to talk about your family with me.'

'Why—am I boring you?'

'No, you're not boring me.' Was he trying to be obtuse? 'It's a bit late for deep and meaningful discussions.' She yawned elaborately to emphasise her point.

'Isn't that what people do late at night?' he suggested softly. 'When the curtains are closed and the rest of the world does not exist. They reveal things about themselves that they would not dream of doing during the day. The night has a way of lowering barriers and thawing reserves.' His liquid dark gaze slid slowly over her body, then returned to her soft, trembling mouth. 'Of course,' he rasped throatily, 'they are usually in bed at the time and they do not spend all their time talking.'

Her sanity was history!

His voice was a sin!

She cleared her throat and tugged fretfully at the neck of her robe. It took all her will-power to wrench her lust-struck gaze from his face. At that moment she was extremely grateful that the towelling was so thick because her breasts were so tense and tender that in normal clothes the brazen changes in them would have been hard to miss.

'Well, we aren't…in bed!' she choked. 'That is, I don't want…you…we…' She closed her eyes and squared her shoulders. She could link more than two words together if she just put her mind to it and didn't look directly into his eyes.

'I'm sure I don't want to pry,' she announced, applying herself to the food even though her appetite had suddenly left her.

Considering his hunger, Nikos did not eat much, but he did watch her; in fact her appetite seemed to fascinate him. She tried not to let his interest put her off—it actually became a matter of principle not to let him see how much he spooked her, though she was beginning to suspect he already knew. He had to have seen the symptoms a hundred times before—he was the sort of man that women reacted to. In fact he probably took their homage as his due.

It occurred to her that he might be comparing her robust enjoyment of the food unfavourably with the more delicate, refined manners of his sophisticated lady friends.

'That was very nice, thank you.' Having started, Katie decided it seemed logical to get all the thank-yous out of the way at once. 'And thank you for saving my cat and giving me a bed tonight…it's kind of you,' she admitted primly.

Nikos looked at her with unsettling intensity for a moment. 'Perhaps you should try and get some sleep?' he suggested abruptly.

Katie nodded, unable to rid herself of the conviction he'd been about to say something quite different. Unable to endure his hard, steady appraisal any longer, she stood up. Aware of a strong and totally illogical feeling of anticlimax, she smoothed down the non-existent creases in her robe.

'I will.' Nikos's dark enigmatic eyes held hers but he still didn't speak. 'Goodnight?' Katie was deeply mortified to hear the word emerge as a wistful question. Her bare toes curled into the thick carpet. Could she be more obvious? She chastised herself, *Why don't you just go ahead and beg the man not to let you leave, Katie? That might be more subtle.*

'Goodnight, Katerina.'

Though his expression was about as revealing as a stone wall and his deep-accented drawl no more enlightening, Katie was totally convinced she read contempt in both. She limped towards the door before she could make any more of a fool of herself.

CHAPTER NINE

DESPITE the fact her body ached with exhaustion, Katie didn't find sleep quickly. Neither, it seemed, did Nikos—as she tossed she was aware of the crack of light under the door and maybe it was her overactive imagination but she seemed to hear his soft tread as he paced the room.

Eventually however she must have slept and when she awoke later in a cold sweat the light had gone and the room was in total darkness. She couldn't recall what she had been dreaming about, but when she had awoken whatever it was had left her with a nebulous sense of dread. In the unfamiliar surroundings it took her several clumsy attempts before she found the switch for the bedside light.

Despite the cluttered condition of her bedside table at home—the surface was crammed with framed snapshots of her family—she could locate the light switch with her eyes closed. In fact she frequently did.

A poignant smile curved her lips as her sleepy thoughts drifted to those well-loved family photos, none of which was going to win any prizes for composition or technique, but each one represented a precious memory for her... The one of Peter soaked to the skin but grinning after he'd taken a tumble into the pond they had picnicked beside. One of her favourites was her mother, who had believed herself unphotogenic, looking beautiful as she held aloft their birthday cake aflame with candles...*aflame*— The sound of the mental block in Katie's head crumbling was deafening.

'Oh, what am I going to do? They've all gone! Everything!' she cried out loud as the full horror of her loss came crashing down upon her.

The photos were gone...everything was gone. There was

nothing…not a single keepsake left of her mother, father or brother. She must have known this all along, but a protective mechanism had kicked in that had stopped her acknowledging it—until now.

Shoulders heaving, she turned over and buried her face in the pillow. Curled up in a tight foetal ball of misery beneath the duvet, Katie began to sob without restraint for what she had lost in the fire.

She was so immersed in this orgy of misery that she didn't hear the knock on the interconnecting door and she remained oblivious to the sound of a deep, concerned voice hesitantly calling her name. She wasn't even aware of the tall figure lowering himself down onto the edge of her bed. The hand on her shoulder was the first she knew of Nikos's presence.

'What's wrong?' He raked a hand through his tousled hair as he received a fresh wail in response. '*Speak to me!*' he demanded, shaking her slightly.

If Katie hadn't had other things on her mind she would have immediately noticed that his accent was perceptibly stronger and his air of calm command considerably frayed around the edges—but she did have other things on her mind.

Clutching the pillow her face was buried in even tighter with one hand, she used the other to hit out backwards. She didn't make contact.

'Nothing's wrong. Go away!' Her words emerged indistinctly through the pillow and the aching constriction in her throat.

'Clearly there is nothing wrong,' Nikos ironically observed. Eyes narrowed, he examined his options…then, giving vent to a harsh, guttural Greek curse, he flipped the hunched figure in the bed over onto her back. Katie didn't alter her position, she kept her knees folded up on her chest and her chin tucked into them.

'No doubt this cheery contentment is causing you to

weep as though your heart is broken,' he said drily as he proceeded to separate her from the pillow. 'You look like a baby hedgehog minus the spikes—on second thoughts, cancel the minus.'

Bereft of her protection, Katie covered her face with her arms, oblivious to how much of her naked state she revealed in the process. 'At least I have a heart!' she exclaimed. 'Will you just go away and leave me alone... *please!*' she added on an anguished note of entreaty as the sobs began to rise in her chest again.

Nikos drew a frustrated hand across a lean cheek, which was liberally sprinkled with an even layer of dark stubble. 'Do not be ridiculous, I cannot possibly leave you like this,' he told her grimly. 'Are you ill?'

'Go away!'

'Do you need a doctor? Is that it? I need to tell him what is wrong. Are you in pain? Does it hurt?'

'Only when I breathe.'

'Your chest hurts?'

'No.'

He released a tense sigh. 'I am going to call a doctor. I won't be long.'

Alarmed at the idea of medical intervention, she lifted an arm from her eyes and glared through jewel-bright, tear-filled eyes at him. 'Don't you *dare* call a doctor!' she snapped, emphasising her prohibition with a finger waved angrily in the general direction of his aristocratic nose.

'That,' Nikos approved, 'is better.' Almost casually he pinned her wrist against the pillow and then, after a very minor tussle, did the same with the other.

Katie's head thrashed angrily from side to side before she focused her wrath on the dark, demonically handsome face of the man looming over her. Her breath slowed and her expression grew unfocused. It was the first time she registered what he was wearing or, rather, *not!*

She had slept in the nude because she had no option;

Nikos obviously did so out of choice, because he clearly didn't have a stitch on beneath that robe. Which wouldn't have mattered so much if it had been a towelling hotel robe he was wearing, but this was a black silky thing that was knotted worryingly loosely about his waist as though he'd thrown it on in a hurry.

'What school of counselling did you attend?' she asked hoarsely.

'Talk to me,' Nikos replied with the air of someone who was not going to be easily distracted from his purpose.

Katie envied his focus; her own couldn't even withstand the warm, uniquely male fragrance rising from his body. To her dismay when he leaned forward to cause the revealing robe to gape even more, exposing in the process most of his chest and a great deal of his flat belly, and if she hadn't stopped herself looking—it hadn't been easy—probably even more.

'Why should I?' she demanded, reasserting control over her wandering eyes. It might be different if he actually cared, she thought dully, and why should he? *First I'm an inconvenient wife he preferred to pretend didn't exist, now I'm an embarrassingly emotionally incontinent guest.* By now he must be wishing he hadn't taken pity on her homeless condition.

'Because you want me to go away, and I won't do so until you have,' he explained simply.

'What,' she asked facetiously, 'do you want me to talk about? The weather?'

Nikos was pleased to recall an annoying phrase that Caitlin was inordinately fond of using. It seemed appropriate for the occasion.

'It is not good to keep things bottled up.'

Katie was so astonished to hear this advice emerging from his mouth that she stopped struggling. '*You're* giving *me* advice on expressing emotions?' She blinked. 'You're priceless, you really are.'

Nikos decided to try another tack.

'What' he asked with a dizzying change of subject, 'are you wearing?'

Katie froze and tried to slide a little farther under the duvet. 'What's that got to do with anything?'

He lifted one brow and smiled blandly. 'Not a thing, but I was just thinking how easy it would be to find out, if I were a man totally without scruples.'

Katie ran the tip of her tongue over the outline of her dry lips and swallowed. 'Are you trying to blackmail me?' she squeaked as she considered her options. He was almost certainly bluffing, but could she risk it? 'Let me go. *Please…*'

Nikos's dark glance dwelt thoughtfully on her face for several seconds and then with a slight inclination of his head he released her wrists.

With a white-knuckled grip on the duvet, Katie slithered a little farther upright, raising the cover to her chin as she did so.

'I was crying because I have lost everything in the fire.'

'Were you not insured?'

Katie threw him a scornful look. 'I'm not talking about things with monetary value; I don't care about them!' she declared with a disdainful sniff.

Nikos's gaze narrowed as he listened to the woman who had married a stranger for money contemptuously dismiss her possessions. Nikos did not like anomalies.

'Some things can't be replaced with a cheque.' She caught her lower lip between her teeth to stop it trembling. 'All the photos of my parents and brother…all the keepsakes… Mum kept the oddest things—a curl from our first haircut, Peter's certificate when he won first prize in the fancy dress competition, the theatre programme from her first proper date with Dad.'

With a cry she rolled onto her side and pressed her hand

over her mouth. Nikos went to touch her but her slim body tensed in rejection and with a twisted smile he drew back.

'They all went up in the fire,' she explained dully, when she had composed herself. She rolled onto her back. 'There's nothing left!' she told him in a tight, controlled voice that couldn't disguise the bleakness in her eyes. Despite her attempt to stay in control, her voice rose as her anguish-filled eyes locked angrily with his.

At one level she knew that it was unfair to make him a target of her anger, but her anger didn't listen to reason, it just needed an outlet.

'Does that constitute just cause in your eyes? I suppose you think I'm being hopelessly sentimental crying about things most people would throw away?' she goaded.

Feeling herself losing control—or was it the emotion she saw in his eyes she couldn't take?—she lowered her eyes to her fingers, which were restlessly picking at the edge of the cotton cover.

'It is just cause, and, as for sentimentality, that is not a crime in my homeland. We Greeks are a sentimental race.'

Katie lifted her head jerkily and looked with astonishment at the grave expression on his face. Would this man ever stop surprising her? she wondered. Every time she thought she had a handle on him he did something that made her retrench.

'But I think you are wrong—you have not lost everything.'

Katie's anger stirred. He'd been in there, he must know that nothing had survived. It was cruel of him to try and raise false hopes just to save himself the discomfort of her tears!

'The fire may have burned paper and twisted metal beyond recognition but some things were beyond its reach...' He reached over and touched the side of her head with his forefinger. 'Inside here you have the memories of a lifetime and nothing can ever rob you of those,' he told her softly.

Her eyes shot to his and what she saw there convinced her of his total sincerity. He was not just mouthing empty platitudes, he believed totally in what he had just said.

'*Oh!*' she breathed, moved to tears by what he had said, but this time they were tears of appreciation not despair. He was right—some things nobody could take away from her. She could keep her memories, treasure and polish them. She lifted her hand to dab the moisture leaking from her eyes and felt the duvet slip; she immediately grabbed it again.

Nikos folded his arms across his chest and watched her contortions. 'Let me?'

Before she could voice a protest he lifted his hand and blotted the salty moisture from her cheek with his thumb. Her body's response to the soft touch was immediate and devastating. The devastation was not confined to the area of her downy cheek he stroked; her entire body was filled with a heavy, throbbing lassitude. Katie's eyelashes brushed her cheek as they flickered weakly downwards.

'There's really no need,' she murmured vaguely.

Nikos looked down into the upturned face of the young woman beside him, his dark eyes touching the blue-veined tracery on her flickering eyelids, the faint, tell-tale flush of blood beneath her pale skin, the vulnerable exposed line of her lovely throat and the pulse spot that throbbed at the base of that throat.

He was barely touching her and she was aroused. The natural progression of his male thoughts led him to visualise how she might respond if he did more than stroke her cheek…such a soft cheek, such smooth skin. Was it equally smooth all over? His heated glance dropped from her lush lips to her smooth, bare shoulders…

'No,' he agreed throatily. 'No need at all.' The statement was noticeably lacking in his usual absolute conviction.

Katie sighed low in her throat, an almost feline sound of

pleasure, and turned her head so that the circular movement of his thumb now moved over an area as yet untouched.

The action caused a section of her long silky hair to fall across her cheek. Nikos brushed it aside, but instead of removing his hand he slid his fingers deep into the thick glossy mass until they could trace the shape of her skull.

Katie gave a voluptuous sigh of pleasure.

'I should go,' he said throatily.

Katie's eyes shot open in protest. *'You can't!'* She encountered the sensual heat of his smouldering eyes and her heart started to slam against her ribs. She moistened her lips with the tip of her tongue and swallowed. 'You could stay?'

Nikos inhaled sharply, the action sucking in his flat belly and swelling his magnificent bronzed chest. His eyes slid from hers, his lush lashes effectively concealing his expression; this didn't stop Katie imagining the embarrassed distaste no doubt mirrored there. Her misery was complete when he turned his head away and expelled his suspended breath with a low, sibilant hiss.

No wonder he can't look at me. Self-respect, pride… remember what those are, Katie?

'No, of course not, that's a silly idea. Take no notice of me, I'm in shock…yes, that's it, I'm in shock!' she heard herself cry in manic relief. 'Let's just forget I said it. I didn't mean it.'

Nikos spun back to her, his eyes blazing. 'Yes, you did!' he contradicted rawly. 'And *I can't forget!*' The explosive pronouncement seemed to be ripped from his throat.

Katie swallowed, mesmerised by the lambent glow in his silvered eyes. 'Why not…?'

'Because,' he said in the manner of someone making an uncomfortable discovery, 'I don't want to.'

Katie gasped as a pleasure-pain knifed through her body.

Sexual longing of a type she hadn't known existed made her bold; it also made her reckless and single-minded. Her tunnel vision saw no consequences, only need—a need that consumed her. Every fibre of her being was mindlessly intent on assuaging the hunger, which no part of her was free of.

'What *do* you want?' she whispered, wondering how much more of this torment she could take.

Her desire for him went bone-deep; she wanted the taste of him, the feel of him, she wanted all of him... She'd never experienced anything like this before and had no defences against it.

'The same thing I've wanted to do since the first moment I met you...' Arms braced either side of her shoulders, he lowered himself with a beautifully fluid movement down until she could feel his warm breath shiver against her skin. He adjusted the angle of his head so his lips were positioned directly over hers and their warm breaths mingled.

Anticipation of his kiss made her dizzy, but despite the tension that every taut line of his body screamed Nikos was in no hurry.

'Your mouth is truly edible,' he rasped smokily as, holding her eyes with his, he took tiny soft bites almost too light for her to feel from the quivering outline.

The sexy rumble of his voice made her tremble. Through the fluttering shield of her lowered lashes she studied his rampantly male features, dizzy with anticipation.

'No!' He shook his head very slightly as her heavy eyelids closed. 'I want you to look at me.'

Katie responded to his instruction without thinking, though her eyelids felt as though they were weighed down. 'I was looking at you, I can't seem to help myself,' she said, not trying to evade his searching eyes. 'What else do you want me to do?'

'I want you to open your mouth for me.'

'I want that too,' she revealed, gazing up at him with unconcealed desire. '*I want you,*' she added simply in a voice that literally *ached* with longing, silently adding that this was what she'd wanted for seven long years.

A hot flood of hoarse words spilled from Nikos as his darkened eyes sealed to hers; he seemed completely unaware that he had spoken in Greek. Katie barely registered it herself. The only thing she needed to understand was in his smoky eyes and they said the same thing in any language—he wanted her! And she wanted him—oh, how she wanted him!

Why didn't I know that surrender felt this sweet, this empowering? Katie thought dreamily. The satisfaction didn't come solely from surrendering to him, it was from surrendering to her own passion.

He rolled onto his side and, with one big hand supporting the back of her head, took her with him, all the while pressing hot, frantic kisses to her face and neck as throaty words of Greek and English spilled from his lips.

The fine tremors afflicting her entire body became deep shudders as he finally fitted his mouth to hers.

Katie whimpered at the expert pressure of his lips, the whimper became a fierce groan as his clever tongue stabbed smoothly deep into the sweet warmth of her mouth and then again and again…parodying a more intimate invasion.

Through the thickness of the duvet Katie curved her pliant body into his muscular frame and even though several inches of duck down separated them she could feel the urgency of his arousal. She took hold of his head between her hands and, meshing her fingers deep in his rich, luxuriant hair, she met his tongue tentatively with her own—then again, more boldly.

If this was depravity she wanted more of it—she never wanted to break the contact; she wanted it to go on for ever and ever.

Nikos continued to kiss her with the same blind, driving urgency as he smoothly rolled her underneath him. He performed the move with the same fluid grace he did every-

thing, but at that moment she was willing to forgive him
for being perfect. Very few things Katie had experienced
had ever felt as incredibly marvellous as the weight of his
warm, hard body pinning her to the bed. The intimate pressure of his erection grinding into her soft belly made her
whimper softly into his mouth.

Panting, they finally broke apart like divers breaking to
the surface in search of oxygen. Nikos rolled away to one
side, his chest heaving; he lifted his arm across his face,
wiping the sheen of sweat from his brow. It remained there,
concealing his expression from her.

Eyes glazed and glittering, face flushed, Katie reached
for him; actually she couldn't bear *not* to touch him. His
body was incredible; every detail of it held a fascination
for her. She had enough oxygen stored up to last at least
another two kisses and she shook with the need to get out
of her depth again—and fast!

'You've wanted to do that all night?' she asked wonderingly as she stroked his arm. His flesh had a deliciously
silky texture and the toned muscles were hard and compact
and beautifully formed beneath her fingertips. She'd had
her suspicions, but it came as some relief to have it confirmed that her lustful fantasies had not been one-sided.

'I've wanted to do that since seven years ago,' he corrected huskily.

Katie's eyes widened. 'I had no idea I made such an
impact.'

'*Impact!*' he echoed, releasing a strange, strangled laugh.
'I think you could safely say you did that, Katerina. When
I walked into that cheap, nasty little room I expected...'
Katie saw the muscles of his strong brown throat work as
he swallowed.

'A cheap and nasty bride?' she suggested sadly. Only
her loyalty to the memory of her brother stopped her explaining there and then why she had taken the drastic decision to buy a bridegroom.

'Well, let's just say I wasn't expecting a girl who looked like a sexy kitten. All enormous, trusting blue eyes, a sexy mouth and a cloud of the most incredible silky hair. It put me in a vile temper to realise I was as weak as any other man; I had considered I was immune to such things.'

He had known of course that she couldn't have been the wide-eyed innocent she'd appeared, which in his considered opinion had made her all the more dangerous. But he had begun to wonder if he shouldn't have followed his gut instincts in this instance and to hell with consequences. He had a strong suspicion that his gut instincts might have been closer to the truth than the judgment he'd made based on more practical considerations.

'Add to that you looked about sixteen.'

'I was eighteen,' she corrected him huskily.

'And you had—correction, *have*—a body that could make a grown man weep.'

A sound halfway between a groan and a laugh was wrenched from his chest as his arm lifted from his face revealing a rigid mask of constraint. As he scanned her face some of his control slipped, offering her a glimpse of a raw hunger that made her stomach muscles clench violently.

'I know that marriages nowadays are not noted for their durability, but how many men who meet the most beautiful and desirable woman they have ever seen marry her then walk away swearing not to remain faithful, but never to see or contact her again?'

He lifted a section of her silky hair and let it slip through his fingers. 'You know, *yineka mou*, I think we have some unfinished business.'

Katie nodded. 'I nearly asked Harvey about you,' she admitted shyly. 'But I couldn't, not after making such a fuss about wanting there to be no contact.'

'Do you still not desire contact?' His low, seductive drawl sent a stab of white-hot sexual desire through her body.

She shook her head and urgently moaned his name. In

her naivety she'd expected his kisses to ease her hunger, but instead they had acted as a release valve for all the pent-up sensuality that had been dammed up inside her for years. Her passionate nature had found a focus—Nikos.

'So sweet, so wild.'

His husky appreciation jolted her. *He thinks I'm going to be good at this. He's expecting a sex goddess—heavens, does he have it all wrong!* Telling him she was a virgin would be just too mortifying; there had to be some other way to explain her lack of competence...?

'*No!*' she denied, twisting to evade his lips. 'I'm not wild—in fact I'm not a sexy sort of person,' she blurted out.

Her revelation did not have any immediate effect; Nikos carried on kissing her neck with just as much dedication as before. Katie's concentration drifted as she felt the resistance slip from her body. 'Did you hear what I said, Nikos?' She hoped so because she couldn't say it again.

Nikos gave her neck a nibble before raising his head. 'You have my full attention. So you are not sexy?' Laughter formed in his liquid dark eyes and his lips twitched. Even with his hair tousled he looked incredibly gorgeous.

Katie observed with dismay that he didn't seem to be taking her very seriously. 'Ask Tom if you don't believe me.' As wrong things to say went, this was right up there in the top three.

She wasn't exactly surprised when Nikos's expression froze over. 'I don't require references from your lovers.'

Lovers! Gracious, he was really missing the point—it being she hadn't had any of the above and he'd had dozens...hundreds probably! Therein lay the problem.

'And I forbid you to *think* about Tom.' His powerful body curved over hers. 'Do you hear me?'

'I hear you, Nikos!' she said, awed and even—quite shockingly—a little turned on by his masterful behaviour.

Nikos scanned her face; whatever he saw there must have satisfied him because then he nodded before he kissed her again, long, deep, drugged kisses that left her craving more.

Katie gave a soft moan as he left her mouth to lick and bite his way down her throat until he reached the wildly throbbing pulse spot at the base of her neck. His breath, which came in uneven gasps, was hot against her bare skin.

'I want to see you,' he informed her in a thickened voice that was not entirely steady.

At his words a white-hot flame of desire pulsed through her throbbing body like a blade. Along with it came a thread of doubt…which she firmly squashed.

Katie had never craved a man's approval before. Taking her courage by the scruff of the neck, she pushed away the mesh of hair that had fallen across her face. Looking directly into his eyes, she peeled back the quilt in one quick motion.

Nikos inhaled sharply. Katie's self-doubt began to flow steadily away from her as he examined her body in an almost reverent silence. A primitive mask of need tautened his lean features as his liquid dark eyes consumed her with the single-minded concentration of a starving man confronted with a feast.

'So pale, so perfect. You are beautiful, *yineka mou*,' he asserted shakily. 'Just looking at you makes me burn.'

Katie ran a finger across his cheek feeling drunk with her newly discovered feminine power. That she could excite such feelings in a man like this…why, nothing seemed impossible now.

'You make me feel very strange,' she confided innocently.

The not-so-innocent sultry smile that accompanied her words provoked an immediate response from Nikos. He laughed huskily and framed her flushed face with his hands. Her pulse gave a lustful surge as she stared in awed wonder at the thrillingly primitive expression etched on his strong-boned, beautiful face.

'You make me feel very hot,' he revealed with a wolfish grin that made her quiver inside and out.

She watched, not daring to breathe, her heart thumping like a wild thing as he curled his hand around the swell of her breast. A voluptuous sigh of pleasure escaped from between her clenched teeth; his touch on her bare skin was electric.

The expression on his face as he traced the tip-tilted profile of first one breast and then the other with his expert fingers was rapt. When his eyes lifted to hers there was a raw, needy look on his face that made her insides dissolve.

His exploration homed in on her nipple; she stopped breathing as he took the prominent bud between his thumb and forefinger, and the resulting friction made her body arch.

'Good?'

Katie opened her eyes. 'Very good. Do it again!' she demanded.

He did.

Lips parted, eyes shut tight, she squirmed restlessly as his thumb moved back and forth across the rosily engorged nipple at the centre. He ran his tongue over the sensitised flesh and sensual overload sent Katie's head backwards into the pillow.

She had barely assimilated the sensual delights of this sensation when his exploration moved lower. His skilful fingers left a burning trail as they skimmed lightly over her belly. As his exploration boldly widened to include the soft fuzz of hair at the apex of her legs Katie found she could hardly breathe for the intense excitement that held her in its vicelike grip.

With sultry abandon she looked up at him through half-closed eyes. The mindless hunger she felt was reflected in the stark mask of need that contorted his dark features. She caught her tongue between her teeth and gasped as, with his eyes melded to hers, he allowed his fingers to slide between her legs into the slick heat of her aching core.

Katie moaned and felt the heat spread across her lower abdomen. Eyes locked to his, she parted her long legs in wanton invitation. With a muttered imprecation Nikos loosened the belt of his robe in a frenzied manner.

'My God, but you have a beautiful body!'

Shooting her a quick, predatory grin, he continued.

Simply looking at his sleek, streamlined, rampantly male body brought an emotional ache to her throat that had nothing to do with simple lust—she wasn't actually surprised, she supposed that deep down she'd always known the feelings he aroused were more complex...more dangerous.

He finally shed his black silky robe, revealing to her mesmerised gaze a fully aroused male in all his glory. 'Oh, my!' she gasped shakily as he rejoined her on the bed.

'Touch me!' he invited, kissing her lips. 'Don't you want to?'

'Oh, yes!' She touched his collar-bone; it was very nice, but there were other areas that interested her more.

Nikos seemed to share her view because, smiling into her eyes, he took her hand and fed it onto a more enticing area of his body. She felt the fine muscles under the smooth skin of the surface of his belly contract violently—she was hooked!

Katie released a long, shuddering breath and, no longer tentative, trailed her fingers over his warm brown flesh, making return journeys to areas that seemed particularly sensitive. The texture of his flesh was incredible; she wanted to taste it.

What's stopping you?

With growing confidence in her ability to excite him, she let her lips and tongue follow the pathway her fingers had previously traced down his tense, quivering body.

Nikos lay, his eyes half closed, accepting her ministrations until her exploration got bolder.

Lying on her back, her arms pinned either side of her head, she was about to protest but he got in first.

'My turn, I think,' he said, slipping down her body.

He seemed to know exactly where, how and for how long to touch her in order to send her out of control and keep her there. Katie didn't want to think how he'd got so good at what he was doing to her, she just wanted to enjoy it, and she did.

'I can't take any more of this,' she gasped weakly, when he eventually returned to her mouth.

'Just a little more…' he promised, settling between her thighs. His face a mask of rigid restraint, he slid into her with one smooth thrust.

A fractured gasp hissed through her clenched teeth at the sharp pain, but then it was gone and he was still there filling her, stretching her in a wonderful way that she could not have imagined. Experimentally she moved; this was when she realised that Nikos was not moving. He was dead still.

She opened her eyes to find him watching her with an expression of white-faced incredulity; his body was quivering with the effort of not moving.

'There's more?'

Katie felt the sound of hoarse amusement that was wrenched from his throat. 'Let me show you, *yineka mou.*'

Her throaty, *Please,* was lost inside his mouth but her awed, *'That is incredible,'* to inadequately describe the sensation of him moving inside her was clearly audible. Pretty soon after that she lost all ability to say anything coherent, though when she felt his hot release pulse into her body a couple of seconds after she'd been blown away by a shattering climax she did manage to speak, but only the one word.

'Nikos!'

It was amazing how much feeling and variation a person

could put into two syllables, especially if you said them over and over and over again!

Once she could speak it seemed better to anticipate any awkward cross-examination.

'Before you ask, yes, I was. But,' she added with a languid smile, 'if I'd known it could be like that I wouldn't have been.' This out of the way, she curled up like a kitten in his arms and went to sleep.

CHAPTER TEN

KATIE woke to the smell of coffee. Eyes closed, she stirred, drowsily conscious that something was subtly different. She tried to focus her thoughts but the extra ingredient remained tantalisingly out of reach. It was several sleepy minutes later when it hit her with the dramatic impact of a force ten hurricane; she gasped and stilled.

Oh, no, it's me, I'm different. Beautifully different. I slept with Nikos Lakis.

A wondering smile drew the corners of her mouth upwards. Rolling onto her side, she reached out. Her smile faded when she discovered only a sheet, its crumpled condition standing a silent accusing testament to the vigour of their lovemaking through the night.

She closed her eyes as a jumbled kaleidoscope of the events of the night slid across her inner vision. What she saw shocked and excited her; it also provided an explanation for the unaccustomed tenderness in several parts of her body.

The only cloud on her horizon was Tom—she had to tell him. She felt ashamed that she had treated him so badly, but she'd always known in her heart that they weren't right for each other. She knew that Tom did too. Not that she had any excuse.

'You are awake?'

Katie's head whipped around, her face bright with expectation and excitement she could not hide.

Nikos was standing at the bedside, a towel wrapped around his narrow hips. The wet hair plastered to his skull and the drops of water still clinging to his shoulders indicated he had just stepped from the shower.

'You shouldn't have let me sleep,' she told him shyly.

'You needed the sleep,' he replied without meeting her eyes.

'I slept as much as you did.' The memory of what they had done instead of sleeping brought a rush of warmth to her cheeks.

'I don't need much sleep,' he replied flatly.

Katie was finding it increasingly difficult to conceal her growing consternation. *Well, what did you expect—that he wouldn't be able to keep his hands off you?* She released a rueful sigh; well, actually yes, she had, but what did she know about the way people behaved the morning after?

Maybe Nikos wasn't a morning person, but in her eyes he more than compensated by being a night-time person.

Her eyes flickered hungrily along his lean, streamlined body; the moisture on his brown skin emphasised the rippling muscles of his spare torso and delineated each individual muscle in his washboard-flat belly.

At the sight of him her doubts dissolved before they had fully formed. What was to regret? Last night had been the most incredible experience of her life. Nikos was the perfect lover and just looking at him made her ache. Her eyes darkened as she recalled waking in the night to find him looking at her. Neither of them had spoken, they hadn't needed words; he had come to her and she'd been ready for him. Just thinking about the urgent primal coupling made her breasts swell and tingle.

Her breath came quickly as she half closed her eyes and imagined touching him, running her hands over the hard contours of shoulders and chest, tangling her fingers in the soft whorls of dark hair that lay against the brown skin there. The heat inside her grew as she gloatingly anticipated running her fingertips over the damp hairs on his muscular flanks and feeling his stomach muscles quiver beneath her flattened palms as she laid them against his flat belly.

She'd save the best until last.

The sexual heat coiled in her belly spilled through her entire body in response to the tactile imagery of holding his silky hard length in her hand...she released a hoarse sigh and lifted her shaken gaze to his.

Their eyes touched and Katie could almost taste the passion flare between them; she felt the electrical current of mutual attraction crackle and spark.

Then as if a switch had been flicked it was gone. Nikos's expression was—actually it wasn't so much what was there that made her feel uneasy, it was what wasn't there.

This couldn't be right.

She smiled questioningly up at him, and got nothing back in response, not even a hint as to what was going on behind those shuttered eyes. Despite this Katie felt an incredible swell of love in her chest as she looked at him. The outpouring of emotion was so intense that she could hardly breathe.

She was seized with an irrational desire to share with him how much the previous night had meant to her. She had to bite her tongue to stop herself blurting out something stupid.

'That coffee smells good.'

'I'll get you some.' A muscle flexed along his strong, angular jaw.

Katie viewed this development with considerable dismay. *Maybe he's regretting last night.*

'Did the phone wake you?'

She shook her head. 'I don't think so.' She took a resolute breath and steeled herself to hear something she didn't want to. 'Nikos, what's wrong? Have I done something?'

His eyes swept over her face. 'You were perfect!' he declared fiercely.

Katie didn't want to be perfect, she wanted to be loved, or failing that at least *wanted*. Being wanted by Nikos would be better than being loved by any other man.

'Then why—?' she began.

Before she could finish there was a knock on the door.

Housekeeping bringing a fresh change of towels, no doubt. Katie would have let them go away, but Nikos called out for them to come in.

With a grunt of frustration Katie pulled the quilt up to her chin. Her mood lightened considerably when, after dropping his towel, Nikos slid into the bed beside her.

With a sigh she insinuated her soft curves up against him, revelling in the strength of his lean body. His body felt cool against her warm skin. Without saying anything he pulled her almost savagely into his arms. Holding her eyes, he brushed his mouth against hers in a tentative, questioning way. She trembled.

'This is wrong!'

'It feels pretty right to me.' She tried to keep the rising panic from her voice.

'Katerina?' he began urgently.

Katie pressed a finger to his lips. 'I know what you're going to say.'

'You do?'

Katie nodded. 'And I feel badly about Tom too, but it wasn't something we planned.'

'Katerina…'

'Don't talk, not now,' she begged huskily.

With a groan he crushed her to him. His kiss was bruising and had an element of desperation about it. Katie felt something equally primitive inside her stir and respond to the demands of his lips and tongue.

Breathing hard, she rested her forehead against his chin, shivering as his hands closed tight across her back, pressing her sensitised breasts up against his chest.

'Nikos, would you really hate it if I fell in love with you?'

Nikos went white and flinched as though she'd struck him. Katie knew immediately that something had gone badly wrong; it wasn't until ten seconds later that she knew just how badly!

'Oh, my God!'

Katie turned and saw a white-faced Tom standing there in the bedroom, staring at them as though his world had just come to an end.

'Tom?' Icy shock, bitter regret, guilt that she was responsible for putting that look of disillusionment on his face hit Katie simultaneously. 'Oh, Tom, I'm so sorry,' she whispered. 'So very sorry.'

Tom didn't reply, he just turned on his heel and walked unsteadily away.

Katie lay there, her hand pressed to her lips, her eyes tight shut, but even with her eyes tight shut she could see Tom's face, see the bleak disillusionment she had put there. Suddenly she sat up and, running a shaking hand through her disordered hair, swung her legs over the side of the bed.

'I have to go to him!' she gritted in some agitation.

'I doubt very much if he wants to see you,' Nikos rasped drily.

Turning to him in protest, Katie was shocked to see the grey, unhealthy tinge to his skin and the grim and bleak light in his heavy-lidded eyes. Of course Nikos must feel every bit as wretched as she did; Tom was his friend. Katie felt a fresh spasm of guilt, this time because she'd been too busy thinking abut how she felt to consider how bad this was for Nikos.

She brought her knees up to her chin and wrapped her arms around them.

'Perhaps later?'

Nikos laughed; it wasn't a pleasant sound. 'Think again,' he advised. 'The man just found you in bed with his friend,' he reminded her brutally.

Katie flinched and buried her face in her hands. 'I wouldn't have had him find out like this for the world!'

Telling him was always going to be a messy, unpleasant business, but this had been awful.

'Perhaps it is for the best this way.'

She rubbed her temples where the pressure had reached critical level. 'I don't see how. What I don't understand is how he knew I was here?'

'He heard about the fire on the local radio station and he rang me to ask if I had any idea where you'd stayed last night.'

Katie shook her head to clear the fog that was making her thought processes slow and stupid. 'He rang you?' she parroted.

'From the lobby,' Nikos confirmed. 'I told him to come on up.'

'You told him, I don't understand…' Suddenly Katie felt cold inside, icy cold and empty. 'But why?' she faltered, seeking an explanation for the inexplicable cruelty in his actions. 'Why would you do that?'

'Tom deserves to know that you don't love him.'

'Of course he does, but not like this…it's not as if I was going to stay with him…I couldn't. I mean, you can't think that I'd have gone through with the marriage after last night? Oh, no,' she gasped. 'You did, didn't you?' Still he didn't reply.

His silence was a reply.

'You set me up!' She said it, but part of her still couldn't quite believe it. How could anyone make love the way he had when all the time they were planning to…? A choked sound of distress emerged from between her clenched teeth.

Nikos started forward and then stopped, his nostrils flaring as she shrank back from him, her expression one of loathing. 'You should lie down.'

She rained contemptuous eyes to his face. 'Oh, you're so considerate,' she snarled.

'I didn't plan this,' he told her heavily. 'You have to believe that I only—'

'I have to believe absolutely *nothing* you say,' she corrected him coldly. 'I suppose you *accidentally* directed Tom in here and you just didn't stage that kiss for his benefit either?' She wiped a shaking hand roughly across her mouth.

Nikos's jaw tightened. 'I couldn't be sure you wouldn't go back to him. I could not permit that.'

What a cheek, he didn't even try and deny it any more. 'I suppose you're proud of what you've done? I suppose this constitutes true friendship for someone as emotionally stunted as you,' she observed bleakly. 'You sleep with a woman you despise to save your friend from her evil clutches and you think that's what a true friend does?'

Hand pressed to her mouth, she ran to the bathroom where she was violently sick.

Grabbing hold of the washbasin, she heaved herself upright. Her legs shook and her skin felt clammy.

She looked at the wet flannel Nikos held out to her and laughed. *'You have to be joking…?'*

Face white as chalk, her expression one of proud disdain, she walked past him, chin held high.

'If you don't mind I'd like a bath—to wash you off my skin.' From the corner of her eyes she caught her reflection in a mirror and registered her naked state for the first time. 'And I need clothes…' she added vaguely.

She turned on a tap and turned back, her cold mask cracking to reveal the aching anguish beneath. 'Did you plan this all along…you planned all along to seduce me?' She could no longer say made love. 'Silly question, of course you did…you planned it down to the last detail.'

'Including the fire?'

'I wouldn't put anything past you!' she declared, glaring at him in simmering distaste. 'But I suppose the fire just made things easier.' *And I was very easy,* she thought bitterly.

'If you had truly loved Tom you would not have been

in my bed last night. If you had had any sort of relationship you would not have come to my bed a virgin.'

'Tom respects me!' she declared furiously. 'Not that you'd know anything about that.'

'You're right there, I wouldn't. Perhaps if Tom hadn't respected you so much,' he sneered, 'you wouldn't have fallen into my bed so readily last night.'

The sound of her hand connecting with his lean cheek resounded shockingly around the room.

'Face it, Katerina, your whole relationship with Tom was a lie. What were you expecting to happen when the ring was on your finger? That passion would suddenly ignite, or were you prepared to sacrifice love for security and money?' he wondered contemptuously.

'You can try and deflect the guilt as much as you like, Nikos, but we both know that you behaved like a rat.'

'I didn't force you to do anything you didn't want to do last night,' he told her quietly. 'And I didn't suggest anything you haven't been thinking of from the first moment we met again.' His burning eyes travelled over the heaving contours of her breasts before dropping to her belly…beads of sweat appeared across his upper lip when he reached the soft dark fuzz between her thighs. 'And we both know that even now if I touched you you'd be begging me to take you,' he declared arrogantly.

'I hate you,' she whispered.

'For telling the truth? If you care so much for the luxuries money can buy, I am far richer than Tom.'

Katie felt a flash of blind rage. 'You think you can buy me?' she quivered.

'Do not be dramatic, that is not what I am saying.' Nikos strove to retain his calm in the face of her determination to misread everything he said. 'I am simply pointing out that lack of funds is not an issue, I am able to provide for you and unlike Tom I have no problem with you working.'

Was he for real? 'My, isn't that big of you?' she drawled.

Nikos felt his control slip. 'Perhaps we should discuss this later when you are able to speak rationally,' he gritted.

'I want to talk now and there isn't going to be any later for you and I, not without a lawyer present anyhow. Let me get this straight—are you asking me to be your mistress?'

'You are my wife.'

Katie laughed. 'Not for very much longer. Sleep with you! I can't bear to be in the same room as you!' she told him in a throbbing voice.

His dark eyes snapped. 'If I go now it will be for good,' he warned her.

'At last,' she sighed. 'Light at the end of the tunnel.'

'You will miss me every day for the rest of your life, Katerina!' Nikos predicted as he turned on his heel and left.

Katie heard the door slam. The awful part was he was probably right; she was a one-man woman, it was just her luck that that man happened to be an untrustworthy bastard!

CHAPTER ELEVEN

'THERE'S someone asking to see you, Katie,' Georgina hissed as she poked her head around the door. 'And she looks like *pure money*,' she added.

'Does this money have a name?' Katie asked, trying to inject a note of animation into her flat voice.

Despite the black cloud of despondency that had positioned itself above her head, she really did make a determined effort to appear her normal cheerful self at work. Nobody liked to be around a misery guts.

'It's CJ Malone,' the older woman twittered excitedly. 'You know, the fashion designer.'

'I know,' said Katie, thinking of the blue dress.

'Actually it's Caitlin Lakis; Malone was my maiden name.' The tall figure who strode calmly into the room approached Katie's desk, hand confidently outstretched.

Katie got to her feet, all the colour leeching from her face. 'Kyria Lakis.' She used the title even though she knew, because the relevant papers that would free Nikos to marry were at that very moment in her bag, this couldn't be strictly accurate.

As the woman who was trying the name on for size— you couldn't miss, it fitted her like a glove—seemed to be studying her with frank, but not unfriendly curiosity, Katie thought it legitimate to return that scrutiny.

What she discovered did nothing to lessen her misery, which had taken the physical form of a tight knot lodged permanently behind her breast bone.

There were no flaws to discover—one little flaw would have been nice, Katie thought wistfully. She'd automatically assumed that Nikos's suitable bride would be Greek, so it was slightly shocking to be confronted by a tall, confident redhead with green eyes and a soft Irish accent. Maybe this woman had been beautiful in her twenties; now she looked in her—what…mid-thirties?—the word seemed too insipid to describe her, she was simply stunning!

An intrigued expression flickered across Caitlin's face at the form of address used by the younger woman but she didn't comment.

'Sit down, my dear, you look pale…' she advised, widening her inspection to include the small cramped office before turning to the elderly woman who had announced her. 'Perhaps a cup of tea?'

Katie felt suddenly extremely sick.

'I don't want tea,' she replied, judging it time to re-establish who was actually in charge here.

'No, neither do I,' her visitor revealed. 'But I wanted to be private.' Without being asked she removed a pile of papers from a desk and sat down. 'Do you mind if I'm frank? It would save time.'

'Nikos told you about me, then?'

'That he married you.' Caitlin gave an irritated click of her tongue. 'Eventually. Seven years and he didn't say a word, when he told me…' she shook her head '…I can't tell you what a shock it was.'

'I can imagine.' This might very well be the strangest conversation she would ever have in her life.

'And of course with the timing I knew straight off that he did it for me. If I'd known I'd have never taken the money, of course, but, well, what's done is done.'

'I don't understand. What has Nikos marrying me got to do with you? He married me for money.'

'Money *I* needed.' Caitlin sighed. 'My business was in trouble, I'd foolishly over-extended myself. My marriage was going through a rocky period.'

'You were married?'

'I still am.'

'Does Nikos know?'

Caitlin frowned. 'Look, who do you think I am?'

'The woman Nikos is going to marry.'

A look of understanding swept over Caitlin's face. 'My dear girl,' she laughed. 'I'm Nik's stepmother.'

Katie flushed to the roots of her hair. 'I feel such a fool.'

'Don't be, I'm flattered.' The older woman grinned. 'I went to Nik when I didn't know what else to do. If I'd been declared bankrupt Spyros would never have forgiven me for disgracing the family, and if I'd asked him to bail me out he would have believed what he half believed already—that I'd married him for his money. The result would have been much the same either way—our marriage would have been over.

'Nikos agreed to act for me, he could not go through the normal channels because Spyros would have heard about it. I asked my old friend Harvey to help us and he came up with you, though I swear I didn't know it.'

Katie stared. So now she knew why Nikos had married her. The past, no matter how fascinating, did not alter the present—Nikos wanted a divorce, which was no doubt why Caitlin was here to hurry things along.

'Right, well, I'm seeing my lawyer to get my signatures witnessed in the morning. So you can tell Nikos that he won't have to wait long,' she promised.

'Oh, heavens, no, don't do that!'

Katie looked at her blankly. 'Pardon me?'

The redhead's beautiful face creased in consternation. 'My dear girl,' she began earnestly. 'That's what I'm here to ask you—please don't give Nik a divorce...well, not yet, anyhow.'

The bizarre request made Katie think she must have misheard. 'I don't understand.'

The older woman sighed and tugged the silk scarf from around her neck. 'I'm not surprised,' she mused, allowing the fine material to slip through her long fingers. 'It must seem a very strange request to you, and it's probably desperately inconvenient. Nik tells me you have marriage plans of your own?'

Katie flushed. 'I don't,' she said flatly.

'But Nikos said he'd made it right with your boyfriend?'
She shrugged. 'Whatever that might involve?'

'It didn't make it right for me.'

Explaining to Tom that she didn't want to marry him even if he did forgive her had been one of the hardest things she'd ever had to do. She supposed she ought to be grateful to Nikos. He'd been right about one thing: she didn't love Tom—at least, not in the way that would make a good marriage, and Tom himself was in love with a Katie that didn't exist. Marrying Tom would mean trying to be that girl and Katie knew she couldn't do that.

'Is that so?'

'Listen...*kyria*—'

'Caitlin, please call me Caitlin.'

'Listen, I don't want to be rude...but I don't understand why you want to delay the divorce.'

'If you sign Nikos will marry that wretched girl, Livia... there's nothing surer.' In her agitation Caitlin's soft brogue deepened. 'And I'd *never* forgive myself,' she declared, 'if I let him do that without making any push to stop him. She'd be the ruination of the boy and I'm terribly fond of him.'

Katie had gathered that much.

'What I need,' she mused, 'is time to come up with a plan and you could give me that time. I don't suppose you've got any ideas?'

Katie, who had been listening with growing fascination, shook her head vigorously. There was no way she was going to get involved in Caitlin Lakis's machinations, though she couldn't help but feel a certain degree of satisfaction that Nikos's chosen bride didn't meet with universal approval.

'I can see what Nikos meant when he said his stepmother was still an active force in his life.'

'Did he say that? How sweet. You know,' she said slowly with a twinkle in her eyes that had Katie been better acquainted with her would have immediately rung warning bells, 'I've just thought of something that *might*, with a bit of jiggling, work...but it would need your assistance,' she added, looking at Katie speculatively.

'I'm afraid that's not possible. It isn't...why are you looking at me like that?'

'I was just thinking that you don't look like the sort of hard-hearted girl who could abandon a basically sound chap to a life of *mediocrity* with the wrong woman...?'

'Nikos is quite old enough to make his own decisions.' *And leave others to deal with the consequences.*

'Oh, you think I'm an interfering old bag.'

Katie laughed—she had never seen anyone who looked less bag-like.

'Oh, I probably am, but the thing is it wouldn't take much. I'm positive he's already got his doubts, but being a Lakis he's just too damned stubborn to admit it. You are fond of him, aren't you?'

This sly rider made Katie start. She gulped, unable to maintain eye contact with that candid green gaze.

'Maybe more than fond...?'

Katie flushed and got to her feet. 'I'm sorry, I really can't help you,' she said stiffly.

Caitlin rose too. 'I'm sorry,' she admitted frankly. 'But think about it, please?' With a winning smile she laid a card down on the table. 'I'm staying here if you want to contact me.' With a smile she turned to go.

'Has Nikos...?'

The older woman turned back.

Katie took a deep breath. 'H-has he mentioned me at all?' she asked with what she knew was a pathetically poor attempt at indifference.

'Hardly at all, despite my efforts.'

Katie's chin went up; she was too proud to let the other woman see how deep her words cut... *Why the shock? It's not as if you didn't already know he didn't care about you.*

'Which in itself is revealing, don't you think?'

Katie raised her downcast eyes, startled by the soft words.

Caitlin smiled back at her, a good deal of understanding in her eyes. 'He's also been in the foulest mood imaginable,' she revealed. 'I'm meddling, I know I am, but after all it's because of me he married you in the first place so I feel responsible.'

Katie sighed heavily. She had thought she'd achieved— what did the psychologists call it? Closure...? Yes, that would be right, closure. If nothing else, Caitlin's visit had revealed that her wounds were still very much open!

Georgina, a dazed expression on her face, re-entered the room. 'You must have been *very* nice to her,' she said faintly. 'She gave me this,' she explained, placing a cheque reverently down on the desk.

Katie looked at the amount written in strong, flowing hand and understood why Georgina looked as if she'd been run over by a truck. 'Very generous.'

'You don't think it will bounce, do you?' Georgina asked with sudden anxiety.

'Relax, it definitely won't bounce.' Of that, but not much else, Katie was sure.

Katie closed her eyes; it felt as if they were dropping out of the sky. It obviously hadn't occurred to Caitlin that Katie had never flown in a helicopter before...so how she'd stare if she knew that before today she'd never flown full stop.

Nobody, she reflected ruefully, could ever have had such a luxurious introduction to air travel. First the private jet to Athens and now Spyros Lakis's personal helicopter, which was just now hovering above the helipad of his yacht—the reason Katie had her eyes closed.

No wonder she was experiencing a sense of unreality.

It was barely forty-eight hours before that she'd rung Caitlin to say that she would go along, but only because she wanted to speak to Nikos herself.

The older woman had not asked what had brought about this change of heart, but Katie wondered if maybe she suspected the reason. There had been something distinctly knowing about her smile when Katie had refused wine with her meal on the flight over.

There was an inescapable irony in someone who had been so openly contemptuous of people who forgot to take the proper precautions, as she had, finding herself pregnant. Katie didn't think it likely that Nikos would see the joke when she told him. She felt sick again as she contemplated doing so—not telling him had never been an option for her; he deserved to know.

She had no idea how active a part, if at all, he would want to take in his child's life, but she was willing to be reasonable up to a point—that point being she wouldn't have another woman bringing up her child!

CHAPTER TWELVE

THE guest list read like a who's who of the rich and famous. Politicians and media moguls rubbed shoulders with famous faces from the fashion and the entertainment industry. It seemed that when her hosts threw a *small* party on board their yacht, people didn't refuse the invitation.

Katie, introduced by Caitlin as a 'dear family friend', mingled and smiled with the best of them and acted as though it were perfectly normal for her to find herself standing next to someone whose love life had been reported in detail in her newspaper the previous week. Similarly she avoided drawing attention to herself by goggling too obviously at original works of art, the like of which she had only previously seen in art galleries, that lined the walls.

Dressed in one of Caitlin's elegant, deceptively simple creations, her hair twisted in a simple knot on her head, she thought she blended in pretty well, but it seemed not everyone was fooled. Her puzzled eyes were drawn once more to the tall, distinguished-looking figure with a head of distinctive silver hair standing alone—he was still staring at her as he had been since she'd entered the room.

Perhaps, she reflected wryly, it was because she was the only female in the room who wasn't wearing a king's ransom in jewellery around her neck. Katie was wondering if she should confront the rude stranger when from amongst the bright chatter around her she picked out the one name—*Nikos*!

Underneath her expertly applied make-up she went desperately pale. *Pull yourself together, Katie,* she remonstrated sternly, *if you go catatonic at the sound of his name just how are you going to deal with the man in the flesh?*

Always supposing Caitlin was right and he did turn up to-night.

'At least that's what my wife says…'

Katie, who had tuned out of the conversation for a vital thirty seconds, had absolutely no idea what the laughing man beside her had been talking about, but clearly he was waiting for her response.

'I believe frills are *huge* this year!' It was only after she'd delivered this inane observation that she recalled that she was no longer in the company of a fashion editor.

The high-ranking diplomat was too polite to come right out and say she was demented, but he did suddenly remember he needed to be somewhere else.

His hurried departure cleared a channel through the crowd of bodies to the other side of the room, revealing in the process a tall, commanding figure who looked quite unbelievably handsome in a formal dark dinner jacket and black tie. He looked exactly what he was, even down to the obligatory blonde in a low-cut dress who was laughing up at him: a rich, incredibly powerful man who was out of her league.

Despite the blonde's energetic attempts to gain his attention, Nikos's dark, arrogant gaze was locked onto Katie's face. Even at this distance she could feel the strong emotions emanating from his still figure.

Seconds later the opening closed over, concealing his face from view; his dark head was still visible above the throng. Sheer panic engulfed Katie as she desperately tried to keep track of the top of his distinctive glossy dark head as it began to weave in and out of the crowds. Someone jiggled her arm, spilling some of her drink on her dress in the process. During the few precious seconds her attention was distracted she lost him.

This had seemed a good idea—*why, exactly?*

What had seemed the right thing to do when she had been in England suddenly no longer seemed such a crash-

hot idea after all. If you believed it was foolish to mess
with something that wasn't broken, it therefore followed
that it was equally foolish to try and fix something that was
smashed to smithereens!

Oh, God!

Every instinct she possessed was telling her to run. It
was only the knowledge that Caitlin had gone to a great
deal of expense to engineer this scene, and of course the
fact there wasn't any place for her to hide that he wouldn't
track her down to, that held her back.

Caitlin has done her bit, now it's my turn. She had
planned what she'd say, practised it down to the last into-
nation so many times she was word perfect, but now at the
vital moment her mind was a perfect blank!

Nervously she lifted her glass to her lips only to discover
it was empty; the contents were now a stain on the silky
silver-grey fabric of her dress.

'Thank you, but actually I was drinking mineral water,'
she began as her glass was almost instantaneously filled by
an efficient waiter.

With a smile she looked up to discover it was not a
waiter standing there with a bottle of champagne in his
hand; the air rushed from her lungs in a silent sigh.

'Oh!'

Unnoticed by either party, Katie's wineglass emptied itself onto the thick carpet and then slipped from her fingers.

'Hello, Nikos.'

Nikos, never one for the polite formalities, just stared at
her. Unblinkingly his densely lashed eyes moved over her
face examining each minute detail with a fierce air of preoccupation. At least it gave Katie the perfect excuse to stare
back. She hadn't appreciated until this moment just how
hungry she'd been for the sight of him.

Everything in her came awake as she looked at him; it
was as if while they'd been apart even the colours in her
life had been muted. The world with him in it was a more

vibrant, exciting place. Her pulses leapt; he was so terribly, heartbreakingly beautiful, her throat ached, desire tightened her stomach muscles as her eyes ate him up.

Her chin firmed. No, she'd been right to come. She had to let him decide if he wanted to be part of the life they'd created. This way she'd know one way or the other.

Still he didn't say anything.

Unable to bear the tension another second, Katie spoke. 'Aren't you going to ask me what I'm doing here?' she asked throatily.

Katie saw his chest lift—a signal that he'd started breathing again? His eyes burned like silver flames into hers, then he smiled. It was not a safe, cosy smile; it was a pulse-racing, dangerous version.

'No.'

The motion was so swift and fluid, him covering the space that separated them and then taking her by the shoulders seemed one single, seamless action. His fingers dug into her flesh as they tightened against her collar-bones; Katie barely registered the pain. Standing this close she could hear the echo of his rapid heartbeat…or maybe it was her own? And feel the fine tremors that were rippling through his tense, greyhound-lean frame.

'You're real,' she heard him breathe. 'I thought I was dreaming again.'

He took hold of her chin between his thumb and forefinger and tilted it upwards. His fierce gaze demanded answers, but Katie wasn't attempting to hide anything! This wasn't the place she would have chosen to go public with her feelings, but she doubted she could have disguised them even if she had wanted to!

This wasn't about disguising her feelings to save face, this was about confronting Nikos with them, and if the result was humiliation at least she'd have the comfort of knowing she'd made the attempt.

They were meant to be together—every fibre of her being

told her this. She was a one-man woman and Nikos was that man. But she was also well aware that things that were meant to be didn't always happen.

Still holding her eyes with his, he took her face between his hands and sealed his mouth to hers. The raw hunger in him was overwhelming; at the instant of contact her body went limp. But at the first smooth, stabbing incursion of his tongue between her parted lips the life flowed hotly back into her limbs.

The wave of sexual energy that surged through her body blasted away all remnants of submissiveness and transformed her from a passive to a very active participant in the kiss.

A lost cry vibrated in her throat as she wrapped her arms about his neck and pressed herself sinuously up against him, revelling in the hard, virile strength of his marvellous body.

The abrupt separation when he tore his mouth from hers made Katie feel cold and empty inside. She soon heated up, however, when the significance of the silence in the room, which moments before had been filled with the hum of laughter and voices, struck her.

She wanted the floor to open up and swallow her. All those people watching…speculating, thinking God knew what… Well, actually she could hazard a pretty accurate guess what they were thinking! That was the trouble.

Nikos took one look at her burning face and muttered a low imprecation. He bent his head towards her and spoke in a voice for her ears only.

'You look like a paralysed chicken,' he informed her cruelly. 'Lift your head up! Show some pride. I will not permit you to cower.'

Not permit. 'Just how exactly are you going to stop me?' she gritted. It was all right for him—he was used to having his every action scrutinised in the media and he didn't give a damn what people thought about him.

Nikos met her indignant glare with a smile of dazzling brilliance. 'That's much better,' he approved warmly. He threw his arm about her shoulders and pulled her to his side. 'I think we will continue this conversation somewhere a little less public.'

'Pity you didn't think about that before you kissed me.'

'I didn't think full stop before I kissed you,' he informed her sardonically.

'This is a nice room.'

'My father's study,' Nikos said without taking his eyes from her delicate profile.

'Won't he mind?' she wondered, running her finger along the spine of a leather-bound volume on the bookshelf. 'This looks old.'

'It's a first edition,' Nikos snapped dismissively.

Katie's hand dropped away from the no-doubt priceless book. First editions, old masters on the walls—this place was like a floating museum with Jacuzzis. The disparity between their backgrounds had never been more apparent to her.

'Where is Tom?'

Katie, her lips still tender and swollen from the unbridled passion of his kiss, the taste of him still in her mouth, turned to stare at him incredulously. Of all the things for him to say! Anger started to build inside her...it escalated quickly.

'Why, did you fancy a threesome?'

Nikos's nostrils flared as he inhaled sharply. 'I do not like it when you speak that way,' he told her austerely.

'How fortunate I care so passionately about what you like and dislike,' she replied sarcastically. The simple declaration of love she had intended to make before her confession was fast becoming a distant memory. 'I think the time to wonder if Tom was around might have been before you mauled me in front of all those people, not after!'

Nikos, his hard cheekbones ridged with dull red, hardly heard what she said; he was recalling how very much she had cared once about what he liked...in fact she had begged him to tell her...to instruct her... She had been a very apt pupil.

'Oh, sorry, was I not supposed to mention you just mauled me?'

'I *kissed* you and you gave every indication of liking it.' His eyes darkened. 'Liking it very much,' he added with throaty satisfaction. 'Tom is not here?' he persisted.

His vague tone and inability to grasp a fairly obvious fact suggested his razor-sharp wits were not working at full capacity.

Katie gave a snort of exasperation, lifted a cushion from one of the sofas and made an elaborate show of looking behind it. 'Tom?' She dropped it and turned back, her expression scornful. 'Nope, it looks like he's not,' she added crisply, then, in a sickly syrupy tone, 'Is your fiancée? I'm just *dying* to meet her...'

'Being facetious does not suit you, either,' he observed harshly. His long-lashed eyes narrowed. 'But that dress does.' He swallowed and tore his eyes from her supple curves. 'What *are* you doing here, Katerina?'

She widened her eyes innocently. 'Where else should a woman be but beside her husband?'

'I was wondering why you had not returned the divorce papers...?'

'Oh, I'm a great believer in the personal touch,' she told him grimly. 'Hand delivery.'

'Do you want me to speak to Tom again?' If he wasn't exactly holding his breath, Katie got the impression her reply mattered to him. 'I thought,' he continued when she remained silent, 'I had made him see...'

'See what? That your leftovers were acceptable? That a quick tumble doesn't mean anything? I'd have loved to be a fly on the wall for that tête-à-tête.'

Nikos's face darkened, he loosened his tie and pushed his clenched fists into his pockets. 'I will speak to him again,' he announced distantly, 'if you wish.' Again the penetrating scrutiny.

Was that what he thought she wanted to hear...? *You are such a stupid man!* Katie took a deep breath and forced herself to unclench her fists.

'No need. Tom,' she admitted, 'was *very* understanding. My shameless behaviour was all a reaction to the trauma of almost being killed in the fire.'

'But you are not together?' For a man who had gone out of his way to bring that about, he sounded quite extraordinarily pleased by her solitary state. Looking a lot less tense, he slipped the buttons of his jacket.

Katie trained her eyes on a point beyond his shoulder to stop them straying to the fascinating dark shadow of body hair clearly visible through the fine fabric of his white shirt.

'Perhaps,' she suggested bitterly, 'I don't want to marry a man who is *understanding* when he finds me in bed with his friend? Call me strange, but I don't think it would be healthy to think about another man when my husband was making love to me.'

A white line appeared around Nikos's lips; with an attitude of seething frustration caused by the knowledge he had actually made it possible, he pushed his fingers deep into his hair.

'You slept with Tom?'

'You look annoyed, Nikos,' she observed mildly—actually he looked incandescent with rage. 'A little bit perverse, don't you think? Wasn't I supposed to sleep with Tom?' She shook her head and pretended bewilderment. 'I mean, you went to such great lengths to smooth things over for me it seemed the least I could do.'

'Do not speak like a tart...'

'Why not? You treat me like one.'

'If you speak to me like that you must expect to face the consequences...Katerina,' he warned her.

'*I'm trembling...*' *Every time you touch me.* 'Male arrogance,' she told him, shaking her head in disbelief, 'is always a reliable form of entertainment. Good luck to you if you can convince Tom to take your leftovers off your hands. Unfortunately this particular reject doesn't want to be passed around like a piece of merchandise. I don't need you or anyone else to make excuses for me! I'm prepared to live with the consequences of my actions...' Would he? That was the big question.

Nikos strode over to the other side of the room, his hand pressed to his pleated brow. He swung back, a strange expression on his face. 'You said that if you married Tom you would think of another man when your husband made love to you...' he quoted with deadly accuracy.

I knew it was too good to be true that he hadn't noticed that one. 'I don't remember what I said.'

'I do. Would this man by any chance be me, Katerina?' he charged huskily.

'You really do think a lot of yourself, don't you?'

'As I am the only man who has made love to you,' he reminded her with a palpable air of smug male complacency, 'it seems a logical conclusion.'

'How do you know I wasn't thinking of someone else when you were making love to me?'

Nikos threw back his head and laughed, perfectly secure in the knowledge, *and with good reason*, that in the bedroom he could wipe the thought of every other man from a woman's mind.

Her shoulders slumped in defeat.

'Oh, all right, then, I wasn't.'

'Before we go any farther I think we should establish why you are here.' Katie found that, now the moment had arrived, she couldn't say it—she just couldn't... *You're scared of his reaction,* she accused herself. *You're a coward.* 'I repeat, why are you here? I demand an answer.'

Demand was the word that did it. Katie saw red. 'That's your problem, you don't ask nicely,' she taunted angrily.

Nikos's face darkened. An errant muscle in his lean cheek jerked as his jaw tightened to breaking-point. Katie watched these danger signs with a strange sense of objectivity. Another little push and he would snap. Briefly she recklessly toyed with the idea of supplying the requisite pressure, but sense prevailed.

'All right, if you must know Caitlin invited me.'

Nikos shook his head. *'What…?* No,' he said positively. 'That is not possible, you do not know Caitlin.'

'I do now. We met quite recently. She told me why you married me,' she added casually.

Nikos stiffened. 'She should not have done that.'

'No, you should have.'

'I don't suppose she told you that my brother engineered her plight?' He saw Katie's confusion and nodded. 'No, she would not. Dimitri, my brother, always resented Caitlin—he didn't like to share our father with anyone.'

'Including you?'

Nikos looked at her sharply. 'Including me,' he agreed slowly. 'He was too clever to come right out and bad-mouth Caitlin, but he had a way of implying things…'

'And if you imply often enough people start to wonder…?'

'You've got the picture. As for the companies that suddenly called in her loans—he'd hidden his tracks well, but Dimitri was behind that too.'

Katie shuddered; the dead brother sounded a sinister person.

'So you see my brother created the problem.'

'And you felt it was your duty to make right what your brother had broken, no matter what it cost you.' Katie sighed. She was beginning to see the sort of man Nikos was: a man with strong principles who would protect those he loved no matter what the cost to himself.

'I think you too know about duty? And paying your brother's debts?'

Katie gasped and went pale. 'How?'

Nikos shrugged. 'It is always easy to track money if you know where to look. As for the rest, I could only theorise.'

Katie closed her eyes—he knew.

'Your brother was very young.'

Katie blinked back tears and nodded. Nikos was looking at her not with scorn as she had feared, but with warmth and compassion.

'He couldn't live with knowing what he'd done,' she admitted. She discovered it was actually a relief after all these years to be able to speak of it with someone, especially someone who didn't seem to be judging Peter.

'And he left you all alone to fix the harm he had done. My poor Katerina...'

'I don't want your pity, Nikos.'

'That isn't what I want to give you.'

She waited with bated breath for him to expand on this infuriatingly ambiguous statement. When he remained silent she said the first thing that came into her head.

'And your father is a dear, isn't he?' Actually calling Spyros Lakis a 'dear' was a bit like calling a lion cute, but despite all her preconceptions she had warmed to the strong, silent man who was clearly besotted by his wife.

Nikos was regarding her with an expression of reluctant fascination. 'You have met my father?' The significance of her presence appeared to finally hit him. 'You are a guest here, on the yacht?'

'Well, I'm not a stowaway.' Katie placed her hands on her slim hips and stuck her chin out. 'And I'm not leaving!' she declared belligerently. 'I'm here as a guest of your parents whether you like it or not and I'll go when they ask me to leave and not before.'

'Did I say I wanted you to go?'

'No, but—'

'But nothing.' Nikos folded his arms across his chest. 'What crazy scheme has Caitlin got you involved in?'

He clearly knew his stepmother pretty well. 'She is unhappy about your plans to marry this…Livia. She asked me not to sign the papers to give her time to…'

'Interfere,' Nikos supplied drily.

Katie was deeply confused by his sudden relaxed almost mellow attitude. He hadn't struck her as the sort of man who took people interfering in his life lightly.

'So you didn't sign the papers.' His eyes narrowed. 'But that doesn't explain your presence here.'

Katie grimaced. 'I wanted to see how the other half live,' she responded flippantly.

'And is it the way you imagined?'

'I feel a little out of my depth,' she admitted.

Nikos reached across and ran his finger over her rounded chin. 'You have nothing to prove to anyone. Remember that,' he instructed, looking deep into her startled face. 'Now why did you really come?'

'I think Caitlin thought I might be able to…*distract* you.'

There was a long, nerve-stretching silence.

'Very delicately put,' Nikos observed slowly.

'Don't worry, I didn't agree. Don't panic.' Pretty ironic advice considering he looked cool and collected and she was about ready to fall to pieces. 'I'm not here to seduce you, Nikos.'

'I feel better already,' he revealed with no discernible inflection in his deep, dry voice.

'You're a grown man quite capable of deciding who you want to spend the rest of your life with.'

'Rest of my life?' An odd expression flickered across his stony countenance.

'Well, that's what marriage is about, isn't it?' she said crossly. 'You must have thought about that.'

'As you no doubt did when you accepted Tom's proposal,' he countered slyly.

Lips tight, Katie flicked back her long silky hair and fixed him with an unfriendly look. 'You can marry who you like, but it might not be so easy after…you know…'

'I know what?'

An irritated grunt emerged from her lips. Even the most besotted and liberal of girlfriends was not likely to view her future husband passionately kissing a strange woman with equanimity. A dreamy, distracted expression drifted into her eyes…it was passionate wasn't it…?

'Well, don't you think that maybe it would be a good idea for you to go and explain to Livia about the…you know…*kissing thing*?' Her eyes, stinging with tears, slid from his.

Virtue might be its own reward but she had yet to see the proof. Katie cursed the wretched sense of fair play that made her act as an advocate for the enemy.

'And say what exactly?' His predatory expression made her stomach flip. 'That I saw you, and could think of nothing but tasting you, feeling your body beneath me…'

'Nikos?' she gasped.

'Do not look at me like that, *yineka mou* or I shall not be responsible,' he warned huskily. 'I will not explain to Livia because she did not see me kiss you.'

'I saw…'

'Not Livia.' Nikos dismissed the blonde with a click of his fingers. 'Even if she had seen me I would still not explain. Livia and I decided we would not suit after all,' he revealed smoothly.

'I'm sorry.'

He grinned. 'You are a delightful but most unconvincing liar. Now tell me, if you are not here to seduce me…a bitter blow,' he admitted solemnly, 'why are you here?'

'It's just there's something I thought you should know…'

'Something so important that you had to tell me face to face?'

Katie nodded.

'It can't be that bad.'

'You'll probably think it is.' She felt it only fair to warn him. 'I just thought you might want to know that you're going to be a father.'

He froze. '*Father…?*' he repeated in a strangled voice. 'Might!' he added in an even stranger tone.

'Nikos!' she wailed, deeply alarmed by the grey tinge of his skin. 'Maybe you should sit down.'

'I'm not the one who is pregnant,' he gritted back.

Katie was relieved to see he had recovered some of his colour. 'I didn't mean to blurt it out like that, honestly. And before you say anything I'm not here to ask for anything,' she added fiercely. 'I just thought that you should know about the baby.'

'You are carrying my child.' His eyes dropped to her flat belly. '*Theos…!*' He clasped a hand to his head. 'Why did I not think of this?' His face hardened with self-reproach that Katie read as anger.

'I'm really sorry, but…'

'You are sure?'

Katie jerked back, her expression indignant. 'Of course I'm sure! Do you really think I'd have said anything if I wasn't?'

Nikos, who appeared to be deep in thought, nodded absently, not seeming to notice her resentment.

'And you have seen a doctor, of course.'

'Not yet,' she admitted. 'But I did two tests and they're accurate,' she added in face of his accusing expression.

'I will arrange for us to see a doctor first thing tomorrow.'

'He'll only say the same thing, Nikos.' He was clearly still clinging to the hope that she was mistaken, she thought, irrationally saddened by his attitude.

'I don't doubt it, but the sooner you receive proper medical care the better.'

'I'm not ill, I'm pregnant.'

'With my child, Katerina…' He dragged a hand shakily through his hair. 'My child is growing inside you,' he groaned wonderingly.

'You're not angry…?'

He looked at her as if she were mad. *'Angry?'*

'Well, this is hardly the sort of news that you want to celebrate.'

'Is that the way you feel?' he demanded tautly.

Katie felt it was significant he'd avoided answering her question. 'Well,' she admitted, wryly, 'I was pretty freaked when I realised.'

'You were alone,' Nikos recognised in a strained undertone.

'But now I kind of like the idea,' she explained with a self-conscious smile. 'It must have something to do with maternal instincts and all that,' she added, a defensive note creeping into her voice.

Nikos nodded. 'I "kind of like the idea" too.'

'That's nice of you,' she replied with a watery smile. 'It really is.' She sniffed. 'But you don't have to pretend.'

An expression of extreme exasperation crossed Nikos's face. 'I am not being kind or pretending. And I do not wish to hear you speak again of our baby as if it is some unwanted burden. Do you think me so incapable of the same feelings you claim for yourself?'

Katie shook her head, bewildered by the deep emotions throbbing in his voice. 'You want this baby?' She gasped.

'Did I not say so?'

'No, as a matter of fact you didn't.'

A brief smile flickered across his face. 'Well, for the record, I am happy. Did you tell Caitlin?'

Katie shook her head. 'I didn't, but she might suspect,' she admitted.

Nikos nodded. 'Do you want a big wedding?'

CHAPTER THIRTEEN

KATIE'S knees sagged and Nikos, his eyes fixed with alarm on her milk-pale face, scooped her up as if she were a child, and, ignoring her weak protests, placed her down on a sofa.

Katie would have sat up if a firm hand on her chest had not prevented her. 'I'm fine.'

'You have clearly been overexerting yourself,' he accused. 'You weigh nothing.'

'I'm being careful, I'm not stupid. It's just that…for a minute there I thought you said *wedding*!' From some hidden reserve she dredged a weak laugh.

'Naturally we will get married—anything else is unacceptable.'

'We are married,' she reminded him.

'Maybe on paper,' he admitted with a dismissive grimace. 'But I want to do the thing properly this time…a priest, a church…'

'People do not get married because they are having a baby, Nikos.' *They get married because they love one another,* she thought bleakly. It had not escaped her notice that love was a subject that Nikos was steering clear of. A loveless marriage, could she bear it? What was the alternative?

'Here they do,' he corrected her drily. 'I am Greek and so is my father. He is a proud man, and strong traditionalist—he would not accept a civil ceremony,' he explained glibly. 'If I produced a bastard he would disown me and he would die of shame…possibly literally. You know, of course,' he added, 'that he had two severe heart attacks a few years ago, and has undergone bypass surgery.'

'So what you're saying is that if I don't marry you I'll be responsible for your father's death?'

Nikos gave a fatalistic shrug.

'No undue pressure, then,' she breathed shakily.

'And our child might be considered an outcast,' he added brutally.

'That's so cruel!' Katie found it impossible to match his pragmatic manner.

Nikos brushed a strand of hair from her eyes. 'I do not make the rules.'

'But you live by them,' she accused.

His finger trailed lightly down the soft curve of her jaw. 'You will marry me...?'

Katie turned her cheek into his cupped palm and gave a sigh. 'It would be a disaster,' she predicted, blinking as her eyes filled with hot tears—Nikos hated tears.

She started when his finger found a single drop of salty moisture on her cheek. He touched it and then he raised his damp finger to his lips and touched his tongue to it.

Katie's insides melted like warm honey as she stared transfixed by the earthy, erotic spectacle.

He framed her face with his hands. 'I will not make you cry,' he promised fiercely.

The emotions she heard in his deep voice moved her once more to tears.

'You already make me break my promise,' he chided huskily. 'I think I shall have to kiss you better? Unless you have a better idea.'

Katie sniffed, trying not to listen to the voice in her head that was calling her a weak fool. *What happened to proudly confronting him with your true feelings, Katie...?*

'I don't,' she admitted with a sniff.

The driver who was sitting in the back of the air-conditioned limo jumped out startled when he saw her approach.

'I'm sorry, I understood you would not need the car for another hour.'

'I won't need it at all,' she told him sunnily. 'I need to go into the city. Don't worry, I'll catch a bus and go from there to meet Mr Lakis.'

'Catch a bus?' the driver echoed with as much horrified shock as if she'd just announced her intention of robbing a bank.

'Could you tell me where this is?' she asked, showing the address written on the note she'd discovered when she'd returned to her stateroom earlier that morning. 'Is this place far from where I'm to meet Mr Lakis?'

The driver confirmed it was in fact within walking distance, so Katie set off with mixed feelings for her assignation.

The short note had revealed its author to be the silver-haired man who had been watching her so intently. He had apologised for offending her and gone on to explain he had been a friend of her mother and he recognised her from the snapshots of her Eleri had sent him when she was a child.

Katie was eager to meet someone who had known her mother; the details she had of Eleri's earlier life were meagre. It didn't even cross her mind to refuse the suggestion that she meet this man in a café before lunch. She could meet him and then go on to meet Nikos as arranged.

She reached the café a little before the arranged time; the silver-haired stranger who had identified himself as Vasilis Atmatzidis was sitting in a corner, and he rose to his feet when he saw her.

'Mr Atmatzidis…?' she said, holding out her hand.

'Vasilis,' he said, taking her hand and raising it with old-fashioned gallantry to his lips.

Katie looked at him curiously. Despite the silver hair she judged him to be in his early to mid forties. Slim and a little above average height, he was extremely good-looking.

'I think I annoyed you last night,' he said after ordering

coffee for them both. 'I was just so surprised to see you there of all places...'

'I wondered why you seemed familiar,' Katie said suddenly. 'You were at the funeral, weren't you?' Her memories of the day were pretty confused but she did recall a well-dressed stranger who nobody had seemed to know who had stood at the back of the church and left without speaking to anyone. 'And it must have been you who sent the flowers with the card written in Greek.'

Vasilis nodded. 'I thought of approaching you, but Eleri always said that you got upset if she mentioned anything about her life in Greece.'

'I got angry. They treated my mother terribly.'

The older man sighed. 'Your grandfather was a proud, stubborn man,' he admitted. 'He missed her terribly, you know.'

'Well, I hope he suffered as much as she did,' Katie responded honestly. She was not inclined to forgive and forget. 'How did you know my mother?'

'I was the man she was meant to marry.'

Katie's eyes went round with astonishment. '*You!* And you stayed friends...?'

'I valued your mother's friendship and once my heart and pride healed we corresponded regularly, and several times when I came to London we met up. She was always eager for news of old friends.'

'I think she was homesick sometimes,' Katie said quietly.

'Perhaps, but she never regretted her decision; she loved your father very much.'

Katie felt the prick of tears behind her eyelids. 'Tell me about her,' she asked huskily. 'Tell me about what she was like when she was young.'

Vasilis was an entertaining raconteur and soon Katie was laughing out loud as, with a roguish gleam in his eyes, he recalled some hair-raising exploits.

'I don't believe she did that!' Katie exclaimed after he recounted one particular episode.

'It's true,' he promised. 'I swear.' The laughter died from his eyes as they swept over her face. 'You know, when you laugh you look like her.'

Impulsively Katie caught his hand and squeezed. 'Did you ever marry?'

'No, he never married.'

Katie started at the sound of a very familiar voice. 'Nikos!' Her welcoming smile faded as she encountered the shimmering hostility in Nikos's rigid face.

Dismayed and alarmed, she watched as he took a swaggering step forward and wedged his thigh up against her chair so that even had she wanted to leave she couldn't have.

'And the reason Vasilis has never married,' he continued loudly, 'is that he is a womaniser, who prefers quantity to quality.'

The look he gave the other man made Katie cringe on his behalf. Anyone would think from the way he was acting he wanted to pick a fight.

'You two know one another, I take it,' Katie said drily. She still didn't have the faintest idea why Nikos was acting so obnoxiously.

'Oh, yes,' Vasilis agreed. 'I've known Nikos since he was a baby.'

'Playing the experience card is calculated risk, Vasilis. There's always the danger that the lady in question will realise that you're old enough to be her father.' The older man's appreciative laughter seemed to infuriate Nikos even more. 'We are leaving, Katerina.'

'I'm not going anywhere with you until you apologise to Vasilis. Honestly,' she said to the older man, 'I don't know what's got into him.'

Nikos inhaled through quivering nostrils and released a flood of Greek for the older man's benefit. Katie might not have been able to understand a word of it, but it didn't sound as if it was anything friendly. Halfway through the diatribe Vasilis's mocking smile faded. He looked from Katie to Nikos with startled incredulity.

'You are married, Katie?' he asked when Nikos had subsided into silent hostility.

'Sort of,' she admitted. 'It's a long story.'

'*Sort of* was enough to get you pregnant,' Nikos reminded her.

'I thought you didn't want the world to know before you told your parents.'

'Don't worry, your secret is safe with me,' Vasilis promised, getting to his feet. He bowed to Katie. 'Until we meet next time, my dear.'

'I'd like that.' Katie smiled, turning her back pointedly on Nikos. You couldn't really blame the older man for leaving—Nikos did look pretty scary.

Not that she was scared. On the surface this seemed a foolish response, but when she analysed it she realised that she knew deep down that Nikos would never hurt her. Whatever else changed in her life this wouldn't; she would always be safe with him.

'If there's a next time,' Nikos informed Vasilis with a belligerent growl, 'I'll break your damned neck. Just keep away from my wife!'

Vasilis seemed to take this threat in good part. Katie was less tolerant.

'*How could you?*' she breathed wrathfully as the other man left.

Nikos pulled a wad of notes from his pocket and slammed them on the table. 'Let's get out of here.'

'I'm not going anywhere with you.'

'You can leave on your own two feet or slung over my shoulder. The choice,' he announced generously, 'is yours.'

Katie examined his grim face; she decided he wasn't bluffing. 'I'm going because I want to.'

'Of course you are.'

'And I hate you.'

'We'll discuss your feelings for me later.'

The fifteen-minute journey to his apartment building was completed in silence, the sort of silence that made the air-conditioning redundant.

If Nikos's temper had cooled by the time the door of his apartment had closed her own had peaked.

'I accept that there was no deception on your part and I am prepared to make allowances for your inexperience, but you have to promise me never again to go anywhere near Vasilis.'

'I will do no such thing and how dare you tell me who I may and may not have as a friend? You behaved like a thug,' she condemned severely. 'I've never been so embarrassed in my life!'

Nikos surveyed her angry, flushed face with outraged eyes. 'I behaved…' His chest swelled. 'I behaved with incredible restraint considering the provocation!' he bellowed. 'If I'd done to that *man* what I wanted to you might have room for complaint. How did you expect me to act? I come back early and find my wife has gone off to meet the most notorious womaniser in the country and she hasn't even had the decency to hide it from me. My own chauffeur told me!'

'Fine, next time I have an assignation I'll lie my head off. Will that make you happy?'

Nikos grabbed her by the shoulders and jerked her to him. 'There won't be a next time,' he ground. 'Because I'm not going to let you out of my sight. *Theos!*' he groaned. 'Why are you doing this to me?'

Her soft heart couldn't take the sort of anguish she recognised in his face. 'I went to meet Vasilis because he knew my mother.'

'Is that what he told you?' Nikos laughed harshly. 'Look,

I know women find him attractive and he's a very plausible guy, but—'

'No, *really*, he knew my mother. He was to be married to her, but she ran away with my father.'

'No, that can't be right. Vasilis was betrothed to the Kapsis girl.'

'My mother.'

Nikos looked dumbfounded. 'Your mother was Michalis Kapsis's daughter…?'

Katie nodded. 'Her family disowned her when she married my father. He wasn't good enough for them,' she recalled bitterly.

'And you have never had any contact with them?'

Katie shook her head.

'This is extraordinary—*Theos*!' he exclaimed suddenly. 'This Greek you taunted me with—the one you lived with—it was your mother,' he breathed.

Katie nodded.

'You are half Greek.'

'I've been trying all my life to forget that…'

Nikos pulled her into the circle of his arms and Katie laid her head against his chest. The hand that stroked her hair suddenly stilled.

'I made a total fool of myself.'

'Yes, you did.' She lifted her head. 'Why did you, Nikos?' Her eyes widened in astonishment as he blushed— he actually blushed!

'Well, I wanted to protect you as any husband would—' He broke off and took a deep breath. 'No, I acted like that because I was insane with jealousy.'

'You were jealous?'

'I am jealous of every man who looks at you. I love you, *pethu mou*, I've known it since that first night, but I wouldn't admit it even to myself. I was so sick at the thought of you going back to Tom that I invited him up to the room. It was despicable and everything you said was right…that's why I tried to make things right between you, I thought I would do the noble thing. I told myself that you being happy was what mattered and if you were happy with Tom then so be it. I think noble is overrated. I went through seven sorts of hell thinking of you with him,' he said hoarsely.

'You love me…' she echoed, still trying to absorb the astonishing things he'd said. 'But why,' she demanded with a groan, 'didn't you tell me? I've been so miserable.'

'Coping with the pregnancy alone?'

'No, sleeping alone, stupid!' she told him lovingly. Clearly he was going to need it spelling out. Her voice dropped a husky octave. 'I love you,' she spelt out, looking up at her incredibly gorgeous husband with shining eyes. 'That's why I let Caitlin bring me here. I decided I had to tell you, but I chickened out at the last minute,' she admitted. 'Because I thought you only wanted to marry me for the baby.'

Nikos's eyes blazed like beacons of love. 'The baby is a bonus,' he said huskily as he gathered her into his arms.

Katie threw him a sultry smile. 'You know, I never did get any lunch.'

'And you are hungry?'

'Always when I look at you,' she admitted simply.

The wedding went like a dream and Nikos had promised her the honeymoon would be even better. Katie, who had learnt her husband always delivered on his promises, saw no reason to disbelieve him.

Katie was sitting wrapped in a golden glow of contentment and not much else besides a few scraps of lace, her wedding gown lying on the bed beside her, when Nikos walked in.

'You make a very provocative picture.'

'Want to do something about it?' she asked with a saucy

smile. Before he could reply she saw the gift-wrapped parcel in his hand. 'A wedding present?'

Nikos nodded. 'From me to you,' he said, handing it to her.

'Why, thank you.' She smiled, tearing the wrapping paper.

Nikos watched her enthusiasm with a proud, tender smile. 'I hope you like it.'

Katie had revealed a leather-bound book. It lay on her knee for a moment before she opened it. 'This is...' Her entire body stiffened as she saw what lay within. She raised tear-filled eyes to Nikos's face before returning eagerly to the contents of the book.

She cried out in wonder every so often as she pored over the pages and by the time she finished she was openly sobbing.

She placed the leather-bound volume reverently down on the bed and ran across to her husband, who folded her in a rib-cracking embrace.

'I thought I'd lost them for ever. I don't know how you did it...' she sniffed emotionally '...but thank you, a million times thank you.'

'It wasn't so hard,' he insisted modestly. 'I contacted friends, the local newspaper had some of Petros when he was swimming competitively, but it was Vasilis who really helped. Your mother had sent him a number of snaps of you and Petros over the years and he had lots of snaps of your mother when she was young.'

'Yes, I've not seen some of them before.' She touched the side of his face with her hand. 'You do know that you are a lovely, *lovely* man, don't you?'

'Shall we keep that between you and me? It is not an asset in the business world for it to be known one has a heart.'

'Nobody needs to know what goes on behind closed doors...' she agreed huskily.

His eyebrows lifted. 'That then leaves us free to do...?'

'Almost anything we want,' Katie completed smoothly. 'Got any ideas?'

'Well, actually...' Katie began. Her eyes twinkled. 'Can I whisper this?'

Nikos obligingly bent his head. 'You know something,' he said when she had finished. 'You are a very bad woman.'

'No, I'm *your* very bad woman. For better—' she sighed happily, tugging at his tie '—or worse.'

Leaving aside the worse part, Katie didn't think it could get much better than being married to Nikos. And as she took him by the hand and led him to the bed she told him so.

THE GREEK MILLIONAIRE'S MARRIAGE

by

Sara Wood

Childhood in Portsmouth meant grubby knees, flying pigtails and happiness for **Sara Wood.** Poverty drove her from typist and seaside landlady to teacher till writing finally gave her the freedom her Romany blood craved. Happily married, she has two handsome sons: Richard is married, calm, dependable, drives tankers; Simon is a roamer – silversmith, roofer, welder, always with beautiful girls. Sara lives in the Cornish countryside. Her glamorous writing life alternates with her passion for gardening, which allows her to be carefree and grubby again!

PROLOGUE

DIMITRI ANGELAKI braced his powerful legs as his launch surged forwards, its streamlined hull scything cleanly through the glittering sea towards the little fishing port of Olympos. He sang softly to himself, an old Greek love song, in a throaty voice that conveyed his passion for life and love.

It had been an odd day. One with stark contrasts of delight and anxiety, during which his senses had been utterly sated—and his nerves had been tested to the utmost.

Glancing around, he allowed himself an indulgent moment of pleasure, letting his gaze linger on his wife's incredible body, and enjoying the gleam of her golden-goddess skin against the luxurious cream leather seat. To his approval, her bikini was minimal: three small turquoise triangles barely concealing the essence of her womanhood.

The dazzling light was turning her hair to white fire where it fanned over her slender shoulders and he felt a helpless little jerk in his chest when he recalled just where that hair had been that day, slithering and sliding over the most sensitive parts of his body in an erotic dance that had driven him to paradise and beyond.

His chiselled mouth curved sensually and a throb began yet again in his loins. That was the joy of sex with Olivia. First would come the anticipation: the fiery glances that ripped his brain to shreds, the messages of hunger and need clearly projected in her sea-blue eyes.

Then, as surely as night followed day, came their un-inhibited lovemaking: inventive, crazy, wild and tender—but always intensely satisfying and releasing the steam valve of their mutual passion.

Finally, he thought, now fully aware of her and with all his senses on high alert, he could enjoy a rerun of every erotic second, from the first glance they'd exchanged to their final sighs of release.

A growl of pleasure rose to his throat and his hands were less than steady when he belatedly turned his attention to steering a straight line again. She got to him, right in the gut, and he loved that because it made him feel alive and utterly male.

Sometimes he wanted to shoot his fist up into the air after their lovemaking, and shout Yes! like a kid who'd just scored a goal. He grinned to himself at the very idea. He, a tycoon whose coolness under pressure was admired the world over! But property deals didn't excite him nearly as much as these exquisite encounters with his wife. It was unfortunate that his work took him away from home so often and that the hectic nature of his breakfast-to-midnight schedules meant that it was pointless for Olivia to travel with him.

Still, the time they were together seemed all the more sweet. That day they had anchored offshore to swim naked in the silken sea. Then they had made love in a lemon grove, the intoxicating scent of a thousand blossoming trees adding to his delirium. Later, she'd fed him lobster and grapes on a hillside overlooking the ruins of an ancient temple dedicated to Aphrodite, the goddess of love.

'Venus,' he'd explained to her. 'A poor second to you, my darling.'

Amazingly, he could still feel the thrilling touch of

Olivia's fingers on his mouth, his throat, his chest…and everywhere else. Each deeply pulsing inch of him bore her imprint. It had been one of the most sensual experiences in all the thirty-two years of his life.

Everything would have been perfect—if it hadn't been for his increasing concern for Athena. A frown creased his sun-bronzed forehead as he willed Athena to ring from the hospital to say she was all right. He felt the tension screwing him up again, ruining the memories of the day. But then it was understandable. He loved Athena with all his heart…

Olivia stiffened when she heard the trill of Dimitri's mobile. It had been ringing far too often that day, but with infuriating stubbornness he'd refused to turn it off.

'Greek moguls,' he'd said with a pretence at pomposity and referring to a standing joke between them, 'need to stay in contact with their minions.'

'Then find a minion you can delegate to,' she'd protested, but had been fatally diverted when his mouth had closed firmly on hers and he'd kissed her complaint away with a breathtaking thoroughness.

Looking back, though, she could be more objective. His obsessive devotion to work had been a problem for some time. When he was away, and she only had her disapproving mother-in-law, Marina, for company, she felt increasingly lonely and unhappy. Her insecurity and doubts over Dimitri's true feelings were painfully reinforced by Marina's sly hints about Dimitri's long absences.

Olivia clenched her fists. From the day of her marriage six months earlier, Marina had taunted her.

'All Greek men have mistresses,' Marina had purred. 'Don't think my son is any different.'

A mistress. Would that explain his lack of consideration? Even this long-anticipated trip today, to the ancient Greek theatre at Epidauros, had been marred by his inattention. She sighed. It could have been deeply romantic. Dimitri had demonstrated the acoustics of the two-thousand-year-old theatre by whispering 'I love you' from the performing area far below. Amazingly, she had heard every impassioned syllable from where she had been sitting, fifty-four rows up.

Quite enchanted, she'd risen to her feet to blow him a kiss. Unfortunately just then he'd received another of his infuriating calls and he had hurried out of the arena so that she couldn't eavesdrop on his conversation.

Recalling how offended she'd been, and with her eyes flashing in anger, she curled up crossly in the luxurious seat of his launch, glaring at Dimitri. He handled the boat expertly with one hand, the other holding the loathed mobile to his ear.

Although his back was to her, she'd seen the tension of his body when the phone had rung. And now that he was engaged in an earnest discussion she wondered at the reason for his relief, which was apparent in the easing of those taut muscles that she knew so well. Something was going on.

Her heart cramped. He was almost cradling the phone, his magnificent body fluid with tenderness. A sense of dread played havoc with her stomach. She sucked it in, not breathing. Perhaps her mother-in-law was right.

Yet…Dimitri couldn't keep his hands off her. Almost from the moment she'd become his secretary two years ago, at the age of twenty-four, they'd been

mad for one another. Every moment in public together
had been a deliciously tensioned ordeal; every second
alone had become a shattering explosion of hunger and
raw need. They had been blind to sense, reckless in
surrendering to the volcanic passions that had seized
them.

Thinking of those blissful stolen moments of abandon caused an instant arousal in her and she shifted her
slim thighs, pressing her legs tightly together to control
the pulsing heat that had begun to massage her with its
irresistible rhythm.

Clouds of helpless longing confused her brain and
ruefully she realised that the pressure of her bikini top
had become unbearable because of the sudden fullness
of her breasts and their tingling tips.

Focusing on him, she noticed that he was laughing
now. The honey-gold naked shoulders shook with
amusement as he murmured something intimate into
the wretched phone.

A fierce stab of jealousy ripped through her. Dimitri
was *hers!* Body and soul, heart and mind! Immediately
she felt appalled by her irrational suspicion and, contrite, she went over to stand behind him, wrapping her
arms around the warm, satin skin of his narrow waist
in a gesture of remorse, the jutting peaks of her breasts
pressing provocatively into his back.

Dimitri jumped as if she'd ambushed him, muttered
into the phone something incomprehensible in Greek—
which *might* have been 'see you tomorrow', though her
Greek was still minimal—and with a hasty *'Adio!'* he
broke the connection.

Beneath her hand, his heart thudded fast and loud.
In fear? she wondered, alarmed. Maybe he did have a
mistress. Business took him away so often he could

even be serving a whole harem of women for all she knew!

Yet when he swung around, his eyes were smouldering with intent. Hauling her slender body against his, flesh to flesh, he kissed her with slow deliberation, one deft hand killing the engine, the other untying her bikini straps.

He was fully aroused. Magnificently, thrillingly, urgently. Whilst she revelled in the hardness of him, she couldn't help but wish she knew if it was for her, or the woman on the phone.

'Who was that?' she demanded, an ominous frown flattening her arched brows.

He was intent on an erotic stroking of her hair, the pale ash-blonde strands slithering over her sun-kissed shoulders. He disturbed the sprigs of lemon blossom, which he'd arranged around her head like a crown, and they drifted to the ground in a generous waft of intense perfume.

Dimitri's marauding mouth savaged the golden skin of her throat before he answered lazily and with a satisfying huskiness.

'A friend.'

To her suspicious mind, that sounded a shade too casual. And he hadn't looked at her, his inky lashes dropping to hide his eyes.

'Do I know him?' she asked with even more studied carelessness.

There was a very slight hesitation but it was long enough for her to know he was about to be economical with the truth.

'No. Forget it, my darling. Concentrate on what I'm intending to do to you, mm?'

She firmed her mouth but he teased it open easily

with his tongue. The magic of his fingers, tantalisingly
laborious as they undid the ties of her briefs, ensured
that she did forget. The glorious surrender of her body
began. Throatily whispering outrageous things to her,
describing in detail what he had in mind, Dimitri eased
her gently to the warm teak deck.

Her hands clutched at the waistband of his swimming trunks and slid them from his body. Beneath her
avid fingers, the muscles of his small buttocks contracted and she ran her hands lovingly over the firm
curves.

As a lover he was insatiable. Sometimes his hunger
startled her, but she, too, could be as wild and demanding. Then there were times, like now, when his
tenderness made her heart contract and his thought for
her pleasure knew no bounds.

Olivia began to lose control as Dimitri's wicked fingers slipped with unnerving accuracy to the swollen
bud of sensation that lay close to her liquefying core.
He did love her, she thought in an ecstatic haze. He'd
married her, hadn't he?

That evening, with the great ball of a startling red sun
hovering low in the sky, she, Dimitri and the recently
widowed Marina sat drinking strong Greek coffee on
the terrace of Dimitri's mansion overlooking Olympos
Bay.

Marina had been sour-faced ever since they'd returned, glued to one another like limpets, after their
day out. Olivia's heart had sunk at the sight of the
woman. It wasn't easy, having your hostile mother-in-
law living with you! Yet she knew how lonely Marina
was since her husband's recent death. She had known

such loneliness when her parents had been killed in a
motorway accident.

In a friendly gesture, she touched her mother-in-
law's arm with a sympathetic hand—which was almost
immediately removed. Unseen by Dimitri, Marina gave
her a glowering glance of deep suspicion.

'It's a wonderful sunset,' Olivia said, offering the
olive branch of peace in an opening gambit and refusing to be put off.

'It always is,' came the slightly tart reply. 'I suppose
you two are leaving me alone tomorrow as well. I remember you are shopping in Athens—'

'Ah.' Dimitri replaced his cup in the saucer.

Olivia knew from the look on his face that he was
going to cancel their trip. This would be the third
time—and he'd said that he wouldn't disappoint her
again.

'Not business!' she protested.

It seemed to her that he squirmed a little. 'Some
local… meeting that I can't avoid. And after that I must
fly to Tokyo for a week. Sorry. I'll make it up to you.'
His smile was perfunctory, as if his thoughts were elsewhere. 'When I return, we'll definitely hit the shops
and wear our credit cards out—'

'I'm not a child to be offered bribes in pacification,'
she said, hurt. So he was going away again. Misery
swept over her.

'No. But this is important. In fact,' he said, rising,
'there are some calls I have to make in preparation—'

'Minions,' she muttered, glowering.

Dimitri paused in mid-stride as he headed for the
door. He was anxious to call Athena to see if her false
labour pains had really gone away, and he didn't take
kindly to Olivia's resentment.

Turning slightly, he gave her a long, steady look. She didn't understand. She had everything: money, a husband and security. In contrast, poor Athena had so little—though he'd make damn sure she didn't go short. He himself had known poverty, and the enervating fear that went with it. When it was born—any time now—Athena's child would carry Angelaki blood in its veins. He would have protected her and her child even if he hadn't promised his dying father that he would do so.

Athena had given Theo, his father, the love and warmth that had been lacking in his marriage. Dimitri had seen his father's new happiness with his young mistress and, though his feelings had been mixed, he had been pleased for him. But he would keep his oath that his mother would never know the humiliating truth. It was a matter of honour—and respect for his mother's feelings.

Preoccupied with Athena's immediate need for reassurance and security, he felt irritation rising at Olivia's apparent dissatisfaction with life.

'Remember that because of my hard work you are enjoying the proceeds of my wealth,' he shot back angrily, and stalked into the mansion.

Seething at that unfair stab, Olivia sat tight and sipped her coffee. She wanted Dimitri, not his millions. Until her marriage she'd always worked, and had always occupied her mind. Now she was experiencing boredom for the first time in her life as she whiled away day after day, waiting for him to come home.

That wasn't healthy. No wonder she pounced on him when he returned from yet another trip. Her Greek wasn't good enough to win her a job to give her an outside interest—not that Dimitri would let her work.

His mother ran the house and gardeners tended the grounds so all Olivia could do was to sightsee and shop. And long for Dimitri's return when the house and she would spring into life again.

Paradise, she reflected, had its downside. She stared unhappily at the million-dollar view. The sun, now a yellow furnace, slipped beneath the horizon. For some reason she felt close to tears. And suddenly homesick for her friends.

'My dear!' exclaimed Marina with false concern. 'Your first quarrel!'

'We're both passionate people,' she said coolly.

'Dimitri does not like women to argue with him.'

'He knew what he'd got when he married me. We'd worked together and slept together for two years,' she reminded Marina. 'He loves my independence. Loves it when I stand up to him—'

'Oh, *then* he did, yes,' Marina murmured. 'But not now you are his wife. He will expect obedience.'

'He can expect all he likes,' Olivia said tiredly.

'Then you must realise that he will turn to someone soft and yielding. Like his mistress. I expect that's where he's gone now,' Marina said with satisfaction.

'Mistress? He wouldn't have the energy to manage another woman,' Olivia told her with unusual frankness, stung by Marina's spite.

The older woman pursed her lips in disapproval of such intimate knowledge.

'My son is more of a man than you know. I'll give you her address. I think her name is Athena. You can see for yourself.'

A cold chill went through Olivia. That had been said with such certainty... Please, no, she thought. She couldn't bear it. Suddenly she felt she must get away from Marina.

'I'm going to bed. Goodnight.'

Shaking with apprehension, she made her way to the master bedroom, where she found Dimitri lounging on their vast bed, laughing and murmuring into the phone. The moment he saw her he cut the call short and she felt a terrible sick sensation sweeping through her.

They stared at one another like two wary opponents in a boxing ring. She saw disappointment in his eyes before he swung off the bed and strode past her.

'Where are you going?' she asked, hating herself for sounding like a nagging wife.

'Out.'

'At this hour?'

Oh, that was stupid! But she understood now why women probed like this. They didn't trust their husbands. And often with good reason.

He studied her soft, trembling mouth and almost told her. Then he bit back the words that were on the tip of his tongue and said curtly; 'At this hour.' And he strode out before she could weaken him.

Olivia stood in the middle of the luxurious bedroom, mistress of all she surveyed, co-owner of the mansion and all its valuable contents, of a penthouse in Athens overlooking the Acropolis, a Georgian house in Berkeley Square, a yacht, a private jet and apparently unlimited funds. Yet never had she felt so bereft, so shorn of everything she valued.

The wealth and its trappings were nothing without Dimitri's love. If he didn't care, then she had nothing. She looked down at her shaking hands. The huge diamond in her engagement ring flashed at her as if in mockery. The diamond necklace, designed to look like

a scattering of glittering daisies at her throat, felt suddenly like a slave's halter.

She was a wife now. A possession. And according
to their marriage ceremony she was supposed to stand
in awe of her husband. At least, she thought wryly,
she'd then been directed to stamp on his foot. Pity
she'd just tapped his instep with her toe.

Olivia frowned, remembering that he had been instructed to love her as if she were his own body. All
right. Either he did love her or he didn't. She wasn't
going to be used purely as a sex object, or a breeding
ground for Angelaki children while he 'played away'.
At times like this it was sink or swim, and she'd never
been the sinking sort.

Her mouth firmed in determination. If he did have a
mistress, she would leave him. She would not be
shared. Tomorrow she would swallow her pride and
ask Marina for that address.

No man made a fool of her. No man would ever use
her purely to appease his sexual appetite. Better a life
without Dimitri than that.

She noticed that the sprig of lemon blossom she'd
placed on the bathroom shelf had withered and died.
Was that an omen? She met her own blazing aquamarine eyes and grim mouth in the baroque mirror, the
full enormity of her situation striking her with chilling
reality. This time tomorrow she could be on the plane
back to England.

CHAPTER ONE

IT WAS three years since she'd last been in Athens. Three interminable years since she'd walked out on Dimitri after wrecking their bedroom in a fit of helpless rage, flinging valuable objects around as if they were cheap souvenirs. It had done nothing to ease the searing pain.

He had been cheating on her. She had seen it with her own eyes. Marina had driven her to a small village near ancient Mycenae, just in time to witness Dimitri's tenderness as he shepherded his mistress towards his car.

His hugely *pregnant* mistress. For a moment she hadn't been able to breathe, so great was the shock. The woman was obviously in labour. That—and Dimitri's loving care—hurt more than anything. She felt that she would have preferred to find them both naked and in the act of love. Seeing his devotion to a woman who carried his child had been infinitely worse.

'Believe me now?' Marina had enquired.

And when Marina had driven them away Olivia had known that she'd never be able to forget Dimitri's betrayal.

She had been devastated. Arriving back at the villa, a gloating Marina had reminded her that Dimitri must now be on his way to Tokyo.

'Go home,' Marina had urged. 'To the people who love you.'

17

'Yes,' she'd whispered, aching for loving arms around her. 'I need my friends.'

Her note to Dimitri had been brief but heartfelt. *When there is no love in a marriage, it is a mistake to continue it.* Yet a little part of her had hoped that their marriage could be saved. Maybe he'd find her in England, to apologise, and beg her forgiveness and they would begin again.

But he had made no contact. It was as though someone had turned off a light inside her. Men seemed pale shadows compared with Dimitri. England was greyer than she remembered and life was less exuberant. Greek life, and one Greek male in particular, had suited her temperament, but she had to move on. And divorce was the first step.

'How are you feeling?' Paul Hughes, her lawyer and friend, solicitously took her hand in his.

She withdrew it on the pretext of tucking a strand of hair back into her tight chignon. 'Ready for battle,' she replied grimly.

'Next month, you could be one of the richest and most powerful women in Europe!' Paul crowed.

Money and power. Was that all men cared about? Why didn't they put love first, like women? She settled back in her seat, crossly smoothing imaginary creases from the figure-hugging skirt of her white linen suit.

Her hand was shaking and she stared at the back of the chauffeur's head, pumping up her courage with cold, clinical anger by thinking of the terrible moment when her love for Dimitri had shattered into bits.

On his yacht, moored near Piraeus Harbour, Dimitri dealt with his e-mails, despatching instructions to his property agents scattered about the globe. Business was doing well—though it should be, since he'd devoted eighteen hours a day to it for the past three years.

Unravelling his six-feet of toned muscle from the confining chair, he escaped from his desk, unable to concentrate, incapable of sitting like a trapped lion for a moment longer. He'd glanced at his watch impatiently. Ten minutes and she'd be here.

She'd been in his mind ever since the call. The scent of her body. The wicked look in her eyes as she wound herself around him, capturing him in her silken web.

'I want a divorce,' she'd said coldly, two days earlier.

'Come and get it, then,' he'd replied, and severed the connection.

He'd sat motionless for an hour, steaming. So many questions had been on his lips. Where have you been? Why run away like a coward? And why the hell did you marry me—for sex and money, as everyone told me over and over again till I doubted even those early months of married bliss? Then had come the most chilling question of all. Did you *ever* care?

He scowled at the glittering sea and wondered why she had waited till now for a divorce. Perhaps she was afraid of his anger. With good reason. Though his mother had said it was because she'd run out of money and that fact had conquered her fear of what he might do to her. It was odd, though. The allowance he paid every month into their old bank account was more than generous.

Sometimes when he lay awake at night he imagined himself putting his hands around that slender neck and throttling her. Or flinging her to the ground and...

He disgusted himself. She'd aroused terrible emotions that shamed him utterly. The raw animal nature of his fury appalled him. He'd believed himself to be a gentleman, but Olivia had reduced him to his basest instincts. Hatred, ungovernable desire and revenge.

His fist descended on his desk with such force that everything on it bounced. He slammed the fist into his palm. His eyes glittered. He was ready.

Taking the stairs three at a time in huge leaps, he emerged onto the deck to find Eleni, the daughter of his business partner. She was outstaying her welcome. He had relented—under persistent pressure from his mother—to take Eleni on a trip along the coast for a couple of days.

With Olivia constantly filling his mind he'd been bad company and Eleni had irritated him beyond belief. Too girly. Too breathless, clingy and starry-eyed. And, at nineteen, too young to be a companion for him anyway. Poor kid.

He took a deep breath to steady his nerves. This meeting with Olivia had to be short and sharp. It would be a merciful release from a marriage that had died with Olivia's curt admission that she didn't love him.

'Time to go,' he announced in crisp tones of authority. 'You're due at your father's for lunch.'

Sulkily, Eleni rose, her bikini-clad silicon-enhanced body voluptuous and tanned, her blonde hair swishing around her shoulders and reminding him sharply of his final day with his wife.

Hating to remember even one second of that deceitful day, he clenched his jaw in anger. It had figured in his dreams as their last perfect time together. Yet all the time they'd been making love she must have been planning her departure. He ground his teeth in impotent fury.

Olivia had made a fool of him and that was unforgivable.

Where she was concerned, their relationship had been nothing but lies, lust and credit cards. Lies he could brush away with contempt. His bank balance could cope with her spending sprees—which he'd encouraged, admittedly, delighting in lavishing gifts on her and watching her slither into fabulous creations by top designers. And out of them again. His hand shook.

But the lust... That was an unbearable loss. Desperate to forget her, he'd made love to several willing women, but they were nothing compared with Olivia. Worse, it crucified him to know that she would be incapable of doing without sex. Through many sleepless nights he'd fumed over his highly coloured imaginings of Olivia writhing beneath some other man. Or men.

Eleni reached up on tiptoe to kiss his cheek. Her mouth seemed to press more firmly than usual and he realised that his fears were real. She was definitely being lined up as his next wife.

Inwardly he cursed as he saw his car approaching the mooring. He'd miscalculated the journey time. Either baggage control had got its act together or the notorious Athens traffic must have been less dense than usual.

'My wife is here,' he said curtly. 'Get dressed and stay out of sight. Go!'

He heard her irritating snigger as she scampered away. Getting rid of a wife was one matter. Acquiring a second bride barely out of her pram before the ink was dry on the divorce papers was another.

As the car had driven into the marina Olivia had identified Dimitri's luxurious yacht immediately—and his tall, arrogant figure standing on the deck. Her heart somersaulted at the sight of him.

But it steadied when she saw his companion. A pneumatic blonde, with hair just like hers and wearing the tiniest of bikinis, was strolling with a hip-swaying walk towards him. The woman was now kissing his cheek and murmuring something sultry in his ear. There was something vaguely familiar about her that she couldn't quite place, as if she'd met her before. Perhaps at a party during their marriage...

'Nice little popsie,' commented Paul.

Olivia's eyes glittered with contempt. Dimitri's mistress had been dark and beautiful with flashing black eyes, another woman entirely. How many dancing girls did he need to fawn over him? She fumed silently. They were all set to discuss divorce and he was intending to parade his latest conquest to show he didn't give a damn!

Well, she'd show him that she didn't care either.

'She's one of Dimitri's *"popsies"*. That's his boat, probably his latest woman, and that's him up there,' she said, proud there was no tremor in her voice.

'Wow. How many million is that worth?' Awed, Paul stared at the luxury yacht, then more warily at the intimidating figure of Dimitri.

'No idea, but he worked for every penny of it,' she said shortly. 'Dragged himself up from nothing, from shepherd's son to property magnate. Worked night and day without ceasing, pitting his brains against the sharpest knives in the box and coming out top through drive, determination and sheer force of personality.'

'Sounds as if you admire the pants off him,' Paul commented sulkily.

Insulted, she turned brightly sparking eyes on the

lawyer. 'I loathe every hair on his head! I'd sooner lie in a pit of venomous snakes and be eaten by rats than be in a room with him!'

Olivia drew in a breath and controlled her temper. She must stay calm. Be dignified. In the privacy of her small flat, she'd rehearsed the right words till she was hoarse.

When she reached the top of the gangplank, regal and icy-featured, she waited for Dimitri to move towards her. Infuriatingly, he just stood like a rock in that conceited way he had, with his legs planted apart, the darkness of his hair and the bright blaze of his obsidian eyes giving her a jolt of surprise.

Long-neglected embers startled her even more by sizzling into life within her. She felt the wonderful, warm, curling sensation in her stomach with some dismay. The hunger was still there, then. Festering like a disease.

Deliberately she put the lid on it. But she still reeled from the impact of Dimitri's magnetism, the lurking strength of his torso beneath the crisp white shirt that was belted neatly into the sand-coloured trousers, and the intense masculinity of his cynical mouth that had once roamed over her body so freely and with such devastating effect.

Her eyes narrowed behind the concealing sunglasses as she surveyed him. She noticed the air of wealth that hung about him and how beautifully groomed he was— in contrast to Paul's drooping and travel-worn appearance.

A glorious hunk of a man. Supremely male and with a raw and magnetic appeal that still had the ability to reach deep into her and stir her senses.

Dimitri was a power to be reckoned with, a man

whose huge personality and vitality could fill a room and draw all eyes. A man in a million.

The air sucked from her lungs, her mouth became dry. Paul, perhaps thinking she was nervous, put his hand in the small of her back and propelled her forward. She had to either go with the flow or stumble, and naturally she chose to move—but silently cursed Paul for giving Dimitri the advantage.

'This is Paul Hughes, my lawyer,' she said coolly and without preamble.

Eyes mocking her, Dimitri nodded with cool indifference and turned away to pick up a towel from the deck, thus neatly ignoring Paul's outstretched hand.

Seething with irritation that this was not going as she'd planned, she glared at the back of Dimitri's head. The raven hair had been cut with its usual precision, the band of olive-toned skin below the sharp black line being a tempting contrast against the crisp edge of his hand-tailored shirt. And his back... Tingles skittered across her skin as she contemplated the gorgeous, so-touchable triangle...

Enjoyed by other women now. That nubile blonde was waiting somewhere below, perhaps waiting for Dimitri's sensitive fingers to arouse her to frenzied delight. A terrible stab of jealousy lacerated her chest.

She heard Paul clearing his throat and found herself jumping in with both feet and firing off her first salvo before the lawyer had a chance to speak. Unfortunately it wasn't what she'd intended to say, but a question she just had to ask before it burned its way out in an unladylike screech.

'Was that your *secretary* I saw you with just now?' she asked coolly.

Immediately he was flung back in time. He saw

Olivia entering his office for her interview as his secretary. Slender and shapely, she had oozed sensuality
despite the modest beige suit and cream shirt, and her
entirely proper demeanour. It was her eyes that had
enticed him, as deep and as mysterious as the sea. And
her mouth, with its high arch and full lower lip, had
made him wonder what it would be like to have her
kneeling before him with that soft mouth sucking the
sweetness from him, that white-blonde hair soft beneath his fingers...

He'd never forget the interview, during which he had
become so heated that he'd opened the windows and
called for a fresh carafe of water. And he had known
that, whatever her secretarial skills, he must have her.

Amazingly she was as efficient as she was beautiful.
Images of her as his secretary filled his brain. The palpable tension as she took his hurried dictation. Then he
saw her spread across his desk, her eyes and fabulous
body reeling him in as he slowly removed her clothes
with shaking fingers.

His jaw tightened, his chest cramping. Enough. It
was over. He turned then, his eyes narrowed as he
thrust his hands into his pockets in a belligerent gesture.

I know your game, he thought. He'd employed it
often enough himself in business not to recognise it.
Disconcert your quarry. Throw them off balance. Find
their Achilles' heel. And she knew all too well that the
sex they'd had together was so incredible that recalling
it would heat him up in seconds.

The same, he thought callously, went for her. Two
could play. But he'd win this one.

'No. Not...my secretary,' he murmured, giving her
the benefit of a long, memory-filled stare.

The richness of his deep voice filled the very air between them with provocative resonances and she felt something inside her give a little shimmy of guilt-laden delight. The curl of his mouth captured her gaze and she had to force herself to remain outwardly cool to hide the oven-heat within.

'Just some woman, then,' she said dismissively.

Did he detect a note of jealousy? he wondered. Mocking amusement flickered in Dimitri's satin-soft eyes. She hadn't recognised Eleni. But then, she had known her before the girl had increased her bust size to its current oversized proportions, dyed her hair and spent some of her father's fortune on liposuction.

'Last time I looked, she was,' he agreed in a sexy drawl, his mouth upwardly curved with salacious, masculine pleasure.

And he let his gaze wander. Linger. Contemplate. Then he reached out and removed her sunglasses before she could protest, slipping them into his pocket. Now he could see her eyes. He smiled into them.

'I need to see into your soul,' he explained.

Olivia glared, even as she felt the knife of jealousy stab deeply in her chest. Dimitri was the most sensual man she'd ever known. It occurred to her that maybe he had never been faithful to her, even in the early days. He was a man of huge passions, vast sexual needs. For all she knew, she could have been merely one of many women he enjoyed.

And did Athena know about this blonde—or had he abandoned Athena and moved on to pastures new? Her head whirled. This was the man she'd married—a man apparently with the morals of a stray dog. It hurt to know she'd been so thoroughly deceived. It made her stomach curdle to think of his betrayal. There had been times when she'd tormented herself thinking of him playing with his child.

Her eyes gleamed like blue glass in the mask of her face. 'You are such a bigoted chauvinist where women are concerned,' was all she could say in icy derision, without revealing how upset she was beneath her frosty exterior.

'Olivia—' Paul began uncomfortably.

'Let me have my say!' she snapped, whirling on him so abruptly that he was forced to take a step back.

Paul put up his hands in surrender, shocked by her vehemence.

Dimitri knew at that moment that this man would never satisfy a woman like her, not for a second. She liked tough men with big passions. A man who could tame her fiery nature and bring calm and serenity to her life. Paul might look at her as if she were the nearest thing to the goddess Aphrodite, the Greek Venus, but he'd bore her to tears in no time at all.

With his mind working like quicksilver, he began to think, to plot and scheme. There was much he needed to know—and that would take time. First he'd get rid of the lawyer. Then he'd inform her that she'd have to stay in Greece while the case was being processed.

He smiled. He'd turn Olivia inside out and get the answers he wanted to all those unasked questions that had plagued him for the past three years. After that he'd find a way—whatever that might be—to prevent her from using her predatory claws on another unsuspecting man. A threat, perhaps. A clause in the divorce settlement preventing her from marrying for some years... He'd come up with something. He always did.

His shoulders squared with resolve. Olivia wouldn't know what had hit her. She'd be putty in his hands.

CHAPTER TWO

'YOU want a divorce, I understand,' he said amiably enough, motioning them to the sun loungers with an authoritative hand.

In a graceful movement of her supple body Olivia slid onto the thick cushion before she realised she and Paul were now at a disadvantage in the low recliners. Dimitri towered over them both, dominating them and smirking with self-congratulation at his cleverness.

She wanted to slap him. 'As fast as we can arrange it,' she agreed instead with a smile that dripped honey. 'And,' she said, adding the vinegar, 'with as little contact with you as humanly possible.'

Filled with a reckless and rebellious need to unnerve him, she kicked off her high-heeled sandals and wriggled her bare toes, making the pink varnish gleam in the sunshine. Then she leant back and unbuttoned her jacket before languidly lifting her arms behind her head to revel luxuriously in the warm sunshine.

Dimitri allowed himself a moment to devour her. She had elegantly arranged her slender, endless legs so that he could admire their length from her small arched feet to mid-thigh. With the raising of her arms, the swelling mounds of her breasts had lifted to gleam provocatively above her simple scoop-necked white top. Delectable. His senses stirred. She was playing her little game to the hilt and beyond.

Crouching close to her, and with his back to Paul, he slowly raked her body with his gaze, watching her

respond, knowing the tell-tale tightening of her thighs
and contemplating with drowsy sensuality the peaks of
her breasts which betrayed the effectiveness of his hungry glance. Or her avid sexual greed. It didn't matter
which, only that she should want him—and be denied.

Aching for her more fiercely than he could remember, he let his eyes meet hers. For a moment he forgot
where he was and what he was doing. She dragged him
in, her soft blue eyes telling him everything he needed
to know.

His heart raced with dangerous thoughts. She
claimed she wanted a quick ending to their marriage
and the minimum of contact. He was tempted to make
her suffer the exact opposite. A kick of excitement
jerked at his solar plexus.

Fighting his way clear of the thickened atmosphere
around them, he flung her a dazzling grin and put his
hand on her shoulder.

'What are you prepared to do to encourage me to do
what you want?' he murmured, resisting the urge to
slide his fingers somewhere more interesting. Though
he stared at the tantalising curves of her breasts, imagining the feel of them as he weighed them in his hands.

'Whatever it t-takes,' she stammered, and he was
delighted to see how dry her mouth was and that her
voice was husky. Though the slick of her tongue over
her lips almost incited him to moistening her mouth in
his own inimitable way.

'You always did put your body and soul into your
projects, didn't you?' he said in husky contemplation.

'Look,' the lawyer interrupted petulantly from somewhere behind his back, 'can we get on with this somewhere more suitable? We will want a list of your assets—'

'Oh,' Dimitri said with a low chuckle, his eyes riveted to Olivia's softly parted lips. He remembered their taste. The soft plumpness between his teeth. His voice grew thick with desire. 'I think Olivia knows all about my assets.'

'Some of them lie below your belt and are virtually the public property of any good-looking woman who passes,' she scathed.

He grinned and his black eyes seemed to dance wickedly, sending her into a haze of hunger. His fingers had tightened on her shoulder in a grip of possession.

'I can't help being virile. Our sex was extraordinary, wasn't it?' he murmured. 'Entire continents moved. Flames scorched our—'

'Look here—!' began Paul, red-faced with disapproval.

'Come.' Dimitri catapulted himself to a standing position and had the lawyer off the lounger and across the deck before Paul or she knew what had hit them.

'Dimitri!' she called, angrily swinging her legs to the deck.

She'd blown it. For hour after hour she'd practised what she'd say, the carefully chosen invective and scorn, the icy analysis of his flawed character. All to no avail. He'd turned her into a helpless mass of fluttering hormones merely by looking at her. She ground her teeth and balled her fists in fury.

'Don't worry. I'll be back in a moment,' he flung over his shoulder, and she seethed silently at his blithe and carefree attitude.

'Lemonade, madam?'

Still glaring, she jerked her head around and saw a man clad in immaculate whites bearing a silver salver with a crystal jug and two glasses.

Two glasses! Dimitri must have *planned* to get rid of Paul—

'Madam?'

Innate politeness made her rearrange her scowling face. With an apologetic smile, she nodded.

'Yes. Thank you.'

She could handle Dimitri. Her needs were small—just a few home truths, the divorce, thank you and goodbye. Olivia sipped gratefully at the cooling drink and felt her temperature settle down to something closer to normal.

Restlessly she wandered to the rail and stared at the glittering sea. A thousand islands lay out there, and all the beauties of Greece. Nostalgia slipped, uninvited, into her heart and soul. If only he hadn't strayed. She would give everything to live in this lovely part of the world again.

Closing her eyes, she dreamed of the Olympos promontory which floated in the sapphire sea on the coast of the Peloponnese land mass—the large peninsula to the south of Athens. On Olympos, white and pastel-blue houses snuggled companionably in the hollows of gentle hills thick with olive trees and vines.

The dazzling light gave the sandy beaches and classical ruins a startling clarity. Nothing was mild or gentle. All was passion, laughter and high drama, and she, with her explosive passions, had felt at home. The people were friendly to a fault...

She scowled. Too friendly, and too many faults where Dimitri was concerned! And where the devil was he—?

'Olivia. Forgive me for leaving you.'

She jerked her head around. Bursting with vital energy that took her breath away, he came striding towards her. Alone. Instantly suspicious, she turned around completely to glare at him, leaning back against the rail for support. Because she needed it, badly.

'Where is Paul?'

Dimitri smiled to himself, poured himself a glass of lemonade and came to join her, his step ominously cheerful. He tilted his head to one side and listened. So did she, and after a moment she heard the sound of a car revving up. At that moment he beamed with pleasure and replied.

'On his way to New York.'

Her eyes hardened. 'New…*York?*' she gasped. And, sure enough, when she looked across at the quayside, she saw Dimitri's car disappearing around a corner.

'Mmm.' He took a thoughtful sip, his mouth hypnotically glistening. Her tongue tipped her own lips before she could stop it and his gaze lingered there, making her skin tingle with excitement. 'He seemed very keen.'

'I bet. How much did you bribe him with?' she asked sourly, hating him.

'Not a lot,' he admitted happily. His eyes crinkled, making her heart jerk as she remembered the laughter they'd shared, the happiness she'd imagined was theirs alone. 'The price of a first-class plane ticket, accommodation, all expenses—'

'Why?' she asked, loathing him more every second that passed.

Dimitri's eyes widened innocently. 'My lawyer's there.'

'I see. Not, then, because you think you can bully me into agreeing to some underhand scheme you have in mind while he's absent?'

To see his expression, Olivia thought scornfully as

he reacted with shock horror at her suggestion, you'd think there had never been such an honest and trustworthy man in the whole world.

'What a suspicious mind you have!' he objected. 'I thought you'd be pleased I took such immediate action. The two of them can get on with making lists of my assets and come up with some figure agreeable to both sides—'

'I just want the divorce,' she told him with an impatient gesture. 'Nothing else.'

His eyebrows shot up. 'You mean...no money? Property? Jewellery?'

'That's it.'

'Please! Don't insult my intelligence by pretending you aren't interested in a share of my wealth!' he scoffed. 'No woman would turn down the chance to be rich. And no court would allow me to leave you unprovided for.' His lip curled in contempt. 'After all, you've worked hard and waited a long time for your share of my fortune.'

She bristled. 'What exactly do you mean by that?'

'You spun your net and threw it out and caught me,' he said, the low growl stiffened with steel. 'You're here to claim your reward. In order to get rid of you I'm prepared to play along and pay you off. I know you'd relish the independence it would give you—'

'I have that in spades, with or without money,' she retorted, boiling with the insult. 'And I can support myself. I don't need a man to provide for me.'

'Is that the line you're taking?' he scorned. 'You intend to impress the courts with your lack of greed— and they'll reward you handsomely for your modest demands? Whereas you and I know that you are owed something for the almost professional pleasure you've given me in the bedroom, on the floor, against the—'

'*Professional?* I'm not one of your whores, to be paid for her services!' she shot back before he listed every single place where they had made love.

'No?' His insolent stare suggested that she might be. 'That's what it comes down to, Olivia. Dress it up any way you like, but marrying a man for his money is a kind of prostitution.'

'I agree,' she grated, so angry that her too-silky tresses were slipping from their confining chignon and she didn't even care. Hauling in a hard breath, she snapped, 'But for your information, I married you for—'

'Sex,' he said softly and the hairs rose on the back of her neck as her body sprang into life. 'That's all it was. Let's not pretend it was anything else. We were great in bed. And everywhere else.' He grinned wickedly. 'Remember—'

'I don't want to remember anything!' she flamed, hating him for the flood of erotic images that were churning up her body and mind. Hating him, too, for killing even the happy moments they'd spent together and reducing their relationship to one base urge.

Dimitri had never loved her. He'd admitted it at last. *Sex. That was all it was.* Well, now she knew, and the truth hurt her more than she could ever have imagined.

'Nothing?'

His mouth had curved into a shape of such carnality that she felt a shudder of desire ripple through her before she managed to drag her wanton body under control again.

'No! It was all a lie, wasn't it? Those declarations of love. The flowers, the little gifts—and the notes you left lying around for me to find… All part of your seduction technique, honed to perfection on…how many women?' she cried heatedly. 'Oh, there must have been hundreds! It was so slick, so smooth! You've probably fathered bastards all over Greece. New York too, for all I know! You humiliated me with your cheating and lying and it gave me great pleasure to disappear off the face of the earth so that you couldn't marry some other deluded female and cheat on her, too!'

Oh, help, she thought. Whatever had happened to her intended cool condemnation of him? Her speech had gone clean out of her head. He just made her *mad*, that was the trouble.

'Me? Cheat?' He frowned as though he didn't know what she was talking about. And then his face tightened. 'I see. You've realised that you are on shaky legal ground in saying there was no love in our marriage. You intend to claim in court that you walked out on me because I was unfaithful.'

'*Claim?*' she stormed. 'Don't insult my intelligence! If you're going to pretend you're as innocent as the driven snow then you're more of a louse than I imagined!'

His scathing glance stabbed into her. 'If you are prepared to malign my character for your own ends—'

'Malign!' she gasped, flinging her head up in outrage and scattering the remaining pins that had held her hair in place. 'I couldn't make your character any worse if I flung it into a sewer and stuffed it full of dead rats!'

It was typical that even at the height of his anger he was able to find her outburst amusing. Their brief, fire-brand rows had always ended in laughter, usually prompted by some outrageous overstatement on her part. And after the laughter had come the making-up…

'Always a colourful phrase on the tip of your tongue,' he drawled, shutting his mind to their passionate reconciliations. The darkness returned to his eyes. 'But I warn you not to make false accusations against me.'

'I won't,' she said grimly, and he nodded as though he'd won a victory. She didn't enlighten him. Her evidence of his infidelity might be needed to secure her the divorce. If so, she'd use it. 'I don't want to discuss your sordid life. I have no interest in it or the way you ran rings around me,' she said coldly. 'Now I'm calling the shots and I want rid of you. As soon as possible. Get that?'

'Your eyes are almost violet with rage,' he mused. 'And you're so flushed, I could almost imagine—'

'Don't try to flirt with me!' she jerked, furious at his murmuring tones.

An innocent, piratical lift of his eyebrow sent a quiver through her. 'I can't help—'

'No. Because you don't value women as people in their own right,' she said, scorn in every line of her uplifted face. Dimitri had never been helpless in the whole of his life. 'You see them as potential conquests and you spin them a line, expecting them to lie down and beg. It's just a knee-jerk reaction to you, isn't it?'

'*Knee?* Wrong place, Olivia,' he murmured. 'Try a little higher up.'

Impatiently she flicked her hair back from where it had tumbled seductively over one eye during her outburst. 'Listen to me. Simple words. Simple solution. I want a divorce. You arrange it—fast.'

'But there is so much to discuss!' he protested. 'Your lawyer's talking of a fifty-fifty division which—'

'He has no right to!' she cried, quivering with indignation.

'Really?' he drawled. 'Sorry, Olivia, but I can't believe he'd take it on himself to decide what settlement you deserve. You'll play the sweet, downtrodden and betrayed wife and tell the courts one thing whilst pushing my legal team for as much as you can get in your greedy little hands.'

Dimitri's mouth had taken on a cynical sneer. She felt like thumping him—and Paul. Dimitri clearly didn't believe her protests and thought she was here for a hefty share of his money. Paul had reinforced that opinion.

Silently cursing the lawyer for launching his own agenda, she decided that Dimitri could wriggle for a while, fearing the ruination of his empire. Serve him right. He'd find out the truth for himself when the time came.

'I just want to be free of you,' she emphasised.

'Come clean, Olivia, and then we can deal. I know that you won't expect to go away empty-handed, not after all the effort you put into driving me so crazy with lust that in a weak moment I proposed marriage in order to keep you,' he reasoned.

Olivia bristled. 'Oh, you were incapable of rational thought, were you?'

'As I said, bewitched. And as you well know.' Their eyes met and she felt herself in danger of falling under his spell, as she had that first day she'd walked into his office and the world had spun around her. 'I feel I owe you something though,' he added. 'You've taught me a lesson.'

'Which is?' she asked unsteadily.

'That I'm not a good judge of women when my loins are on fire,' he growled.

A silence fell between them. Olivia struggled to keep her head. Dimitri was weaving his old magic over her and yet she hated him as much as ever. The pressure of the atmosphere seemed to increase and she found herself fighting for breath. Infuriatingly, Dimitri wasn't affected at all, because he broke the heavy silence and spoke quite casually.

'Tell me. What will you do when you are a free woman again?'

'Start a new life,' she shot back, her entire demeanour daring him to obstruct her goal.

'With Paul?' he queried.

'What's it to you?' she demanded.

Everything, he thought, raked with hatred for any man who might look desperately into those sultry blue eyes and slide into her hot little body. He managed a shrug, which gave him time to swallow away the harsh rage filling his throat.

'I'd hate you to be frustrated.'

'No chance,' she assured him, and was surprised to see the flash of anger that lit his eyes.

'So he excites you?' he said, sounding faintly belligerent.

'Good grief! I'm not discussing my personal life,' she replied airily, and half turned, only to be halted when his hand closed firmly around her arm.

'He's very interested in my money—and how much you'll eventually win,' he purred silkily. 'Tell me, Olivia. I need to know…was that what drove you to marry me? Was it a bonus that there was the prospect of good sex? Did you think we'd have fun for a short while, till you struck out for independence and wealth when you judged you could legally sever our bonds? If so, I admire your single-mindedness, your tenacity and patience—if nothing else—for playing the long game.'

How could he believe that of her? It suggested that he held a very cynical view of women—and her in particular. It was outrageous to suggest she'd married him with a view to a lucrative divorce. Vile-minded rat. Deeply insulted, she picked off his fingers one by one, her mouth tight with contempt.

'You don't know me at all,' she snapped.

'I know you well enough to realise that Paul is only half the man you need,' he bit.

'At least he's not the philandering kind,' she countered.

He grinned. 'I agree. He hasn't, if you'll pardon the expression, got the balls.' It pleased him when her mouth twitched in amusement, acknowledging that he was right. 'He might have a fight on his hands.'

She looked up at him in alarm. 'What…do you mean?'

Dimitri gave a low laugh. 'Oh, not that I'll challenge him to a duel for you. I'm not interested in having a whore for a wife—'

'I'm not!' she yelled, pink with indignation.

'Matter of opinion. No, I could contest the divorce. Make things difficult for you.'

'That's spiteful and beneath you,' she croaked.

'Mm. It might be in my interests, though,' he mused. 'What will I get out of legally severing our marriage— other than a halving of my fortune?'

'Freedom,' she told him, agitated.

'I have that,' he told her. 'I do what I like.'

He always had. 'To remarry?'

'Maybe I don't want to.'

'You want children,' she said bluntly. 'Even you can't create blood heirs without the help of a woman. And however many you father on the wrong side of the blanket, I know you would want at least some of your children to be legitimate. It's definitely to your advantage to divorce me so don't pretend it isn't.'

He smiled. 'You're trying to tell me you're doing me a favour?'

'Well, we can't go on like this, being neither single nor married!' she said crossly. 'I want out of this relationship, Dimitri. I want to wipe you from my shoes, where you've been for these past three years, and never see or think of you again. You have influence. See to it that we're divorced quickly. You can play the field all you like then with a free conscience—that's the little voice in your head that tells you when you're doing something morally wrong, by the way,' she added scathingly.

He smiled, clearly amused by her stinging jibe. 'I don't think a divorce will instantly erase me from your memory,' he purred.

A shudder rippled through her in acceptance of the fact that he himself had made too powerful an impact to be forgotten. Somehow she turned it into a shudder of disgust.

'I sincerely hope it does,' she said stiffly. 'Now. This divorce—'

'Ye-e-s. There's a little snag, though. It will take some time, I'm afraid,' he said with feigned regret.

'Then pull some strings.' She wasn't falling for that one.

He shrugged as if he had none to pull. 'I made some

preliminary enquiries after you rang. The courts are overburdened with work.' Reaching forward to lift back strands of hair which had blown across her face, he came closer, his breath reaching her in a tantalising whisper that caused chaos in her frantically thudding heart. 'I hope you realise that you'll need to stay here while the proceedings are taking their course.'

'That's ridiculous!' she cried. 'I'm flying back tomorrow morning—'

'As you like. But there'll be no divorce. If work's a problem—'

'No.' She frowned. 'It's not. Just that I don't want to stay anywhere near you—'

He shook his head as if in regret. 'It's your choice, of course. There are officials to see, papers to sign… You'd never believe the complications. Even if you stay, it could be three or four months before our case even gets onto the list. Then there might be a year's wait while—'

'A year? That can't be right!' she protested, closing her eyes in dismay.

'Would that be a problem?' he murmured. 'Staying here, discussing each stage with me…'

She couldn't do that. Even now his seductive voice was creating havoc within her. It felt to her as though she might drown. Her senses were taking over. Dimitri's eyes had been as liquid as her bones. Every bit of her was screaming for a sexual release—a kiss, a touch, to be crushed in his arms…

Olivia floundered, trying to keep her head above water. It wasn't over between them, she thought bleakly. She hated him. Despised him. Yet the terrible bond was as strong as ever.

'I could, perhaps,' came his voice perilously close

to her mouth, 'hurry things along a little…if I so wished.'

She gulped and surfaced, opening her eyes to find that he was kissing-close, his head already angled as if he was contemplating his assault on her mouth. The drowsiness of his eyes and the sultry set of his lips sent any rational sense to the four winds.

Ruthlessly she gritted her teeth and reminded herself that he'd be unbearable if she ever let him touch her again. He wasn't worthy enough to clean her shoes, let alone have access to her body. Adulterer. Man of few morals… She searched for words to strengthen her resolve. Yes, she thought grimly, and with the self-restraint of a rutting stag!

'Then wish. Find a four-leafed clover, a black cat, a fairy godmother—I don't care, but *wish!* Bribe someone if necessary, but hurry everything up,' she told him, her tone deliberately acid.

His smile would have beguiled her in times long past. He took her glass from her trembling hand and put it, with his, on the table beside the loungers. Then he took her hands in his, moving his thumbs rhythmically over her skin. And all she could do was to look at him, washes of warm heat turning her body into a glowing furnace.

'I'll do that,' he agreed.

'Good,' she husked.

'For a price,' he said thickly.

Her body slumped. Yes. If it's sex, she thought in a crazy moment of weakness, she'd say yes. One last moment together before she shut down her hunger for him and became celibate again.

How awful! she thought, appalled by her feebleness. What was she thinking?

Despairing, she fought her appallingly wayward, abandoned nature and tried desperately hard to remain indifferent. But he had taken her in his arms now and his body almost touched hers. Every inch of her wanted to strain forward so she could feel the hard, muscular torso against the softness of her breasts and enjoy the pressure of his narrow hips as his pelvis settled against hers.

'I won't pay your price!' she croaked. They fitted so well. Always had. Her head spun.

'I think you will,' he countered with soft certainty.

He was exultant. Her arousal had astonished him. But then they'd always matched one another in their demands. No doubt Paul had starved her of true satisfaction. He had a powerful urge to erase her lovers from her mind and body.

She would definitely pay the price he demanded. He'd see to that. Dimitri touched her quivering mouth, a knife-wound of excitement shafting through him when she gave a little gasp. Oh, yes. To have that glorious body in his bed, to remind her how good their sex had been, that would ease his ache. He would keep her until she didn't know which way up she was. And then when she was utterly dependent on him he'd dump her so fast her feet wouldn't touch the floor.

But hell. He wanted her. *Now!* For the time being, a quick retreat might be wise.

'Wait there. I'll see what I can come up with,' he whispered. And couldn't resist touching her lips with his, intending the kiss to be brief and casual.

Yet in seconds they were wrapped around one another. The ferocity of their passion startled even him. A warning voice in his head told him that he must get away before he showed his desperation.

'Mm. Very nice. But I have a call to make.' Everything throbbed. His blood raced around his body, turning his head to mush. He pushed a hand through his hair and steadied himself, mentally, physically and emotionally. 'I will see what I can do to speed things up.'

Somehow he found his way to the cabin door, though he felt as intoxicated as a drunk. But then he was addicted to her and the more he had the more he wanted. This time, however, it would be on his terms and he would be emotionally detached. The safest way, where his harlot wife was concerned.

Not for nothing did he come from 'under the ditch', the ditch being the pet name for the Corinth Canal that cut off the Peloponnese peninsula from the Greek mainland and turned it into a technical island. People from his area were considered to have a particularly devious mental agility. They could assess a situation and turn it to their advantage, which was why so many Greek politicians came from his homeland.

He headed for the salon, his brain fizzing as if it had been plugged into a socket, his body vibrantly alive. An idea had come to him of such startling simplicity that it left him breathless. He'd deal with Olivia and the Eleni problem at the same time.

A sense of elation made him want to shout and he caught himself grinning stupidly. He'd have one hell of a roller-coaster ride with Olivia. By the time he'd finished with her, she'd be begging him to let her stay as his wife and she would know for herself the humiliation and pain of being rejected. And he'd make sure she realised that he'd treated her like the callous little tramp she really was.

CHAPTER THREE

FOR a moment or two after Dimitri had disappeared into the cabin, Olivia remained at the rail, clinging on to it for dear life because her legs were in no fit state to do the job for which they'd been designed.

No wonder she hadn't been interested in those other men who'd been keen to take her out. Over the past couple of years she'd accepted a few invitations to dinner, hoping that she could forget Dimitri in some other man's arms. All too soon she had discovered that the experimental dates had only reinforced the hold Dimitri still had on her.

Being with him again was like leaping into a maelstrom of emotion and feeling, where her senses became heightened and every cell in her body hummed and vibrated as if they'd been connected to a power source.

She paced the deck, horrified by her arousal and deeply ashamed that her sexual hunger could override her contempt for Dimitri. He really imagined that she'd leap into bed with him, given the chance—and perhaps she might, she thought with a groan.

Hearing him flinging open the cabin doors again, she spun around, her heart pounding at the sight of him, his passionate eyes dark and unwavering as he strolled towards her trembling body.

'I can offer you a quickie if you like.' He smiled at her, one eyebrow lifted in query.

Olivia inhaled sharply and raised her hand to slap his face but he caught it, laughing, the sudden crinkling

45

of his eyes and the warmth of his expression making her knees liquefy.

'How dare you?' she whispered.

'Sorry. Your language sometimes has too many meanings. I meant a quickie divorce,' he said, amused.

Sceptically she narrowed her eyes. Dimitri knew exactly what he'd said. His English was impeccable. If she'd gone all coy on him, he would have grabbed her and rushed her down to his cabin without a second thought. Though what the pneumatic blonde would think of that, she wouldn't know. It shocked her that Dimitri could juggle two women, only a few feet from each other, without turning a hair!

'Do it, then,' she said coldly, snatching her hand free.

'And you'll agree to what I want?'

'Not to anything illegal or immoral!' she declared.

'Absolutely not,' he said, sounding prim and shocked. She stared at him witheringly and he grinned again. 'Well?'

'Depends. I can think of several things I *won't* do for you.' Her wary eyes searched his and met a wall of blandness.

'Don't worry. It's something well within your capabilities,' he said, not calming her suspicions at all. 'I'll explain to you over lunch.' He motioned her to the cabin but she stayed put.

'Is this a pretext to get me into your cabin and your bed?' she asked, trying to keep a rein on her runaway desires.

'Is that a round-about way of asking?' he enquired silkily.

A flush spread from her neck to the roots of her hair. 'It certainly isn't!'

'Uh-huh.' He didn't sound too convinced.

'I loathe you, Dimitri. Do you honestly think I'd want to slip between the sheets with you?' she derided.

His shoulders lifted in a typically Greek shrug. 'It doesn't have to be sheets. I have a very wide desk... Still,' he hurried on, seeing her furious expression, 'it looks as if I must settle for lunch and a discussion, then. Hungry?' he asked.

She blinked. It was hours and hours since she'd eaten, her nerves preventing her from touching break-fast—or even her meal the night before. There was no point in starving. And Dimitri always ate well. He had the most wonderful chef who prepared sumptuous meals for when he was on the boat. Her mouth watered.

'I could eat a horse,' she admitted.

'I think we can come up with something a little less controversial than tucking into one of our equine friends.'

Olivia almost smiled at his dry comment, but stopped herself in time when she remembered that the blonde was hanging around somewhere and they might not be alone. There was safety in numbers, but she wasn't too keen on watching Dimitri play footsie under the table with one of his gooey-eyed groupies.

He picked up her shoes and politely handed them to her, then led the way to the cabin.

Olivia felt suddenly nervous. 'Will your blonde... *friend* be joining us?'

Dimitri pulled a face. 'Not if I can help it.' He put out his hand to help her down the steps but she ignored it.

'Not into threesomes, then?' she said sarkily.

'No. Are you?' he enquired.

Her glare answered him. 'I don't particularly want

to meet one of your…popsies,' she began, her mouth twitching when Dimitri roared with laughter at her choice of words. 'But it seems rude to eat separately—'

'Believe me,' he said as they moved into the panelled dining room, 'I want to stay separated from…the popsie. She's the reason I need your help. One of the crew is discreetly putting her ashore now we're in the dining room.'

Callous brute, she thought, feeling a little—only a little—sorry for the woman. She supposed that Dimitri was used to shuffling his mistresses around in order that they never met. How tacky.

They'd eaten their *mezedhes*, choosing delicacies from the countless small dishes of tempting snacks, and had been served with a beautifully presented dish of red mullet before Dimitri ended his non-stop commentary on the delights of Greek cooking.

She'd listened patiently, sipping champagne with the strangely loud notes of a haunting Greek folk tune swirling about them noisily from a hidden music system, and wondering when he'd get to the point.

During his monologue, Dimitri had leaned confidentially towards her. Because of the deafening music she had been forced to do the same, so that she could hear what he'd said. It had given an uneasy intimacy to the meal.

The haunting notes of the bouzouki filled her head and stirred her emotions. She wondered if that was deliberate and she tried to remain unaffected, but it was difficult with Dimitri's handsome face so close, the faint scent of aftershave lingering in the air whenever he threw back his head and laughed.

The waiter deftly slipped dishes of artichokes, courgettes and green beans beside each of their plates and then exited, discreetly closing the door. She almost felt like calling him back, because being alone with Dimitri seemed increasingly risky.

The tender flesh of the fish seduced her tastebuds but Olivia instantly adopted a businesslike air and broke in on Dimitri's lyrically sensual praise of the dish. Before she knew it, he'd be moving from food to other things...

'I have to check in to my hotel this afternoon. There isn't enough time for a tour around Greece's gastronomic delights,' she rebuked. 'Tell me what you want me to do in exchange for a quick divorce. And don't suggest sex. You can find that elsewhere.'

In a leisurely movement, Dimitri leaned back in his chair, eyeing her over the rim of his flute. He looked very satisfied with himself.

'You could get me out of a difficult situation,' he said casually. Olivia popped a forkful of green beans into her mouth and made no comment. Dimitri sighed as though the weight of the world lay on his shoulders. 'It's my mother.'

Her lashes flicked up in surprise. She'd thought the blonde was his problem. 'Go on.'

He tried to sound concerned. It wasn't easy when his pulses were hammering with the cleverness of his plan and every inch of him surged with hard-to-suppress excitement. Carefully he produced a frown and another sigh.

'Once I am a free man she wants me to marry a suitable woman—'

'As opposed to an unsuitable one like me,' Olivia said drily.

'I've never understood why you two have never got on,' he told her. 'The fact is, all these years she's been hassling me to trace you, to divorce and remarry and to provide heirs for the Angelaki empire.'

'You…didn't search for me at all?' She sounded surprised and disappointed.

He scowled, hating to remember that time. Of course he hadn't. She'd made it clear that she didn't love him. What was there to be gained—other than heartache and a series of heated arguments?

With cold precision he had cut her from his heart and sealed up the wound. In time he had found that his anger and frustration eased. And soon he had discovered that his married status kept scheming women and their mothers at bay so that he could get on with burying himself in non-stop work.

'I saw no point,' he replied cuttingly.

Olivia winced. So much for vanity. Yet his indifference hurt. He hadn't even bothered to find her in the hope that their marriage might be saved. That told her how deeply he felt about her—and marriage itself. It confirmed what she'd feared. Dismayed, she hung her head. All she could do was make a quick exit and try to forget that he'd ever shared her life. That seemed pretty unlikely at the moment. But time healed, so they said.

'I loathe you, Dimitri. Every conceited inch. The sooner I can get away, the better.' It gave her no pleasure to say that. Unsteadily, she met the black satin of his eyes. 'Tell me your price. What you want me to do.'

The tense muscles around his mouth relaxed into a triumphant curve. 'Play a role you've played before.'

Games, she thought, her heart sinking. No. It was actually leaping. Her lower lip trembled. Heaven help her. He wanted her to indulge him with some sex game and she found that thrilling! Somehow she dredged up a disdainful look.

'Secretary?'

His grin was deliberately lecherous. 'You fancy trying my desk out after all?'

'Don't flatter yourself,' she muttered, though the pulses in her body were urging her to do just that. 'And I'm not wandering about with a spiral-backed notebook and sitting down with my skirt hoiked up so you can relive some of your lurid fantasies.'

'The thought of you taking dictation while I ogle your legs is certainly an attractive idea,' he admitted, 'but that's not what I have in mind—for now.'

She didn't like the 'for now'. 'What, then?' she asked ominously.

'Unfortunately my mother has found a suitable woman to be my next wife. A young Greek heiress.'

Olivia felt a tremor of shock run through her. Was that why he needed her help with Miss Pneumatic?

'Not…the blonde you hid in a cupboard somewhere on board?'

'Eleni, yes,' he replied, suppressing a smile. 'Don't you remember her? The daughter of Nikos Kaloyirou, my late father's business partner—'

'I do!' she said in surprise. 'And I remember him. Very aristocratic but an absolute sweetie.'

Dimitri grinned. 'He spoke highly of you, too.'

Her puzzled frown cleared. 'Are you saying that the woman I've just seen is little Eleni? She…' Olivia remembered the girl's large nose and chin, and how as a teenager she'd hung around Dimitri as if he was God's gift to womanhood. 'She looks so different now!' she declared in amazement.

The flat chest and heavy hips had gone. Eleni looked fabulous.

'Courtesy of a good surgeon and a doting father. But…' He paused and gave a grimace, shaking his head.

'Don't tell me she doesn't appeal,' Olivia said in disbelief. The woman was gorgeous, right up Dimitri's street. He'd kissed her, too…

'Oh, physically she looks stunning,' he replied, making her entire body tense up with crippling jealousy. 'But that isn't enough, as I learnt from the experience with you.' He flashed her a disarming smile, which she returned with a look of withering scorn.

'If she's that gorgeous, what's wrong with marrying her and having mistresses?' Olivia asked tartly. He'd done that before, after all.

He raised his eyes to the ceiling. 'Everything. She's giggly and stupid and I'd end up throttling her. I'd hate my children to inherit her simpering ways and butterfly brain. My children will need to be quick-witted to run the Angelaki business—and to fob off fortune-hunters. You see my predicament.'

Again he produced a dazzling grin. She felt puzzled. It wasn't just the way Dimitri kept smiling at her but something she couldn't quite fathom. Mischief lurked in his eyes.

She remembered how he'd once told her of a property coup in which he'd outsmarted several high-powered rivals. He'd been the same then, simmering with a very appealing elation that had made his eyes dance as they were dancing now. Her suspicions deepened.

'What happened to your acclaimed art of persuasion?

Can't you use your famed diplomatic skills?' she suggested cynically.

'I *am* using them—by using you, Olivia,' he silked. 'Let's keep our prejudices out of this. You need something and so do I. We can do one another a favour. I want to let Eleni down gently, without insulting my friend and partner and causing a rift that would damage the business. Family honour is a very serious matter to a Greek. I can't appear to insult Eleni. My partner would be obliged to split with me and that could cause mass staff redundancies and ruin many lives.'

'So where do I come in?' she asked, frowning at him from beneath lowered brows.

He beamed back at her, the brightness of his eyes intensifying. 'You already know that you will need to be resident here while the divorce proceedings are being dealt with. During that time you can make yourself useful.'

'Oh, as in warning her off, you mean?' Her eyes gleamed. 'I could tell her what a terrible husband you were. How you left me to the mercy of your mother's viperish tongue and jetted about the world trying out the springs on other women's beds—'

'No thanks, I think I'd prefer something that leaves my good reputation intact,' he said, laughing.

Olivia shot him an incredulous look. 'Good reputation! Huh. Like what?'

He inhaled deeply then said softly, 'I want you to pretend we've met up and have fallen in love again.'

She stared at him, aghast. 'You're kidding!'

'Never been more serious.'

'But...but that's the most ridiculous thing I've ever heard—!'

'No, Olivia. People would believe it. We could put on a good show—'

'*No!*' She went pale at the thought of the kind of show he envisaged.

'You could throw things at me in private,' he offered, his mouth twitching with a horribly appealing humour.

'I'd find it hard not to throw *up* in public,' she muttered.

He chuckled. 'I'll provide you with medication to prevent that. It'll be worth your while. The quickest divorce in Greek history.'

'That appeals,' she conceded. 'But pretending to love you…!'

'Bizarre thought, isn't it?' he said cheerfully. 'But think of the end result. If I'm willing to suffer *you*, I don't see why you shouldn't suffer *me*.'

She scowled, bridling at his comment. Was she that awful to live with? 'That's because you'll enjoy making me simper over you. Whereas I'll hate every moment.'

Even as she said that, she knew she wasn't being entirely honest with herself. And she knew that her protest had sounded half-hearted.

'Olivia.' Dimitri had put on his most coaxing, satiny voice. And while she knew that he was insincere, she still felt inescapably seduced by it. 'We could do one another a good turn. Perhaps even part without rancour. I need you to agree, to get Eleni off my back. If it seems that we are together once more then Eleni, her father and my mother would have to accept that fact.'

'Would they?'

He leaned forward earnestly, fixing her reluctant gaze with his. 'They couldn't in all conscience come between man and wife,' he argued. 'They would immediately set their sights on some other man. The result would be that Eleni wouldn't lose face and she'd detach herself from me without a showdown. She's a nice enough kid underneath. Just…young, spoilt and raw around the edges. Her feelings would be saved from hurt, and my employees will be secure in their jobs.' His thick lashes lowered and lifted lazily. 'You wouldn't like to see people on the poverty line because you can't be bothered to give this a try, would you?'

'Don't use emotional blackmail on me!' she cried indignantly. 'You'll be telling me next that if I don't agree hundreds of people will be begging for grass cuttings to eat—while entire families throw themselves off high buildings—'

'A slight overstatement.' He chuckled in delight. Olivia was mesmerised by his laughing mouth, and he must have known this because he leaned even closer. 'However,' he murmured, 'I can definitely foresee employment problems if I insult Eleni and her father by rejecting her as a bride. In Greece we defend family honour. As I said, the very least my partner could do would be to cut our business ties, causing untold devastation to the Angelaki empire. You can do this, Olivia—'

'You're wrong! I can't!' she protested, scared stiff of being close to him for any length of time.

Already a wicked little voice was urging her to agree so that she could be with him. Yet she didn't trust her seesaw emotions and had no intention of falling for him all over again.

'You can,' he coaxed. 'It won't be for long. When Eleni is safely off the scene, you can slip away a free woman and never see me again. It won't be a difficult task to pretend you love me.' His tone grew cynical. 'You managed it for six months while we were married, after all.'

Olivia hardly registered that, her brain refusing to move into gear. 'It's…horribly manipulative.'

'Thank you! I'm flattered.' Flashing his white teeth at her again, he raised his glass to her and then drained it.

His mouth was moist and relaxed. Olivia stared at it, mesmerised, imagining them together again. Pretending…

'How…?' She grabbed her own glass and took a hasty gulp to ease the dryness of her throat. 'How long might this take?'

'I'd hope two weeks. Maximum. Take time off work—'

'I'm between jobs,' she said, and could have kicked herself when he beamed.

'No big deal, then, is it? You don't even have to lie about your feelings. Just a puppy-dog look here, a sigh there…' Enthusiastically he tackled the vegetables on his plate, pushing them into the exotic sauce and closing his eyes in ecstasy. 'Bliss,' he sighed and then his black lashes lifted, his eyes burning holes in her.

She had the unnerving impression that he wasn't talking about the food, but the prospect of having her dancing to his tune.

'I don't think so,' she muttered.

'It is. Try it,' he said, choosing to misunderstand her.

His fork hovered close to her mouth. Bemused, she opened her lips before she realised she was playing into his hands. The fish melted in her mouth, the velvety sauce stimulating her tastebuds. Dimitri's eyes melted into hers, stimulating every other sense she possessed.

It seemed that the electrified air sizzled and crackled between them, connecting their bodies in a fatal circuit. Feeling faint, she reached for her glass, realising as she sipped frantically that somehow it had been refilled.

Her head whirled. Whether that was from alcohol or the nearness of Dimitri, she didn't know. Only that she had to cut this cosy tête-à-tête short before she found herself leaning forward a fraction more and...

'Olivia.'

She swallowed as the throaty tones vibrated deep inside her. Music swirled erotically about them, the insistent rhythm eating into her brain. In an agonisingly tender gesture, his hand touched her cheek in a light caress and her eyes closed against her will.

'Are you afraid,' he said softly, 'that we would end up in bed together?'

Her eyes shot open. 'No!' she lied in an awful squeak.

'Then you have no reason to refuse,' he said, casually peeling a leaf from his artichoke and dipping it in butter.

She watched, hypnotised, as he delicately sucked the butter off and slipped the fleshy part of the leaf into his mouth. His challenging smile made her blood boil. He thought she'd be good for a quick lay. The arrogance of the man! Maybe she did keep falling for his practised seduction techniques. But she hadn't actually succumbed.

It would give her the greatest satisfaction to prove that he wasn't the irresistible Lothario he imagined. All she needed to do was to remember he had at least one illegitimate child—and that he thought women were merely toys, designed for his pleasure. That would keep her from making a fool of herself over a man who could well be a serial adulterer.

She hated him, after all.

In genuine disgust, she gave a shudder, as if she was repelled by the thought of spending time with Dimitri.

'My only hesitation is that I'd have to pretend to like you,' she said, grimly attacking her fish, stabbing it with her fork as though it might be his body. 'And what about your mother? She won't be too pleased.'

'She thinks badly of you for leaving me,' he agreed. 'But she must learn that I run my own life. One day I might fall in love. She must be fully prepared to accept the woman I love, whoever and whatever she is. I want my mother's blessing when that time comes.'

Olivia winced. Something tore in her chest. Jealousy, she supposed. Dog-in-the-manger. How small-minded of her. She didn't want him but couldn't bear to think of him being in love.

She wondered if he wanted to marry Athena and legitimise his child. Or if he had grown tired of her and discarded her long ago.

It was hard to think, what with the heavy beat of the music and her scattered wits.

'I don't know…'

'Do this, or I'll see to it that our divorce takes years to settle,' he said in a steely tone.

Her heart sank. He meant every word—and had the money and power and ruthlessness to carry out his threat.

'You are an opportunistic swine!' she muttered.

'That's right.'

It annoyed her that he had the upper hand. It didn't matter to him if they were divorced or not—in fact it had probably kept Eleni from demanding that he set a wedding date. Olivia glowered, feeling like kicking something. Preferably Dimitri. She wanted to get her divorce signed, sealed and delivered so that her new life could begin. Perhaps two weeks swooning over Dimitri wasn't too much to ask.

'I need to think this over.' Suddenly feeling fragile and desperately vulnerable, she pushed her plate away.

'Of course.'

He nodded and they ate their puddings in silence. Or, at least, he did. Trying to remain objective, she toyed with her *bougatsa*, even though it was her favourite dessert, and considered his extraordinary suggestion.

Everything was conspiring to make her say 'yes'. Despite seeing no other way to make him do what she wanted, the music had somehow tapped into her emotions. The food reminded her of the exotic tastes she'd enjoyed so much. And above all, there was that beautiful country waiting outside.

If she did have to remain in Greece for a while then she had to admit that it would be lovely to stay at his mansion, even if she had to play the loving wife to do so. She loved the old Venetian house and had missed it with a deep ache in her heart that had astonished her. But it was perfect. The views across the Saronikos Gulf were spectacular, the furnishings luxurious and comfortable, yet the ultimate in good taste.

Every day she could revisit the places she adored. The little town of Nafplion, with its Venetian houses and fountains and squat fortresses guarding the harbour. The golden beaches and savage crags, the spectacular ruins of ancient Greece and Rome atop verdant hills, every path and stone richer in drama and history than anywhere else in the whole of Greece.

It was the land of Agamemnon and Helen of Troy. Of Hercules, gods and goddesses. Magical.

She thought of the silent glades and crystal-clear rivers, the intoxicating scent of the wild flowers and the inviting warmth of the sea, as deep a blue as her eyes, Dimitri had murmured once.

All this she had lost and mourned because of his infidelity. For two short weeks it could be hers again, to record on her camera and to smile over in future days when the hurt and emotion had become just a distant memory.

'Come.' His hand was on her arm and she was rising blindly, obediently from her seat. 'I think we both need a shot of coffee,' he murmured, guiding her to the salon.

In the doorway he spoke briefly in Greek to the waiter, who was arranging a tray of coffee and chocolate peppermints on a low table inlaid with mosaics. The evocative sound of Maria Callas singing of her lover's betrayal in the opera *Madame Butterfly* filled the room, the plaintive, soaring pure notes reaching deep into Olivia's wounded heart and tearing relentlessly at her emotions.

'Olivia, we don't have much time. Have you come to a decision?' Dimitri asked quietly, turning her around to face him.

She looked up at him and hastily averted her eyes. But she could smell that masculine aftershave and could feel his power energising her. He was too close for comfort. Any moment now and she'd lift her face for a kiss—and be thoroughly humiliated by her lack of sense. Panic jerked at her. Anxious to escape to the safety of a chair, she blurted out suddenly, 'Yes. I'll do it.' And added in defiance, 'For me, not for you.'

He smiled, the corners of his lips curving appealingly. And, oh, she could drown in those velvety eyes. At that moment she panicked, worrying that she'd committed herself to something she couldn't handle.

'For you?'

Aware of the danger she'd risk if she continued to look up at him, she coolly focused on the third button of his shirt. 'Why not?' she replied, miraculously assuming a casual air. 'It'll be a nice holiday. Luxurious surroundings, use of a car—which I insist on—and the chance to explore.'

'I will spare no expense in amusing you,' he drawled. He had been right. She could be bought. Almost every woman had her price, it seemed. Disappointment wiped out his pleasure at having her in his power. 'In return, you must give me your word you'll do this. That you won't back out. I have to know my plan has every chance of succeeding.'

Her eyes flicked up then; the darkest aquamarine like the sea at the mouth of the caves on the east coast of the Olympos promontory. Enticing. Fathomless.

'Shake on it,' he said, more curtly than he'd intended, and he put out his hand. 'Swear that you will see this through to the end.'

'I promise.'

Hesitantly her fingers touched his palm and then her hand had slid into his.

It wasn't what he'd intended—not yet—but he found himself drawing her close until she lay in the circle of his arms. Warning voices were telling him that he could scare her off at this delicate stage, but to his surprise he discovered that he wasn't capable of holding back.

Suddenly they were kissing. Hot, frantic kisses that

burned and seared. Their hands were clutching and possessing, bodies crushed together in a desperate need for every inch to be touched and caressed and relieved of terrible, unsatisfied hungers.

Their mutual lack of finesse startled him, he who'd always been so proud of his skills at wooing a woman and the smoothness of his approach as he coaxed and kissed his way to his goal. But his feelings were overwhelming him, shutting down his brain, his mind focused only on the glorious sensation of her plush mouth on his, her body fitting into him as if they had been made for one another.

His mouth found the soft warmth of her throat and she flung her head back with a groan of sheer pleasure. The shock of her beauty ripped through him. She was so lovely that it hurt, great, scything shafts of pain slicing him from head to toe.

His weight moved her backwards till she hit the panelled wall with a dull thud. Slipping his hand down, he pushed up her skirt and let his fingers enjoy the softness of her thigh. With a little shudder, she raised her leg and hooked it around his back. Hardly able to contain his excitement, he concentrated on lifting her T-shirt over her head.

The languid stretch of her arms made his pulses drum loudly. And she left them raised above her head, open to him, boldly and unmistakably inviting his invasion.

'You are incredibly beautiful,' he whispered, then dipped his head to kiss her scented breasts where they heaped generously above a lacy bra.

He closed his eyes, sensing the arching of her spine, the urgent thrust of her hips, and he responded with a fierce onslaught of impassioned kisses that left him breathless. And more frantic than ever to take her.

Even if she had used him… Angrily he ripped off her briefs and shuddered when she sighed as though in relief and melted against him, her teeth savaging his shoulder, his throat, his jaw…

This was pure sex in its rawest state. And yet he could feel his heart aching for more than that as he let her snatch at his shirt and forcibly wrench it open, scattering buttons in all directions.

Her mouth was moving over his naked torso, driving him wild, the slick of her tongue and the nip of her sharp teeth jerking his body into a frenzy while her hair slid with more tantalising delicacy, reminding him of other times when he had imagined they were making love as a couple who adored one another.

Tormented and tortured with this betrayal, he caught a hank of golden hair and raised her head. Their eyes blazed, liquid jet meeting bewildered sapphire. Something broke in him. His heart, his control, any contact with reality.

Olivia knew this was madness but couldn't stop herself. All her solemn resolutions had been swept away the moment he had taken her into his arms. There was such a joy in her heart when he looked at her and touched her that she knew with an almost chilling certainty that she still loved him and always would. Like an animal craving water, she needed him to make her live again, to make her whole. Without him she was nothing.

Whimpering in a confusing muddle of dismay and delight, she began to drag off her bra with infuriatingly clumsy fingers, almost weeping when the hooks refused to be released. Dimitri reached around her back and yanked it free. Her naked breasts touched his chest tentatively, their dark centres immediately hard and exquisitely painful. She let her body sway a little so that they brushed his quivering muscles, rejoicing in the sound of his quickened breathing.

They would make love. Their feelings for one another had been reignited. It would be like old times, she dreamed.

And all the while his fingers were slipping relentlessly between her thighs, slicking backwards and forwards in a ruthless rhythm that was becoming unbearable.

She touched him. His groan echoed hers when her hand closed around the hot smoothness and suddenly he was impatiently pushing her hands away and was thrusting inside her with an urgency that took her breath away.

It had never been like this before. Never so uncontrolled, so primitive or needy. Her arms locked around his neck and she buried her head in his shoulder, feeling the silken slide of him against each unfurling nerve within her, wondering at the ecstasy and despair that battled in her heart.

Their mouths clashed. Teeth and tongues fought together as all the years of longing and anger welled up within her. She cried out, called his name, heard him huskily whisper hers as his thrusts became faster and more vigorous, wiping away the past and focusing her on the here and now.

Gasping, she felt the rising ripples of an orgasm, enhanced by his skilful, wickedly arousing fingers. On the summit of it, she hovered and began to subside, only to be driven there again and again.

Dimly she was aware of the thick carpet beneath her

back. Then of them rolling, locked in a passionate embrace, unable to release one another till the silken pressure within her had swelled again and they had reached a shuddering climax together.

Slowly the madness faded and she felt calmness descend on her. Limp and glowing with delirious delight, she lay silent and still in Dimitri's arms, dreaming of their renewed love. She had never been so certain of anything in her life. He had been so frantic for her, muttering what had sounded like sweet Greek words of adoration.

With a long exhalation of breath he rolled away. Hearing him stand up, she smiled, stretched luxuriously with the satisfied conviction of someone who felt deeply adored. Lazily she opened her reluctant eyes.

She blinked. Instead of smiling down at her, he was heading for the door. There was something about his beautifully muscled back that told her he was controlling huge emotions. Ice froze her veins.

'Dimitri?' she whispered. A sudden panic took hold of her.

He jerked to a halt as if she had caught him with the tip of a whip. 'I didn't expect you to act the loving wife with such enthusiasm,' he muttered, his voice shaking and hoarse.

She felt as if he'd punched her in the stomach. But she fought her horror. He must never know how she felt.

'I've always enjoyed a healthy attitude to sex,' she flung recklessly.

'Perhaps that's why it's so enjoyable with you. No strings. Every man's dream. Have a shower. You know where to go.' And he slammed the door behind him with an unnerving finality.

CHAPTER FOUR

SHE felt desperately cold, even though the rays of the sun were streaming in through the huge picture windows and shimmering on her nakedness. Shaking uncontrollably, she snatched up her clothes, flushing with embarrassment to find them so thoroughly scattered about the room.

As she moved, she felt unsteady on her feet. At first she thought this was the after-effect of Dimitri's lovemaking. And then she discovered that the boat was moving and there was no sight of land.

Her head cleared as if it had been doused in water. Seething, she realised that the music must have drowned the sound of the purring engines and she'd been too overwhelmed by the glorious sensation of being loved to notice the gentle movement of the boat over the glass-like sea.

Loved! As if.

At the time, every instinct she possessed had assured her that he cared. But she had been wrong. It was just his technique. He'd taken what he'd wanted and then mocked her for her abandon.

A sharp pain of pure reality sliced into her chest. There would be no future for them. She had been fantasising. And she had misunderstood his eagerness. Of course he'd been seductive. Where women were concerned, he was driven by his loins. There had been no tenderness. Just sex. And she'd been conned. Bitterly she wondered how she could ever feel good about herself again.

Refusing even to think about what had happened, she held her clothes strategically around her body to hide her nakedness, and headed off to the nearest shower. She stayed there a long time, letting the relentless power of the water sluice her heated skin.

Her mind was in such a turmoil that she didn't know what to think. And so she blanked everything out, concentrating only on soaping herself with a punishing vigour.

'Olivia!'

She glared at Dimitri's abrupt call, thinking sourly that she wasn't ready for visitors. Hoping to drown out his knocking on the door, she turned the shower up to its most ferocious level.

'Leave me some privacy!' she yelled.

Her eyes were full of angry tears. She didn't want him to see her like this, vulnerable and humiliated.

The door opened, causing her to hastily get a grip on herself. It annoyed her intensely that Dimitri had walked in on her as if he had a right. But then he had always done exactly what he wanted and to hell with everyone else. Well, this time, she vowed grimly, she'd do the same.

Adjusting the bath sheet that was wrapped around his slim hips, he lowered his head and looked at her from under heavy brows. Silver droplets of water slid from his tousled hair and with an impatient hand he pushed his fingers over his scalp, smoothing his hair back to its normal sleekness.

Magnificent in his half-nakedness, he stepped into the spacious bathroom, his tanned body glistening with the sheen of water.

He looked composed, though his eyes were a hard black, like a slab of jet. The set of his mouth, the lift of his chest and shoulders, suggested that he was still struggling to master some tempestuous emotions. Nervously she wondered what they were. Triumph at seducing her? Scorn, disgust…

It was on the tip of her tongue to ask. Only pride stopped her. Avoiding his unnerving eyes in case she betrayed her misery, Olivia shut off the shower and grabbed the nearest towel, binding it around her body tightly.

'What's so urgent that can't wait till I'm dressed?' she snapped.

'I want to say that nothing has changed. I hold you to your promise,' he stated, a dangerous light in his narrowed eyes. 'With or without the sex.'

She gave a shrug of indifference as if the whole episode had been merely an indulgence on her part.

'I wouldn't like to embarrass you with my enthusiasm,' she said tartly.

'I'm not complaining. Enthuse as much as you like,' he growled.

'No thanks. I don't think I want to repeat that,' she clipped.

'It's of no importance,' he dismissed insultingly. 'Your promise is, however. Well?'

Thinking of spending two hours—let alone two weeks—with him made a quiver ripple through her glowing body, electrifying all the parts he had touched with such devastating results.

Whatever she claimed to the contrary, she knew that if they carried out this extraordinary plan of his they wouldn't be able to keep their hands off one another. There would be nights of unbelievable pleasure. Then

would come the scouring emptiness that followed loveless sex.

Maybe she could live with that. She knew the score.
He didn't love her.

To her eternal shame, she wanted him—with an all-
consuming hunger that appalled her. Yet she didn't
want the pain. Olivia bit her lip. The choice was stark:
two weeks with him, or years spent fighting to be free
of the chains that bound her to him like a prisoner to
a stake.

And she had made a promise. She studied him.
Arrogant, hard-jawed, implacable. A flare of anger
surged through her. That was how he cut a swathe
through the business world—and women.

Maybe he'd feel different if he was on the receiving
end of such callous behaviour. Her eyes narrowed and
she closed her heart to him. There was nothing wrong
in enjoying sex with one's husband.

She would take what he had to offer—if she felt like
it—and would bid him a cool farewell when her divorce came through. That would astonish him. His ego
would be dented if she waved a cheerful goodbye. She
smiled to herself.

Two weeks. She could do it because she needed him
and hated him with equal passion. He was totally incapable of being faithful and she could never truly love
a man who didn't put her at the centre of his universe.
Whatever she felt for him, it wasn't love. Obsession,
perhaps. Infatuation. But nothing deep and spiritual.

This was something she had to do, like an ordeal by
fire. To sate herself with him until she was sick of him.
Absence hadn't helped. Maybe this would.

Aware of his tension, she smiled and said casually,
'All right. I won't go back on my word.'

'So…we will be together.'

The vibrations of his deep tones raised goosebumps on her skin. 'Of course. We agreed to put up with the temporary discomfort as a means to an end, didn't we?' she said with a lift of her slender shoulders.

There was a long pause and he held her gaze while his eyes liquefied. He took a step towards her and she felt her heart slamming into her ribcage.

At that moment, the boat unexpectedly lurched forward and then back again. Losing her balance, she fell into Dimitri's arms. Although she tried to pull away, he held her tightly and after a moment she felt her flesh weaken and begin to flow into his. Quiescent, she looked up at him guardedly, allowing her body to respond—yet not her emotions.

'Yooo-hooh!' shrilled someone on deck. *'Ti yinete?'*

Dimitri froze. Olivia was wide-eyed at the sound of clattering feet. 'We've docked,' he explained hurriedly.

'But who—?' The words dried in her throat.

'Pedhi mou—'

Olivia recognised the voice at once. Purring the Greek equivalent of 'my boy', Dimitri's mother, flush-faced and excited, had come to the open doorway of the bathroom. Olivia swung around and Marina's elation turned to horror when she saw Dimitri apparently embracing his estranged, towel-clad wife.

'You!' Marina croaked.

Olivia blushed, her bare toes curling with embarrassment in the thick carpet. 'Yes. Me.' Her eyes narrowed, seeing the disappointment on Marina's face. 'You thought I was someone else. Who were you expecting to find?' she challenged.

It dawned on her that Marina's tone had initially been indulgent, almost frisky. She hadn't been surprised or horrified to see her son snuggling up to a semi-nude blonde. Perhaps, she thought darkly, Dimitri and Eleni's relationship had gone further than he'd said.

'Eleni! I—I thought it must be her!' Marina stammered, confirming Olivia's suspicions.

She tightened her mouth. Maybe Dimitri had already made Eleni his mistress, but drew the line at marriage with the girl. Rat!

'She has gone to meet her father,' Dimitri explained. 'Good afternoon, Mother. I'm sorry if we have embarrassed you. We weren't expecting anyone to drop in unannounced,' he added drily.

It was a mild rebuke, though affectionately spoken, and his mother's bean-thin body stiffened. Olivia felt sorry for her, though she remembered how her mother-in-law had frequently interrupted them, deliberately destroying their romantic picnics and quiet walks, intruding on their much-needed privacy.

'What's happening?' Marina quavered. 'Why is she here—?'

'I will tell you in private,' Dimitri said gently. 'It concerns the divorce. I'll meet you back at the house and we'll go into the details later. Olivia, I suggest you get dressed. You know where the bedrooms are.'

With that, he turned her around and gave her a light and playful husbandly slap on her rear.

Olivia whirled, intending to give him a piece of her mind in return, but he put a finger on her lips and sent her warning messages with his eyes.

'Remember your promise,' he whispered into her burning ear. 'And let me judge when it's best to tell Mother. She'll get the message soon enough.'

She glared at him suspiciously, wondering if he'd

stage-managed this moment. It was mighty convenient that his mother had walked in on them before they'd had the chance to get their clothes back on.

Their gazes clashed. His was amused and simmering with mischief; hers ignited immediately at the thought of turning the tables on him. A tingle spread through her body, setting it alight with excitement. She'd never felt so fired up.

Right, she thought, enjoying the challenge ahead. You want an adoring wife, then hang on to your hat. Because you'll get one with knobs on.

Languorously she wound her arms about his neck and kissed him on the mouth. She had one weapon. Her body. And she'd use it to good effect.

'Anything you say…*darling*,' she murmured, delighted when he shuddered and his eyes glazed over.

'Dimitri!' gasped Marina in alarm.

'Don't worry, Mother. She's a minx. I can handle her,' he murmured.

Flinging him a wonderfully warm and loving smile, she faced the woman who had helped to ruin her marriage. Marina seemed to be panic-stricken. Olivia's expression saddened. She pitied the woman. Marina would go through hell during the next two weeks or so.

'Please excuse me while I dry my hair and make myself presentable,' she said pleasantly. Her mouth quirked. 'See you in a moment, darling.'

Apparently cool and controlled, she patted Dimitri's bottom, gathered up her clothes and strolled past her bristling mother-in-law.

Dimitri watched Olivia's swaying body. Luscious. With the most clutchable rear he'd ever seen. A flawless back, her skin a glowing gold.

His entire body throbbed with memories of their lovemaking. She had quenched his passion in the most spectacular fashion. Dangerously, she'd come close to touching his emotions, but he'd remembered in time that she had used him—and was still using him to ease her own insatiable appetite.

'She's trying to win you back!' his mother declared anxiously.

He smiled at her in reassurance. Olivia had played the vamp for his mother's benefit with alarming sincerity. A woman who could lie so convincingly could never be trusted.

'I must dress,' he said with unusual gentleness. He went to her and held her stiff, bony body in a loving embrace. Then he kissed her cheek and pretended not to notice the tears which had sprung into her eyes. 'There's nothing to worry about, I promise. All will be well in the end. I have a scheme.' He saw his mother's face brighten. 'I'll see you at the house, as I said. We'll talk.'

'There's no time! I'm so busy! I planned a surprise party for you. It's all arranged for tonight,' she said in an unrecognisably small voice. 'To celebrate your coming divorce. You will be there, won't you?'

Dismayed, he knew he couldn't shame her by making her cancel it. 'Of course.' Tenderly he patted her hand. 'Thank you.'

Even in her expensive white designer dress and coiffed and tended by countless beauticians, his mother looked unsure of herself. It was as if she'd never been comfortable with wealth and might have been happier remaining a poor shepherd's wife.

He felt a strong sense of sympathy for her. His father had embraced the new life, working to build the business into the billion-dollar property empire it was now, with Angelaki developments springing up all over the world. But his mother had suffered from intense insecurity, terrified of doing and saying the wrong thing, unnerved by the social occasions she was expected to co-host. Gradually she had hidden behind a cold hauteur to disguise her lack of confidence and rarely let down her guard.

He wanted to find the laughing, tender mother he remembered from his childhood. The woman who had baked fat little bread men for him, who had run into the garden barefoot with him to watch sunsets. She was there—and he would find her.

He took her hand and kissed it with great tenderness. 'See you in a moment,' he said fondly and slipped into the stateroom to dress.

When Olivia emerged into the brilliant afternoon sun some twenty minutes later, she saw what she had surmised—that they had docked in the small fishing port of Olympos. Dimitri was leaning on the rail, lazily observing the sleepy little village whose cube-shaped houses clambered haphazardly up an olive-clad hill behind the harbour.

'Has your mother gone?' Olivia asked when she came to his side.

'Back to the house.'

'What did you tell her?'

'That you would be staying with us to keep our arguments as private as possible.'

'How did she take that?'

'Badly. I think she's afraid I'll find you irresistible,' he drawled.

She tilted her head insolently and put her lashes to good use. 'Maybe you will.'

His eyes caressed her and she surrendered to the delicious melting of her bones. 'I think we'll both enjoy our pretence. You know that's all it is, don't you?'

She snorted. 'I want to be free of you,' she said fervently.

Free of the compulsion to yield up her heart again. Free from having him constantly on her mind and in her dreams.

'Olivia…' Unusually, he seemed to be struggling for the right words.

'What?' she asked, frowning.

'I don't want to announce we're back together immediately. I want my mother to see for herself what is happening and to accept it willingly.'

'She won't! Not ever!' Olivia said fervently.

He frowned. 'You're wrong. She will if she thinks it's what I want. She accepted my marriage in the end—'

'No. You're wrong. She didn't.'

'That's ridiculous! I know what you think of her. You've told me often enough—'

'Everything I've told you is true,' Olivia said doggedly. Marina had been a bone of contention between them throughout their brief time together. 'You never believed me because she was always careful to keep her spiteful comments for when you were not around. But she undermined me and made my life miserable while you were away—'

He stopped her with an impatient wave of his hand. 'I'm not going over old ground. The past is past. Although she had reservations—and made them plain—she didn't say a word against you after our wedding day. Reading between the lines, it seemed to me that you made no effort to be friendly.'

'I did!' she insisted. 'I tried to fit in, to be a good daughter-in-law, but—oh, what's the use? It doesn't matter any more.'

'No, it doesn't,' he snapped. 'Except that I don't want to hurt her. She can't be unaware of the sexual chemistry between us, but our reunion is supposed to be something more. We need to convince everyone that we are falling in love. Understand?'

'Agreed,' she said quietly and, feeling a sudden flurry of nerves, she turned her attention to the scene before them.

'You think you can handle this?' he asked.

'It's worth it to get shot of you quickly. And there's the compensation of being here,' she whispered with a sigh of pleasure. There was nowhere like it on earth.

Fishermen mended bright orange nets, their heads bent low in concentration as their fingers flew in and out, deft and sure. The diamond-faceted water slapped gently against the streamlined sides of Dimitri's yacht. Children played happily on the nearby beach, their joyous voices ringing out excitedly.

She saw Dimitri's thoughtful gaze on the children and the spasm of pain that crossed his face at the same time that an echoing pain slid into her heart. How lovely it would be to have children to adore. Dark-eyed, dark-haired, strong and vigorous like Dimitri…

Impatiently she snapped out of her futile dream, wondering glumly if he still saw Athena and his child. The question burned inside her but she couldn't bring herself to ask. Instead, it sat like a cold stone in her heart.

'Shall we go?' she suggested, her tone hard with the effort of concealment. 'I'm looking forward to seeing the house again and swimming in that glorious pool.'

'I won't deny you the enjoyment of luxuries.' He looked disappointed, his eyes oddly dead as they walked to the gangplank. 'I'd better warn you that Mother has laid on a party at the house. A celebration of my divorce-to-be.'

'She doesn't waste much time,' she muttered. 'I'll hide in my room.'

'I want you there.'

'Your runaway wife? Won't people think that odd?'

'Unusually civilised, perhaps. But a public occasion will be ideal for our purpose. I have the impression that Eleni will be there.'

Olivia grimaced. 'How far do we go?' she asked.

'Lingering looks. Dancing too close. Too much touching,' he drawled.

She thought she could cope with that. Most of it would be for real, anyway. She just had to make sure she remembered that all his feelings were centred below his belt.

'OK,' she said airily.

'You have no problem with that?' he queried, clearly surprised she could contemplate being close to someone as compelling as him and not fall under his spell.

'Yes. One.' She produced a siren smile, her eyes dancing with amusement when he interpreted that as a tribute to his irresistible appeal. She simpered and sighed, 'I don't have a thing to wear!'

He laughed, but there was a challenge in his eyes. 'If only my problems were that small,' he observed in a drawl. 'However, all the clothes you left behind are still in your dressing room.'

'Are they? I'd have thought you would have flung them in the bin ages ago,' she said in surprise.

'The room was shut up the day you left,' he said abruptly. 'Come on. Let's go ashore.'

Olivia could hear the cheerful strains of lively music while she was trying on dress after dress, and discarding each one in a frenzy of indecision. Running to the window, she peered out at the pool terrace, where the party was to take place. White-coated waiters scurried about importantly among the classical statues and ancient urns, bearing silver salvers of food to a long buffet table. A small Greek orchestra gently switched from a traditional folk tune to a more sentimental ballad, a famous local singer huskily crooning passionate words of love and desire.

Marina hurried here and there, her thin frame resplendent in a long, glittering gown that must have cost Dimitri a fortune. This was a party to set him up for Eleni, she thought. How ruthless Marina was, to virtually sell her son to enhance her family standing with Greek aristocracy!

People began to arrive. Assured and elegant, they strolled around the pool, admiring the exotic plants and romantically lit statues.

Olivia's nerves grew worse. In despair she stared at the clothes heaped on the silk counterpane, uncertain whether to be demure and wifely or—as her instincts urged—to be a flamboyant temptress and thoroughly put Eleni's nose out of joint. It would be fun to explode on that scene. And, in the back of her mind, she knew she wanted to make Dimitri's tongue hang out.

'Not dressed?'

She whirled, flustered, glaring while Dimitri ran a raking glance up her stockinged legs to her lacy black suspender belt. He dwelt for a heat-seeking moment on her minimal briefs, then let his gaze wander up to settle on her breasts, uplifted by her balcony bra.

'Fantastic deduction,' she scathed when she'd got her breath back. 'Don't you ever knock?'

'It's my house.'

'But I'm not your woman!' she scowled.

'To all intents and purposes you are,' he pointed out.

She was trying not to look at him. One glance had been enough. Her heart had always fluttered when he wore a formal dinner suit and this was no exception.

The way his jacket had been moulded over his beautiful chest made her want to run the palms of her hands over his torso. His smoothly shaven face invited her touch or the pressure of her lips. Already she was aching for him. And they hadn't even begun their little play-acting for the evening. She groaned.

'This is a private room. I can throw things, you said so,' she muttered obstinately, contemplating a marble figurine with an air of menace.

'Throw whatever you like,' he said obligingly. 'But I must be seen to come in and out of your bedroom. Tongues must wag.'

'I suppose so,' she said grudgingly, and blindly reached for one of the dresses on the bed.

'Not that one.' He strode forward and took it from her hands. 'A nun could wear that and not be ashamed. This one.'

He held up the scarlet sheath she had longingly stroked and rejected without even trying it. This was her favourite—and had been his. But she hadn't dared to wear anything so blatant.

She wrinkled her nose in doubt. 'Isn't it a bit tarty?'

'Not at the price I paid,' he said. 'It's a knockout.

All eyes will be upon you. No one will be surprised when I spend most of the evening by your side.'

'Aren't you worried that Eleni and her father will be offended?'

'Everyone else will be willing us to get back together,' he said, holding the dress out for her. 'People are sentimental at heart. My business partner won't be able to show open disapproval, not when marriage is so important, so sacred.'

Sacred. Her lower lip quivered. If it was that special, why had he destroyed it?

'But your mother will go ballistic!'

'Not in public. And she will be consoled by the fact that the family will be spared the shame of divorce.'

'Until you reveal the truth and we really do end our marriage,' Olivia pointed out.

He smiled with infuriating self-belief. 'I'm confident that I can persuade her then that divorce is the only answer.'

'Oh, I'm sure she'll agree with you there,' she said wryly. 'She'll help you put the flags out.' Dimitri laughed, but she didn't. There was a sick sensation in her stomach. 'Two weeks. And then we'll both be free,' she mused.

'So let's make our bid for that freedom,' he purred, encouraging her to step into the dress. 'The sooner we start, the sooner we're rid of one another. Put this on.'

'I've only worn this dress once,' she said, hesitating.

'In New York,' he said throatily, his eyes glistening like melted chocolate. 'The Starlight Ball.' He smiled beguilingly, his gaze fixed on her parted lips. 'All those celebrities and you outshone them all. Everyone was talking about you. And I felt a hundred feet tall, having you on my arm.'

Her lashes dropped to hide her sadness. She'd been a bit of arm candy. An accessory to make him proud. And the bonus was that she was good in bed, too.

That decided it. She'd wear the dress and show him what he'd lost. One hell of a woman who'd loved him more than life itself. Who would have given him sons by the yard and daughters he could pet and adore. If only he hadn't been greedy and vain. If only he hadn't needed the flattery of other women.

The dress slid up her body, following her curves and hugging them possessively. On the pretext of smoothing creases, his hands shaped around the female swell of her hips and swept into the enticing dip of her waist.

He could hardly breathe. Obediently he responded when she turned her back, and slowly zipped up the dress. His fingers skimmed her warm buttocks and when he fastened the hook and eye almost at the base of her spine where the dress finished, he fumbled like a teenage kid who'd been offered his first chance to stroke a girl's nakedness.

'Let's see,' he growled.

Her eyes were bright and sparkling when she turned around again. He tried to cast an objective eye over her but it didn't come off. He knew he'd tensed. His teeth were jammed together, his loins were doing their own thing as usual and making him forget he had a brain at all.

At that moment, Olivia heaved in a breath, causing her incredibly high and generous breasts to swell alluringly above the low-cut neckline. He couldn't help himself. His head dipped and he was letting his lips move experimentally over them while his hands curved around her small and curvaceous rear.

She gave a little gasp and his mouth scalded hers.

He bent her backwards, revelling in her compliance, the silky material sliding sensuously over her willowy body. The pressure of her knee between his legs made him groan and intensify the pressure of his searching mouth as it travelled along the line of her jaw and then her pulsing throat.

Beneath his fingers the naked small of her back arched as she writhed against him, her arms dragging his head harder towards her in a satisfyingly fierce demand.

'Dimitri!' she whispered.

And brought him to his senses. He straightened, a mocking look in his eyes to hide his need.

'Isn't that proof enough? Your dress sets *me* on fire,' he commented tightly. 'Every man tonight will wonder why I don't put you over my shoulder and carry you off. Nobody will blame me for wanting you.'

'What a shallow lot,' she snapped, breathing heavily and adjusting her dress. He noticed the thrusting dark nipple of her left breast and wished he could surround it with his lips and tug it until she begged for mercy. But she had wriggled the scarlet silk back to its proper place and the moment was lost. She had seen his gaze, however. 'I'm just a body to you, aren't I?' she flung, hot and flustered. 'Nobody seems to care if I have a mind—'

'I did,' he objected, moving away and cooling himself down by standing at the open window. 'Once,' he added, before she got the wrong idea. 'Are you ready now?' he asked imperiously.

'Nearly.'

Her voice seemed to be shaking but he didn't turn around to see why. He needed a moment to steady his nerves. Many a time in the early days he'd been almost sick with apprehension before a big deal. But the way he felt now beat that hands down.

Tonight he must subdue his raw lust and dig out those long-forgotten gestures and glances of love that had been shut away in his heart. He knew that tapping into his emotions like that would be dangerous. Olivia had hurt him so badly that he'd vowed never to let any woman near his heart again.

He stared into the dark velvet night, inhaling the night scents. Behind him, Olivia fiddled with some jewellery. Perhaps she'd chosen the ruby necklace she'd left behind in the safe when she'd disappeared, and which he'd placed on the dressing table earlier, with the rest of the jewels that had escaped her voracious hands.

'Dimitri.' He stiffened against the softness of her voice.

'What?'

Olivia gulped. Her nerves were in shreds and he was barking at her! 'I need your opinion,' she managed, reasonably evenly. 'Tonight is important for both of us.'

With an irritable sigh, he moved from the window and faced her. For a moment his angry expression faded and she saw admiration in his eyes. Then the warmth vanished, to be replaced by coldness.

'You'll do.'

'Oh, thanks,' she muttered, slamming down the hairbrush.

His hands came down on her shoulders. They were burning hot, searing her skin as if he was branding her. In the mirror she saw his dark, enigmatic face close to hers.

She lifted her head in an unconscious effort to re-

main cool and detached and watched her pendant ear-
rings swaying gently, the rubies flashing in the centre
of the diamond star as if they were on fire.

'You look and smell wonderful. How much more
admiration do you want?' he grated.

She scowled, hating the way he treated her. When
he wanted sex he coaxed and purred. All other times
he walked all over her.

Huffily she replied, 'I only wanted to know if the
rubies were right—'

'They are. Time to go.'

Olivia felt like throttling him. But she'd get her revenge another way. Gracefully she rose and deliberately she lifted her narrow skirt to expose a generous
length of leg. Taking her time, and enjoying the fact
that Dimitri's breathing seemed all over the place, she
tucked her feet into a fabulous pair of jewelled sandals
before letting her skirt swish back to brush her ankle
bones.

'I'm ready,' she announced with a sweet smile.

It wasn't returned. Glowering, he muttered, 'I'll go
down first. Follow in ten minutes.'

'But—!'

'We can't arrive together. You need to make an entrance. I'm sure it will be a memorable one.' His assessing glance all but stripped her naked and the hunger
in his eyes made her stomach clench. 'I have no doubt
that we will leave together, however, and spend the
night inventively. You will surrender to me as you
never have before. And I will pleasure you until you
wonder if it is possible to die of that pleasure.' His
eyes blazed into hers. 'Keep that in mind all evening.
Think of it, anticipate it, hunger for it,' he murmured,
and was gone before she could draw breath from her
collapsed lungs.

CHAPTER FIVE

FROM her vantage point, with her shaking hands gripping the window sill, she watched Dimitri make *his* entrance down the broad flight of steps that led to the pool terrace.

Everyone seemed to stop talking for a moment. The women frankly stared. Men eyed Dimitri with open envy and admiration. He flashed a general smile at his guests and began to move among them, the genial and dazzling host she remembered from the parties they'd held here in the past.

Olivia saw Eleni detach herself from a group of giggling young women and head determinedly towards Dimitri, virtually pushing people aside in her eagerness to reach his side. He reeled under Eleni's enthusiastic hug, stepping sharply back so that Eleni's rapacious grasp was dislodged.

Enough was enough, she thought, loathing the way the girl simpered up at him. Now Eleni had begun to paw him on the pretext of admiring his jacket. Olivia felt as if her territory had been violated.

But she must remember that her role this evening was to *act* the swooning wife, not to *feel* it. And it annoyed her that she must seem to be besotted with him. It would flatter his ego too much.

Simmering still from Dimitri's searing promise, she told herself that his parting words had been part of the power game he meant to play. He wanted her passion to look real. She sighed. It might be. But she intended that his would also be real. It would be an evening *he'd* never forget. She had weapons too. And he'd go to bed frustrated.

Battle stations, she decided. Knots tied themselves in her stomach as she checked herself in the mirror. Would Athena be there with Dimitri's child? She couldn't bear it if she was. Though she imagined that since Marina had arranged the party, Athena wouldn't have been invited, not with Eleni taking centre stage. Was Athena still on the scene? She wished she knew— *needed* to know.

She heard the laughter below and bundles of nerves leapt and jiggled inside her. But this was too important. She couldn't let a few jitters hold her back from her purpose. The sooner Eleni had realised she wasn't likely to be Dimitri's next wife, the sooner she, Olivia, could escape Dimitri's clutches.

Brazen it out, she told herself. Enjoy rendering her arrogant husband helpless with desire for her! Tonight she was The Other Woman, despite being technically Dimitri's wife! She giggled.

Recklessly she teased her hair forward so that it curved seductively over one eye and she practised a sultry look. Laughing at the result, she took advantage of the fact that humour had eased her nerves a little, and sallied forth, every inch the seductress.

The walk down the marble steps was the longest she'd ever made. Her body ached from being held in tension as she gazed with apparent interest at the now silenced crowd and gingerly felt for each step with the backs of her ankles.

To her relief, Dimitri moved into the space at the bottom of the steps, his hand outstretched. The abandoned Eleni stared, wide-eyed.

She could have heard a pin drop.

'Olivia,' he said, as cool as cucumber and kissing her on both cheeks. 'Welcome.'

'Hello, darling,' she purred throatily, her arms curving around his neck so he couldn't escape. Her lashes batted flirtily. 'What a lovely party. I'm going to have such fun,' she purred.

His eyes twinkled. 'I can see that,' he said drily. With sheer force of strength he shifted to one side and broke her linked hands. She realised this was born of years of practice. There had probably been a whole list of women he'd grown tired of, and had given the brush-off to in the exact same way. 'Come and say hello to my mother,' he said forcefully, driving her relentlessly towards Marina's rigid figure.

Olivia swallowed and fixed a smile on her face as she dutifully kissed the cold, powdered face. 'Good evening, Marina,' she said, managing to keep the shake out of her voice. Marina was trembling and she felt pity for the woman. Dimitri had put them both in a very difficult situation. 'You look lovely, Marina,' she said truthfully. 'And I see you've arranged the party with your usual flair and efficiency. It all looks wonderful, and the lighting is just magical.' She admired the starry lamps, softly illuminating the scene, and the subtle floodlights which made the garden look mysterious and inviting.

'Thank you,' Marina said with a stiff inclination of her head. 'Do you know why I've thrown this party?'

'Yes,' she said brightly. 'To celebrate our forthcoming divorce. Such a good idea.'

Marina blinked, disconcerted by Olivia's level and uncritical tones. 'I...I didn't think you'd want to come,' she blustered.

'Dimitri insisted,' she replied with a smile, throwing the blame on him.

'I couldn't leave her in her room while we celebrated down here. It would offend my sense of Greek hospitality,' he explained with great gentleness. 'I'm sure everyone will think you are enormously tolerant and adult about my forthcoming divorce, Mother. They'll imagine you personally invited Olivia—and they'll applaud you for your generous spirit.'

Marina fluttered a little coyly and Olivia knew he'd made his mother feel better about the peculiar situation.

'I suppose it doesn't matter as Eleni is here.' Marina put her hand on Olivia's arm in an apparently confidential gesture. 'She and Dimitri have been very close over the past few months,' she whispered.

'Lovers, you mean?' Olivia said with a frankness that startled both Dimitri and his mother.

'Oh! I wouldn't know that!' Marina assured her archly, though it was clear she believed they were. 'But Dimitri has a man's needs—'

'Mother!' Dimitri said quickly. He was crushing Olivia's hand in his to stop her from bursting into laughter and she knew that he was controlling his laughter too. 'We mustn't keep you from your guests. And I think we should mingle, too. Excuse us.'

'A man's needs!' Olivia murmured when they'd moved off. 'You get carte blanche to do what you like, don't you?'

'Pretty well,' he agreed with a grin. 'And when I don't, I do what I like anyway.'

'No wonder you think the world turns around you.'

'Don't frown or they'll think we're having an argument. Smile sweetly and adore me,' he urged.

'*Pretend* to adore you,' she corrected, blinking stu-

pidly at him till he lost control of his twitching mouth
and broke into delighted laughter.

'What a night this is going to be!' he said cheerfully.

'*Evening.*' She didn't want him to be too sure of
himself. It would give her pleasure to refuse his advances. 'Cinderella is leaving at midnight and Prince
Charming will turn back into an ugly rat.'

His eyes twinkled. 'I said night and I meant night,'
he murmured into her ear. 'And I think you've got the
fairy tale a little muddled. Prince Charming was always
the hero—'

'Not from where I'm standing. He has all the characteristics of a class-one rodent,' she shot, enjoying
herself enormously.

'You can't accuse me of having cold blood,' he protested.

'A cold heart. And you scavenge for pickings from
any heap of female flesh you come across—'

'Cinderella,' Dimitri said with a laugh, 'we have social duties. We'll continue this in bed.'

'We most certainly won't—!'

But he was already greeting his friends and she was
forced to hold her tongue. 'Olivia,' he said with convincing warmth, 'I think you know several people
here—but not, perhaps, my more recent business
friends. My wife, Olivia.' She smiled at everyone a
little nervously. 'She's here so we can arrange our divorce.'

There was a moment's shocked silence and then people began to introduce themselves. His easy-natured
acceptance of her made it plain sailing after that.
Clutching a glass of champagne, she found herself being directed from one goggle-eyed huddle of people to
another.

During the ensuing conversations, she and Dimitri made sure they cheerfully explained their separate plans for the future—whilst flinging fond glances at one another. Olivia added the occasional flutter of her lashes, too.

She became aware that his hand was lingering on her naked back. That he was drawing her closer. And occasionally he seemed lost for words because he was staring at her as if hypnotised.

So she smiled up at him and let her widened-in-awe eyes do the talking. Her body was soon leaning in to his. It was like old times and it hurt, but she played along because she must.

Gradually she became bolder and flirted outrageously, reminding him constantly of things they'd done in the past. Although he seemed to be laughing with his friends at her witticisms and teasing, several times there was a warning light in his eyes. That only spurred her on to defy him.

'You have met my partner, Nikos Kaloyirou, before,' he murmured, whisking her away from a handful of people who'd been fascinated by the familiarity of their repartee.

Olivia sobered at once. This was Eleni's father, a distinguished-looking grey-haired man with pleasant features and a dark, assessing stare.

'Yes,' she said warmly as Nikos took her hand and kissed it gallantly. 'You came to London a couple of times when I was Dimitri's secretary. And of course you came to our wedding with your daughter, Eleni. But our paths didn't cross after that.'

Nikos nodded amiably. 'You probably know that I left immediately after with Eleni to set up the New York side of the business. We spend most of our time there now.' He lifted his glass in a silent toast. 'I remember how kind you were when I was in London and caught flu. You visited me every day, interrogated me as to my likes and dislikes and hobbies, and sought out books and magazines to amuse me. And you took my darling Eleni shopping.'

She'd forgotten that. The girl had been impossible: spoilt, rude and petulant, the vilest fifteen-year-old she'd ever known.

'It was fun,' she said, focusing on the attention she'd paid to the ailing Nikos at that time. 'I'll never forget the look on the newsagent's face when I walked off with a stack of fishing magazines, a book on fly-fishing and tying your own flies, a book on—'

'Dirty dealings while orchid hunting in South America and one particularly gruesome one on whaling in the eighteenth century!' Nikos finished with a chortle. 'I enjoyed your selection so much that I was almost sorry to be well again!'

During this exchange, Dimitri kept a smile on his face, but she knew he was uncomfortable and she wished they weren't deceiving this decent, honest man. She was about to make some excuse and leave when Eleni's raised voice made them all turn in surprise. She seemed to be berating a cowed waiter. Dimitri frowned and detached himself from Olivia, till Nikos stayed him with his hand.

'My dear daughter has such passions!' he said fondly. 'She'd give you a good run for your money, Dimitri!'

'I'm sure she would,' he agreed.

Nikos grinned, winked at Dimitri meaningfully and strode off to placate his daughter.

'He adores her,' she commented.

'And is blind to her bad habits.'

'Does he know you sleep with her?' Olivia dared to ask.

Dimitri choked. 'That's the second time you've accused me of that! What gave you such a stupid idea?' he spluttered.

'Things,' she muttered with a vague wave of her hand. 'You said she was physically stunning. Since that's all that registers with you where women are concerned, I assumed—'

'Smile,' he murmured. 'Your claws are showing.'

She pinned on a particularly soppy expression and he laughed, annoyingly dropping a kiss on her nose.

'You didn't confirm or deny your relationship with Eleni,' she persisted.

'I don't have to. The only thing you need to know is that I don't want to offend Nikos. And that I am determined not to be hustled into marriage. I especially need to beat it into Eleni's head, and my mother's, that I am not interested in nineteen-year-old girls who have temper tantrums. Like that,' he added grimly.

For a moment they watched the red-faced Eleni stamping her foot while her father ineffectively remonstrated with her.

Olivia chuckled. 'I almost feel sorry for you,' she said with a grin. 'If I were truly vindictive, I might consider leaving you to Eleni's mercy.'

'Mercy?' he said ruefully. 'She'd have me committing suicide in a week.'

'Rubbish. You love life far too much for that. Come on.' She wrapped her arm around his waist, feeling extraordinarily cheerful. There was something wonderfully abandoned about being The Other Woman! 'Let's do a bit more play-acting. *Darling.*'

'Wicked witch,' he muttered, and nibbled her ear.

Olivia allowed her shudder of delight to surface, knowing that they were being watched and that people near by were leaning in their direction to listen to their conversation.

'Naughty.' She retaliated with a little nose play of her own, tapping him there with her forefinger. His eyes gleamed and she giggled as she continued, 'What will your divorce lawyer say to such behaviour?'

'Right at this moment, I don't care,' he growled sexily. 'Tonight you are my wife and I intend to claim my rights.'

He pulled her roughly into his body and she only just kept her head, remembering that this was all make-believe. So she lifted an arched eyebrow and purred seductively, 'Ohhh! I *love* it when you're so dominating, like some puffed-up little potentate!'

His mouth twitched at the dubious compliment. And he whispered in her ear, 'Watch it. You might regret that remark by breakfast time.'

'Sounds thrilling,' she said, eyes sparkling with devilry.

'It will be. I promise.'

She laughed in delight and dragged him a short distance to four of his male friends who'd been riveted by their banter. They were all over her like a rash and seemed to find it almost impossible to unglue their eyes from her cleavage.

Dimitri played it to the hilt and became even more possessive. She loved every minute of his growling attention, and several times found herself gazing up at him with real adoration when she forgot that he was only pretending to be jealous.

He was appalled at the ease with which she flirted.

Years of practice, he supposed. And in between she was managing to look at him with such melting love in her eyes that it made him want to shake her till she begged for mercy. Now he knew how she'd deceived him in the years up to their marriage. Even her eyes could lie convincingly.

'Tell me, Olivia,' said his friend Vangelis, his voice flatteringly croaky. 'Will you stay in Greece after the divorce?'

'You'll be very welcome,' butted in a bemused Andros, addressing her bosom. 'Especially in my house.'

'All of me or any particular part?' she asked with a grin, and Dimitri's irritation was swapped briefly for a smile.

'Oh, all, yes!' Andros said fervently. Dimitri worried cynically for his friend's blood pressure.

'That's very kind,' she murmured with a sweet smile. 'Thank you.'

'Time we circulated,' Dimitri growled, and the men all looked at his menacing face warily. 'I'd better tell you that Olivia is less certain about her future now we've met up again. And I'm becoming more and more uncertain about mine.' He let his gaze rest on Olivia, staring deeply into her eyes.

'Does that mean…you two…?' Vangelis left the rest in mid-air.

Dimitri's hand stroked her shoulder and she looked up at him with naked adoration, before fluttering her lashes and adopting a more flirtatious glance.

Lying eyes. Lying little tease! he thought, barely controlling his anger. He touched her parted lips with his forefinger, cynically admiring her clever little gasp that had his friends completely fooled.

'Can't comment now. Watch this space,' he said in a parting shot, and whisked her away to a quiet, unobserved corner.

It would have given him the greatest pleasure to put her over his knee and slap her tight little rear. Hell. Why was he so jealous?

'I knew you'd make an impact,' he muttered tightly through his plastered-on grin, 'but I hadn't expected my intellectual friends to mislay their brain cells quite so comprehensively.'

'That's the trouble with men and breasts sometimes,' she said perkily. 'The face doesn't get a look-in. All normal communication is diverted southwards.'

'You encouraged them,' he growled.

'I was only doing what we agreed,' she defended.

'And so very well,' he mocked. 'But it didn't include making eyes at everything in trousers.'

'It's good for people to see that you can be jealous,' she said, suspiciously demure.

He caught hold of her impatiently. 'I just don't like men thinking you're up for grabs. You're still my wife. Behave with some decorum and don't bring your London morals here.'

'Is this for real, or are you merely *staging* a show of Jealous Husband Syndrome?' she asked, her eyes wide with wonder in the semi-darkness.

And he realised he was in danger of betraying the fact that he was behaving 'for real'. So he conjured up a thin smile and tried to make his eyes join in.

'Me? Jealous? If I wanted you, I could have you. There'd be no competition in sight. It would all melt away.'

Her hand stroked his cheek. 'Such unbelievable conceit,' she sighed. 'And so misguided.'

'Like hell it is!'

Provoked to the limit, he kissed her. Hard at first, then softening his mouth as hers began to yield. When he released her, he saw that her eyes were unnaturally bright.

'What an exhibition we're making of ourselves,' she commented, desperate to hide her misery. Her mouth burned. Her heart felt sore. But she'd never let him know what he did to her.

'I think my intention is clear,' he rasped. Placing his hand on her rear, he added, 'Isn't it?'

'Painfully so. Is mine?' she countered sweetly.

And she risked a saucy wriggle against him before she squeezed his hard, neat rear too, while she kissed him back, pulling away when he tried to prolong contact with her lips.

He looked annoyed. 'Crystal. It seems we have the same goal in mind,' he growled.

No, she thought. Yours is domination and bed. Mine is escape from a ridiculously obsessive relationship that's destroying me.

'This'll be interesting,' he said, before she could come up with a quip. 'Eleni's heading this way. Think you can deal with her on your own?'

'Coward,' she chided.

'With good reason. I'm trying to prevent two inches of pancake make-up from being plastered all over my dinner jacket,' he grunted.

'Well, you disappear, then,' she said, giving him a push. She didn't want Eleni slithering all over him either.

He hesitated. 'I think,' he said hurriedly as Eleni bore down on them, 'it would be a good idea if we catch each other's eyes across the crowded terrace a couple of times. OK?'

Olivia nodded and held her hands out obediently, ready to 'catch' his eyes. Always quick on the uptake, Dimitri laughed, kissed her cheek and slipped away just as Eleni barged past her last obstacle—two teenagers ogling Dimitri as if they wanted to eat him whole.

'Hello, Eleni,' Olivia said cheerfully, getting in first. 'It's ages since we met. I remember taking you shopping—'

'I was a kid then. It was before I got these.' Eleni defiantly thrust out her shiny breasts at the startled Olivia. 'I must say, you've got a nerve, flirting with Dimitri! Don't you know he's mine? He is my *lover*. So don't muscle in or I'll scratch your eyes out.'

Lovers. Who was telling the truth—Eleni or Dimitri? After all Dimitri's lying in the past she'd rather take Eleni's word. It seemed that Dimitri would take sex in any form, even when he despised the woman involved.

Olivia winced. Dimitri despised *her* and yet he wanted to make love to her. Maybe he felt like that about all women.

Soberly Olivia gazed at Eleni. The girl seemed very confident, but when Olivia looked more closely she saw that beneath the glamorous make-up was a very young and possibly insecure young woman. Studying the sullen, resentful face, Olivia decided that she couldn't blame Eleni for adoring Dimitri. He'd turn any woman's head.

So she smiled with some sympathy, making no reference to Eleni being Dimitri's mistress. Even if the jealousy scoured a hot well of anger inside her.

'It's three years since Dimitri and I were last

together,' she said evenly. 'We're having fun, reminiscing.'

'Is that what you call it?'

Olivia shrugged. 'It's amusing to tease him. Too many people treat him like some kind of god. He needs bringing down to earth.'

'You can do that without draping yourself all over him!' Eleni protested. Olivia dared not comment. 'How long are you staying?' Eleni asked bluntly.

'As long as it takes to get the divorce.'

'In that case, why are you making eyes at him? You don't love him!' Eleni blurted out. 'You never loved him!'

She looked at Eleni sadly, every raw wound suddenly exposed. 'He was my life, once. My soul mate…'

Something made the hairs on her neck tingle. Something compelled her to turn. And when she did, her gaze honed in on Dimitri like a heat-seeking missile. He was staring at her, and the impact of his impassioned eyes made her draw in her breath and she found herself walking in his direction as if propelled by an unseen force.

Remembering her manners, she flung back confusedly over her shoulder, 'Excuse me.'

Eleni was looking at her in astonishment, blinking at Olivia's dry-throated whisper.

'I must go. You see how it is,' Olivia breathed.

And she glided away, seeing that Dimitri was striding purposefully towards the garden, politely but briefly replying to comments from the guests he passed whilst constantly checking that she knew where he was going.

Around her she could hear the buzz of conversation increase in volume and she knew they were talking about them both, about the strange powers that drew them together.

But this was what they'd planned. A very public recognition that the sparks hadn't died in their marriage. It was also very true.

Stooping to remove her shoes, she padded over the billiard-table lawn to Dimitri, feeling as if her body flowed towards him with the same inevitability as a river flowing to the sea.

Her eyes were almost midnight-blue when she looked up at him. He gave a shudder, his longing apparent in every inch of his tensioned muscles.

'I want to make love to you, here and now,' he muttered, his voice riven with passion. 'I want to see your limbs spread on the grass, your arms reaching up for me.'

She shivered, rivulets of pleasure rippling through her pliable body. 'A rather extreme way of indicating to everyone that we're getting back together,' she croaked.

His head inclined and he gave a wry smile. 'My conclusion too. Unfortunately.'

He sounded rawly husky, as if he too had trouble with a desert-dry throat. Olivia felt weak. They'd always have this incredible chemistry between them. Nothing, no one, could ever affect her as deeply as Dimitri did. So she blurted out the first thing that came into her head.

'I—I had to get away. It...seemed a good idea to wander over here,' she said, her eyes huge in the darkness at the telling of the little white lie. But she couldn't let Dimitri know that he had caught her in his web as a spider caught a fly and rendered it helpless.

So she babbled on. 'I thought Eleni might throw her drink over me and I didn't want my dress ruined.'

Her heart began to pound when his arm lifted and he reached out to lightly stroke her hip. 'No. It would be a shame. It suits you so well,' he said jerkily. Retracting his hand and thrusting it deep in his pocket, he frowned and cleared his throat. 'I'm afraid she regards me as her property.'

The atmosphere thickened between them as if the air was being filled with silent messages they dared not speak. She swallowed, trying to keep the thread of the conversation in her dazed mind. Yes. Eleni. Her eyes flashed.

'With good reason.'

'Nobody owns me,' he growled.

'No. But some people have rights where you're concerned,' she said sharply.

It was appalling that he thought he could treat his mistresses with such contempt. First Athena, then Eleni. And goodness knew how many in between.

'Was she being bitchy?' he asked, ignoring her comment.

'It wasn't a conversation I wanted to continue,' she admitted.

Dimitri sucked in a long breath and let it out slowly. 'I know she's difficult but she's had a strange upbringing. Her mother died when she was tiny. A series of nannies have spoilt her,' he said gently. 'And it can't help that Mother gave her the impression this was *her* chance to shine and yet everyone's talking about *you*.'

'Oh!' she said, flustered, her face flushed from the compliment. 'I don't think so—'

'I can assure you they are. They're all bowled over

by your beauty, your poise and your easy manner. I am constantly being told what a fool I am.'

She went pinker still, reluctantly but undeniably weakened by the throbbing richness of his low tone.

'I'm not surprised they're gossiping about us,' she said, attempting levity. 'It's not often a man entertains his wife and his wife-in-waiting at the same party.'

He chuckled. 'With any luck the wife-in-waiting will become the one that got away.'

'She'll be devastated.' Olivia frowned, worried for the girl. She'd lost her virginity to a monster. 'You shouldn't have slept with her,' she reproved.

'How many times do I have to tell you? I haven't!' His scowl suggested that her accusation offended him.

'That's what she says!' she persisted.

'Then she's lying. Wishful thinking. I swear it. She has a crush on me, nothing more, and she was trying to warn you off. I'm far too old for her,' he replied, and she felt certain he was sincere. Her spirits lifted. Maybe he wasn't such a heel after all. 'There are several young men of her age who are more than eager to step into my shoes and they'll suit her much better. She won't have to pretend to be sophisticated and she can take off those layers of make-up and be her nice, natural self. It's buried there somewhere.'

'I hope you're right. I don't like hurting people,' she said slowly.

'Really?'

Her lashes flicked up at the note of disbelief in his voice. 'I make an exception with you,' she muttered.

His grin slashed the darkness. 'I thought so. Now, to scandalise everyone a little more and to get the sentimentalists sighing, I suggest we walk up and down in full view,' he directed. 'Take my arm and talk to me.'

They strolled through the garden, lit by huge, guttering candles. Its beauty tugged at her heartstrings and added to the turmoil of emotions that threatened her judgement. She felt as if she might suffocate with the tension that hung around them and prevented her from breathing normally.

Aching with the effort of walking without stumbling, she was glad when they paused to look out at the lights of Olympos village twinkling in the darkness and the necklace of lamps edging the waterfront. Tantalising perfumes teased her nostrils as they drifted in on the breeze. She could smell lemon blossom and it was so sharp and poignant that she began to tremble from the memories it evoked.

'I want to go back to the party,' she said, weak-kneed, weak-willed and frantic to go before she said something she'd regret. Like *I love you and I always will.*

'You can leave any time,' he murmured, as if he understood the reason for her sudden distress. 'I'm sure people here have got the message about us.'

The gentle expression on his face tore into her heart. In a moment of madness she reached up and drew his head down, kissing him tenderly. Then she pulled away abruptly before she confessed her true feelings.

'In case they haven't, I hope that does the trick,' she croaked out with as much brightness as she could manage, and hurried back to the fascinated throng as if she was escaping from a dangerous animal. Which she was, she thought wryly.

'What exactly are you up to?' snapped Eleni, accosting her with angry belligerence.

'I've no idea,' she blurted out honestly. 'I wish I did.'

Blindly skirting the crowd, *en route* to goodness-knew-where, she was halfway across the empty dance floor when Dimitri caught her up.

'Dance with me,' he said in a tone that brooked no refusal.

Not that she wanted to refuse. She was in his arms and swaying to his every movement before her brain could warn her against such a silly move. And she was loving it. Her head nestled in the hollow of his throat. His breath seared her scalp hotly. The glory of his body lured her in until her curves lay against his, her breasts leaping into sharp peaks where they were rubbing the soft wool of his jacket. The burning pillar that heated her pelvis grew harder and harder and his grip on her hand grew tighter as their breathing shortened.

'Look at me!' he whispered in hoarse command.

Helplessly she did so. He stopped in the middle of the floor. Took her face between his hands and looked at her for what seemed an eternity, her eyes swimming under his impassioned gaze, before he swept her into his arms again and continued the dance, even closer than before.

This couldn't go on. It was beginning to hurt, the pain of loving him tearing at her heart so fiercely that she almost cried out loud.

'Wait,' Olivia ground out when they were level with the small orchestra. She managed to push herself free and begged the bandleader for something lively.

Dimitri laughed when she returned to him. 'Can't stand the heat?' he murmured.

'Can't stand being pawed. Darling,' she whispered, plastering a sweet smile on her face.

'Like a bit of action, instead?' he drawled and, catching her by the waist, he whirled her around the floor till she was breathless.

Despite her reluctance, she began to enjoy the hectic excitement of dancing with a man who knew how to lead, whose movements she could anticipate so well that it seemed the two of them had rehearsed for hours. And it was a release for her pent-up emotions.

Soon the dance floor was empty and they were working through their repertoire of energetic jive-cum-rock and roll, to suit the rumbustuous music.

Bright-eyed, laughing and exhausted, they finished with an exhibition twirl that evoked a storm of applause. Dimitri looked down at her flushed face, his heart thundering.

He'd forgotten what it was like to feel like this. To have his heart and mind dominated by something other than luxury apartments and executive houses. She made his bones sing. Little witch. But it was a great feeling and he meant to string it out as long as he could. He was enjoying himself too much to let her leave Greece quickly—though he needed to stay in control. She must dance to his tune, not the other way round. That meant he had to call a halt now.

'I must dance with my mother,' he said with private reluctance, wanting to hold Olivia in his arms all evening.

Her luscious mouth parted in a pout. 'In that case, I'll share myself around too,' she sighed.

His grip tightened before he could help it. 'Not too enthusiastically,' he muttered. And hastily added in harsh warning, 'You're supposed to be falling in love with me.'

'Oh, I'll fling you plenty of soppy glances,' she said, patting him like a pet dog.

With gritted teeth that made his jaw ache, he watched her closely for the rest of the evening. It seemed to him that she was having more fun than she should. His friends had claimed her, one after the other, holding her tightly to their chests and gazing down at her with stupefied expressions.

Propping up the bar, he glowered to see her lapping up the admiration. Eleni was hanging on his arm, chattering away. Every now and then he nodded or made a comment on her inane babbling.

But his mind was elsewhere, captured and tied up in ropes by a stunningly beautiful woman who lit fires in his veins, whose supple swaying body had been burnt on the backs of his retinas so that wherever he looked he could see her, and wherever he was he could hear her musical voice and flirty little laugh.

'Dimitri! You're not listening to me!' Eleni shook his arm crossly.

'Sorry.' He dragged his brain back. 'What were you saying?'

'It doesn't matter. You're hooked on her, aren't you? And she's a bitch, deliberately trying to make you jealous. Can't you see that?' sulked Eleni.

There was pain in the girl's eyes. Tenderly he took her hands in his. 'Olivia and I—'

'Her flirting is deliberate! She knows I'm a rival!' she said with a sniff.

'Eleni!' he said in consternation.

Olivia was nibbling canapés at the huge, flower-garlanded buffet table on the terrace when she caught sight of Eleni disappearing into the house. Closely followed by Dimitri.

Her stomach contracted in horror and she slid her

plate onto the table, her hands shaking. He couldn't. Wouldn't. He'd sworn they weren't lovers. Yet the way he hurried after his partner's daughter—as though he was eager to catch her up and kiss her and sweep her into his arms—suggested otherwise.

She would find out. Perhaps expose him for the liar that he was. With a mumbled excuse to Andros, she made her way up a set of side steps to the house.

Where she found Eleni wrapped in Dimitri's arms.

CHAPTER SIX

QUIETLY she slipped away before she was seen, her heart thundering in her chest and her mind teeming with confused thoughts. How could she be so stupid as to love such a man and give her heart and soul to him so comprehensibly? He'd never been true to her. Had never been honest.

And the stupid thing was that she'd *known* they were playing a game. He'd made it plain that she was just a body that he'd virtually hired to rid himself of an unwanted bride-to-be. Yet she realised now to her intense shame that unconsciously she'd harboured wild, crazy hopes that maybe...*maybe*...

She'd been incredibly gullible. Dimitri only had to murmur a few lying sweet nothings and she was his. She ought to have known better. Past experience should have told her that all he wanted was sex without strings from any willing, beautiful woman who happened to be around.

Sure, he found her desirable. But, she thought miserably, he thought loads of other women were desirable too. Whatever had given her the impression that she might be someone special?

Huddled against a marble pillar on the upper terrace, she morosely surveyed the glittering scene. Then with a sigh she glanced down at her fabulous dress. Right now, she'd gladly swap all the glamour here for a little house and a man she could love, who respected her and was utterly faithful.

Wearily, sick of it all, she found another door into the mansion and stumbled to her bedroom. Remembering Dimitri's promise of a night of passion, she jammed a chair beneath the handle on the bedroom door.

He could make do with Eleni, she thought, violently unzipping her dress and slinging it in the direction of a chair. It missed and fell to the floor, but she let it lie there, hoping sourly that Eleni would spend the entire night giggling into Dimitri's ear and numbing his brain with inanities.

Too tired to think, she prepared for bed mechanically and eventually slipped on her black silk nightdress and crawled into the soft linen sheets with a sigh of relief. But as she lay there, longing for sleep, her mind began to replay the evening in full Technicolor.

There was Dimitri, dark, handsome, apparently adoring. There he was again, laughing. The whiteness of his teeth and the amusement on his face caused her body to tighten even now. He seemed to be everywhere in her head. Deceptively loving. Painfully good-looking and desirable.

She put her hands to her head, desperate to be rid of him. With a groan, she sprang up and poured herself a glass of wine from the carafe by the bed, thinking that a good slug of alcohol might make her drowsy. It didn't.

Muttering angrily under her breath, she paced the room, and even tried counting backwards from a thousand. Somewhere around nine hundred and thirty she lost the plot and found herself quivering at the memory of Dimitri's touch.

It was going to be a long night. Resigned, she

stomped over to the window to glare at the few remaining guests. No Eleni in sight.

Surprisingly, Marina was still up, dancing with Nikos. Olivia wondered if her mother-in-law might be a little drunk, because she seemed to be melting in her partner's arms, her gaunt face so remarkably relaxed and happy that she looked quite pleasant for a change.

Olivia tensed. Dimitri was there, too, chatting amiably with a handful of friends in that easy, male style. Her eyes softened. He sat in a wicker chair, every inch the Greek tycoon, his arms draped casually over the arms, one long leg crossed over the other. And he looked immaculate as ever and totally unperturbed, as if he hadn't spent the past hour or so smooching with a nineteen-year-old girl.

Suddenly he stiffened and glanced up at her window, as if he'd known she'd been staring at him. Olivia hastily moved away, upset that he'd seen her. With his giant ego, she thought crossly, he'd probably think she was mooning over him like a lovesick fool, while she'd been mentally firing lasers at his steel-clad heart.

Dimitri's head reeled. There had been an uncharacteristic droop of her shoulders that warned him something wasn't quite right. The narrow straps of her nightdress had been slipping down her arms. In fact, her whole demeanour had been strangely listless. Despite the distance between them, he was sure her mouth had been set in an unhappy line. He had to go to her. He didn't know why, only that he must.

Using well-honed tact and skill, he managed to persuade the last guests to leave. Stifling his impatience, he thanked the orchestra and the caterers, then hugged his mother, who hadn't said a word about his extraordinary behaviour throughout the evening—presumably because, as he'd guessed, she dared not object in public that it looked as if his marriage might be saved.

'Don't worry about me. Everything's under control,' he said, anxious to put her mind at rest.

'I won't,' she said before he could continue. She smiled with unusual warmth at Nikos, who had brought two brandies over. 'I know you're up to something. Besides, I've decided that I have my own life to lead and you must make your own mistakes.'

Astonished, Dimitri looked from one to the other, noting the new softness of his mother's face. Nikos gave him a sheepish look and a helpless shrug. A little dazed, Dimitri said his goodnights and left them to it.

All he had on his mind was Olivia. In truth, she had drowned out almost everything else all evening. Racing up the stairs, he tried to open her door. And found it wouldn't budge more than an inch.

'Olivia!' he called. 'It's me.'

'I hardly thought it might be anyone else!' she shouted back crossly.

He frowned. 'Let me in, then.'

'If you think I'm entertaining you after you've been canoodling with another woman, you're sadly mistaken!' she yelled.

What was she talking about? Irritated, he pushed the door again and it yielded slightly.

'Open this door or I'll break it down!' he ordered.

'You've been watching too many American movies!' she retorted. 'Go back to your lover and leave me alone!'

He had no choice. Refusing to discuss her wild accusation through two inches of oak, he took a few steps back, steadied himself, and charged, thinking to shock her into opening the door. However, there was a re-sounding crack as something gave way and he was hurtling into the bedroom.

'Get out of here!' she cried, shocked.

Cringeing against the bed hangings and clinging on to them for dear life, she looked so terrified that he calmed down immediately. He kicked aside the broken chair which had allowed him entry, then pushed the door shut and leaned against it, trying to look harmless.

'So—other than you—who am I supposed to have made advances to tonight?' he asked in amusement, loosening his bow-tie and undoing the top button of his shirt.

'Good grief! Don't you know?' she hurled.

'No. And I think I would have noticed,' he pointed out with a grin.

'It's not funny! Allow me to jog your memory,' she seethed. 'Curvy blonde. Spectacular body. Giggles a lot.'

'*Eleni?!*' He laughed at the very idea. 'Heaven help me, I've told you before—she'd be the last woman on earth I'd approach.' His eyes twinkled. 'How could I fondle a woman whose breasts are solid marble?'

'How do you know they are?' she demanded hotly.

'I don't,' he replied with great patience. 'I'm assuming they would be since they don't move a lot.' He looked pointedly at hers, which were moving more than he could personally withstand.

'You don't deny you've looked, then?'

He heaved a sigh. 'It's difficult to escape them when they're sitting like cannonballs on top of her dress. Olivia, I keep telling you. I'm not interested in her—'

'Then it was her double who I saw in the salon in your arms—'

'Ahh. That's it.'

'You're not denying it now, are you?' she flung, sounding at the end of her tether.

She was truly jealous. For some reason that delighted him. Vanity? No. Something else that he dared not investigate.

'Olivia.' His voice and his entire demeanour softened. 'Eleni *was* in my arms. But, as I recall, we were fully dressed and we remained clothed throughout the time I comforted her.'

'Oh, yes?' she muttered sulkily.

'I saw that she was upset,' he explained. 'I decided to enlist her as an ally.'

'That's ridiculous! You're lying to me,' she accused.

'Not at all. I am aware that she needs people to think well of her. Therefore I remarked on the fact that she and I had always been good friends and that I knew she would want the best for me. I said she'd always seemed like a kid sister to me—'

'Bet she hated that.'

'It made her blink,' he agreed with a wry smile. 'And while she was temporarily speechless I managed to talk at length about marriage being a sacred union between a man and a woman—'

'What a liar you are!' Olivia glared.

'And,' he persevered, 'I got her to agree with me on the sanctity of marriage. She'd realised what I was doing by then, but she could hardly say that it meant nothing.'

'Devious.'

'I thought so,' he said, pleased. 'I told her I was entrusting her with a secret and that you and I were getting back together. She burst into tears and I said I knew how sentimental she was and how kind of her to feel so happy for me that she felt like crying. I imagine that's when you saw us, because almost immediately she pulled away and wiped her eyes before stomping off to dance with Vangelis.'

He willed her to believe him. But he didn't tell her what else he'd said to Eleni.

'You…didn't…do anything else? Like…kiss her?' Olivia asked in a small voice.

He winced at the very idea. What would convince her? 'I swear I didn't, on my father's head,' he said simply.

There was no arguing with that. Dimitri would never use his father to support a lie. She bit her lip, cursing herself for jumping to conclusions. Dimitri had been acting kindly to Eleni by letting her down gently.

'I'm sorry,' she mumbled.

'It was an understandable mistake.'

'Yes, it was, considering your reputation!' she muttered.

'And what reputation is that?' he asked mildly.

'As a womaniser.'

'Ah.'

No denial, she noticed. 'You're pretty untrustworthy where women are concerned.'

'Am I?'

She glared. 'Don't tell me you've been celibate ever since we parted!'

'No. I haven't.'

She flinched at his honesty, wondering how many, how often, how beautiful those women had been.

'I suppose I should be pleased,' she said jerkily, 'that you have persuaded Eleni to abandon her hopes of marrying you. We can bring this awful charade to a close…'

She gulped. Why was she appalled at the thought of a rapid divorce? She ought to be celebrating, but it felt as if she were at a wake. Turning away to stare sightlessly out of the window, she tried to control her swamping misery.

Dimitri's hands rested lightly on her bare arms and she felt a jolt of lightning flash through her.

'And we can be free to do whatever we want,' he finished for her.

All she wanted was to love him. To trust him. To be the only woman in his life. Some chance.

When he tried to turn her around she resisted and escaped, backing away, her eyes wide with apprehension.

'Well, I want you to leave,' she said in a low voice.

'No, you don't.'

His sheer arrogance made her eyes flash with instant defiance. When he smiled, and took a step towards her, she picked up the half-full glass of wine and hurled the contents at him.

'I do!' she cried, as most of the wine fell to the floor.

Unperturbed, he shed his wine-stained jacket and shirt, letting them drop in a heap.

'That is a lie,' he said calmly.

Alarmed by the determination in his glittering black eyes, she grabbed the carafe and began to eject its contents at him, backing nervously as he advanced on her. Wine gleamed darkly on his chest, trickling over its planes into little valleys and wetting the dark hairs that curled in a dark, tapering line that led towards his loins.

'I'm going to make you lick all that up,' he growled, unhooking his belt.

'Dimitri...no!' she croaked, dazed by the thought of sliding her tongue around the hard contours, and teas-

ing each tight, male nipple into an erection... Her hand
went to her mouth and she blushed, finding that the tip
of her tongue had already moistened her lips as if in
eager preparation.

'Could be a glorious way of getting tipsy,' he
breathed.

It was the way he looked at her that sent electric
thrills pulsing into every nerve of her body. She could
feel her flesh softening beneath the sensual impact of
those wicked black eyes, which were heating her like
blazing coals till a furnace burned inside her.

'Why should I want to do that?' she demanded,
clinging by a thread to normality.

'To throw off those peculiar inhibitions you seem to
have acquired since I last made love to you. Put down
the decanter, Olivia. It's cut glass and will cause damage to those bare feet of yours if it smashes. Those
beautiful feet... I wouldn't want them scarred.'

The hunger was eating away at her, unfairly reminding her of long-ago pleasures. Dimitri, taking each foot
in turn and exploring every inch with his mouth.
Sucking her toes while watching her with blazing hot
eyes.

Shakily, she put the decanter on a marble table.

'This isn't what I had in mind!' she whispered.

'Isn't it?'

Somehow she shook her head instead of letting herself drift into his arms. 'No. You said we'd pretend to
be crazy about one another in *public*. Well, no one is
here to see. We can behave normally—'

'I am.' He spread his hands in innocence.

She glared. 'I'm sure that's true. You'd come on
strong to any woman who looked vaguely willing—'

'Not at all. I'm very fussy,' he purred. 'I only like

women who make my body quicken with a mere glance. Who are so aware of their sensuality that it characterises every movement they make. Who can abandon themselves to the possession of their senses and lure a man on till he thinks he's going crazy. Women who respond to my touch. Who shiver and shudder and love bodily contact—'

'Don't!' she whispered, aghast at what he was doing to her.

He was talking about *women*. How many did he know who'd given him such exquisite pleasure? And…how had he got so close to her? She hadn't noticed him moving. Only the dark promise in his velvety eyes. She took a step back and found that the wall was touching her spine. Trapped. She had only her wits left to keep him at bay—and they seemed hell-bent on deserting her.

'Go and find one of those women, then,' she scorned, tossing up her head with a defiant swirl of her hair. 'I'm only here as a means to an end—our *divorce*! I'm willing to continue the farce of gazing at you idiotically in public, but don't get any ideas that I'm game for a little light sex in private—'

'It won't be little and it won't be light.'

The soft murmur ran through her like a hot wave that melted where it touched. His mouth curled in anticipation and she found herself unwillingly watching its sensual curve. Her breath shortened and she almost leaned forward to kiss those amused lips, wanting to shut him up, to impose herself on him and to remind him that he could be *her* slave when it came to sex. Because she didn't want him to seek out another woman. She wanted him for herself. Exclusively.

An impossible dream and she knew it. 'You have to leave!' she jerked out.

He smiled, as unconvinced by her breathless order as she was. 'It seems such a waste when you're here, those gorgeous summer-sky eyes sending me enticing messages I can't ignore—'

'They're telling you to go!' she cried, but lowered her lashes, knowing they were doing nothing of the sort. And her gaze hovered again over his intensely masculine mouth. The urge to drive her lips into his and kiss away all her tension was overpowering.

'Olivia, be honest,' he murmured as her hands screwed into tight fists. 'Admit what you feel. I see it in every line of your body. The way you tremble. The swelling of your lips. The thrust of your nipples, forcing against the black silk so hard that I can hardly keep my hands from touching them. You don't know how difficult it's been for me, trying to get you to own up to your feelings instead of ripping off those straps and letting your nightie fall to the floor so I can see and touch and claim your body.' He paused, his voice husky. 'We are virtually free agents. We can do what we want,' he whispered. 'And at this moment I want *you* with every beat of my heart.'

She gasped with fury, his near-seduction ending as if he'd dropped her into cold water. 'At this *moment*?' she spluttered. 'Oh, thanks! I'm pleased to be considered for your diversion *at this moment*. And who might you want at any other moment? Like this afternoon, tonight, tomorrow? How *dare* you! I'm not someone to be picked up and put down as the fancy takes you! Maybe you didn't want to spend the night with Eleni sniggering in your ear, but that doesn't mean you can turn to me for your sexual comforts just because there's no one else suitable around!'

She had never looked more beautiful, with her eyes sparkling, mouth parted and ready for his kiss, her head flung back and that lovely neck exposed. He had never wanted her more. Or been so determined to have her.

'I'm not treating you as a poor substitute for anyone,' he said, croaky with need. 'I have spent the entire evening waiting for this moment.'

His hand reached out, surprising him by the way it shook. Quickly he let it rest on her moon-silvered shoulder, then slowly slid it to linger on that slender, silken throat. She gave a little gasp, which emboldened him to move closer. His other hand slid into her perfumed hair till he could feel the warm curve of her head.

'The love between us might have died,' he said quietly, 'but the sexual attraction is hotter than ever. Isn't it?'

She didn't reply, but gazed at him in consternation. It was agreement enough for him. But he wanted her to say it. So he leaned forward a little and lightly touched her lips with his. He felt her breath heating his mouth in fast, jerky little bursts.

'Isn't it?' he persisted, tasting her with the tip of his tongue.

Her eyes closed, seemingly in despair. After a long, breathless moment, she whispered with a moan, 'Yes!'

The silk slithered down her body in an agonisingly erotic movement. He felt an odd little stab in his chest. Standing there, naked and glorious, she seemed vulnerable. Beaten.

'Olivia!' He took her in his arms and held her close. At first she remained stiff and tense, yet trembling like a leaf. But because he did no more than hold her she slowly relaxed. And when she lifted her head and looked at him he saw something of the old Olivia, a passionate and proud woman who rejoiced in the extraordinary chemistry between them.

And then her mobile rang.

Dimitri groaned. 'Leave it,' he muttered, kissing her throat.

'No... ' She drew in a sharp breath as his teeth nibbled her lobe. When he began to suck it, she pulled away and snatched up her bag. Sitting on the bed, she avoided Dimitri's eyes and dragged the duvet over her nakedness.

This was her chance to cool down. To give her brain an airing instead of letting it sink like a stone beneath her appalling lust.

'Hello?' She cringed at her quavering, froggy voice.

'Olivia?' Paul sounded puzzled.

'Oh, yes!' she said brightly. 'Paul! How *lovely* to hear from you.' Dimitri sat on the bed, much too close to her. Covering the mouthpiece, she flung him a false smile. 'It's Paul,' she said unnecessarily, then, crushed by Dimitri's mocking eyes, she jerked her head away and attended to what the lawyer was saying.

'...fabulous time. Angelaki has an entire skyscraper for his company alone. We've got a brilliant settlement—'

'But—'

'You'll be free of him pretty soon,' Paul hurtled on. 'And a multimillionairess! How about that? Don't you think I've done well?'

'Paul, I—' She slapped Dimitri's hand away. It had slid beneath the duvet and was slinking its way up her leg.

'It's OK. Don't thank me. I'm hoping you'll come over to New York,' Paul said smugly. 'I've some fantastic news! Guess what, Olivia!'

She grabbed the corner of the duvet, which Dimitri was tugging free. Glaring at him, she snapped an irritated, 'What?' into the phone.

'Are you all right?' Paul asked, just as Dimitri flung his weight across Olivia and bore her back to the bed. 'It's not too late, is it? I tried to work out the time difference, but frankly I'm in such a whirl that I'm not sure—'

'I'm fine,' she gritted, fending off Dimitri's determined assault on her bared thigh. His hand was smoothing it with an infuriating rhythm and she seemed to be getting short of breath as her need began to dull her brain.

'Good. Well, this is my news,' crowed Paul.

'Oh, help!' she whispered, feeling herself surrendering to the passionate kisses being rained on her jaw and throat.

'I,' Paul announced proudly, 'have been offered a job by the Angelaki New York office.'

'A…job?' she said, incredulous. The news was like an ice-cold shower. Stiff and resisting, she glared at Dimitri, who was openly listening to the conversation while kissing the line of her jaw.

'That's right. And you know what American lawyers can earn! This is my chance, Olivia! And—well, I don't need to tell you this because I know you and I had a kind of understanding—together we could be a great team—'

'Paul,' Dimitri murmured, having snatched the phone from her, 'take the job and be grateful. You're not having Olivia as well. Is he, my darling?'

'Give that back!' she gritted, struggling. Dimitri grinned at her. His body effectively held her a prisoner and she couldn't reach the phone.

'One more thing,' Dimitri said, his tone edged with steel. 'Learn the time differences if you want to keep your job. It's the early hours of the morning here and we're in bed.'

'Bed?' she heard Paul screech.

'Luckily we weren't asleep—if you know what I mean,' Dimitri drawled, then disconnected the call and flung the mobile on the floor. 'Now, where were we?' he mused. 'Here? Or here—?'

She jerked her head to one side and he just managed to avoid kissing the pillow. 'Don't *touch* me!' she breathed in fury.

His hand cradled her cheek and he pushed firmly till she was forced to face him again. His eyes had darkened dangerously.

'Is your conscience troubling you?' he muttered. 'That's the little voice in your head, by the way, that tells you it's not decent to chat to an ex-lover on the phone while your husband is about to ravish you.'

She ground her teeth together. 'Why did you instruct your people to give Paul a job?' she demanded furiously. 'I know you have an ulterior motive in doing so—'

'Correct. I'm ensuring he's off the scene.' Dimitri's mouth came down hard on hers in a long kiss that left her gasping for breath. 'It was obvious to me what he had in mind. He wants to marry you and I can't allow that.'

'Why?' she defied, as if she might contemplate the idea.

'Because he's not man enough for the job.'

'And you are?'

His eyes gleamed. 'Definitely. I intend to remind you of that. Right *now*.'

CHAPTER SEVEN

THE sun was gently turning her body a golden brown. She knew she ought to turn over to do her back but she didn't have the energy...thanks to Dimitri.

With a slow and languid lift of her arm, she tipped back her floppy sun hat to observe him. He, too, had been utterly still for the past hour, stretched out on one of the steamer chairs beside the pool.

The effort of holding up her hat was too much and she let it drop. But she could still see him in her mind. There was a warm glow inside her when she thought of his hard, toned body gleaming in the sun. His arms hung limply to the ground as if he was exhausted, too. Dimitri's sensual mouth seemed at odds with his strong, masculine profile and she wondered if he was thinking of the hours they had spent in bed—and out of it—till mid-morning.

Faint quivers trickled deliciously in the channels of her limp body and seeped into her very bones but she was too sated to be aroused.

It seemed as if time had been suspended. The air hummed with the heat, a slight breeze bringing tantalising scents to her nose. A stillness had descended on the garden, broken only by the gentle swish of the palms surrounding the pool.

She heard the maid, Maria, offering lemonade. The sound of it being poured and the clink of ice.

'Olivia,' murmured Dimitri.

A cold glass touched her fingers that draped negli-

123

gently on the hot tile and she gave just a drowsy 'mmm' of thanks. Her hand was grasped, kissed, then released. She heard him returning to the lounger and settling himself with a contented sigh. As well he might.

She loved him. Not because of the unbelievable, earth-shattering sex, though that would have made any woman feel she'd found paradise on earth, but because they had talked and laughed too, and she had felt truly happy, utterly at ease with him.

All the feelings she'd had for him in those heady, early days when they'd first begun to work together were back in force, but far stronger now.

Dimitri had caressed her and loved her until she'd thought she might die of pleasure, and even at this moment a little sigh was escaping from her kiss-swollen lips at the very memory of those hours of bliss. But for her the sex was a part of something greater that involved her deepest emotions. He was more than a drug—he was essential to her happiness.

The thought filled her with alarm. She sat up abruptly and sipped the cold drink, hoping to steady her wild thoughts. Because if that was true then she had to fight for him. To make him love her more than he loved his freedom to enjoy other women. And how could she ever do that?

Dimitri reached out lazily, his hand touching her arm. 'I will never forget last night,' he said huskily.

'Nor will I.'

She hesitated, tempted to pour out her feelings, to take the risk that he'd laugh and say it was great but not for keeps. But the familiar voice of Eleni trilled out behind them and she groaned and clamped her lips together instead.

'Did I drive all thoughts of Paul from your head?' he probed.

'Yes—'

'Dimitri!' Wearing a crop top and brief skirt over a bikini, Eleni flung her arms about his neck and virtually sprawled over his body. Olivia groaned. 'Lovely party, darling,' she purred, toying with the lock of hair that had fallen onto his forehead. And she began to murmur under her breath to Dimitri.

'Get off, wretched child!' he complained.

Olivia put down her drink and went for a swim, even though she was too tired to do much more than drift about aimlessly in the silken blue water, floating on her back with her eyes shut against the sun.

After a moment, two splashes at the far end of the pool told her that Dimitri and Eleni had joined her. She lifted her head to watch. They were fooling about, ducking one another as if they were the greatest of friends. No, she thought, seeing how often Eleni managed to slide her body against Dimitri's. More like prospective lovers taking every opportunity to touch.

Tears stung her eyes. Every time she thought Dimitri really cared, she discovered that it was merely part of his seduction technique. If he did care, he wouldn't fool about with Eleni.

She turned and began to swim to the edge but suddenly she found herself being grabbed and pulled under water. She kicked out and emerged spluttering to see Eleni's laughing face a few inches away.

'Got you!' Eleni crowed.

'You certainly did,' Olivia said without amusement.

'Jealous?' Eleni taunted.

She looked for Dimitri. He'd disappeared. 'Should I be?'

'Oh, yes. I'm Greek and his partner's daughter. And I accept that the men of my country are passionate and have many affairs.'

Olivia blinked in astonishment. 'You'd let him have affairs?'

'Sure. If it meant he'd stay married to me. It's rumoured that his father had a mistress. I'd have to accept that Dimitri would probably have one too.'

Olivia knew that Dimitri had idolised his father. When Theo had died she had spent hours talking to Dimitri and comforting him. After he'd returned to England from the funeral she had done everything possible to ease his grief. A week later he had proposed.

Perhaps, she mused, it had been a mistake to marry on the back of tragedy. Maybe Dimitri had needed emotional support after losing the father he loved, and had thought marriage would provide that. It wasn't a good enough basis for a long and stable relationship, though.

One thing she did know: if his beloved father had maintained a mistress then Dimitri would have accepted that as the norm. It wouldn't be surprising if he believed that fidelity wasn't important—at least, not where he was concerned. Her spine felt as if a cube of ice were sliding down it.

'I don't know how you could contemplate sharing him,' she said soberly.

Eleni shrugged. 'Better that than nothing, so long as it's discreet. Though if he upsets me once we're married, or if he harms one hair of my head, my father will see to it that the Angelaki empire collapses.'

Olivia was appalled by the girl's ruthlessness. Eleni had set her sights on Dimitri and wouldn't be put off.

'Personally,' she said quietly, 'I'd rather have the

devotion of a man because he adores me, not because he's been threatened with financial ruin.'

Olivia swam away and climbed out of the pool. The girl had been spoilt and given everything she wanted. Eleni might idolise Dimitri, and imagine that being married to him would be all roses, but she didn't love him. Love was more than sexual attraction and starry-eyed dreams.

Thoughtfully she rubbed her hair dry with a towel. Love weathered all difficulties. It grew... Pausing in her reverie, she smiled at the masses of geraniums in a terracotta urn near by. Grew like a flower. She'd been madly in love with Dimitri from the moment she saw him. The seeds of passion had been there already, but she had grown to love him more profoundly as time went on.

Her heart thudded painfully. Perhaps she was giving up too easily. At least Eleni was fighting for the man she wanted.

Maybe it was worth the risk of being hurt. She could try persuading Dimitri that a deep and loving commitment to one person was infinitely more satisfying than casual affairs. Slowly she dabbed at her damp skin, trying to decide whether to follow her heart or her head. Her brow furrowed. Was she thinking like a woman, and forgetting that men felt entirely differently?

From inside the house, he watched Olivia tensely, knowing she was chewing over something that troubled her because she'd been drying the same part of her firm little rear for the past few minutes.

With difficulty, he dragged his mind from those tempting curves, irritated with himself for being so easily distracted. But her body was gorgeous, the sun gleaming on it lovingly, and he couldn't help but relive his recent exploration of every squirming inch.

He slapped his hand against his forehead in rueful exasperation. Olivia invaded his mind so thoroughly that sometimes he wondered if every brain cell he possessed had her image emblazoned there.

His greedy gaze enjoyed the rhythmic movement of her hands, a stab of remembered sweet agony slicing through him. She could drive him crazy with those delicate, wicked fingers. With her wholehearted, utterly abandoned responses to his touch.

She was biting her lip and frowning. He hoped she wasn't worrying about Eleni's behaviour. That girl needed a firm hand. If he hadn't left the pool when he did, he knew she would have done something outrageous and he would have been forced to slap her down—with disastrous consequences. He knew how vindictive Eleni could be.

His tension softened at the sight of the pensive Olivia. Their odd sense of psychic communication ensured that her head lifted and she saw him watching her. She gave a little gasp, then, flinging down the towel in a determined way, she tied a colourful wrap around her body and walked towards the salon, where he stood, still in his swimming trunks.

He smiled, anticipating the kiss they would share. As she approached, he opened the double doors that led to the terrace.

'Your little chat with Eleni didn't work. She intends to marry you,' she said bluntly, stepping past him into the room so quickly that her hair whisked over his bare shoulder.

He made the quivers die down in his body, but the

scent of her remained to provoke him. Here were the
memories of last night, of the morning, crowding in on
him, rendering him weak with desire.

'I know.' He cleared his throat of the huskiness that
betrayed him. 'She told me so a few moments ago and
I tried to laugh it off—without success, it seems.' His
eyes gleamed with slumberous pleasure. 'We must try
harder to convince her that we're back together again
and she doesn't have a chance.'

Olivia frowned and the tip of her small pink tongue
touched her lips. 'Yes. Or I'll never… ' She bit her lip
this time. 'Never get the divorce, will I?' she finished
rather shakily.

He sensed a reluctance in her, which suited his purpose very well. If he played his cards right he could
spin this out till he was rid of his addiction to her. A
year, maybe. Studying her huge blue eyes and the thick
fringe of lashes, he felt a thrill start its journey through
his body.

Her face assumed an expression of drowsy longing.
He began to plan a day of unrestricted lovemaking, his
gaze wandering avidly over her curves, outlined by the
clinging wrap. And she gave a little gasp, her breath
shortening like his.

'Olivia!' he whispered, managing just a croak.

'Yes?' she mouthed, and he felt compelled to move
forward, to seal her hot lips with his in a long and
thorough kiss.

His hand drifted into her hair. He tipped up her chin
and smiled, shaking with overwhelming feelings for
her. Sexual, of course. Nothing more. He'd sealed off
his heart three years ago and she was the last person
he'd allow to break that seal. But she made every cell

in his body leap with life and he wasn't intending to let her go till he'd exhausted his passion for her.

'More passion,' he ordered thickly.

'What?' Her voice shook very satisfactorily.

'Eleni is watching,' he whispered, and took her mouth in his, crushing it in an explosive kiss that had her whimpering in need. 'Convince her!'

'Yes!' she moaned.

Dizzy with love, she writhed hungrily against him, finding joy in being in his arms. For a moment she could pretend that he cared. She knew she was taking a risk with her emotions but she couldn't help it. If there was a chance that Dimitri might recognise how well they were suited, then he might learn to love her.

She lifted a long bare leg and slid it down his thigh. He gave a shudder and beneath her palm she felt the acceleration of his heart.

'It's good, isn't it?' she whispered.

He groaned, hating her, wanting her. His mouth savaged her throat as she sighed and pressed her warmth against him; he felt his skin scorch where her naked flesh met his.

He had to tell her. She must agree to stay. The uncertainty was gnawing at him till he thought he'd go mad.

'You know it is. You know that you drive me crazy,' he muttered.

'Do I?' she murmured with a languid smile. Her sharp teeth nibbled at his lower lip.

He pulled her deeper into the room, out of sight, and took her head in his hands to focus her attention on what he was saying. 'I don't want you to go,' he said hoarsely. 'Stay with me.'

She gasped. 'Dimitri—' she whispered.

'Stay.'

He saw her eyes fill with tears. The radiance of her face made his stomach clench. This was what she'd wanted, he thought helplessly. She thought she'd got him back for good. But it was only till he'd had enough. The mother of his children would never be a gold-digging tramp.

'For…how long?' she asked, her tear-washed eyes searching his.

He hauled in a shaky breath and kissed her, losing himself in the taste of her mouth, the feel, the smell of her.

'I don't know,' he said honestly.

'I'm afraid.'

He frowned, his finger idly brushing back and forth across her nipple. 'Of what?'

'Being… ' A faint moan fluttered from her parted lips. She moved his finger to her other breast and began to breathe hard when its peak surged into life beneath his rhythmic touch. 'Being sh-aa-red,' she jerked.

'Listen to me.'

He looked down at her closed eyes, the soft lashes thick and luxurious on her beautiful cheekbones. Her head was thrown back, her mouth moist from his kiss. He would do anything, promise anything to make her stay. Night and day he thought of her. Some time he had to drag his brain back to work, but while she possessed it so utterly he was useless.

So he stepped back. Held her at arm's length. 'Olivia,' he said, 'I wouldn't be interested in other women if we were lovers again. I'm not that much of a stud!' he added with a smile, and was curiously flattered when she seemed to doubt that. 'You take everything I have to give and leave me sated—until you look at me with those hungry sapphire eyes and then I want to devour you whole. There will be no other women. You have my promise.'

'Not…even a brief fling with…with any of the women you've been involved with since I left?' she asked in a small, anxious voice.

His face cleared. 'Absolutely not!' He laughed. 'They were a disappointment. I'm afraid I compared them with you and found them wanting.'

'No one…special?' she probed, concern in every line of her face.

He pulled her into his arms. 'No. You will be the only one. I swear on my father's head. Please stay.' And he waited, holding his breath while she stared at him, perhaps making up her mind, perhaps keeping him dangling. He didn't know, didn't care, only that she should say yes.

She held her breath. It was worth trying. She must put the past aside and think of their future. Maybe she was gambling with her happiness, but she'd never forgive herself if she didn't make the attempt.

When she smiled, hope leapt in his chest. Her smile widened and lit her eyes till they gleamed like jewels.

'Yes,' she murmured, and a strange delirium hurtled through him.

Steady, he warned himself. But her palm lovingly shaped the contours of his chest and her mouth sucked delicately at his nipple. The familiar wildness came over him. Olivia would be his and his alone. Exulting, he lifted her head and drove his mouth hard on hers while his fingers slid to the tie of her bikini. Her hand closed over his.

'Not here. Not with Eleni hovering in the background. I want us to go somewhere,' she murmured, flushed and bright-eyed. 'Somewhere romantic.'

He smiled and showered kisses on her face. 'I know just the place,' he breathed. 'I'll tell her we're leaving. Get dressed and collect what you need. We'll take a trip out in the boat away from here, away from Eleni and Mother. Just you and me, enjoying ourselves.' His hungry mouth nibbled her warm shoulder. 'The bonus is that it'll look good, the two of us sneaking off together.'

It sounded wonderful. And perhaps it would be her opportunity to show him how much she loved him. They'd spend the day together, just as they used to. She wanted to remind him how comfortable they had been with one another. If she could revive that sense of belonging, of deep conviction that they had always been destined for one another, then he might realise what he would lose if he ever risked playing the field.

Her dreamy smile made her face radiant with happiness. It was quite possible that they might be together for ever, she thought. And let out a long, satisfied sigh.

'I'd like that very much, Dimitri,' she murmured. Winding her arms about his neck, she eyed him with open adoration and was rewarded by his indrawn breath. Her forefinger touched his mouth and he gently savaged it with his teeth. They would talk. Make love. Forget everything but the future. 'Somewhere private,' she whispered. 'Where we can swim and...sunbathe.' Closing her eyes, she let her soft lips close on his.

Briefly she felt the flicker of his tongue, and then he was gently unpicking her fingers. 'Go,' he said thickly. 'I can't wait.'

She shuddered, running an exploratory finger over his biceps and down his arm, her eyes holding his in a long, loving look. 'I'll be ten minutes,' she whispered, joy lighting her face.

Hand in hand, they strolled to the harbour. She wore a simple sky-blue top with bootlace straps and a matching skirt that swirled about her legs. Dimitri looked edible in a cream open-necked shirt and chinos.

Joyfully she joined Dimitri in greeting the black-garbed women with merry eyes that they passed, and the wrinkled old men who drowsed in the sun on rickety chairs outside tiny cafés dripping with bougainvillaea.

'*Kronia pola,*' she said happily. Many years.

'*Epsis,*' they replied. And the same to you.

Olivia thought of the many years she might spend with Dimitri and couldn't stop smiling.

Her senses seemed acute. She could smell garlic and lemon, and the sound of sizzling came from the small taverna on the quayside.

Her heart seemed to expand. This was where she wanted to be. This was the man she wanted to share the rest of her life with. Providing he committed himself to her.

A tremor of uncertainty collapsed her confidence, but when she looked up at him and he smiled down at her, squeezing her hand affectionately, she remembered his oath and told herself she was being unnecessarily neurotic.

In companionable silence they clambered on board his small motor launch, and Olivia stood with her arm around Dimitri's waist while he eased a passage between the sturdy fishing boats.

'Where are we going?' she asked, enjoying the wind whipping her hair back from her face.

He gazed down at her with heart-jerking affection. 'Wait and see.'

Snuggled up to him, she felt his back muscles expand as he manoeuvred the boat around the rocks scattered like broken beads at the tip of the island before heading out to the deeps, the breeding ground for sharks.

After a while they passed the volcanic island of Methana and seemed set for Poros Island. Slipping through the narrow channel between Poros and the mainland, they began to hug the coast. And Olivia knew where they were headed.

She couldn't stop smiling. He had remembered.

He drew the boat up on a small sandy beach and lifted her out as if she were a new bride crossing the threshold of the marital home. Symbolic, she thought, her heart catching with happiness.

Setting her down gently, he collected the small rucksack he'd brought and took her hand.

'I can smell the lemon blossom,' she said softly.

He smiled. 'I thought it would be a good place for a picnic.'

'Perfect,' she sighed as they left the beach and began to walk through a field of poppies, starred with white daisies. Flowers bloomed everywhere, as they did in Greece: in the ruined walls of some long-forgotten temple, in rock crevices, and—exuberantly flooding the area with a tapestry of colour—beneath the trees in the lemon grove.

'Fabulous.' Drenched in the heady scent of the lemon blossom, she could hardly speak for joy.

They sat on a low hill with views down to the lapis-lazuli sea, their backs to a warm wall where tiny lizards basked. Olivia put her head on Dimitri's shoulder and they remained in awed silence for a long time, their arms around each other.

It was so peaceful they might have been the only people in the world. Olivia thought dreamily that he *was* the only person in the world for her. And it was enough just to be with him, her troubled mind calm at last.

'Look. Swallowtails.'

She followed Dimitri's pointing finger and saw the butterflies hovering over the rock roses and sage. Now she could see little blue butterflies too, flitting about the wild lavender and rosemary bushes which were dotted about the lower ground.

Drugged by the lemon blossom, choked with happiness, she let her gaze wander over the orchids, fritillaries, anemones and blazing, blowsy poppies.

'I thought of this place so many times when I was in England,' she said quietly.

He kissed her, the first of many kisses that day. They kissed and touched and hugged one another often, and it seemed to her that he too was in a hazy dream.

Lazily they ate their simple meal of olive rolls with herbs, cold *kleftedes*, cheese, and cinnamon doughnuts soaked in honey syrup. Dimitri licked the syrup from her fingers and her lips, then fed her cherries and sweet oranges. They stayed in the grove for a long time, sipping wine and talking.

'You said you were between jobs. I hope you didn't have a male boss in the last one,' he muttered.

Olivia laughed and her expression told him that she was intent on teasing. 'I *did*. But he was seventy-one and could never catch me when I ran around his desk!' Dimitri glowered and gently sank his teeth into her bare shoulder. 'I'm fooling,' she said. 'He finally retired and

his son took over. I didn't like the way he looked at
me or the comments he made—as if he fancied his
chances—so I gave in my notice. And that's when I
decided it was a good opportunity to call you and say
I wanted a divorce.'

Dimitri stared out to sea, his heart thumping. A tiny
suspicion formed in his mind. 'So you don't have a job
now.'

'No. Which means I can stay.'

He was silent. Had she planned this all along?
Handed in her resignation and deliberately set out to
ensnare him again?

She began to kiss the side of his face and after a
moment he turned his head back to her, his eyes shuttered.

'Fortunate,' he rasped, and pushed her back to the
ground.

She felt dizzy from the perfume around them, the
wine, his searching, demanding mouth. Her arms
wound around his neck and she lured him with her
eyes.

'Let's go for a swim.' He had pulled her to her feet
before she could comment.

But she loved him, so she indulged him. They
stripped and walked into the sea, which was as warm
as a bath. She was too sleepy to do much more than
float or tread water, but Dimitri powered his way up
and down the little bay as if his life depended on it.
Amused, she waited till he emerged, water sluicing
from his body, and slowly joined him on the beach.

They dried one another and she felt such love for
him that she thought her heart would crack. They
walked to the headland to watch the sun set. As the
crimson sky turned to a dusky black, the cicadas began

to whirr in a deafening chorus. Fireflies speckled the darkness as they wandered back to the launch.

Olivia curled up on the sumptuous leather cushions, weak with rapture. He hadn't even made love to her. Sex had been superseded by something deeper: the delight they shared in being together. Sighing, she flung her head back and stared at the deep velvet sky and its pinpoints of tiny stars. She wanted this to be her destiny. And yearned for it to be permanent.

CHAPTER EIGHT

SLEEPILY, aware of the morning light, she flung a loving arm to Dimitri's side of the bed. Her eyes shot open. Her hand had landed on an empty space. She listened for the sound of the shower, but all was silent, except for the low murmur of voices below on the terrace.

Curious, she slid naked from the bed, her body still humming from Dimitri's tender lovemaking.

He was having breakfast with his mother, drinking *sketo*, the unsweetened coffee he favoured, and talking to her earnestly. Olivia smiled, guessing that he was giving his mother the news that their marriage had been saved.

Yawning, she stumbled to the shower and pulled on a pair of briefs and a simple white sundress, pleased with the golden tan she'd acquired the day before. Pausing only to put a pair of pearl studs in her ears, she fiddled impatiently with their fixings before hurrying down to the terrace.

'Olivia!'

Dimitri leapt to his feet when she appeared and came to kiss her cheek.

'Hello, darling!' she beamed. 'Hello, Marina.' She bent to kiss her mother-in-law. 'How are you?' she said, taking the chair Dimitri held for her.

'Very well,' smiled Marina vaguely, making Olivia blink with surprise. And then she discovered the reason for Marina's rather distracted manner. Nikos appeared, greeting them all—but with his steady gaze lovingly fixed on Marina.

Dimitri and Olivia exchanged amused glances. Nikos had stayed the night. And in whose bed? they signalled to one another.

'Nikos,' Dimitri said quietly, 'I want you to be one of the first to know. Olivia and I are back together again. I hope you are pleased. I know how you feel about wedding vows.'

He looked shocked for a moment, then his inbred courtesy came to the rescue. 'Of course. Congratulations,' he said a little stiffly.

'I imagine you'll be organising Eleni's wedding soon,' Dimitri went on tactfully. 'There are so many men buzzing about her I think she's spoilt for choice.'

Nikos gave a grin of pride, his disappointment eased. 'She's a catch.'

His eyes strayed to Marina, and Olivia wondered if Nikos would beat his daughter to the altar. She began to relax, feeling like the cat who'd got the cream, and tucked into her breakfast of yoghurt, fruit and honey with enthusiasm while Marina and Nikos chatted like children on a spree.

'I don't think they even noticed us going,' she giggled, when she and Dimitri stole away.

'Mother's a different person,' he said softly. 'Being in love changes everything.'

'Yes,' she agreed. 'It does.'

And she waited for him to make some kind of declaration to her. Or even to suggest they found another romantic spot—where he could tell her how deeply he was committed to her. Pulses fluttering, she waited in vain and bit her lip to conceal her disappointment.

They had reached the hall and he had remained si-

lent, engrossed in thought. At that moment she heard
his mobile ring. She automatically stiffened, her heart
sinking at the familiar and much hated sound. Many
times in the past that wretched tune had heralded a
change of plan, and she didn't want that to happen this
time, not when so much should be said about their
future together.

'Shan't be a moment.' He glanced at the read-out
and stiffened. 'Go up. I'll be with you in a moment.'
Preoccupied, he gave her face a casual caress then
pushed open his study door and slipped inside.

As she turned away despondently she felt her earring
slip to her shoulder and then fall to the ground, its weak
fastening probably dislodged by the brush of Dimitri's
hand. On her knees in search of it, she found herself
staring into the study past the half-open door. Her
stomach wrenched at the sight of Dimitri. It was obvious that he thought she had gone upstairs and had no
idea she was still around.

She froze. Noted the way his voice softened. The
pleasure on his face. The way he was murmuring in
such velvety tones.

He lounged against a bookcase, utterly relaxed and
content and then turned so that his back was to the
door. But she heard the word he uttered.

'Athena.'

For a moment she stopped breathing. It was unmistakable amid the flow of liquid Greek. And murmured
with a breathtaking tenderness that knifed straight
through her.

'Avrio,' he said. Tomorrow. She knew that much
Greek.

She walked in, unheard on the thick carpet, intending
to ask what was going on. That was when she saw the

birthday card. Blinking in disbelief, she stared blankly at the cheerful elephant holding three balloons. There was a cake in front of the animal, with three candles on it, and a badge marked with the number three. It could be for any child he knew, she reasoned, trying to stop her heart from beating so hard and fast it physically hurt.

Or, she thought in growing dismay, it might be a card for Athena's child. *Dimitri's* child. After all, it had been three years ago that she'd seen him lovingly helping Athena into his car.

The woman's forehead had been slicked with sweat. They had paused while her contractions made her gasp and Dimitri had kissed Athena's beautiful face and held her firmly in his strong arms, murmuring something soothing and encouraging.

Everything he'd done, every look he'd given Athena, had shown the love he felt for his pregnant mistress. Wouldn't any man be the same? she had thought at the time. His child was about to be born. A time of joy and masculine pride. A time of tenderness.

Olivia winced. She had been frozen with horror, unable to move or speak. After all, she had been married for six months. That meant he'd known his mistress was pregnant when he'd walked down the aisle between those wreaths of white flowers linked by satin ribbon. When he had been exhorted to love her as if she were his own body. Lies. All lies. All deceit.

She had stared at Dimitri and Athena, a thousand thoughts racing through the turmoil of her mind. During their wedding, all the time they had circled the altar whilst being pelted with rose petals, sugared almonds and rice, had he thought of Athena and his child growing in her womb?

Tortured by this, Olivia had half fallen out of the car after Dimitri had driven away with his pregnant mistress. She had been violently sick. The man she had idolised and respected and loved so deeply had proved to be worthless and shallow. She had battered her fists on the car until the pain was too much to bear any more. But she hadn't cried. Her anger had been too intense for tears.

She feared that Athena might be still in the picture. If so, he had lied to her yet again.

She took a shuddering breath, her sad eyes lingering on Dimitri's gently angled head. Obviously he must feel some kind of love for the mother of his child. But she wondered if this might be the future wife he'd spoken about, the woman he must persuade Marina to accept one day.

Her world seemed to tilt and then steady again. She winced, remembering that she had been close to declaring her own love—and unwittingly facing the humiliation of Dimitri's rejection.

Without a word she crept out, emotion filling her throat like a hard pebble. Tears began to sting her eyes and she found herself stumbling through the hall, half tripping over her own feet.

'Olivia!'

Silently she groaned at Marina's peremptory tone. Dimitri's mother was the next-to-last person she wanted to see at this moment. Incapable of speaking, she flapped a hand of dismissal in her mother-in-law's direction and continued on her way.

'Are you drunk? What is the matter with you?' Marina persisted.

'Dimitri! Who else?' she flung wretchedly, and headed blindly for the stairs.

'Wait.' Marina caught her arm and spun her around.

'No! Leave me alone!' Desperate for somewhere quiet to nurse her wounds, she tried to wrench away, but her mother-in-law was surprisingly strong and determined.

'I want to know what he's done,' Marina said sharply. 'I insist.'

'So you can enjoy my misery?' Olivia shot.

'No. Because I want him to be as happy as I am.'

Olivia slumped in capitulation. Why not tell her? What did it matter any more?

'Not here,' she jerked out, feeling venomous. She glared at the study door. 'The way I'm feeling, if he comes out of there I might damage his face permanently.'

Marina registered shock. 'Come into the salon,' she ordered hastily. 'I think I should know what is going on.'

Imprisoned by the firm fingers that held her wrist in a vice-like grip, Olivia trailed after the thin, upright figure into the sunny room. She knew that she had to be careful what she said. If Marina knew the marriage was really over now, then that would leave Eleni free to pester him. It would be ages before the divorce came through and she'd be stuck in Greece, with her life on hold.

And yet... Olivia paled. They couldn't continue with their ridiculous pretence. Not now. It would be unbearable, living here day after day, exchanging kisses and loving looks with him. Even worse to watch him drive away, wondering if he was heading for Athena's arms. She just couldn't trust him.

Hell, she thought grimly, he wouldn't know love if

it were burnt with a hot poker in capital letters on his steel-hard heart.

'I'm waiting.'

Olivia heaved in a hard, hurting lungful of air. Determined to keep the angry tears at bay, she lifted her chin.

'I—I had thought that Dimitri and I might be able to forget the past and start again—'

'So he said at breakfast. Don't you love him after all?'

'No,' she said flatly. 'I don't.'

Marina's eyes widened. 'So I was right all along!'

'Not exactly. I really thought he'd changed. But I'm not sure any more. Sometimes I think he might have the morals of an alley cat.'

'It sounds as if you hate him,' Marina said.

'I do!' she hurled emphatically.

'So tell me, if you hate him, why are you upset?' her mother-in-law demanded. 'Is it because you've lost the chance to live a life of luxury again?'

'No!' Olivia yelled. 'Because I love him to distraction!'

'I'm confused. The note you left when you disappeared said the opposite,' Marina pointed out.

Olivia frowned. 'No, it didn't. I said there wasn't any point in staying when *he* didn't love me! Heavens above, you saw how devastated I was when I saw him with his mistress! I've always loved him, more fool me. I know what you thought. That I went after him because he was rich. Well, I didn't know that he was wealthy to begin with. We went to small, intimate restaurants. His apartment was functional rather than luxurious. He drove an expensive car—but then a lot of men go into debt to get the car of their dreams. And by the time I knew he actually headed the vast Angelaki empire I was madly in love and I didn't care what or who he was, so long as we could be together.

'I'm stupid enough to have fallen for him, like all the other women who worship him and leap into his bed whenever he crooks his finger! Every time I'm with him I think that I'm the only woman in the world for him and it's the most wonderful feeling I've ever known. He has me dangling on a string and dancing to his tune like some wretched puppet. But I've got feelings, Marina! I love him and I hate him because he can hurt me so deeply that I can barely bring myself to continue living!' She put a hand to her aching forehead. 'I have to go,' she said weakly. 'I can't allow myself to stay near him. He's destroying me, inch by inch. I have to be shot of him. And I want you to help me to find somewhere to live in Greece while I'm waiting for the divorce. I'm sure you'll be willing,' she added with bitterness.

Her mother-in-law seemed stunned by Olivia's outburst. 'I—I had no idea you felt like that,' she said eventually. There was a long silence.

'You believe me?' Olivia mumbled.

'Yes,' Marina said softly. 'I recognise what you are saying. I felt the same about my Theo.' She smiled when Olivia blinked in surprise. 'Yes. The Angelaki men have a habit of rejecting the love of their wives. You left my son because you'd been hurt by his affair with that woman we saw—'

'I think he's still seeing her.' Olivia tried unsuccessfully to hide her pain. 'Perhaps because of their child. Perhaps because… ' She couldn't bring herself to say any more of her fears.

Marina frowned hard. 'My dear, I'm going to give you some advice that might surprise you.'

'I want practical help, not advice,' Olivia muttered.

To her surprise, her mother-in-law's eyes softened. 'You'll get it. But…first, something that will interest you… It may astonish you to know how awful Dimitri has been since you left. Bad-tempered, difficult to please, with little time for friends or family.'

'Why are you telling me this?' she asked.

'Because Nikos has been talking to me about you. He thinks well of you and I trust his judgement. So I'm telling you that Dimitri was deeply affected by your disappearance.'

What did she care? She shrugged. 'I imagine his pride was hurt.'

'Or maybe he was devastated when you left and wanted you back.' Marina sighed. 'Who knows? All I can say is that he was not happy and his mistress was obviously not giving him what he wanted. However, he has been happy since you returned. I will tell you this. If you truly love him then you must accept him as he is.'

'An unfaithful cheat?' Olivia spluttered.

'You wouldn't be the first to turn a blind eye to adultery,' Marina said, an unhappy light in her dark eyes. She hesitated. 'Olivia, I know my Theo had a mistress somewhere. But I saw no reason to leave him just because he'd found a younger woman sexier than me.'

Olivia stared in amazement. 'You didn't mind?'

'Of course I did. But I wanted him,' she said simply.

It seemed an awful compromise. And she wondered if that was why Marina seemed so bitter about life. 'Were you happy at all?' she asked gently, astonished that her mother-in-law had told her such an intimate confidence.

There was a fleeting flash of anguish tightening the gaunt face. 'No,' she admitted. 'And I confess I probably made him miserable with my sharp tongue and drove him even further from me. But I couldn't help it, I loved and needed him so much. Maybe I even drove him to another woman's arms in the first place. I was intensely possessive.'

Olivia could feel Marina's sorrow because she knew the same pain of rejection and humiliation. On an impulse, she put her arms around her mother-in-law in an understanding hug.

'I couldn't do what you did. You're much stronger than me,' she confided.

'Or more pig-headed,' Marina said with a rueful sigh. She pushed away slightly and looked at Olivia with sympathy as she tucked an escaped strand of hair behind Olivia's ear in an almost gentle, motherly gesture. 'But I couldn't bear being cast aside so I pretended not to know the truth. It seems that Dimitri is like his father. Let him have his freedom. You must decide on your course of action. Either divorce him— or stay married and ignore his absences.'

Olivia gazed at Marina helplessly. 'I can't live without him,' she admitted. 'Yet I can't live *with* him if he's having affairs. Or even one affair. How could I lie in bed wondering if he was coming home, wondering who he was with? It would crucify me. And yet I don't really feel I'm alive without him. Oh, Marina!' she whispered, as the finality of the situation began to hit home. 'I have to go. Help me, I beg you—'

'There you are!' The two women jumped at the sound of Dimitri's strong voice. He stared in amazement at their friendly embrace. 'What on earth is going on?'

Olivia's mouth tightened into a thin, hard line. 'Character assassination on my part.'

He looked puzzled by her hostility. And so sublimely innocent that her knees automatically weakened. He was utterly desirable to her as he pushed a hand through his silky hair and it tumbled boyishly onto his broad forehead.

'But…I thought you… We were going out somewhere today—'

'Oh, is that still on?' she asked coolly. 'I imagined you had better things to do or other people to see.'

There was a tightening of his face. His lashes dipped and lifted again and he shot his mother a sharp glance. To Olivia, he looked taken aback—and highly embarrassed. Proof, if she needed it, of his guilt.

'The phone call! Of course. I'm sorry I had to leave you.' He smiled with agonisingly tender affection and she melted, as she always did, her heart pounding with love, her head, however, bursting with ungovernable anger. 'But I'm here now, and we have the day ahead of us. You choose where we're going—'

'*We* are going nowhere. I am leaving this house and getting out of your life for good,' she said, ice dripping from every word.

He was instantly alert. 'Leaving? I don't think so,' he sliced at her.

Tactfully, Marina muttered something and slipped from the room past the granite-faced Dimitri.

'Watch!' Olivia spat out.

He folded his arms across his chest, his entire body taut with menace. 'Care to tell me the reason for your change of mind?'

'With pleasure! I'm sick and tired,' she ground out, 'of being used by you!'

'You might be tired but that, I imagine, is because you were unusually enthusiastic last night,' he growled, looking offended that she'd apparently forgotten the eager part she had played.

'I like sex!' she hurled. Liked? Adored it passionately—with him—until she had come to her senses after that phone call and realised that she was probably nothing but a toy for him to play with!

Dimitri's eyes narrowed. She had reduced a memorable day and night to basic lust. His heart pounded as he realised with mounting dismay that for him it had been a deeper experience. Fool that he was. He knew she had never loved him. She'd made that perfectly clear.

His fists clenched. Every instinct was now driving him to punish her. To exact some kind of revenge. He would break her. He had to. No woman was going to treat him with such contempt.

'You don't need to tell me you like sex. I'd noticed for myself,' he drawled.

She flushed. 'I respond to you because you're good at it. I hear that comes of continual practice. But what we did last night doesn't mean I like you, or that I accept your peculiar morality—'

'Just a minute. What has my mother said?' Putting two and two together, he moved forward, till he was just a foot away, studying her with shrewd eyes. Olivia had radically changed her mind about their arrangement. There could be only one explanation. 'I thought she was happy for me that you were staying. But…has she offered you money to go?'

Olivia gasped and cracked her hand across his face.

He caught it a second too late, and for a moment she was terrified by the black glitter in his eyes. Then he did something extraordinary. He pulled her against him, tipped her head back roughly and kissed her hard.

She fought him—and herself. Felt her body sliding against his. The fierce beat of his heart. He cupped one breast and bent her backwards, dominating her, firing her with his skilful, hateful caresses till she sank into them, her defiance blown away by her own body's betrayal.

'You want me!' he gritted. 'That's obvious. OK. We'll deal. Shall I offer you even more money to stay?'

Olivia drew her head back, hot blue eyes blazing into his. 'I can't be bought or bribed!' she grated. 'I don't want your mother's money or yours—'

'You took the maintenance I sent you,' he said in a cynical drawl.

Her eyes widened in utter bewilderment. 'What maintenance?'

'Paid into the English bank where we had a joint account, remember? Or was that small change for you?' he scathed.

'You don't know which bank I use! I go to a different one in—' She firmed her mouth, remembering not to tell him where she'd been for the past three years. 'If you've put money in our old bank,' she said grimly, 'then it's still there untouched, with the rest of the cash we'd put by. There are probably statements heaped up on the mat of your London apartment. Haven't you been there?'

'No. Avoided it like the plague,' he muttered. His eyes narrowed. 'Are you telling me you haven't taken a penny?'

She applauded. 'Well done.'

He scowled at her sarcasm but he looked uncomfortable. 'I thought—'

'I know what you thought,' she snapped. 'That I worship money.'

'Don't you?'

'No more than the next woman. Of course I like new clothes and eating in restaurants and trips to New York. Of course it was wonderful to have financial security. But that came at a price—'

'Me.'

'You,' she agreed, deciding not to elaborate any more.

His mouth tightened. 'How did you manage when you left?'

She glared. 'I told you. On my own earnings. I don't need a man to provide for me. Does that tell you something about my money-grabbing tactics? Does that suggest I might *not* have taken a bribe from your mother?'

Clearly surprised, he touched his face where the marks of her fingers still lingered. 'I deserved this, it seems,' he said stiffly.

'And more!' she muttered.

His eyes flashed but he nodded. 'I apologise. However, it doesn't explain why you are so determined to leave. Only last night you seemed perfectly reconciled to amusing yourself with me for an indefinite period.'

'And now I want to go home,' she muttered, not daring to tell him that his cavalier attitude to women distressed her. He might think she cared—and that was the last thing she wanted him to know.

'This is an attempt to wring more alimony out of me, isn't it? Yes,' he said when she opened her mouth to protest, 'I know you haven't touched the maintenance, but that's because you didn't know it was there. The fact remains that you admit you like financial security. Your lawyer has already accepted a substantial sum on your behalf which you want to increase—'

'I don't want it!' she snapped.

His eyebrow arced up in surprise. 'Really? Then ring him. I am calling your bluff, Olivia.'

'I don't know what time it is—'

'Excuses, excuses.'

'All right!' Eyes glittering, she picked up the phone on his desk and made the call, instructing the astonished Paul that she didn't want one penny from Dimitri.

'He's forced you to do this!' Paul protested. 'Olivia, if he's seduced you with the sole purpose of—'

'Maybe he has, maybe he hasn't,' she snapped. 'I don't care any more. I just want to wash my hands of everything connected with him as soon as I possibly can. I refuse to be accused of whoring. As far as I'm concerned, whatever has the Angelaki stamp on it is contaminated and poisonous.' Shaking, she put the receiver down. 'Satisfied?' she flung at Dimitri. 'You can't accuse me of marrying you for your money now. Or divorcing you for it.'

'Why the devil did you marry me, then?' he flung angrily.

'If you don't know, I sure as hell am not going to tell you!' she yelled.

He went very still. His eyes searched hers. 'Love?'

It was the way he said the word that made her tremble, imbuing it with such tenderness that she felt her heart would break.

'Love,' she agreed, her face mournful. 'It's terrible when it dies.'

So that was it. She had loved him once—maybe in

the early days of their relationship. But when they were married she'd been restless. After she'd run away, the passage of time must have killed whatever feelings she'd once had for him. At least now he knew the truth and could act accordingly. She would regret ever giving him the impression that their love had been reignited.

His teeth clenched. She looked suddenly vulnerable, her lashes thick crescents on her cheeks. Her mouth seemed carved in sorrow and he had the urge to kiss it into smiles. Instead, he scowled and sought to bind her to him. Because he wasn't finished with her yet.

'We're getting nowhere. The plain fact is that you can't leave,' he said in cutting tones, 'because you would be breaking your promise.'

She stared at him in loathing. 'I didn't promise that I'd live here!'

'No,' he said, his mouth savage. 'But you agreed that you'd pretend we were in love until Eleni gave up her quest to be the next Mrs Angelaki. And lovers don't live in separate places, not if they're married and rebuilding their relationship.'

She swallowed the ache in her throat. Tried to ignore the nausea swirling around in her stomach. He looked utterly ruthless and determined. The set of his body and the hardness of his eyes intimidated her. He actually wanted her to stay around and flatter his ego in bed and out of it, while she slowly died inside!

'You can't and you won't hold me to that!' she cried, distraught.

'Believe me, I can and I will,' he growled, his brows a dark line above coal-black eyes. 'It was a promise. And one I'll make you keep.'

'I can't bear to be near you!' she cried raggedly.

His eyes flashed a warning, and then his hands descended on her shoulders as if intent on crushing her slender bones.

'Do it,' he gritted. 'You want this farce of a marriage annulled in record time. It's the only way.'

'I can't keep the pretence going! I feel sick at the thought of being touched by you—'

'Then,' he said, frighteningly tight and angry, 'I have to congratulate you on your performance to date. You almost convinced me that you enjoyed every second.'

'Let me go,' she said feebly.

'No. You won't wriggle out of this.'

She gave a helpless groan. 'Please, Dimitri!'

'Nothing would give me more pleasure than to see the back of you,' he snapped. 'But you have a job to do. I'll make it easier for you, though. You will continue to live here. We will leave for trips together and return together. This place is a hotbed of gossip and Eleni will soon discover that we are rarely separated—'

'I'm not spending all day with you—'

'You'll do whatever I say,' he growled. 'At night—'

'I won't sleep with you!'

'I can't remember us sleeping much before,' he said drily. 'But I agree. You will sleep in my room for appearances' sake, but I will go elsewhere—'

'Where?' she demanded, thinking of Athena.

'Anywhere. Does it matter?' he said impatiently. 'Agree to this and I'll get my lawyers working around the clock. You'll soon be free of me. And I will be free of you,' he finished under his breath.

If only she hadn't given her word. He had trapped her in an impossible situation. She lifted a haunted face.

'I have no choice,' she muttered. And ran from the room before she burst into tears.

CHAPTER NINE

THE boat sped once again across the aquamarine sea, leaving behind the small community where her happiness had been found and lost for the second time. The white houses faded against the background of olive trees covering the hills and soon the harbour and the little boats there were no longer visible.

The contrast between how she felt on this day and how she had felt the previous day was too painful to contemplate.

She knew that Eleni had watched them leave the house from the drawing-room window. And Olivia had felt a pang of sympathy for her, knowing what that misery was like and how horribly it could possess and destroy. She didn't like what she was doing—and wished it were all over.

They headed for a sickle-shaped beach backed by tamarisk trees where they had spent many glorious hours in the past. She tried hard not to think of those days. What was the point? They'd been a fantasy strictly of her own making, after all.

Dimitri killed the engine and let the boat drift on the gentle swell towards the shore. Like her, he wore beige shorts, though his T-shirt was blue not white, and more close-fitting, hugging the contours of his broad chest.

He might have been a fisherman but for his imperious manner that marked him out as a man used to being obeyed. With a shiver of apprehension she watched him leap into the crystal water. The muscles

of his arms stood out as he hauled the boat further up
the beach and she jerked her head away to stare at the
distant islands out to sea because she didn't want to
moon over him any more. Those days were over.

'Take my hand.'

So many times they had done this. She had ended
up in those strong, supposedly loving arms and they
had kissed and murmured their adoration while the water swirled around their legs.

'No.'

Determined to be independent of him, she stood up,
preparing to jump into the shallow water.

'Olivia,' he snapped, 'she can see us from the
house.' He jerked his head at the promontory. Of
course she knew that. She could easily make out the
mansion rising from the trees. 'Just do it.'

She did. With bad grace. And she didn't know how
it happened, but one minute she was upright, the next
she had fallen into two feet of water. On top of Dimitri.
They surfaced, spluttering. His arms held her securely.
Too securely.

For a moment she responded, her mouth seeking his
in a terrible knee-jerk reaction. How wrong could her
instincts be?

'Very good,' he rasped, fastening his mouth greedily
on hers.

She could feel the anger in him and fought to be
free, gasping when the water swirled over their partly
submerged bodies.

'That'll do.'

Abruptly he let her go. Clamping his hands on her
waist, he hauled her up. Water streamed down his contorted face. His eyes were small black chips of glass,
his mouth a tight, grim line.

She had never seen him so close to losing control. He bit out a single word with frightening venom. *'Bitch.'*

Blindly she staggered to the shore and concentrated on twisting her hair to wring out the water. She was trembling, afraid of what he would do. And suddenly she knew she couldn't stay here all day, in full sight of the house. He'd be demanding that they gave a convincing performance of two lovers enjoying themselves and she shuddered to think how far he expected her to go.

'I refuse to sit on a beach all day while you pretend to make advances and Eleni watches, poor girl,' she said stubbornly. 'I'm not an exhibit. And I won't have you grope me more than you have to! Take me somewhere else.'

With a mutter of irritation, he swept his palms over his wet face and shot, 'Where, then?'

'I don't know. Anywhere would be hell,' she snapped.

'Helpful,' he clipped.

Her temper flared. 'If we *have* to go anywhere together, I'd prefer a drive into the hills. I can sit on one side of a mountain and you can sit on the other, out of my sight,' she said coldly.

'You're right,' he growled to her surprise. 'I'd prefer not to touch you. Get into the boat. We'll return to the house and change our clothes—and our destination.'

Mutely she obeyed. In a horrible, deadly silence, they returned to the harbour. Clearly in a filthy mood, Dimitri helped her to the quayside.

'Face me.'

'No.'

Ruthlessly he grabbed her arms and stared into her

mutinous eyes. 'A few minutes of simpering, that's all we need,' he bit. 'My arm around you while we walk to the house. Your head leaning on my shoulder. And if you imagine I'm enjoying this, then think again. I have finally discovered what you are, Olivia. A cold-hearted little tramp who seeks only to satisfy her own selfish needs.'

'And you,' she slashed, 'are a swaggering bully, with no concept of love or decency, who must hate women because all you do is betray them and hurt them!'

His arm wrapped around her waist. Stiffly they moved up the little road. Olivia knew she couldn't keep this up. Being with him like this was a living nightmare.

To her relief, there was no sign of Eleni when they reached the house. When Dimitri enquired, he was told that she had gone out with a young man in a sports car. Perhaps their ruse was working. She hoped so.

Walking indoors, she changed into a blue cotton sundress and met Dimitri by the garage block.

'I suppose this stupid trip is necessary?' she asked haughtily.

'I wouldn't be doing it otherwise. I'd rather be sitting behind my desk dealing with a mountain of mail,' he snapped. 'But I'm prepared to do this to get you out of my hair. Get in.'

He looked cool in stone cotton jeans and T-shirt, but when their fingers brushed as he opened the car door for her she discovered that his skin was burning hot. She snatched her hand away and cradled it on her lap as if it had been scorched.

The moment Dimitri flung himself into the driver's seat she felt crowded. A hurried, slanting glance at his granite face told her that the hostility between them had reached epic proportions.

Silent and rigid with tension, she cringed back in the seat and clipped on the safety belt. He drove with grim concentration into the mountains. Miserably she stared out of the window, hardly noticing the scenery. Ruined classical temples flashed by. Tiny domed churches, secret villages designed to be hidden from marauders and the Ottoman tax collectors. The road zigzagged up a steep hill terraced with vineyards and they only came to a stop when a flock of goats blocked their way.

'Health to your hands,' Dimitri said courteously to the men amiably moving the goats along, and smiles and greetings returned his traditional acknowledgement.

It was sickening the way everybody adored and admired him, she thought bitterly. He was a fraud. A man without a heart.

The car crawled along at a snail's pace till Olivia felt like screaming. Her head ached from the tension and misery she was keeping under tight control. This hideous situation was making her ill and she resented that.

'Where are we going?' she muttered through her teeth.

'I've no idea.'

She drew in a sharp breath. 'Find somewhere quickly where we can stop. I'm not spending the whole day cooped up in this car with you.'

'I'm killing time. If you have any ideas, then share them,' he said sarcastically.

'Any hill will do, providing you're on the other side of it!' she muttered.

He stabbed a hard finger at the radio. The soft strains

of a sad love song murmured through the icy silence. Olivia closed her eyes, squeezing them tightly to stop the tears from escaping. Unable to bear the tug on her emotions any longer, she punched the 'off' button and slumped back miserably in the seat.

He shot her a quick glance and wished he hadn't. Her lashes were wet with tears and there was a tell-tale shiny trail shimmering down her cheek to the corner of her mouth. Why her distress should upset him, he didn't know. But it did. He wanted to scoop her up into his arms and soothe her, to say that everything would be all right—when he knew full well that in a few days they'd be parting for ever.

And what of his revenge? He had meant to make her dependent on him. To hunger for him and beg to be loved in return. Then he had intended to reject her so that she knew what it was like to feel passionately for someone and be callously dismissed, as she had dismissed him. But now he couldn't do that. His feelings were too raw, his own emotions too disturbed. She was slowly destroying him. All his instincts were telling him to call a halt to the charade they'd agreed to play. He couldn't stand this disruption of his mind and body any longer.

'Olivia,' he began huskily.

A movement told him that she had averted her head. Quickly estimating where they were, he pulled off at the next turning and drove down a bumpy track. They had to work out a strategy for ending this as soon— and as painlessly—as they could.

Nikos was already lining up eligible young men for Eleni—and apparently she had dates every night that week. He was sure that soon she would no longer be a problem.

That meant he could risk putting Olivia on the plane home that evening. As that thought permeated his consciousness, his eyes widened at the sharp contraction in his chest. Astonishingly, his head seemed to explode with pain. And he screeched to a stop in a flurry of dust and burning rubber.

'What?' yelled Olivia, clutching her chest. 'What on earth are you doing? You nearly broke my ribs!'

Slowly he turned, dazed, stunned by his realisation. In her anger she looked unbelievably beautiful, her huge blue eyes fixed on him in searing fury. There were small freckles on her gold-tinged nose, winging across her cheekbones in such a heartbreakingly appealing way that he felt his hand move out to touch them before he knew what he was doing.

'Keep your hands off me!' she stormed, slapping it away. 'And explain why you're practising emergency stops!'

Such a soft mouth. Designed for kissing. The heat in his loins intensified and he had to look away. He needed to think. To talk to her. To put an outrageous suggestion to her.

The risk to his pride was incalculable, but if he didn't he'd never forgive himself.

'I'm sorry. I had an idea,' he croaked, his mouth dry with nerves.

'Let's hope it involves imminent separation.'

Muttering something rude under her breath, she folded her arms and waited for him to drive on.

It took a moment before he could clear his brain and find the gearstick. When he did, his gaze lingered on the long, tanned length of her leg and he knew he'd do anything to keep her.

Olivia felt the heat of his eyes and tugged her skirt

down over her thigh. 'Don't even think it,' she snapped.

Without a word, he put the car into gear and drove on carefully down the rutted track, at the end of which he parked.

'I think we should talk,' he said quietly.

'Is that so? First, I don't trust you,' she muttered. 'Second, it's a bit late for that. Third, I have nothing to say.'

'I have, though. I think I will surprise you.'

A quick glance at his face told her what she'd feared on hearing his low, seductive tones.

'You sit here and surprise yourself, then,' she said, flinging open the door. 'I'm going for a walk. Alone.'

The way her body moved as she strode away just made his breath choke in his throat. She held herself proudly, the tilt of her beautiful head a little too high on that slender neck. The stiff swing of her arms and the jerky movements of her legs were touchingly child-like in their anger. That, more than anything else, made his heart do a small skip.

There was no woman like Olivia. Dazed, he watched the resolute figure of his wife, with her blonde hair flying in the breeze, and prepared to use every weapon at his disposal to persuade her to stay.

When she reached the top of a small rise Olivia found herself looking down on a small circular theatre, rather like the one at Epidauros but with only ten rows of marble seats. It had been poorly preserved and had become overgrown with scrub and wild flowers, though the central court—where the actors had stood perhaps two thousand years earlier—was still intact.

Determined to while away the time until she could return to the privacy of her own room at the mansion, she began to walk around the upper rim, blanking her mind to everything.

The tread of her feet disturbed brightly coloured lizards, their quick, darting movements making it look as if they were jewels flashing in the bright sun. As she brushed the low bushes of thyme and velvety sage their leaves released powerful oils, scenting the air heavily.

Her heart jerked. She would miss so much. There would be perhaps one or two days left here and then she would be going home. Away from Dimitri…

The pain in her bruised heart stole her breath, and she sat down on the cold marble seat. Everything had been so perfect. Dimitri, the love she'd thought they'd shared, this beautiful, fierce blue sky, the warmth of the sun on her aching body, the fabulous views and fascinating history.

'I want you to listen to me, Olivia.'

She blinked and looked down to the source of the voice. Dimitri stood in the circular court below, as he had in Epidauros that fatal day when he'd said he loved her—shortly before she had discovered him with Athena. The acoustics were perfect. Although he spoke quietly, she could hear every word.

Coldly she stared down at his dark head. He had nothing to say that would touch her. Not now.

'It doesn't matter that you don't love me,' he said, his face lifted up to where she stood. She tensed. He looked as if he was pleading with her. 'The fact is…' He sighed, with a helpless spread of his hands. 'I don't think I can bear it if you go…'

Liar! Rage and pain seared through her. Turning her head away, she tightened her jaw. Now what? Did he need half an hour of sex? She would have left him there, spouting his lies, but she felt suddenly bone-tired. Let him ramble on. It wouldn't make any difference.

'...and when it dawned on me that you'd be almost certain to leave in a day or two, I...'

Oh, clever, she thought, jerking her head back to see what fake attitude he was adopting now. Contemptuously she noted the dipped head, the clearing of his throat. What an actor he would have made. If she didn't know any better, she would have been convinced of his misery.

Especially when he raised his head. Even from where she sat it was possible to see that his eyes were shining a little too brightly. Her tender heart contracted, and then she came to her senses and anger once again filled every cell in her body. Hard-eyed, she let him continue, to see how far he'd go to get what he wanted.

'It's true, Olivia. I can't live without you!' he blurted out throatily. 'Do what you like here. Live where you like, so long as it's not too far away. But let me see you sometimes. Let me prove to you that...' His chest rose high and fell again, and she heard the long hiss of his breath as it emptied his lungs. 'Olivia,' he cried in ringing tones, 'I love you more deeply than I ever imagined. I always have, always will. Let me love you. Take care of you.' He knelt on the dusty stone floor, and she stared at him, mesmerised. 'I do love you, Olivia. With every inch of my body, every breath I take, every thought in my head. I want you to be the mother of my children—'

She jumped to her feet, unable to stand any more. And she walked back to the car. Too late, she thought unhappily. He was making his pitch at the wrong time, because it just hurt her to hear him protesting his love, to be offered the chance to bear his children.

Stumbling, she tripped and fell onto the stony track with a cry of pain as her head hit a small rock. For a moment she lay there, all the stuffing knocked out of her by Dimitri's cruel pretence. And suddenly he was with her, gently turning her over, gathering her into his arms.

'Leave me!' she moaned, and thudded her fists weakly into his chest.

'You're hurt,' he said in a choking whisper.

His finger lightly explored her forehead and she winced, her eyes narrowing at his devastated expression. Why would he look so miserable? It didn't make sense. Unless he was upset at being turned down.

'Anything else damaged?' he enquired, still croaky.

Her heart. It had been smashed beyond all repair, she wanted to tell him. But he was gently rubbing at her elbows and the heels of her hands, which were white with road dust, and she had to bite her lip to stop herself from releasing a small sob of self-pity.

Because the care and concern in his expression just made her ache.

'I want to go back,' she said in a tone as dead as her eyes. 'I don't want to do this any more. I've reached my limit.'

'Of course.' He swallowed and looked at her as if his world had come to an end. 'I love you, Olivia,' he jerked hoarsely.

She turned her head away and stared coldly into the mid-distance. After a moment his hands slid away and he helped her to her feet.

'There's a first-aid kit in the car,' he muttered.

Snatching her arm away from his supporting hand, she grimly stomped back along the track. Mentally she left the beauties of Greece, and one Greek in particular, far behind.

When he came up to where she sat on the ground, with the first-aid kit on her lap, she pointedly ignored him and continued to dab at her forehead with the calendula cream. The silence seemed to crush her like a heavy weight. Briefly she looked up at him, to see why he was standing there, staring at her, and she stopped breathing.

His face was dead. The vitality and vibrancy had gone. His skin had a greyish tint and his eyes were no longer a gleaming black but a cold, muddy brown. The liveliness of his mobile mouth had become a pained, downturned line. And the change in him made her want to cry.

'You drive,' he growled.

She blinked as he spun on his heel and sat in the passenger seat. Slowly she got to her feet, stunned by the extraordinary way that Dimitri's vigour had ebbed from his body. And for the life of her she couldn't understand why—unless it was because he feared that marriage to Eleni was inevitable now.

It wasn't until they drove up to the mansion that Dimitri spoke again. 'I'll arrange a flight for you to England this evening,' he said in strangled tones. 'My jet is in Paris. It'll have to be a commercial airline.'

'Fine.' Numb with misery, she crawled out of the car. To her surprise, he immediately moved behind the wheel. 'Where are you going?' she blurted out in astonishment, alarmed that he would be driving in his odd state of mind.

'I don't think it's any of your business,' he said wearily, and stamped his foot viciously on the accelerator.

She stared after him in consternation. And in a flash

of inspiration she knew where he could be heading. To Athena, the ever-loving mother of his child, who'd stood by him all these years.

Olivia's eyes took on the colour of slate. She fished out the car keys he'd given her and grimly marched to the garage block.

All the time he'd been slinging her that line about loving her—and looking as if he believed every wretched word—he had fully intended to keep Athena on, as a back-up.

Well, she thought, her fingers gripping the wheel as if it were her lifeline, she would confront him at Athena's house and then he'd be forced to admit that everything he'd said was a lie.

CHAPTER TEN

ATHENA stroked his forehead, but her gentle fingers did nothing to smooth the deep furrows there. The pain was too deep. Unreachable.

She had gasped when she'd opened the door to her cottage. Stumbling in, almost drunk from the turmoil raging around in his mind, he'd caught a glimpse of himself in a mirror and had realised why she was so shocked.

He hardly recognised himself in the zombie who stared back with graveyard eyes. Love and Olivia had done this to him.

Now he sat listlessly at Athena's feet in the garden overlooking Selonda Bay, two glasses of wine poured and forgotten, while little Theo played happily with his toy cars.

Warm and loving as always, Athena asked no questions but waited for him to speak. He didn't know where to begin. His future seemed utterly bleak and uninviting. He would have done anything for Olivia. Given her whatever she wanted. And she'd turned him down.

Bone-weary from hurling his emotions into a void, only to have them slung back at him, he leaned his head back against Athena's knees and closed his eyes. But he still saw Olivia. If it was anything like the last time she left him he'd see her there for a long while.

He groaned. Lightly Athena's fingers caressed his face. And then they stilled abruptly.

169

Looking up, Dimitri was astonished to see Olivia. He blinked, thinking he must be hallucinating, because she didn't know where Athena lived or where he might have gone, but she was definitely there, by the low gate that led into the garden. She flung it open angrily and strode towards him, her face set, hair streaming behind her in golden waves.

'What a pretty scene!' she scorned. 'And you claim you love me?'

'Yes,' was all he could manage—and that was hardly coherent.

'You're living in a make-believe world, Dimitri!' she flashed. 'Get real. While you're with one woman you love her. You honestly seem to believe that. Then five minutes later you're with some other lover—and you offer undying love to *her!* It's not normal,' she snapped. 'Either you know full well what you're doing, in which case you're the lowest form of life that exists, or you are deluded, in which case you need a psychiatrist—'

'I don't have any confusion,' he husked. 'I love you. It's that simple.'

Olivia seemed shocked. She looked at Athena and then back at him again. 'You can say that in front of her? I can't understand how Greek women accept infidelity so easily,' she jerked.

'They don't,' Athena said quietly. 'What are you trying to say, Olivia?'

At the gentleness in the other woman's voice, Olivia's eyes filled with tears.

'I loved him!' she sobbed. 'He was everything to me! And when I came back to Greece and saw him again I knew I would always feel that way! Then he lied to me and deceived me and pretended he cared when all the time he was two-timing me! I can't bear it! And I hate being so feeble and crying like this over such a louse!' She rounded on Dimitri. 'You've broken my heart! I hope you'll be miserable as hell and some woman will hurt you as you've hurt me...'

She broke down in a storm of weeping. Athena hurried to her and led her inside the cottage, frantically waving Dimitri back when he made to follow.

'This is my bathroom,' she said gently to Olivia. 'You can freshen up here and then we can talk. Dimitri isn't the kind of man you claim he is—'

'See him for what he is! You've been taken in by him, as I was!'

Olivia wrenched on the tap and glared at Athena in the mirror. The woman was older than she'd seemed from a distance. Perhaps forty-five, with several grey hairs. Probably good in bed, Olivia thought bitterly. She sluiced her face and dried it.

And then she noticed a photograph of Athena with Dimitri. No, not Dimitri...

Olivia whirled, and went to study the snapshot. It showed Athena and Dimitri's *father*, Theo, looking adoringly at each other. She held her breath in shock and looked around. On a shelf was a photo of Theo, smiling into the camera with that besotted look adopted by all lovers.

She strode into the adjoining bedroom and swallowed hard. There were pictures everywhere. Theo on a beach somewhere, laughing. Theo...

Wide-eyed, she spun around to stare at the puzzled Athena. 'Dimitri's father?' she breathed.

Athena smiled fondly and stroked one of the photos. 'My darling Theo,' she said softly.

It was too much for Olivia. She went outside and

faced the tense-looking Dimitri, who was standing by a wrought-iron table, a glass of wine in his hand. When he saw her, he drained the glass and put it down, a wary expression on his face. No wonder he seemed agitated, she thought in contempt.

'Whose child is that?' she demanded.

Dimitri frowned. 'I can't tell you.'

'I will.' Athena spoke up. 'He is Theo's child. But Marina must never know. We don't want to hurt her. I hope you will not tell her our secret—it would be too cruel.'

Shaken, Olivia tried to steady herself. Dimitri's morals were worse than she'd ever imagined.

'I don't believe you two! Is it a Greek tradition to take on your father's mistress?' she demanded angrily.

He blinked. Very slowly, a smile spread across his face, and then he was laughing with Athena, who was doubled up and clutching him as if she had never heard anything so funny in the whole of her life.

Their easy intimacy outraged her, and she had to sit down on a low wall because of the cutting pains in her chest. How dared they laugh at her?

She sat with a forlorn expression on her face, though her fists were clenched as if she might attack him at any moment. Dimitri sobered, hating to see her so hurt, so misled.

'Athena isn't my mistress. I've never been her lover—'

'I saw you!' Olivia whispered, her eyes huge and silvered with distress. 'She was in labour and you were helping her into your car—'

'Oh, hell! So that's it!' He groaned, and a wave of regret churned at his stomach. 'How on earth did you find us?'

'Your mother guided me,' she said, her voice taut and strained.

'My...mother?' He and Athena looked at one another in consternation.

'Yes.' Olivia flung up her head defiantly. 'She'd been telling me you had a mistress ever since the day we met. Finally I became suspicious about your secretive phone calls. She offered to take me to your mistress's house.'

Poor Olivia. What she must have thought... 'And that was the day you left—?'

'Of course it was!' she cried, slamming her fist on the hard stone. She winced, and he reached out to take that wounded little hand in his but she glared at him so fiercely that he thought better of it. Her lower lip trembled and his heart somersaulted with love and tenderness.

'Olivia,' he said gently, 'Why didn't you tell me what you'd seen? I could have explained—'

'I wouldn't have believed you!' she hurled tightly. 'You were loving and k-kind to Athena, and it was obvious that she must be the mother of your child... Oh.' She looked confused. 'He's Theo's child. I don't understand.'

'I can assure you that he is Theo's child. And I have never loved or made love to any other man but Theo in the whole of my life. Why don't you two sort this out somewhere private?' Athena suggested, as little Theo ran to her and clung to her knees, his huge Dimitri-eyes round and anxious.

Olivia's hand flew to her mouth. 'I'm sorry! I wouldn't have upset your little boy for the world—'

Jumping to her feet in agitation, Olivia was dazed by Athena's gentle smile.

'It's all right. I'll explain to him,' Athena said. 'Just go. And tell her everything, Dimitri. I mean *everything*,' she added, kissing his cheek and lifting Theo up for a cuddle. Dimitri buried his face in the toddler's little neck and then set about tickling him, till his half-brother giggled, his little face sunny once more.

'Olivia,' he said quietly when he'd set Theo down. 'We have a lot of explaining to do, the two of us. I want to clear the air. Will you trust me and give me an hour of your time?'

Hardly breathing, he waited for her nod, and when it came he felt as if he'd been reprieved from a prison sentence.

His heart pounding, he drove her to the ruined temple by the sea, dedicated to Aphrodite, and they sat on the base of a fallen column, amidst a drift of wild sea lilies, the air heavy with pine scent and herbs.

'I'll begin with Athena. She was from my father's village,' Dimitri said when Olivia looked at him questioningly. 'They'd known one another as children. He always remained a simple, uncomplicated man at heart, loving the land, happy with his old village friends.'

'He was wrong to love her,' Olivia reproved. 'He was married.'

Dimitri sighed. 'Only because he felt he had to marry Mother.'

'What do you mean?' she asked, her curiosity aroused.

'Initially he'd been going out with Marina, and she adored him. But she was a little too possessive, and as he realised he didn't love her he decided to break off the relationship. He'd drunk a little too much, trying to pluck up courage, and Mother—knowing what he intended—seduced him. He began to court Athena, but Mother then told him she was pregnant.'

'With you!' She looked startled.

'Me,' he agreed with a smile. 'And Father, being a man of honour, married the mother of his child.'

'Marina had what she wanted,' Olivia began.

'But she knew she'd ruined Father's life.'

Olivia sighed. 'How sad.'

'She paid for it,' Dimitri said, sympathy etched deeply on his face. 'At first she diverted her love to me. But that wasn't enough. Father never stopped loving Athena. When the marriage became unbearable, he went to her for comfort. She and Father adored one another and were happy together. You've seen her, Olivia. That's the face of a kind and gentle woman, unwillingly caught up in the life of a married man. She wouldn't let Father ask for a divorce. She was content with the situation as it was. And when he died I made sure Athena was secure.'

Now Olivia was sitting with her spine erect, her beautiful eyes fixed intently on him as she tried to untangle the story.

'That day on the boat, the day when you said you stood in the theatre at Epidauros and said you loved me, you had several secretive phone calls—'

He nodded. 'Athena had been rushed to hospital with labour pains. They turned out to be false and I teased her about being a drama queen. Though they were real enough the next day, when you saw us together. That was the day little Theo was born.' He smiled fondly, thinking of his little half-brother. 'Olivia, Athena was all alone and had lost the man she loved more than anything in the world. She needed my support—'

'Of course she did. But Dimitri,' she mourned, 'why didn't you tell me?'

'I had promised her that I would tell no one,' he said gently. 'My mother once accused me of being Athena's lover—she knew where she lived, and I think she'd seen my car outside one day. I couldn't say anything. Couldn't hurt Mother, you see. She was unhappy enough. I believe that when she met you and saw your happiness she was desperately jealous. She envied the intensity of our love. But now she is loved again and her bitterness has gone.'

Seeing how appalled she looked, he moved close to her. Taking her hand, he found that she was trembling.

'Are you saying that I left you,' she croaked in dismay, 'because you were being kind and thoughtful to your late father's lover? Dimitri, I was so certain...' She buried her face in her hands. And then looked up again sharply and he knew the doubts were still there. 'I'm not sure if I dare believe you. You said...you said our marriage was based on sex and that was all!' Her eyes blazed blue fire.

'Not as far as I was concerned. I was talking about *you*. It seemed to be all you felt,' he said, hurting. If she didn't love him, he didn't know what he'd do...

'That's not true!' she protested indignantly. 'I've loved you since we first met! I've always loved you!'

He wanted that to be true. Yet she could be settling for his love, and a comfortable life. That wouldn't be enough for him. She'd told him quite baldly that she no longer cared.

'I want the truth from you, Olivia. No more lies, no more pretence. You've forgotten your farewell note,' he reminded her, his body stiff. But they had to get to the truth, however painful that might be. She must be honest with him. 'You said in that note that when there was no love in a marriage it was a mistake to continue it. You can't deny that. Those words are burnt in my heart.' His voice shook but he didn't care. He was exposing his emotions because this was his last chance to do so.

Her fingers stole into his. He dared to meet her eyes and tried not to be fooled by what he thought was tenderness there. And yet hope leapt inside him, jerking his pulses into a fast, erratic beat.

'Dimitri, I wasn't referring to *my* love when I wrote that note. I meant yours. It seemed clear enough to me at the time, but now I see it wasn't. I believed that you loved Athena, not me. I wasn't going to let you live a lie. I couldn't trust you, and that made every day a torment.'

'But you were mistaken to doubt me,' he said gravely.

'I so want that to be true! I refuse to share the man I love! You must believe me, Dimitri. Whatever happens between us, whatever we decide to do, one thing is certain and you must know it. I love you with all my heart. Don't you know that? Can't you tell?'

It was his turn to hesitate, to doubt. And those doubts haunted him, stretching him on the rack.

'I want to believe you. More than you can ever know,' he muttered. Her grip tightened. He ploughed on. 'But when we were married you seemed so distant sometimes. When I came back from trips abroad our sex was fantastic, but you were quiet. Almost reticent—'

'I was lonely,' she explained, her face earnest. 'All I did was explore the country and shop. I seemed to have no purpose in life except to be your wife. Wonderful though that was, it wasn't enough.'

His arm crept around her. 'I'm sorry. I thought you'd love a life of luxury—'

'Not if you weren't there to enjoy it with me,' she sighed. 'I need to keep my mind active. And I was fed the most awful stories by your mother about what you might be doing. I know you've always denied her part in my misery, but she fed my suspicions. Perhaps that was because she truly believed you to be Athena's lover. I think she might have been preparing me for the truth, so I wasn't hurt as she'd been hurt by your father's suspected infidelity.'

'I'm sorry. To me, Mother seemed so pleasant to you that I couldn't imagine she was being two-faced and making you unhappy. But you must believe me when I say there were no other loves in my life. I slept and ate and dreamt of you. I haven't stopped loving you, not even in those years I wished hell on earth for you. And when I saw you again…I couldn't breathe for the hunger that filled my bitter heart. I wanted to throw that lawyer of yours into the sea, just because he'd spent time with you and on the offchance that he might have…might have…'

'I've had no other lover but you,' she said softly, touching his beloved face. 'I had some dire dinners in the attempt to start my life without you!' She giggled. 'No man matches up. They didn't even come close. I have loved you despite trying to forget you. I always will. But…you…' She bit her lip. 'What about you? You mentioned women…'

'Yes. I went out with other women,' he said, his cheek soft against hers. 'I made love to three of them. A one-off, each time. Such a mistake. A disaster. You were always there, luring me with your wicked eyes, sighing the way you do...' His arm tightened around her waist. 'I suppose it kept Eleni at bay for a while,' he said ruefully. 'I told her how I felt about you. That I was obsessed, addicted—'

'But you didn't say you loved me?' she murmured, lights glinting in her eyes.

'I couldn't admit it to myself, let alone her. I knew you were out of my reach and I had to resign myself to that. Acknowledging my love for you would have torn me apart. I was devastated when you left. An absolute bear. Eleni thought she'd slip into your shoes but I didn't want anyone there. Only you.'

Contented now, she leaned her head into his shoulder. 'She kept trying because she didn't know how you really felt,' she mused.

'Yet she was aware that I'd raged and rampaged about the house when you left.'

'Perhaps she thought your pride was hurt,' Olivia said wryly.

He smiled. 'Perhaps. But...why did you run away? If you'd confronted me, I could have explained—'

'I barely knew what I was doing,' she confessed. 'I hurt so much. Imagine what I'd seen, Dimitri! Imagine the corrosive half-truths your mother poured into my ear! I'd long been unhappy, lonely, unsure of your love and seeing you with Athena just confirmed my worst fears.'

'I was a fool. I left you alone too much. I know that now,' he said quietly. 'I was trying to continue working as I had before I was married. I thought you must be blissfully happy, enjoying your life of leisure.'

'I felt I wasn't part of your life any more.' Her face was sober as she remembered how isolated she'd felt.

'That day when I saw you with Athena, my instincts were to go back to people I knew and loved. My friends. I needed to think—and I couldn't in that oppressive, intense atmosphere. You were in Tokyo, your mother was keen to see the back of me so you could find yourself a Greek wife. And…' She hesitated. 'To be honest, I thought that you'd lie your way out of the situation and I'd be so desperate to believe you that I'd be tempted to pretend you didn't have a mistress and a child. I'm so weak where you're concerned. I didn't dare risk being coaxed by you into accepting your infidelity and turning a blind eye to it.'

'I would have persuaded you,' he pointed out sadly. 'Because I would have shown you the photos of Athena and Theo and there would have been no doubts left in your mind.'

'I know.' She hung her head. 'Sometimes I'm not rational where you're concerned.'

He gave her waist an understanding squeeze. 'I know. I lose all sense of rationality too.'

'Where…?' She swallowed. Could they begin again or had their chances been soured? 'Where does this leave us, Dimitri?'

'Do you trust me now?' he asked. She nodded. 'I am totally committed to you and always have been. I regret my prolonged business trips without you. This time we've spent together has shown me how much I need you, that you must come with me—or I must learn to delegate more.'

'Does that mean…?' she breathed, not daring to say more.

Gently he turned her to face him. 'I love you and you love me. I want us to spend the rest of our lives together. But we must never again be silent about our doubts or worries. Not that there will be any in the future, will there?'

Her smile lit her face with a joy that took his breath away. So he kissed her warm, inviting mouth and forgot everything else.

Some time later they broke away. 'Eleni,' she said anxiously, remembering.

'She will find someone else. Her head was filled with me, but there are many young men longing to love her,' he assured her. 'We'll be kind to her. Give her a party and invite some hunks to adore her.'

'And your mother?'

He touched her soft, concerned mouth. 'She's happy with Nikos. If I'm happy then she'll be content. I think that she will be the mother I remember as a child,' he said contentedly. 'Love will bring out the best in her, you'll see. And we must make sure you're not neglected. You need a project of some kind, something worthwhile—'

'I thought,' she whispered, running her hand inside his shirt, 'motherhood might occupy me thoroughly.'

'Oh, my darling,' he murmured, passionately kissing her. 'Let's have a selfish year to ourselves first. Come with me wherever I go. Be my social secretary. Charm and dazzle my clients. And then,' he said, carefully unzipping her dress, 'we will start our family. For now,' he breathed, kissing her throat, 'we'll just practise our technique.'

She smiled her Venus smile, stood up and slithered out of her dress. Dimitri groaned and held her close. Lovingly she stroked his dark head. Children, she thought happily. Dark-haired, dark-eyed and beautiful.

'Love me,' she whispered, overwhelmed by the joy in her heart. 'Just love me for the rest of our lives, as I will love you, Dimitri.'

EPILOGUE

'EVERYONE on the beach must think we're mad!' laughed Olivia, scarlet in the face from exertion.

'Be quiet, woman, and *hop!*' muttered Dimitri, his eye fixed on the finishing line.

But she was giggling too much. Hampered by the tie wrapped around their ankles as they stumbled across the sand, she finally overbalanced and brought Dimitri crashing down with her.

'Ha!' exclaimed a triumphant Lukas, hopping by and thrilled to be on course to win the three-legged race with his sister, Helen. 'We're the best! Hurray!'

Dimitri laughed and pretended to grab his son's foot, but Lukas was too agile and triumphantly went on to breast the tape held by his proud grandmother, Marina, and his step-grandfather, Nikos.

'The winners!' cried Marina, holding up her grand-children's hands in delight.

Olivia and Dimitri, still chuckling, staggered to their feet. 'And what happened to Eleni?' asked Olivia, looking back.

'Huh. Smooching with Vangelis. And they're married! Yuk!' said Lukas, with all the scorn of a ten-year-old who knew that winning a race on your birthday was far more important than kissing.

'You'll think differently in five years' time,' admonished Athena, hobbling up, still tied to Theo, who was now taller than his mother.

'Never!' Lukas declared.

Dimitri's eyes warmed as he put a loving hand on his son's shoulder. 'Never say never. All is possible. Love will hit you with the speed of a bullet one day, if you're anything like me.' He looked lovingly at Olivia, her arm around their golden-haired daughter. 'And you'll live in a glorious haze from that moment on.'

'Hmph. It's the sack race next,' declared Lukas, dismissing such rubbish out of hand.

'And then pass the orange,' announced Helen happily. 'I'm organising the teams.'

Dimitri perked up, knowing this involved holding the fruit under your chin and trying to pass it to the person next in line. A lot of close contact was necessary, and he had every intention of standing beside Olivia to make the most of the intimacy. He smiled to himself. All these years and he still thrilled to be near her, still found excuses to touch her. Loved her more than ever.

'Men and boys against women and me,' Helen insisted.

Olivia laughed at Dimitri's crestfallen face. She knew what he'd been thinking. 'Save it for later,' she murmured.

His eyes kindled. 'To hell with later. Share a sack with me?'

'Rogue! We'd stand no chance of winning!'

'Who cares about winning?' He swept her into his arms, not caring that his son groaned in despair. 'I love you,' he said, brushing the strands of wind-blown hair from her face.

'And I love you,' Olivia whispered, her eyes adoring, their surroundings forgotten. He held her closer.

'Sack race, Mother!' Lukas was tapping her on her

arm, his face so imperious and like Dimitri's that she had to stifle a smile.

'Are you enjoying your birthday, darling?' she asked, obediently hauling the sack to her waist.

Affectionate as always, he impulsively kissed her and then his father. 'It's great. Quite mad, of course, but that's English parties for you. The cake's *huge*. I'm so lucky to have you and Gran and Nikos, and Eleni and Vangelis, and Athena and Theo.'

Olivia hugged her son and Helen, a burgeoning long-legged beauty even at the age of eight. 'We're the lucky ones, your father and me,' she said softly. 'We were given a second chance and this lovely family is the result.'

Dimitri kissed her. 'Not luck. We were driven by love.'

'Yes.' She smiled up at him.

'They're in that haze again,' sighed Lukas extravagantly. 'I think we'd better start without them, Helen, don't you?'

'Definitely,' agreed Helen. But her gentle blue eyes met her mother's and the two of them smiled warmly, acknowledging their belief in the joy of true love.

THE GREEK SURGEON

by

Margaret Barker

Margaret Barker has enjoyed a variety of interesting careers. A State Registered Nurse and qualified teacher, she holds a degree in French and Linguistics and is a Licentiate of the Royal Academy of Music. As a full-time writer Margaret says, 'Writing is my most interesting career because it fits perfectly into my happy life as a wife, mother and grandmother. My husband and I live in an idyllic sixteenth century house near the East Anglian coast. Our grown-up children have flown the nest but they often fly back again, bringing their own young families with them for wonderful weekend and holiday reunions.'

CHAPTER ONE

DEMELZA looked down over the stone wall bordering the terrace to find out what all the commotion was about. In the courtyard of the apartment below her she could see two small boys chasing each other round and round, laughing and calling to each other in Greek. Their skin was bronzed by the sun, one of them darker than the other. The lighter-skinned boy glanced up at her and she caught a glimpse of strong white teeth in a happy little face.

She felt a sudden pang of sadness. The boy looked about six years old, the same age as her own son would have been. Tears pricked behind her eyes, threatening to run down her cheeks. Well-meaning friends had told her that time would heal but the years had gone by and she was still hurting inside. She took a deep breath, brushed the moisture from her eyes and smiled down at the little boy.

He paused for a moment, looking up at her, before his playmate gave him a playful push and they continued their game. As she watched them she tried to imagine what it must be like to be so happy and carefree that you had to let off steam like that. They were both wearing the uniform of the nearby school, but from the rumpled state of their shirts it was obvious they'd had a hectic day.

The church clock above her on the hillside chimed six. The sun was dipping low in the sky behind her. It was still early in May but the afternoon had been very hot and she was looking forward to the comparative cool of the evening. Looking down at the two delight-ful little boys, she began to wonder who they belonged to.

They probably lived in the apartment below hers, but when she'd arrived from the airport this afternoon the place had seemed deserted. The door to the enclosed courtyard was now wide open, she noticed, and she distinctly remembered that she'd closed it. She'd felt suddenly nervous to be moving into this large old Greek villa, knowing no one, hundreds of miles from familiar territory.

There was the sound of footsteps on the old cobble-stones outside the courtyard and a small, plump woman burst in, wiping her hands on her apron and beginning a tirade in Greek, directed towards the boys. It was obvious to Demelza that these two happy lads weren't supposed to be there. The woman was pointing towards the open gateway at the same moment as a tall man appeared.

He was carrying a black leather bag, which he put down on the flagstoned floor as he began to talk rapidly in Greek to the woman. She smiled, seemingly reas-sured as she dropped her agitated hands to her side. The boy who'd smiled up at Demelza ran with a whoop of joy towards the man and began chattering excitedly, his little arms fixed, limpet-like, around the man's waist. The woman put out her hand towards the other boy and led him away.

As the sturdy iron door of the courtyard clanged to behind the woman and her child, the tall man stopped speaking in Greek.

'Ianni, how many times have I told you that you

mustn't play here without telling Katerina where you are?'

Demelza was amazed by his flawless English. His suntanned olive skin, the handsome, rugged Mediterranean features, proclaimed him to be Greek, but his English accent was perfect. He was carrying the jacket of his grey suit over his arm, his open-necked white shirt almost as crumpled as the boy's. He looked tired, one hand now running through dark, tousled hair as he straightened up from speaking to the boy.

The little boy had assumed a contrite expression as he gazed up at the tall man. 'I'm sorry, Dad. Lefteris and I didn't mean to come in, but we were playing in the street outside his house and we just sort of found ourselves at this end. I only wanted to see if you were home.'

Perfect English again. Demelza was beginning to wonder who this bilingual father and son were as, for the first time since he'd arrived, the man looked up and noticed her. The sun, dipping down behind the hills, was in his eyes and he screwed up his eyes.

'Hello, you must be the new sister at the resort clinic. They told me you were coming today. I'm Nick Capodistrias.'

She remembered his name from the instructions the travel consortium who employed her had supplied. So this was Nicholas Capodistrias, the doctor she was to contact if there was something she couldn't handle in her new position.

She leaned further over the wall of her large flag-stoned terrace. 'I'm Demelza Tregarron. It's a relief to find we're going to be neighbours. I'll know where to get in touch with you if—'

She broke off, feeling that she was assuming an awful lot. Maybe Dr Capodistrias would think it an imposition if she asked for too much help, especially in his off-duty time. She'd been told he worked at the local hospital and he looked as if he'd welcome a bit of peace and quiet.

'I've been asked to look after you until you find your feet,' he said, his voice steady, giving nothing away as to how he felt about the arrangement. 'Why don't you come down and have a drink with us? We can't talk like this with you up there and the sun in my eyes.'

Young Ianni was jumping up and down excitedly now. 'Dad, can I have some lemonade?'

'Sure!' Dr Capodistrias turned to look up at Demelza. 'Are you coming?'

She was intensely aware that she hadn't finished unpacking and her belongings were strewn everywhere in her apartment, but she also knew that the sooner she began learning the ropes the easier life would become. And there was something intensely intriguing about this father and son. Was the little boy's mother inside, preparing supper and pouring drinks? If she was, why hadn't she come out to greet her husband?

There was so much to find out besides the useful information she needed to run the clinic. For the first time in six years she felt a spark of enthusiasm running through her. Taking the plunge and leaving the old life behind had been a good idea. At the ripe old age of thirty-two, she'd been in danger of stagnating.

'I'll be down in five minutes,' Demelza called, as she dashed inside her apartment to find something suitable to wear.

She couldn't go down in the skimpy shorts and sleeveless top she'd thrown on after her shower. First impressions were important and she didn't want Dr

Capodistrias to think she wasn't suitable to take charge of the new clinic at the beach resort. She mustn't look as if she was just another tourist out for a free holiday funded by a bit of work thrown in on the side.

She surveyed the chaos. The new white cotton trousers would go with her old tried-and-tested lime-green T-shirt. She wanted to look neat, informal, like an off-duty professional. A professional again! It had been a long time since she'd been in paid work and she wanted to give it her best shot.

Fully dressed, she glanced at herself in the long mirror as she ran a brush through her long auburn hair. She usually wore it coiled up on top of her head during the day, but in the evenings it felt so relaxing to have it tumbling casually over her shoulders.

She nudged herself along. Come on, girl, it's only a drink you're going for! As Demelza hurried down the outside stone staircase that led from her apartment to the courtyard, she noticed that whoever had converted this rather grand old villa into two apartments had done a good job. They'd kept the ancient ambience of the place whilst putting in all the mod cons that made life comfortable.

The plumbing left something to be desired but she'd been warned this wasn't a strong point in the Greek islands! But at least the shower had worked, even if she'd had to hold the shower head with one hand while she'd soaped herself with the other. Maybe she could persuade someone to attach it to the wall? Or perhaps she could do it herself. She'd been pretty nifty at DIY when she'd been running the domestic side of the farm.

She crossed the flagstoned courtyard and waited in front of the open door through which she'd seen the doctor and his son go into their apartment.

'Come through!' she heard Dr Capodistrias call from somewhere beyond the open door. 'We're out at the back.'

The interior of the apartment seemed dim after the bright sunlight. Demelza stepped straight into a large, rather grand living room, furnished with antique chairs, a table and a glass-fronted cupboard displaying delicate porcelain cups and saucers, antique silver ornaments and a large amount of cut glassware. Numerous portraits of family figures and groups adorned the walls.

She smiled as she noticed a bunch of spring flowers in pride of place in the middle of the table. It had been stuffed untidily inside a jam jar, obviously by Ianni's small hands, and it seemed charmingly incongruous with the rest of the decor.

She looked around her at the deserted room. There was no sign of his mother.

Nicholas Capodistrias suddenly appeared in the doorway that led to the outside terrace and extended his hand.

'Welcome!' he said impassively, as he shook her hand.

Demelza felt a strong hand enclosing her own and didn't pull away. It was good to have some physical contact with a fellow human being. She was startled by the warm feeling it gave her as she stood looking up into his dark brown eyes.

'Come and sit down.'

Young Ianni was already sitting at a small, rough-hewn wooden table, happily ploughing his way through a dish of crisps. He looked up at Demelza and tried to smile, but it was obviously difficult with his mouth full and the little boy gave an involuntary splutter of acknowledgement instead.

'Hey, save some for us!' his father said good-naturedly, moving the dish towards the centre of the table. 'What can I get you to drink?'

'Whatever you're having, Dr Capodistrias,' she replied politely.

'Call me Nick. And may I call you by your fascinating name? I've never met anyone called Demelza before.'

'It's Cornish. I was born in Cornwall and I was called after my grandmother.'

He was studying her with his expressive eyes. 'It's a lovely name. Now, you've asked for the same drink as me. I'm drinking ouzo, Demelza. Have you ever had any?'

She shook her head. 'I'd like to try some.'

He smiled, and she noticed how much younger and more approachable he looked with a smile on his face. He couldn't be older than his late thirties but the care-worn expression he'd carried on his face when he'd first arrived home had given her the impression of an older man.

She noticed that the trousers of his grey suit had been replaced by a pair of old, worn jeans which outlined the strong muscles in his thighs. There was no doubt that he was a strikingly handsome man. A man who could speak fluent English and Greek, working out here on a sun-kissed island, in charge of a small, bewitching little son who'd already stolen her heart. The situation was intriguing her. She knew very little so far about him, but she found herself avid to find out more.

He was still smiling, but now with a hint of mischief. 'I feel I ought to warn you, ouzo's an acquired taste and it's very strong. I'll give you a small one and mix it with water.'

She watched as the clear liquid turned cloudy with the addition of the water. Raising the glass to her lips, she took a tentative sip. The liquid hit the back of her throat and made her gasp.

Father and son burst out laughing at her reaction.

'I did warn you!' Nick said.

Ianni had jumped to his feet and come round to her chair, patting her gently on the back with a small, soothing hand.

'Would you like some of my lemonade, Demella?'

She smiled at Ianni's mispronunciation of her name. What a perfectly charming boy! Demelza swallowed hard as she turned to look at the concerned little face so close to her own, peering over her shoulder.

'Lemonade would be lovely, Ianni. Thank you very much.'

The boy hurried away into the house to return with a large bottle. Solemnly he unscrewed the cap and was about to pour it into her ouzo glass.

Nick reached for a fresh glass and carefully supervised the pouring of the lemonade.

'See if you like it, Demella,' Ianni said anxiously.

She took a sip and gave it her serious consideration. 'It's excellent.'

Ianni smiled happily and settled back in his chair.

'Try Demelza's name again, Ianni,' Nick said. 'It starts off with Demel.'

'Demel...' Ianni said, carefully.

'Then finishes with za.'

'Za. Demelza, Demelza,' the little boy sang. 'Show me how to write it. I'll get my copy book.'

'Talking of which, did you do your homework at Katerina's?' Nick asked.

Ianni grinned. 'Most of it. I've only got to copy out some letters and then it's finished. Look, Demelza!'

She was amazed by the neatness of the little boy's exercise book and also by the fact that he was doing homework at such a tender age.

'Ianni is learning to read and write Greek and English at the same time, but he doesn't seem to have a problem with the work,' his father explained. 'Do you want to go and finish your homework inside the house so we don't disturb you with our chatter, Ianni?'

Ianni smiled. 'OK! I won't be long. And then can we go to Giorgio's for supper?'

'Didn't you have supper at Katerina's?'

Ianni pulled a face. 'I didn't eat much because I like having supper with you, Dad.' He glanced at Demelza. 'Why don't you come with us, Demelza? You'd like Giorgio's. Do you like dancing?'

Nick put a hand gently on his son's shoulder. 'Finish your homework and we'll see,' he said quickly.

As the little boy disappeared inside, Demelza turned to Nick. 'I really ought to get myself sorted out this evening.'

It was the talk of dancing that had alarmed her. She wasn't ready yet to throw herself into the social scene. One step at a time. She'd got herself out here and she didn't want to rush into things. Besides, she was sure that Nick wouldn't want an extra person intruding on his family supper. Especially someone who'd been dumped on him as an extra responsibility.

As if reading her thoughts, he leaned across the table towards her. 'If it's the dancing you're afraid of, don't worry—nobody has to join in unless they want to and it's only at the weekends that I let Ianni stay up for it. Tonight being Monday, I'll have him whisked away and in bed early enough to get a good night's sleep before school. So, if you'd like to taste the local cuisine, you'd be most welcome to join us. I don't expect you've got any food in the apartment.'

His voice was polite. She knew he was being the dutiful professional but she was loath to leave this warm family atmosphere to return to her lonely apartment.

'It's a very tempting idea,' she said carefully. 'And I do have a lot of questions to ask you about the clinic.'

'I'll fill you in and then you can ask me about anything you don't understand. When you start work in the morning you'll soon get the hang of the place. Basically…'

She listened attentively while Nick explained that she would be expected to do a morning surgery at the clinic on five days each week at the beach resort half a mile away. If there was anything she couldn't handle, she was to contact him at the hospital in the town. In between surgeries and at weekends, if there were any emergencies, the staff at the resort reception would contact her on her mobile and Demelza would decide if it was a case she could handle or if a visit to the hospital was required.

'You're not going to be rushed off your feet, Demelza. This is a new venture, which was deemed necessary because of the expanding number of tourists. Basically, you're the intermediary between the resort and the hospital.'

He paused. 'One thing puzzles me. Having read your qualifications and the fact that you were Sister of a busy surgical ward in London for a couple of years, I was wondering why you'd want to take such a relatively undemanding job?'

She raised her eyes to his but his enigmatic expression gave nothing away. 'My post in London was nearly seven years ago. I left it when I got married. Since then I've been running the domestic side of my husband's family farm.'

His dark eyes searched her face enquiringly. 'I didn't know that you'd had such a long gap in your career, but I'm sure the interview panel in London was satisfied with your curriculum vitae otherwise you wouldn't have been appointed.'

Demelza bristled at the cool tone of his voice. 'Don't worry, I'll be well able to cope with this job. My nursing training, my years as a staff nurse and my two years as a sister have equipped me to cope with any medical emergency. And my contract is only for six months, so if at the end of that time it isn't renewed then—'

'We'll see how things work out, Demelza,' he intervened. 'I wasn't questioning your ability to do the job. You may decide you want to take up a more demanding post in the UK, in which case you wouldn't want to renew your contract.'

He was staring intently at her as he cleared his throat. 'What does your husband think of all this?'

She felt the familiar churning of emotions whenever anyone referred to Simon. 'I'm a widow,' she said quietly.

An expression of deep compassion crossed his face. 'I'm sorry. Nobody told me. Yes, I can see why you might want to make a fresh start.' He paused and his voice became gentler. 'How long have you been widowed?'

'Six years.'

Nick looked surprised. 'And you haven't thought of going back to work before now?'

'It wasn't as simple as that. I've often wanted to but it wasn't possible.'

'And now it is?'

'Yes. You see, my husband's brother has recently married a very capable girl and I felt she could safely take over my duties, so I seized my chance.'

It all sounded so easy when she put it like that, but she wasn't going to fill him in on any of the details, not yet anyway. Not until she knew him better. First she'd lost her husband, then her son, followed by the long years when she'd often felt like a prisoner at the farm, having to cope with her own emotional suffering and that of Simon's parents, who'd clung to her as if she were their real daughter.

Then she'd had to see if the new daughter-in-law had been willing to replace her and had the necessary skills to cope with what had become a very demanding job, both physically and emotionally. Only when she'd been absolutely sure that Jane could fill her shoes had she planned her escape.

She raised her eyes and saw that Nick was still watching her with a puzzled expression.

'You look like a woman who's suffered,' he said quietly, his hand reaching across the table to cover her own.

The touch of his fingers unnerved her. A woman could lose herself looking into this charismatic man's eyes, those dark brown pools of compassion. He would be an excellent doctor. She wouldn't mind being his patient if he put on that expression when he cared for her. It was a poignant moment for her. Another step towards joining the human race again.

Ianni came dashing outside, holding his copy book for Demelza to read. She looked at the beautifully formed characters, one page in Greek and one page in English.

'It's very good, Ianni.'

The little boy smiled. 'So, are we all going to Giorgio's, Dad?'

Nick looked at Demelza enquiringly.

She smiled. 'I'd like that very much.'

Ianni put his small hand in hers and began to tug her away from the table. 'Come on, then!'

Giorgio's taverna exuded warmth and hospitality. Giorgio himself, a gnarled, weather-beaten character of indeterminate age, definitely on the wrong side of fifty but with the mischievous grin of a twenty-year-old, was playing an accordion and singing a lively song in Greek. His eyes lit up as they walked in and he nodded his head towards Nick before quickly finishing the song, putting down his accordion and hurrying over to greet the newcomers.

'Nico!' Giorgio greeted the younger man with an enthusiastic hug, before reaching down to hoist little Ianni onto his shoulder, chattering to the young boy in rapid Greek.

Ianni laughed at what was said to him and replied in a rapid torrent that had the taverna owner laughing along with him. Demelza felt sure that whatever was under discussion had something to do with her. She hung back, reluctant to break up the warm ambience of the group, but Giorgio, still with the boy on his shoulder, held out his hand and grasped hers.

'Welcome,' he said enthusiastically. 'What will you have to drink? Any friend of Nico is already a friend of mine. Drinks on the house! Ouzo? Retsina…?'

'Lemonade, please,' Demelza said quickly, as they

were shown to a table on a large, vine-covered terrace overlooking the bay.

Giorgio raised one dark, bushy eyebrow at her request. 'Lemonade is for the children. I will bring you a bottle of beautiful wine. They make it across the water in Crete. You will like it, Demelza.'

'And a bottle of water to go with it, please, Giorgio,' Nick said quickly.

He was smiling contentedly as he settled himself against the back of his ancient iron seat, looking at Demelza across the table. Ianni had pulled his chair close to hers. Giorgio had already returned to his accordion and was singing again whilst a couple of charming young waiters were setting out wine, glasses and a basket of bread on the table.

She found herself relaxing as she hadn't done for years. Looking out beyond the terrace, she saw the sun dipping down behind the mountains across the bay, casting variegated shadows over the water. The sun was a fiery red as it disappeared and the sky glowed with a diffusion of pinks and orange.

'Come and choose what you would like to eat.' Nick stood up and led Demelza over towards the interior of the taverna.

The kitchen was chaotic. A middle-aged woman—Giorgio's wife, presumably—was standing beside a huge cooking range, stirring something in a large pan. She lifted one hand to wave across at Nick and Demelza before continuing her stirring, smiling at them as they surveyed the vast array of dishes set out for their inspection. Nick explained what each dish contained as he gave Demelza a guided tour of what was on offer.

Lamb stew, moussaka, various kinds of chicken, aubergine, beef stiffado, which was a kind of savoury casserole, fish, lobster, prawns… She found it difficult to decide. It had been a long day since she'd checked in at Gatwick Airport and all the new experiences were beginning to overwhelm her.

'Would you like me to choose?' Nick asked quietly.

She nodded gratefully. 'Something small for me. Perhaps—'

'I'll get something we can share,' he told her.

When the food arrived at the table, Demelza found she could pick and choose from the plates of mezze, different succulent Greek dishes set out in an appetising way. The small helpings of aubergine, stuffed vine leaves called dolmades, prawns, grilled fish and chicken stimulated her appetite and tasted delicious washed down with the Cretan wine.

'I hadn't realised I was so hungry,' she said, as she put down her fork and leaned back against her chair.

The sky was now dark, but lit up by a crescent moon. Behind the taverna, she could just make out the outline of the mysterious hills, waiting to be explored whenever she was able to find the time in her new life. She was sure she could detect the smell of the oregano which she'd noticed on the hillside above her apartment. It was an idyllic setting in which to live and work.

Ianni, pulling his chair even closer to hers, had laid his head on her lap and closed his eyes. Automatically, she reached for the small boy and pulled him onto her lap, where he fell into a deep sleep.

Demelza looked across the table at Nick who was watching her, a strange expression on his face.

'Here, let me take him,' he said quietly. 'Ianni can become a bit of a weight when he's dead to the world.'

She shook her head. 'I don't mind,' she said softly.

That was an understatement if ever there was one! She was revelling in the feeling of this small, sleeping child on her lap.

The noise of plates clattering onto tables, people laughing and joking, Giorgio playing his accordion and singing loudly didn't disturb young Ianni.

'I'd better take Ianni to bed soon,' Nick said. 'I usually have him settled by now.' He continued to watch her across the table. 'You look as if you're used to children.'

She realised that Nick was trying discreetly to find out if she had any of her own. Everyone always did. Sooner or later the dreaded question would surface and she would have to steel herself to make a reply.

'I love children,' she said slowly. 'I was expecting a little boy, six years ago, but I miscarried when I was six months pregnant.'

She swallowed hard, breathing deeply as she'd learned to do—anything to prevent herself from crying. She should have got over it by now. Other people did but for some reason the dreams of what might have been wouldn't go away. If Simon hadn't died before she'd lost the baby they would have had another child and her miscarriage would be a distant memory.

'I'm sorry. That must have been awful for you.'

Nick's voice was sympathetic and sincere. She raised her eyes from the sleeping child and looked at him. She felt she could trust him.

'Sometimes I feel as if I'll never get over it.'

He reached across the table and took her hand in his. 'You'll never forget, but you will get over it in time. Grief doesn't last for ever even though it seems as if it will.'

'Yes, but six years!'

She bit her lip. Why was she confiding in this relative stranger? She'd said more to him than she'd admitted to anyone for a long time.

'If you'd been able to have another child, that would have eased some of the grief in your heart,' he said, his voice husky with emotion.

She gazed into the dark, expressive eyes. Here was a man who was used to counselling his patients in their unhappiness. He'd understood her feelings exactly. It was good to find someone she could really trust. For so long she'd kept her feelings bottled up, trying to appear strong and brave for the rest of Simon's family.

'I was surrounded by Simon's family, but there were times when I felt I was totally alone in my grief,' she said quietly. 'I felt there was no one who understood what I was going through.'

Nick nodded his head sympathetically. 'It's a terrible thing to lose your partner in life.'

She swallowed hard. From his understanding tone, she began to wonder if Ianni's mother was dead.

'Are you...bringing up Ianni by yourself?' Demelza asked carefully.

Nick's eyes flickered but his expression didn't change. 'Ianni's mother lives in England.'

'Does Ianni spend time with her?'

'Sometimes, but Lydia leads a very busy life and finds it difficult to fit Ianni into her complicated schedule. Actually, she's coming out for a holiday some time this year.'

'That will be nice.'

Nick raised an eyebrow. 'Nice for Ianni, I hope. Lydia will be staying at the beach resort, of course. I couldn't cope with having her at the apartment. We're divorced.'

Demelza felt a sudden change taking place in her emotions. She had no designs on this charming, sympathetic doctor whatsoever—indeed, on any man who might cross her path—but the fact that he was relatively free made him certainly more interesting.

Nick stood up and came round to her chair, reaching down to take his sleeping son into his arms. She felt the brush of his strong hands against her as she released the small boy. It was a warm, comforting feeling, this contact with a compassionate man. He hadn't told her to snap out of it, to pull herself together, to get on with her life. But for the first time in years that was exactly what she felt she should do.

CHAPTER TWO

DEMELZA found the clinic better equipped than she'd expected. Everything was brand new. The travel consortium had spared no expense and Nick had told her the previous evening that if there was anything she found she needed she was to put in a request.

'We're hoping for super-efficient medical facilities down there at the beach resort,' he'd said, just before he'd gone into his apartment, carrying his sleeping son.

They'd talked in hushed whispers as they'd hurried along the narrow street from the village back to the old villa. The conversation had been completely professional. It had almost been as if both of them had felt they'd been too familiar during this first evening together, but on leaving the warm atmosphere of the taverna they'd become purely professional colleagues.

Climbing the stone stairs to her apartment, Demelza had wished the warm rapport had been maintained to the end of their evening together. But perhaps it had been a good idea to get back on a professional footing. It had been obvious that Nick was totally wrapped up in his medical work and caring for his son and she…well, she wasn't ready for anything other than a friendly relationship with anyone.

Least of all with a handsome Greek doctor, she thought as she looked out of her surgery window across the smooth sweep of the sandy beach and the dazzling blue of the Mediterranean. Children were already playing out on the sand; adults, semi-clad in bright, garish, sometimes fluorescent holiday clothes, were trooping down to spread their towels on the sunbeds nearest the sea.

She wouldn't mind an hour or two in the sun herself to try and put some colour in her pale skin. Perhaps at the end of the morning, if there were no demands on her time, she could have a picnic lunch out there. She looked at the computer on her desk; it was all very high tech for a Greek island. She'd been warned about power cuts, so she would make sure she saved all vital information onto floppy disks.

There was no patient list to tell her who was coming in this morning. Tourists simply turned up and waited their turn. She could hear a murmur of voices in the waiting room outside and pressed the bell that told the first one to come in.

'Bryony Driver.' A tall, thin woman of about forty announced herself as she came in. 'I had to come and see you, Sister, because I feel absolutely lousy. In the middle of the night I felt terrible. Yesterday I was OK but today...ugh!'

Demelza pulled her chair closer to Bryony's. She preferred to sit on the patient's side of her desk. It helped to break the ice and remove any barriers the patient might feel.

'Have you felt as bad as this before, Bryony?'

'Oh, yes! My doctor says I've got some kind of depression. He gave me some pills, which seemed to help, but I don't want to be relying on pills for the rest of my life. So I thought if I went on holiday I could try and manage without them. I mean, it's so lovely out here, I feel I ought to be able to pull myself together and shake off my depression without needing pills.'

'What pills are you on, Bryony?' Demelza asked carefully.

Bryony shrugged. 'Some kind of tranquillisers. My doctor at home keeps changing them.'

Bryony was fishing about in her large shoulder-bag, placing lipsticks, a comb, a cheque book and purse on the corner of Demelza's desk.

'Here they are!' Bryony brought out the box of pills with a triumphant flourish. 'I thought doing nothing in the sun all day would cheer me up. I was planning to flush them down the loo just to show I could...'

The air of bravado disappeared completely. Bryony's face crumpled and she began to sob. 'I just can't forget him.'

'Who can't you forget?' Demelza asked gently.

'That two-timing husband of mine! Oh, he's given me plenty of money and the house so I can't grumble about that, but I just can't forget that he's with somebody else.'

Demelza nodded sympathetically. 'I see. How long are you staying out here, Bryony?'

Bryony shrugged. 'All summer if I want to. I've got nothing to go back to England for. They've told me I can have my room in the resort for as long as I want it.'

Demelza glanced at the box of tablets, making a note of the name. One of the newer brand of tranquillisers which had been well received in the medical press and had no known side effects. Throughout the years when she'd been confined to the farm, she'd made a point of keeping up with the medical trends in her reading, hoping that one day she would be able to return to the profession she loved. This had enabled her to answer all the questions the interview panel in London had put to her about contemporary medicine.

'I think you should go back on your pills, Bryony,' she told her patient. 'Take them for a week and then come back and see me again. If you're worried, don't hesitate to come before then.'

Bryony's face relaxed and she smiled. 'It's good to talk, isn't it? Sometimes that's all it takes, a shoulder to cry on. I didn't sleep all night, never do. I've got some sleeping pills with me, but I'm trying not to get hooked on them.'

'Well, don't take the sleeping pills while you're on your other pills,' Demelza said quickly. 'You mustn't mix your tablets. Stick to the tranquillisers and if you're awake in the night, read a light book or glance through a magazine. You can snooze on the beach if you get sleepy during the day. Just try to relax and take things easy.'

Bryony stood up. 'Thanks ever so much. What's your name?'

'Demelza.'

'What a lovely name! Sister Demelza. Has a nice ring to it, doesn't it? Do you know, Sister, you're the first friend I've made here at the resort. I'll look forward to seeing you again next week.'

Demelza smiled. 'Take care of yourself, Bryony.'

As the door closed behind her patient she was thinking, Poor woman! Which was more painful—to be widowed or for your husband to leave you for someone else?

She pressed the bell for the next patient.

There was a steady stream of minor complaints throughout the morning, including a couple of patients with upset stomachs. They seemed to be improving already and she didn't envisage an epidemic. That was one thing that she must check on in a resort of this size where tourists were living side by side. One of the things she told her patients was the importance of drinking only bottled water.

One patient had a hacking cough which had kept him and his wife awake in the night. Fortunately, he'd brought his prescribed medication with him from England and merely needed some reassurance from Demelza after she'd given his chest a full examination. It was only the second day of his holiday and Demelza assured him that the sun and the relaxation should speed his recovery. If there was no improvement in a few days, she suggested he should come back and see her again.

There was a mild case of sunburn from a fair-skinned patient but it looked as if this had been caught in time. She'd told the patient to stay out of the sun and given her a soothing cream to apply at intervals. Looking out of the window as the midday sun beat down on the beach, she could see a few potential patients for tomorrow! When would they ever learn to take it easy and apply high-factor sun creams or, better still, stay under the sun umbrellas for long periods?

She finished her notes for the morning and switched off the computer. Everything seemed quiet in the waiting room. Irini, the helpful young Greek nurse who doubled up as receptionist, had already gone off duty now that there were no more patients.

Demelza went across to the fridge and took out the food she'd prepared that morning. She'd bought a couple of bread rolls from the village bakery and a few slices of salami from the shop she'd passed on her way to the beach. She could change out of the white uniform dress supplied by the company into her shorts and sun top before finding herself a sunbed and umbrella near the edge of the water.

Glancing through the surgery window, she could already imagine the feel of the warmth on her sun-starved legs. Mmm...

She picked up the sports bag that held everything she would need for this relaxing afternoon and opened the door of the waiting room.

A woman in a sandy swimsuit was hurrying inside from the beach, carrying a small boy in her arms.

'Oh, thank goodness I've caught you, Sister! They told me the clinic would be shut by now. Harry was jumping off the rocks and he's hurt his arm.'

'You'd better come into the surgery.' Demelza ushered them through, all thoughts of the sun instantly forgotten. 'Now, Harry, will you let me have a look at your arm?'

The little boy continued to whimper as he sat on his mother's lap, staring with frightened eyes at Demelza.

'I'm not going to hurt you, Harry,' Demelza said reassuringly, as she placed her fingers gently on the boy's arm.

It was obvious to her, even without examination, that one or both of the bones in the lower arm were fractured. The unnatural angle at which the hand was now flexed was the deciding factor in her diagnosis. She decided not to put the little boy through any more stress until the arm could be manipulated and set in its correct position. An X-ray was essential to confirm her diagnosis and for that he would need to go to the hospital, but first she would make her little patient as comfortable as possible.

Gently, she explained what was happening to the

anxious mother, before fixing the injured arm onto a splint and into a sling. Picking up the phone, she dialled the hospital and asked to speak to Dr Nicholas Capodistrias.

Her spirits lifted at the sound of his deep, calm voice. 'Nick Capodistrias here.'

'Nick, it's Demelza. I've got a young patient with an injury to the lower right arm. From the angle of the hand, I suspect he's fractured the ulna.'

'The resort driver will drive you to the hospital. Will you bring him in, Demelza?'

Nick was professional to the point of abruptness. Demelza replied in the same tone and agreed to be at the hospital as soon as possible.

As soon as Harry's mother had thrown a dress on over her swimsuit they were on the narrow, winding road that led from the beach towards the town a couple of miles away. Stavros, the resort driver, drove as if he were a competitor in a rally. Demelza, sitting beside him, found herself hanging onto her seat whilst Stavros drove, one hand on the wheel, gently humming to himself a haunting Greek melody which she remembered hearing the night before in Giorgio's taverna.

Demelza glanced behind her to reassure herself that her patient wasn't coming to any harm as the resort people-carrier swayed from side to side. She was glad she'd put the arm in a sturdy splint. Little Harry's eyes were closed as he leaned against his mother, but he'd stopped whimpering.

The whole journey took only a few minutes but Demelza felt great relief as she stepped out and opened the back door for her patient and his mother.

It was a small, new hospital, not more than three or four years old. A nurse in Reception took them along to a small accident and emergency department. Demelza recognised Nick before he turned round from bending over a patient.

He moved towards her with that languid, athletic swing she'd come to admire. His white shirt was open at the neck in a casual manner, but the crisp grey trousers were still impeccably pressed. He looked every inch the successful, efficient doctor.

'So this is our new patient,' he said gently. 'What's your name?'

'Harry,' the little boy said. 'Are you going to make my arm better?'

'I'm going to try,' Nick said, carefully unwrapping the splint. 'First, I'm going to take a picture of your arm so that I can see what's wrong with it.'

'My mum thinks it's broken,' the little boy said.

'Nothing that can't be fixed,' Nick said reassuringly. 'I've been mending broken bones for years. How old are you, Harry?'

'I'm six, but I'm big for my age. Everybody thinks I'm seven.'

Nick smiled. 'Yes, I think you could pass for a seven-year-old. I've got a little boy who's six and I think he's a bit smaller than you.'

'What's his name?' Harry asked.

'Ianni,' Nick replied, gently stroking the boy's hair in a soothing gesture.

They were already in the radiology department with Harry on the table, waiting for the X-rays to be taken. Demelza was impressed by the calm way that Nick worked, keeping up a constant flow of conversation with his patient so that the little boy seemed to have lost his fear of the unfamiliar surroundings and the antiseptic smell that pervaded the hospital.

'He's a super doctor, isn't he?' Harry's mother whispered to Demelza as Nick busied himself with the X-ray. 'I wonder where he learned to speak such good English.'

'I don't know,' Demelza murmured, thinking that was one of the mysteries surrounding this man that she intended to solve.

The thought crossed her mind that it might have been pillow talk with his wife that had improved his English. She was surprised how she didn't like to think about that! She'd become fond of this helpful doctor in the few hours she'd known him and she liked to think of him as being completely unattached, apart from his delightful son, of course.

'You were right, Sister,' Nick said, coming across to show her the developed films. 'Transverse fracture of the ulna. Can you see it?'

She nodded as she studied the X-rays. 'Have you got a plaster technician on duty?'

Nick smiled down at her. 'We all have to turn our hands to everything in this hospital. I took the X-rays and I'll set the arm myself. Would you help me, please, Sister? We haven't any spare staff at the moment. At the end of the morning there's a general exodus for the long midday break. Unless there's an emergency, the hospital has only a skeleton staff in the afternoons. We've all got mobiles so there would be no problem to call back staff early if they were required.'

'Of course I'll help,' Demelza said quickly. 'Just show me where you keep the equipment and—'

'Through here. We do have a small plaster room, even if there's nobody in there at the moment.'

Harry was curled up on his mother's knee, watching Demelza as she soaked the bandages in preparation for application. Nick carefully lifted the little boy up onto the treatment table, carefully but expertly manipulating the bone into the correct position.

'You can pass me the first bandage now, Sister,' he said, quietly. 'Are you OK, Harry?'

The little boy nodded. 'When you've finished winding that stuff round my arm, will it be mended?'

Nick smiled. 'Well, it's not quite as quick as that, Harry. It's going to take about five weeks for the broken bones to mend. I expect you'll be back in England by then, won't you?'

'We go home at the end of next week, Doctor,' Harry's mother said.

'Can't we stay out here until my arm's better?' Harry asked brightly. 'It would be much better for my arm, wouldn't it, Doctor? I mean, that plane journey can't be good for broken arms, can it?'

Nick laughed. 'Good try, Harry! What does Mum think?'

Harry's mother thought that Dad needed to get back to work to earn some more money so they could come out again next year.

'And you'll have your nice new plaster to keep your arm safe on the plane, Harry,' Demelza put in. 'If you let me know your flight details I'll send a note to the airline and ask them to take extra special care of you.'

'And I'll give you a letter to give to your own doctor when you get home,' Nick said, putting the final touches to the plaster. 'There we go! You'll be as good as new in a few weeks, just so long as you don't start jumping off any more rocks. Promise me you won't do anything like that, Harry.'

Harry pulled a wry face. 'I promise...but I can play a bit, can't I?'

'Of course you can.'

Harry's mother was smiling as they walked with her to the outer door.

'Stavros will take you back to the beach resort,' Nick said.

He turned to look down at Demelza. 'You don't have to go back just yet, do you, Sister? I thought you might like to look round the hospital while you're here.'

She smiled. 'I'd like that very much. I've got a bag in the car with everything I need for the day so I'll just get it out before Stavros goes back to the resort.'

She went out to the car and helped to settle Harry and his mother in the back, smilingly requesting Stavros to take great care of her patient. Perhaps drive a little more slowly over the bumpy road down to the beach?

Stavros grinned back at Demelza. 'No problem, Sister,' he told her, letting in the clutch and hurtling off along the road, leaving a cloud of dust trailing behind him.

Nick was studying some case notes as he waited for her in Reception.

Demelza was shaking her head worriedly as she joined him. 'He's a fiendishly fast driver, our Stavros, isn't he? Where did you recruit him from? The Monte Carlo Rally?'

Nick smiled. 'Don't worry about Stavros. That's the way most of the young men out here drive and he can't drive any other way. We haven't lost a patient yet.'

'Well, that's reassuring.'

Nick was giving the notes back to the duty nurse. He turned round and put a hand under Demelza's elbow, guiding her gently towards the corridor.

'I thought we'd start with the wards—the medical

ward is just along here. Like all our departments, it's very small compared with the other hospitals you will have worked in.'

The touch of Nick's hand under her arm was pleasant as Demelza walked along the corridor. What a kind man he was, and so courteous. She was definitely beginning to feel that she wasn't a burden to him, that he wasn't regretting having had her foisted upon him.

'It's good of you to show me round,' she said politely as Nick pushed open the door to the ward. 'I mean, I suppose this is your lunch-hour.'

Nick grinned, his features taking on the appealing characteristics she'd noticed in his charming little son. 'You obviously haven't lived on a Greek island before. Everything grinds to a halt at midday and relaxation takes over. As I said before, unless there's an emergency, we have a long lunch and rest afterwards. Things get back to normal about five or six.'

There were only six beds in the medical ward, with a curtain dividing the male section from the female. Two men and a woman were sitting at a table at one end of the ward, having lunch. There was a bottle of wine on the table, and Demelza could see a large crusty loaf, some feta cheese and a dish of olives and tomatoes amongst the other appetising-looking dishes.

A nurse in a white cotton dress was just about to sit down at the table with her patients. She smiled at Nick and said something in rapid Greek.

Nick replied, before turning to explain to Demelza that the nurse was asking if they would like to have some lunch.

'I said we had to get on with our tour of the hospital.'

'The patients look so happy!' she remarked. 'What a great atmosphere you have in here!'

'They look forward to a glass of wine or two with their lunch. And unless they're really ill or on medication that contra-indicates wine, there's no reason why they shouldn't indulge themselves. The lady is recovering from pneumonia. Both the men have had cardiac problems which have been resolved and, as they keep on reminding me, a reasonable amount of red wine is supposed to be good for their arteries.'

Nick spent a few minutes chatting with the patients who were all obviously delighted to see him. Then it was on to inspect the surgical ward, which was of a similar size. Two male patients were sitting at the dining table while a nurse was helping a couple of bedridden patients.

Demelza was beginning to feel a warm glow about this tiny hospital. There was a lot of tender loving care going on in here. Even in the small operating theatre, she found a nurse lovingly polishing the handles on the cupboards.

'Shouldn't that nurse be having her lunch?' Demelza asked as she and Nick went out into the corridor.

'Eleni will go when she's satisfied that the theatre is perfect in every way. We don't have set hours here.'

'I'm very impressed with the hospital,' Demelza said. 'I'm beginning to see what life out here is really like.'

Nick paused in the corridor outside the small obstetric ward. 'Well, as you're so interested, if you'd like to spend the afternoon with me, I could also show you something of my island.'

She heard the pride in his voice as he'd said 'my island'.

'Your island?' she queried gently.

'I was born here,' he said proudly. 'Oh, I had to live in England for many years but I came back as soon as I could. There's no place on earth like Kopelos.'

There was a catch in his voice as he finished off his sentence. She wanted to ask so many questions about why he'd had to live in England, but it was early days and she didn't want to appear too inquisitive. Little by little, she hoped he would reveal the story of his life to her during the long hot summer she was to spend on this delightful island.

'I want to get to know this island very much,' she said. 'Thank you. I hadn't made any plans for this afternoon except to relax in the sun on the beach.'

'Ah, not the crowded beach at the resort!' Nick said. 'I'll take you to a quiet beach where you'll hear nothing but the sound of the sea, the bleating of the lambs on the hillside...' He broke off and smiled. 'We'd better get on with the tour before I get carried away. This is the obstetrics ward, as you can see...'

There were a couple of young mothers looking after their babies in the tiny ward. A nurse came over to talk to Nick in rapid Greek. He introduced Demelza and the conversation changed to English.

Demelza smiled at one of the young mothers who had finished feeding her baby and was proudly dressing her in a tiny white gown.

'What a beautiful baby!'

'Here, take!' the mother said, handing the baby over to Demelza.

As she snuggled the baby against her, Demelza noticed that indefinable smell all babies had when they'd just been powdered and pampered and put into clean clothes. A lump rose at the back of her throat as she looked at the dear little rosebud mouth, the tiny dim-pled cheeks, the dark lashes like a curtain over the baby's precious eyes.

If she was to work with babies again she would have to steel herself and be totally professional. She couldn't allow the loss of her unborn son to colour her treatment of babies. Maybe it would get easier with time, but for the moment…

She forced herself to keep smiling as she handed back the baby. A lifetime of other people's babies spread ahead of her and she was going to have to cope with her emotions better than she was doing at present.

Back home on the farm she'd deliberately banished the dream of having babies of her own. It had been impossible to imagine being in another relationship. And babies should be born with two loving parents. Yes, she'd had a wonderful loving relationship but it was a beautiful experience from the past. She had to move on. It was early days, but she recognised that leaving the farm and starting a new life out here had been the best move she could have made.

She gave herself a mental shake as she concentrated all her attention on getting to know the hospital and how it worked. There was no doubt she would have to work closely with Nick and the hospital staff, and it was essential that she find out all she can.

'It's a great little hospital, Nick,' she said, as he escorted her out through the front door.

'It's very compact, but we can deal with most un-complicated cases of medicine, surgery, obstetrics, gy-naecology and orthopaedics. Obviously, the cases we can't handle are taken to hospitals in Athens or Rhodes.'

He was striding ahead of her along the small parking

area in front of the hospital. 'Here's my car, Demelza. As you can see, I parked it under the largest tree for the sake of the shade, but it's going to feel very hot until the air-conditioning kicks in.'

It was a sturdy-looking, four-wheel-drive vehicle. Nick unlocked the doors and Demelza climbed up into the front passenger seat. The hot leather felt scorching through her thin cotton dress. She put her bag by her feet.

'Will it be possible to change into my shorts when we get to this beach?' she asked.

Nick was turning on the air-conditioning. 'Of course. And we can have a swim to cool off.'

They headed away from the town on a narrow road carved out of the hillside.

'When I was a boy, this was a mere donkey track,' Nick said, changing down into a lower gear. 'We used to come up here to play sometimes. My mother would send me out to get fresh herbs and I'd take a couple of friends and we'd forget what time it was. Sometimes we even used to forget the herbs! That was when I was only about five or six. It was a big change when I went to live in England and found that children couldn't roam around freely like we do here.'

'Why did you go to live in England?'

Nick took a deep breath. 'Ah, that's a long story.'

Demelza glanced across, but Nick's eyes held a veiled expression. He was making it perfectly obvious that he didn't want to talk about it. There was a sadness in the way his shoulders had suddenly drooped. The air of devil-may-care was missing as he kept his eyes studiously on the narrow road ahead.

She leaned back against her seat and allowed the welcome cool air from the air-conditioning to revive her spirits. Beneath Nick's confident exterior there was a deep vulnerability about him. He obviously loved living on this island—who wouldn't? She was already in love with the place. So it must have been terrible for a young boy to be transplanted to England. She sensed there had been some sort of crisis in the family.

His handsome, dark features and Mediterranean mannerisms proclaimed him to be essentially Greek, but perhaps his mother had been English? She didn't want to pry. If she managed to gain his confidence he would perhaps fill her in on his background. She was intrigued by him, by the depth of his character and the secrets which seemed to be hidden beneath the surface. She found herself longing to know more about him and felt surprised by the way she was feeling. It was a long time since she'd been so curious about a man.

Since Simon's death she'd felt like a nun, having absolutely no interest in the opposite sex. But here she was, driving along beside a very handsome, drop-dead-gorgeous man and not feeling the least bit intimidated. Feeling, in fact, nothing but admiration and the desire to get to know him better.

'There's the bay we're going to!' Nick pointed ahead as they crested the hill.

She glanced sideways at him and caught the flash of strong white teeth in his dark, animated face. The car lurched from the metalled road onto a stony track and Demelza found herself hanging onto her seat. She was glad of the restraining seat belt as Nick carefully negotiated the potholes in the track.

'We had a lot of rain during the winter and it will be weeks before anyone gets around to attempting to mend this section of road. Very few people use it so it's not a priority on the island. I asked the mayor of

Kopelos town about it a few days ago and he simply smiled, spread his hands in front of him and said, "*Avrio!*"'

'Which means?'

Nick laughed. 'Tomorrow! You'll hear that word a lot around here. The philosophy is that most things can wait until tomorrow. It leads to a relaxed style of life but some very bumpy roads.'

Demelza glanced out of her side window and felt a shiver of fear at the sight of the sheer drop.

Nick took one hand off the steering-wheel and patted her hand. 'Don't worry, Demelza. I've driven down this track many times. You're quite safe.'

He removed his hand to steady the wheel. She was surprised to find that she missed the touch of his fingers but was relieved to see the intense concentration on his face. Glancing sideways again out of her window, she concentrated on the beauty of the ravine below her rather than the danger of the road. Fir trees sprawled up the sides of the hills and somewhere in the depths of the valley she caught a glimpse of water, a precious commodity on this island. It was only a small river, she saw, making its way to the blue expanse of the bay.

'Nearly there!' Nick said. 'That's the worst bit over.'

Demelza breathed a sigh of relief as the track eventually opened out into a wide, sandy swathe of land, bordering the sea.

'We'll leave the car here and walk down to the beach. It's too rocky to go any further. I'll get the food out of the back. Do you want to change here? It's pretty hot out there.'

Demelza nodded, feeling suddenly embarrassed about undressing. She only had to pull her bikini on under her uniform dress and then whip off the dress but…

'I'll take the stuff down to the beach and you can follow when you're ready,' Nick said, in a matter-of-fact voice.

Problem solved! She flashed him a grateful smile as she climbed down from her seat. The afternoon heat hit her. It was only May. What was it going to be like in the real summer months?

She stood behind the car and quickly changed into her new white bikini, noting that it was only slightly whiter than her own skin. Extricating the sunblock from her bag, she applied some to every inch of her bare skin. She wasn't going to take any chances. Besides which, she had a whole six months in which to acquire her safe tan.

Glancing around the side of the car, she saw that Nick had disappeared beyond the trees onto the beach. Picking up her bag, she hurriedly followed in the direction she'd seen him going. She felt a certain excitement rising up inside her. It was so amazing to be a long way from England on a deserted beach with a handsome stranger. She felt as if she'd shed ten years since arriving on this island. She was alive again after the arid, desert years.

She saw him immediately as she walked over the small dune at the edge of the beach. He was spreading a rug on the sand. She noticed that he'd already changed into black, figure-hugging swimming shorts and with a shock she recognised the frisson of excitement that ran through her. It wasn't desire exactly, or was it? If it wasn't desire, it was something dangerously similar.

He raised his head and waved his hand as he saw her coming. She took a deep breath to steady herself.

CHAPTER THREE

Nick stood up and came to meet Demelza as she hurried down the beach. He was reaching down to take her bag when he paused to give her a quizzical look.

'You're out of breath, Demelza. You should have taken your time. It's too hot to hurry in this heat.'

Her breathlessness had nothing to do with hurrying! She was experiencing the strangest feelings at the sight of Nick in those flatteringly macho swimming shorts. It was a long time since she'd seen a handsome man like Nick with so few clothes on and at such close quarters. It was having an unnerving effect on her which she could only describe as pleasant...well, actually, if she was truly honest, which she was trying not to be, it was more than pleasant!

She tried to banish the thoughts but they wouldn't go. She recognised that it was all part of her reawakening and she would have to deal with it very carefully.

'We'd better swim first before we have lunch. As we all know, it's not a good idea to swim on a full stomach,' Nick said, putting Demelza's bag on the sand beside the rug.

'I've only brought a couple of bread rolls and some salami,' Demelza said, quickly. 'I hadn't anticipated coming out for a full-blown picnic.'

Nick smiled. 'Don't worry. I've brought enough for an army. When I'm leaving the village each morning, I've got so many friends and relatives who're convinced I don't eat enough that I have to take extra bags to put the food in. Ianni goes to school laden with home-made pastries to share with his friends. I usually share mine among the hospital staff so, as you can imagine, both Ianni and I are very popular. I haven't had time to open up my goodies this morning so I'm glad you came along to help me eat it all.'

They were already walking down towards the sparkling blue sea. The sand was impossibly hot under Demelza's feet.

'Ow!' She began to run the last few steps into the sea.

Nick laughed as he streaked ahead. 'I always went barefoot as a child whenever I could and the soles of my feet are as hard as nails.'

Demelza felt nothing but relief as her feet touched the cool water.

'The sea is amazingly cool, Nick,' she called as she waded out towards the deeper water. 'I always thought the Mediterranean would be warm.'

'The sea doesn't warm up until later in the summer. Most Greeks say the sea is too cool to swim in before August. But I'm half-English so I take my life in my hands and swim when the tourists do, in the spring.'

'So you're half-English?' Demelza felt she wasn't prying now that Nick had brought up the subject.

They were treading water, out of their depth, but the salty Mediterranean was so buoyant it required little effort to stay afloat.

He moved nearer to her, his strong, dark, muscular, bare arm almost touching her pale white skin.

'Yes, my mother was English. She came out here when she was a young student, fell in love with the island and then with my father. I don't know which love was stronger, because it broke her heart to leave the island—mine, too, but I was only a child and more adaptable.'

'Why did you have to leave?' she asked carefully, as she turned onto her back with her eyes closed, allowing the buoyant water to hold her up.

Demelza felt as if she were lying on a water mattress. A small fish was tickling her toes. She spread her arms out from her sides, her fingers lazily stroking the surface of the water. The sun on her face felt so blissful. There wasn't a sound to be heard except the occasional bleat of a goat on the hillside and the gentle lapping of the water as she and Nick made languid movements with their limbs.

She heard Nick, beside her, drawing in his breath. For a few moments he didn't reply to her question. When he did, his voice was quiet, devoid of all emotion.

'My mother had to return to England...for medical reasons. So I had to go with her. It's a long story. Anyway, let's finish our swim. I'm starving!'

She heard the deliberate return to an animated tone. It was obvious that Nick didn't want to talk about it and, lying here in this idyllic paradise, she didn't want to hear anything that would change the atmosphere.

'I'm starving, too!' she said, quickly turning onto her front before setting off back. 'Race you to the shore!'

Nick broke into a strong crawl and streaked past her. He waited for her on the sand. He held out both his hands towards her as she emerged from the sea, and it seemed perfectly natural to take hold of them. She looked up into his eyes and gave a shiver.

'You're cold,' he said in a concerned tone. 'Come and dry yourself.'

She wasn't in the least bit cold. It had been the touch

of his hands that had produced the involuntary shiver. Whatever was the matter with her? She didn't dare to think.

She took a towel from her bag and went behind a tree to strip off and put on her spare bikini. This one was black and she'd only tried it on in the shop. The top was a little bit risqué, leaving not very much to the imagination, but the shop assistant had assured her it was what was being worn this year on Mediterranean beaches.

She'd felt decidedly daring to even consider a bikini in the first place, but the old swimsuit she'd had for more years than she cared to remember was literally falling to pieces. And when she'd investigated at the shop in the nearest town to the farm, the shop assistant had been adamant that she would be much too hot in a one-piece on a Mediterranean beach. Apparently, her over-helpful adviser had been on lots of package tours to the Med and knew what was required. So Demelza had emerged from the shop with two expensive bikinis, having spent an enormous amount on four very small strips of material.

She shielded her eyes as she looked up at the hot sun. Her skin was already dry and she felt more comfortable in a dry bikini. Nick, she noticed, was standing in the hot sun, towelling himself dry and slipping into dry shorts. She caught a glimpse of the brown skin at the top of his muscular legs and hurriedly averted her eyes. Her pulses were racing enough already!

Nick's dry shorts were black, like the other pair. She was now resigned to the effect they had on her and sauntered out from behind the tree as if she were used to taking lunch on a deserted beach with a handsome man she'd only met the day before.

'A glass of wine, Demelza?' Nick was uncorking a bottle.

'Lovely!'

She was going to suspend judgement on her wayward behaviour until the end of the meal. Sitting down on the rug, she smiled her thanks as she accepted the glass and took a tentative sip. Mmm! The wine was most refreshing. She leaned back on one elbow as she sipped.

Nick was smiling down at her. 'I think you're beginning to relax and get used to life on our island, aren't you, Demelza?'

She nodded and took another sip as she wiggled her toes in the sand at the end of the rug.

'Last night you seemed very nervous,' Nick said slowly. 'I wasn't sure you would fit into such an easygoing place, but now…'

She sat up straight, so that her eyes were closer to his. 'I've been out in the cold for such a long time that I find it hard…' She paused, searching for the right words. 'I find it hard to relate to people…especially men.'

'Ah! So that's the problem, is it?' He narrowed his eyes. 'Have you had a bad experience with men?'

'No, no! Quite the reverse. I've loved…too much… but always the same man, and now…'

He leaned forward. 'Love is very precious, isn't it? And when it's gone, how can you replace it?'

His voice was husky with emotion. She swallowed hard as she watched him straightening up before leaning back on his own side of the rug. For a brief, mad moment she'd imagined he was going to kiss her. And the idea that this could happen had been extremely pleasant…more than pleasant. She knew that it would have been an experience she would have enjoyed enormously.

But she realised that she'd completely overestimated Nick's intentions. She'd already witnessed that he was a kind, caring doctor, so he was merely giving her sympathy. But, oh, the touch of his lips would have meant so much more to her!

Nick seemed totally unaware of the emotional turmoil he'd caused as he reached out to remove packages from his large bag.

'Try one of these spinach pies. Anna makes the best spanokopita on the island.'

'Who's Anna?' Demelza asked as she bit into the flaky pastry. 'Mmm! This is delicious!'

'Anna is my aunt, my father's sister. She's married to Giorgio who owns the taverna. You may remember seeing her in the kitchen last night. She was busy cooking so there wasn't time to introduce you. Anyway, last night I didn't know you well enough to make a proper introduction.'

Demelza wiped the crumbs of the spanokopita from her lips with a paper napkin. 'Do you think you know me well enough now to introduce me to your aunt?'

He gave her a strange, enigmatic smile. 'I think the real you is hiding behind an iron curtain but I also think I've had a few glimpses of what you're really like. Maybe if you told me something about yourself, I'd get a better picture.'

Was she really hiding her real self? It was a startling thought, but Nick was probably right.

She took a sip of her wine and leaned back on her elbows. The fir tree they were picnicking under was providing some welcome shade and the view of the sea with the sun shining on it was breathtaking. She could feel herself relaxing even more.

'It's so long since I thought about myself as a person in my own right that sometimes I wonder who I really am. Since Simon died, I've simply looked after other people. I was so grief-stricken after his death that I didn't have the strength to see what was happening.'

'And what was happening?' he asked quietly.

She took a deep breath. 'The day that Simon was killed, I wanted to die as well.'

'He was killed?'

Nick's startled yet sympathetic voice gave her the strength to confront her fear of talking about the awful day that had changed her life for ever. She'd never actually used the word 'killed' before in connection with Simon's death...but that's what had happened. And the unexpectedness of it all had plunged her into deep shock.

'It was four months after our wedding. I was three months pregnant—very happily pregnant. Simon and I felt as if we were in heaven. We'd wanted to start a family—a large family—as soon as possible, and our wish had come true.'

Demelza cleared her throat. It seemed important to tell Nick the whole story, not just the bare outline which was what she usually came up with when it was absolutely essential to tell someone about Simon's death.

'Simon's last day started just like any other. He went out early to supervise the milking with a couple of farmhands. He always came back for breakfast after-wards and we would sit at the table and plan our day together...'

She broke off. 'I don't know why I'm telling you all the details. You don't want to know…'

'Oh, but I do!'

His strong voice reassured her again. Looking across into those dark, expressive eyes, she knew that she'd found a true friend.

'Take your time, Demelza,' he said huskily. 'I think it's good for you to relive the past. It can have a healing effect on your sadness.'

She nodded as she recognised that he was speaking as an experienced doctor again, a doctor who was used to listening to his patients. But she also knew that he was the sort of man in whom she could confide in a way she hadn't been able to since Simon's death.

'I remember, I got up to have my shower after Simon left, and then I went downstairs to prepare breakfast. I was lifting out a box of eggs from the cupboard when I heard the most alarming shouting going on outside the cowshed. I was still holding the eggs as I looked out of the window and saw… I remember my hands simply stopped working and the box of eggs slipped onto the kitchen floor…'

Demelza put her hands over her face. She didn't want Nick to see the uncontrollable tears. Gently, he moved to her side, carefully parting her hands with his own as he dabbed her face with a tissue.

'Don't be afraid to cry, Demelza. You've stored up this awful memory for a long time.' He paused before speaking quietly. 'What did you see?'

She swallowed hard, leaning back to prop herself against Nick's comforting shoulder. His strong arm was supporting both of them as they leaned close together on the rug.

'I saw Simon lying on the ground, partially covered

by the tractor which our youngest farmhand had reversed over him. I ran outside, but there was nothing anyone could do. I knew as I knelt over him that he was dead. I won't go into details, but all the clinical signs... I tried to revive him but I knew it was hopeless, even though I kept on until the ambulance arrived and...' She broke off, unable to go on.

Gently, Nick put his arms round her and held her close against his strong muscular chest.

'Cry if you want to, Demelza,' he said softly. 'Let it all come out. You need to get rid of all that grief.'

Her sobs were subsiding as she leaned against him. And for the first time in six years she felt a sense of calm stealing over her.

She pulled herself gently away so that she could look up into those dark, comforting eyes.

'Thank you, Nick,' she whispered. 'Thank you for listening so sympathetically. I think maybe I just glimpsed some light at the end of the tunnel.'

'I hope so, because I think I just glimpsed the real you. The woman behind the mask. Did you have any family to support you?' he asked gently.

'My own parents had died a couple of years before that. They'd been on a touring holiday when their coach crashed and unfortunately...'

She took another deep breath as the memories flooded back.

'Simon's family begged me to stay on at the farm. His parents said they couldn't manage without me, which was certainly true. They came to rely on me for everything. Soon I was running the farm and I couldn't see any way out of my... I don't want to seem melodramatic, but it used to feel as if I was serving a prison sentence. There was so much emotional blackmail from

Simon's mother that sometimes I felt I couldn't take on any more dutiful tasks.'

'You said you were three months pregnant when Simon died,' he said. 'What…?'

'I lost the baby at six months,' she said, in the even tone she always employed when it was essential to talk about her miscarriage. 'A scan had showed my baby was a boy. He was the only thing that kept me going immediately after Simon's death. And then, when he was gone, I simply lived from day to day. But last year Simon's younger brother got married and his wife wanted to live with him at the farm.'

'So you saw a way out after all that time?' Nick said, gently.

Demelza made an effort to smile. 'I saw an escape route and I took it.'

What would Nick think of her, crying like that? But it was his encouragement that had prompted her to open up. She felt a lifting of her spirits. He was going to be a good friend.

Perhaps more than a friend? She knew she was certainly attracted to Nick. It was more than mere admiration at the sight of his handsome, muscular frame. It wasn't the fact that she was starved of love and affection—even though that certainly was true. No, it was pure, unadulterated attraction for Nick, the man himself. But how would she react if their friendship moved on? She'd had so little experience of men in social situations. In fact, she was a complete novice! It was wonderful to think of becoming involved with Nick, but at the same time she was afraid she wouldn't be able to cope.

She reached for her wineglass, which had fallen over in the sand.

'Do you think I could have another glass of wine?'

Nick smiled. 'You most certainly can.'

She watched his strong, firm fingers as he reached across with the bottle. He would make an excellent surgeon, she was sure of it.

'Where did you train as a doctor?' she asked, raising the glass to her lips.

He propped the bottle up against a stone and turned to face her. 'In London, at St Celine's hospital.'

'And you prefer to work out here?'

He smiled. 'Don't you? Is there any comparison between living on a dark London street and spending your days on this warm sunny island?'

She moved to the edge of the rug and propped herself up against the sun-warmed smooth surface of a large rock. 'You're absolutely right. There's absolutely no comparison.'

'Come on, you've hardly eaten anything! Catch!' Nick picked up a ripe, juicy tomato and tossed it in her direction.

Demelza laughed as she caught it.

'And then you must try some of this cheese pie that Anna made. We call it theropita.'

'Theropita,' Demelza said carefully. 'I've brought a teach-yourself-Greek book with me, but I haven't had much time to study it yet.'

'I can teach you,' Nick said.

'I'd like that,' she said softly, knowing that she would enjoy any activity that brought her into contact with Nick.

From somewhere amongst the pile of Nick's clothes a phone was ringing. He pulled a mobile from his trouser pocket.

Demelza heard him speaking in rapid Greek, his face

stern and concentrated as he listened. He cut the connection and stood up.

'That was Nurse Krisanthe. She's admitted a young woman who's about thirty-five weeks pregnant. Apparently, she's been in labour at home for several hours and hadn't realised what was happening. The foetus is showing signs of distress and Nurse Krisanthe thinks a Caesarean section might be necessary.'

Nick was pulling his trousers on over his shorts. Demelza leapt to her feet and began extricating her dress from her bag.

'Have you got the necessary staff for a Caesarean?' she asked after she'd buttoned up the front of her dress over her bikini. They were already trekking back over the sand, Nick's long legs outstripping her so that she had to take two strides to his one.

'I've told Krisanthe to contact our anaesthetist and have him standing by. I'll perform the Caesarean if it's necessary. I may find it possible to deliver the baby naturally, but I won't know until I've examined the patient.'

'But if the baby is displaying obvious signs of distress then the sooner we get the baby out the better,' she said, breathlessly climbing into the Land Rover beside Nick.

'Yes, yes, of course,' he said, a trifle irritably.

All trace of her relaxed companion of the last couple of hours had disappeared. Nick was totally focussed now on the medical task in hand. She'd better confine her remarks to the minimum.

Nick gripped the steering-wheel hard as he drove the rugged vehicle up the hill. Demelza tried not to think about the sheer drop at the side of the bumpy road as she stared straight ahead.

'I believe you've had experience in obstetrics, haven't you?' Nick said tersely.

'Yes. I staffed in Obstetrics Theatre for a while. We—'

'Would you assist me today? My obstetrics sister is off sick and I don't want to call her back until she's completely recovered.'

'Of course I'll assist.' Demelza knew she was very experienced but she felt a little scared. She tried to convince herself that her practical and theoretical training wouldn't desert her. You never lost the medical and surgical skills that you'd practised over the years, did you?

'Good!' Nick flashed her a grateful smile and her spirits lifted. It would be good to take on some real nursing after all this time.

She thought about the patient waiting for them to arrive as Nick increased his speed when they reached the metalled road. The sooner they could get back to the hospital the better.

A young nurse was waiting for them in Reception. Her face broke into a relieved smile as they arrived.

'Come quickly, Dr Capodistrias!'

They followed the slight, white-clad figure down the corridor to the obstetrics ward. Nurse Krisanthe was leaning over her patient, wiping a damp cloth over her brow. The young father-to-be was sitting beside the bed, holding tightly to his wife's hand. He looked up in relief when Nick arrived, and began a torrent of agitated words.

'Michaelis tells me that Katia, his wife, has been experiencing pain since the middle of last night but they had no idea she was in labour,' Nick told Demelza as they scrubbed up before examining their patient.

Demelza was alarmed to see that the dilatation of the cervix was very poor. They couldn't deliver the baby until the birth canal was much wider. Meantime, glancing at the foetal monitor, it was obvious that the baby was suffering acute distress. It needed to be delivered as soon as possible.

'We haven't time to try dilating the cervix with drugs,' Nick said evenly. 'I'm going to take Katia into Theatre.'

A small man came hurrying through the swing doors.

'This is Dr Patris, our anaesthetist,' Nick told Demelza. He spoke briefly to the man before outlining what was happening to the young mother and her anxious husband.

There was no time for the usual pre-operative preparations. Without any preamble, the patient was wheeled into the small operating theatre and anaesthetised.

A young nurse dressed Demelza in a sterile gown. As she stood at the other side of the table from Nick she felt her strength and confidence returning. She'd been in similar situations many times before. Her skills were still intact. Carefully, she swabbed the patient's abdomen before handing Nick a scalpel in preparation for the incision.

Nick leaned across their patient and carefully cut through the abdominal wall and into the lower segment of the uterus. He paused briefly before placing his gloved hands in the cavity and removing the baby.

Demelza had seen this performed many times but it never ceased to move her. The sight of a newborn infant, saved by Caesarean section, was always miraculous to her. Without their intervention, the baby would have had very little chance of survival.

'It's a girl!' Nick said, his eyes smiling above the mask as he clamped and cut the umbilical cord.

Demelza looked across at him and felt a rush of happiness. Her happiness was momentarily tinged with sadness as she remembered her own son. But only momentarily. She wouldn't allow any morbid thoughts to spoil the moment. She was a professional again and, as such, there was no time for self-pity.

'Nothing wrong with her lungs!' she remarked as she took the lustily bawling infant from Nick's hands and carried her over to the nearby examination table. Carefully, she cleaned the wrinkled newborn, wrapping her in a sterile dressing sheet before beginning the routine postnatal checks. When Nick had finished treating the mother he came across to check the baby's heart and lungs.

'No obvious complications, Demelza. We've been very lucky here. I think young Katia got her dates muddled up. She hasn't been into hospital for any antenatal check-ups. She told me she thought she was about thirty-five weeks pregnant, but I would say she was nearer full term. What's the birth weight?'

'Three and a half kilos. Not bad for a first baby.'

Nick smiled down at her. 'Definitely full term, I would say.'

He lowered his voice. 'I remember Katia's and Michaelis's wedding about six months ago. Since then, I've had the distinct impression Katia has been avoiding me in the village. These things still matter out here. It's such a pity she put the baby's life at risk. Katia and Michaelis are both only seventeen, so they're still very much under parental control. I may have to corroborate a fib to her grandmother and say that Katia's baby came early.'

Demelza smiled. 'Are you willing to do that?'

'If a little white lie will keep the family happy I'm willing to go along with the general conspiracy, even though I know Grandma will have her own theory when she sees the large baby with her lovely black hair and long nails.'

'I can see I've got a lot to learn about the customs on Kopelos.'

'Plenty of time,' Nick said, as he watched her wrapping the newborn girl in a cotton sleeping gown.

'I've only got six months out here,' she said slowly, as she lifted the baby into her arms. The warmth of this newborn miracle brought a lump to her throat, which she swallowed rapidly. No looking back now. She was going forward.

'Ah, yes, I'd forgotten how short your contract was. As it's a new venture, the travel company want to make sure there is a need for this new clinic. The beach resort closes down in the winter months. Well, thank you very much for your help. If you'd like to escort mother and baby back to the ward, I'll see them shortly when I've finished my rounds.'

Demelza held the baby against her as she watched Nick striding out of the theatre. She'd been dismissed and she should feel relieved that her work was finished. But she didn't. She and Nick were back on professional terms again. It was as if the picnic on the beach had been a dream.

As she stood outside the hospital a short time later, she knew she was free to go, but she felt reluctant to leave. The evening stretched ahead of her and she felt suddenly at a loose end. The sun was already dipping lower in the sky and the islanders were preparing to socialise. Across the road from the hospital she could see a group of old men sitting outside at a table, having a loud discussion as they sipped their glasses of ouzo.

She ought to make the effort to join in somewhere, find out more about the fascinating culture of this island. She felt a sense of loss stealing over her and knew she would have to pull herself together. There was a sense of anticlimax after the excitement of the emergency Caesarean. That was what was hitting her now, she told herself unconvincingly.

In her heart of hearts she knew that it was more than that. Since midday she'd been with Nick, roused by his enthusiasm for life, encouraged by his *joie de vivre*. And she missed him already, although it was only about an hour since they'd parted in Theatre.

She'd just been another pair of willing hands to him and she shouldn't take him too seriously. In this re-awakening process he was the first man who'd stirred any interest in her.

She was a complete novice again where emotions were concerned and she had a lot to learn about not going overboard. She looked along the road that led to the village. It couldn't be much more than a mile. The walk would do her good and she might snap out of this dreadful mood that had claimed her.

Walking along the road, her spirits began to lift again. It was difficult not to get the feel-good factor when you started to absorb the atmosphere of this vibrant island. She passed a couple of tavernas where the evening socialising was developing. The haunting strains of Greek music followed her along the road and she found herself smiling.

So much had changed since she'd met Nick. He was good to look at, wonderful company in an off-duty situation. It was a relief to find that her interest in the opposite sex was re-emerging. But could she cope with the emotional turmoil that was already making itself obvious?

She jumped to the side of the road in alarm as a vehicle ground to a halt beside her.

'Sorry, I didn't mean to scare you!'

Nick was leaning across, holding open the passenger door of his Land Rover. 'Can I give you a lift back to the village?'

She hesitated. Having admitted her confused feelings about Nick, she knew it might be safer to say she preferred to walk. But that just wasn't true and, anyway, Nick would wonder why she was spurning his offer.

'Thanks.' She climbed up into the passenger seat. 'I was actually enjoying the walk.'

'I'm sure you were, but I wanted to talk to you. I'd hoped to catch you before you left the hospital but my rounds took longer than usual. I do like to get home as early as I can for Ianni. Katerina is very good with him but I know he's happiest when I'm home.'

'I'm sure he is. What about his mother? Doesn't he miss her?'

Nick hesitated, his eyes firmly fixed on the road ahead. A donkey ambled out of an alley and wandered onto the road. Nick slowed until the donkey's owner had got the animal under control again.

'Ianni has got used to our life being just the two of us. It was an acrimonious divorce and I think, young as he was, Ianni soaked up some of the unpleasant atmosphere. It was a relief for him when everything became resolved and the two of us had a home together away from Lydia.'

Demelza recognised the emotional overtones in Nick's voice and decided it wouldn't be fair to pry.

Nick would tell her more if he wanted to. And it was really none of her business, she reminded herself. She was trying very hard to remain detached from Nick's affairs.

'I'm sure it was a difficult experience for both you and Ianni,' she said, quietly.

'You're absolutely right, Demelza. I couldn't go through that again.'

He gave a harsh laugh. 'In fact, if I'm honest, I'd run a mile if I ever felt I was going to commit myself to a scheming woman again.'

'Was she scheming—your ex-wife?'

In spite of her better judgement, Demelza found her curiosity was getting the better of her. And was it her imagination, or did she feel that Nick was relieved to be able to talk to her? Just as she'd found it helpful to talk to him about her past life when they'd been on the beach that afternoon.

It was nothing to do with her interest in the man, she tried to tell herself. She was merely providing a willing, sympathetic ear.

'Tell me about it!' Nick said, his voice full of emotion. 'You name it, Lydia tried it on.'

He paused. 'Funny thing was, as soon as we'd settled custody of Ianni, it became easier.'

He broke off and smiled. 'Talk of the devil!' He pulled the vehicle to a halt at the entrance to the narrow village street where motorised vehicles were prohibited. The street was only wide enough for motorbikes and Demelza had learned that even they had been banned when they'd become too much of a nuisance.

'See what I see?' Nick said, pointing down between the ancient houses of the narrow street.

Two little boys were chasing each other outside one

of the houses, whooping with laughter. As Nick reversed his car into the parking space at the end of the street, Ianni looked in their direction.

'Daddy!' the little boy shouted happily.

Lefteris, his little friend, was completely forgotten as Ianni charged down the street to meet his father.

'I was waiting for you, Daddy. Katerina said it was too soon but...'

Ianni flung himself into Nick's arms. Nick hugged him closely, a contented smile on his face.

'Remember Demelza?'

Ianni smiled. 'Of course.' The young boy moved around the front of the car and held up his arms towards her.

Demelza knelt down, smiling happily as Ianni hugged her, not so enthusiastically as with his father but certainly showing that she was his friend.

'Are you coming to Giorgio's with us again, Demel...Demelza?' Ianni asked, his young, beguiling eyes shining with innocent excitement.

'Well, I—'

Nick's mobile rang. She was glad of the interruption. There was nothing she would like better than to immerse herself in this family situation but she was so afraid of overstepping the mark...and so afraid of becoming too involved. Far better to make her excuses sooner rather than later.

She glanced at Nick who was having an earnest conversation in Greek. He looked worried as he ended the call.

'I've just agreed to go back to the hospital,' he said to Demelza. 'Katia is complaining of abdominal pain. I have to check her out. The thing is...' He was glancing down at Ianni who was frowning. 'I'm sorry, Ianni.

You'd better stay on with Katerina for a bit longer. I'll be as quick as I can.'

'Can't I go home and be with Demelza?' Ianni asked plaintively. 'She lives upstairs and...I could get my homework done, couldn't I?'

Nick's face creased into a grin. 'You really are a manipulative little—'

'Don't worry about Ianni,' Demelza heard herself saying. 'I'll take care of him till you get back.' She glanced down at Ianni who had wrapped his arms around her legs in gratitude. 'But it's homework first, remember?'

Ianni grinned and said something to Lefteris, obviously indicating that they'd finished their game. Demelza felt the little boy's hand taking hold of hers. It was a wonderful feeling to be wanted like this.

'Well, if you're sure,' Nick said. 'I'll call in and tell Katerina where Ianni is, and if you want to go out, Katerina will be willing to—'

'Stop worrying. I'm perfectly happy to look after Ianni.'

'Go on, Dad!' Ianni said. 'The sooner you go, the sooner you'll get back, and there might still be time for us all to go to Giorgio's.'

As Demelza's eyes met Nick's she was thinking that young Ianni was old beyond his years. He'd probably suffered over the divorce of his parents but it didn't seem to have done him any harm.

'See you later,' Nick called as he reversed the car and went back along the road to the town.

Ianni was tugging her impatiently. 'Come on, Demelza.'

Her plans for the evening were now mapped out. Everything was beyond her control, but she found herself happily looking forward to the next few hours. Looking after Nick's child wasn't becoming too involved, was it? It wasn't as if she'd actively sought to become involved in this family. It had just sort of happened. But she hadn't felt so light-hearted in a long time. Not since…

She didn't want to think about how long it was since she'd felt so happy. It was merely a release of the emotions she'd kept cooped up. That and the effect of the warm sun and the sparkling blue sea. It was like taking a holiday from herself. She would have felt like this even without the comfort of this ready-made family, wouldn't she?

CHAPTER FOUR

DEMELZA was sitting on the edge of Nick's sofa, trying desperately to keep her eyes open, when Nick returned from the hospital. The small pyjama-clad figure in her arms stirred at the sound of his father's voice, but his eyes remained closed.

Nick sat down beside her on the sofa. 'I'm sorry I took so long, Demelza. As I said, when I phoned you from the hospital, it wasn't a straightforward case. If I hadn't known Katia's background I wouldn't have been able to sort out what was happening.'

He leaned back against the sofa and closed his eyes wearily. 'Katia was insisting she had these terrible abdominal pains and it was only when I called her bluff and said I would have to take her back to Theatre that she admitted she wasn't in pain. She was desperately worried about her family's reaction to her baby arriving too soon after the wedding.'

'So what did she hope to achieve?' Demelza whispered, shifting the position of the little boy in her arms.

Nick leaned forward and picked up Ianni, cradling him over his shoulder and whispering soothing noises. 'I'll put Ianni into his bed and tell you all about it.'

'He wanted to see you before he slept,' Demelza said softly, 'so I thought, as he didn't know me very well, I wouldn't insist on putting him to bed.'

Nick nodded. 'Back in a moment.'

He was carrying a bottle of wine and two glasses

when he returned. 'Ianni's fast asleep. Would you like a glass of wine?'

She nodded. 'Yes, please. Strange how easy it is to slip into the sun, sea and wine culture. I can't believe I've only been here a couple of days.'

Nick laughed as he handed her a glass. 'You'll be a proper native by the end of the summer. You look different already…sort of more relaxed, as if you're blossoming in the sun like the flowers.'

Demelza tried to stop herself from blushing but she could feel the heat on her cheeks as she met Nick's gaze.

'I certainly feel as if I've survived a long cold winter and suddenly been brought out into the sun,' she said.

He reached forward and gently touched her cheek. 'Yes, I can see the colour in your cheeks already. You've been starved of all the things that make life worth living for far too long, but now…' He spread his hands wide as if to indicate that all things were possible.

She could feel a magical tingling of her skin where his fingers had touched her face as he clinked his glass against hers.

'Thank you very much for looking after Ianni. He seems to have taken a shine to you. He's happy enough with Katerina but she can be a bit too bossy for his liking. I think I've probably spoiled him since his mother and I split up. Anyway, I was going to tell you about our patient, Katia,' he hurried on, as if reluctant to dwell on thoughts of his wife.

'Was Katia really putting on an act simply to get your attention?' Demelza asked.

'She was pretty convincing at first, but when I'd examined her thoroughly I started to have my suspicions.

Just to give her some peace of mind, I've said that if I meet her grandmother I won't deny that the baby was early.'

Demelza was shaking her head in disbelief. 'I can't believe it matters. As you say, I've got a lot to learn about life on Kopelos. How is the baby?'

Nick smiled. 'Thriving. Katia's feeding him, lying down because that's more comfortable after a Caesarean, and there are no problems there.'

'That's great,' she smiled back, realising that for the first time, it didn't hurt to talk about babies. She drew in a breath, aware that Nick was watching her closely. She felt as if she'd achieved another milestone and she wondered if he knew.

She put down her glass as she thought how nice it was to chat with Nick at the end of a long day. This was something she'd missed when Simon had no longer been there. Simple companionship. Simon's parents had begged her to stay in the sitting room with them during the evening, ostensibly to talk but more often merely to be another person watching the endless television until it was time for her to heat the milk for their bedtime drinks.

'You've got that far-away look again,' Nick said quietly. 'Are you getting homesick?'

Demelza laughed. 'You must be joking! No, I was just wondering how Mark and Jane are coping with life on the farm. I hope Jane isn't getting fed up with the constant demands of the family.'

'Well, as you say, you served your time. And it will be easier for your sister-in-law because she has her husband to help her. You were on your own and suffering the double sorrow of losing your husband and your son.'

She leaned back against the sofa and smiled. 'I'm glad you said that. Between the sorrow and the dutiful demands I found it hard to think straight sometimes about where I was going to end up.'

'And where are you going to end up?' Nick asked gently, as he moved across to top up her glass, staying beside her on the sofa, one arm stretched along the back.

She laughed. 'I'm probably going to end up feeling quite woozy if I drink any more wine. Let's say, I'm not looking too far ahead in the future at the moment. It's enough that I've escaped to live my own life.'

He nodded. 'I know how you feel. It felt like an escape when I finally got away from England, Lydia and the divorce and started a new life out here with Ianni. All I want from now on is a life free from personal complications.'

She felt Nick's arm move along the sofa behind her. She turned to look at him and was touched by the plaintive expression in his eyes. Yes, he, too, had suffered a great deal and was now enjoying his freedom.

'It's good to feel that I've found a friend with the same outlook on life,' she said, quietly.

Gently, his fingers closed over her shoulder and he pulled her gently towards him. She felt her body responding to his touch. Wasn't this a dangerous move for friends to be making? Slowly, he bent his head and kissed her lips very gently.

Moments later, the kiss was over. She moved to pull herself away and he let her go, a tender smile playing on his sensual lips.

'Don't be afraid, Demelza. I meant that to be a friendly kiss.'

'I know,' she said quickly. 'We both know where we stand on friendship, don't we?'

'I thought we did,' he said carefully.

Now, what had Nick meant by that? Had their kiss had as devastating an effect on him as it had had on her?

Demelza stood up. 'It's time for me to go. I had a call on my mobile from Irini, the nurse who assists me at the beach resort, reminding me that we've got an early clinic tomorrow.'

He was standing looking down at her, once more merely the friend and medical colleague. Her knees felt weak and wobbly as she looked at the rugged features surrounding the mouth that had just kissed hers, causing such an unnerving reaction deep down inside her. He was tall, very tall. She was aware that he towered over her and she had long legs herself. She was also aware of his strong muscular arms beneath the thin cotton shirt, arms which she suddenly ached to have close around her.

'Well, thanks again for looking after Ianni,' he said.

'My pleasure,' she said, knowing that she'd enjoyed every minute of taking care of such a delightful young boy.

The fact that he was Nick's son wasn't influencing the way she felt about Ianni. She was trying to remain detached from the little boy in the same way that she was trying not to allow her attraction towards his father to distract her too much.

He stood at the door of his apartment as she climbed the stone steps to her apartment. The moonlight was strong enough to light her way and there was an outside light over her door which she'd put on when she'd first got back with Ianni. The little boy had been intrigued

by her apartment and had asked if he could come up
to see her another day. She'd insisted he must ask his
father first, and had hoped fervently that Nick would
say yes. There was nothing she would like better than
young Ianni playing around her apartment and sun terrace.

She paused at the top of the stone stairs and leaned
over to call, 'Goodnight!'

Nick waved a hand. 'Goodnight. Sleep well!'

Oh, she would sleep well tonight! It had been such
a memorable day. Memorable and enjoyable, nothing
more than that.

She closed the door and leaned against it, breathing
heavily. She tried to convince herself that nothing had
changed. Nick had said he wanted an uncomplicated
life and so did she. Well, to a certain extent! The memory of Nick's kiss was having a devastating effect on
her.

As she stripped off her clothes and sat down in front
of the small, wooden dressing-table she was still trying
to calm her confused thoughts. She picked up her hairbrush and vigorously stroked through her long auburn
hair. Watching herself in the mirror, she could see the
excitement still dancing in her green eyes, eyes that
had held a dead expression for far too long.

It's all part of the breaking-out process, she told herself. Coming to life again after years of lying dormant.
Nick had called it blossoming. That was such a lovely
idea! And it would have happened even without meeting Nick…wouldn't it?

No, she wouldn't have felt like this! But Nick, with
his own complicated life, wouldn't want her as anything more than a friend. Or would he? How was she

to interpret his tender kiss? When a mere friend kissed you it shouldn't cause such havoc with your emotions.

As she tried to sleep the confusion of her feelings for Nick continued to plague her and she realised once more how inexperienced she was with relationships. She'd only ever had one man in her life. So getting to know Nick was like taking a step in the dark.

Demelza had a busy morning at the clinic. As she'd predicted the day before when she'd looked out at the tourists stretched out on their sunbeds, soaking up the sun with insufficient protection, there were several people suffering today. Fortunately, there was no one bad enough to require hospitalisation, although one fair-haired girl had come pretty close.

'You'd better stay inside for the next few days, Jenny,' Demelza said, as she applied lotion to the most badly affected areas.

'But I'm only out here for a week,' the young woman said. 'That's why I was trying to get a tan quickly.'

'It doesn't work like that,' Demelza told her patient. 'A suntan takes time and lots of protection. You can't rush it or you end up looking like a lobster and feeling as if you've been boiled alive.'

Jenny pulled a face. 'Next time, I suppose I'd better start off with a strong sunblock and come out here for a longer time.'

Demelza nodded. 'That's the only way to do it. Or you could apply a fake tan and sit under the umbrella. Fake tans from reputable cosmetic firms are perfectly safe—but not this time,' she added quickly. 'Your skin's too damaged at the moment.'

It was a surprise to see that her next patient was

Bryony Driver, the woman suffering from depression that she'd seen only the day before.

'Hello, Bryony. Hadn't expected to see you back so soon. How are you?'

Bryony slowly settled herself in the patient's chair, giving Demelza the impression that she had plenty of time to spare—unlike herself! She could hear the hum of voices outside in the waiting room but was well aware that she had to give her patient a few minutes at least. But she hoped it wasn't going to turn out to be a lengthy consultation. The patients suffering from depression that she'd treated during her professional life had all taken up a lot of time. There was no quick route back to normality.

'I've gone back on my pills but I had a terrible night, Sister,' Bryony said, in a dull tone. 'Tossing and turning and—'

'Did you read a book like I suggested, yesterday?'

'I couldn't concentrate. It was a love story and I couldn't stop thinking about Vinny, wondering if he was in bed with that scheming little minx and…'

Demelza let her patient ramble on for a while, going over the same ground they'd covered previously. One thing that alarmed her was that, although it was only just after nine o'clock in the morning, there was a definite smell of alcohol on Bryony's breath. When there was a pause long enough to break in, Demelza carefully tackled the question.

'You do know you mustn't drink alcohol with the pills you're taking, don't you, Bryony?'

Bryony's eyes widened as she stared across at Demelza. 'Sister, I wouldn't dream of abusing alcohol.' She paused. 'Well, I might have had a little nip of brandy in the middle of the night when I was feeling so desperate, but—'

'And again this morning perhaps?' Demelza said.

Bryony nodded sheepishly. 'You don't know what it's like being me, Sister. Waking up each morning and having to face another day without—'

'You're right. I don't know what it's like to be you, Bryony,' Demelza said sympathetically. 'But I'm going to try and help you all I can.'

Her patient couldn't help the fact that she had other patients to see and that their current discussion was leading nowhere. Bryony needed to see a psychiatrist.

'I really think it might be better for you to go home, Bryony,' Demelza said carefully. 'You're not responding to the medication you're taking but I think if you talked over your problems with a good psychiatrist, then—'

'I don't want to go home. I'm all on my own in England. At least out here I can mix with other people when I want to. Aren't there any psychiatrists out here?'

'I'll make enquiries,' Demelza said. 'I'll get in touch with the hospital and let you know. Otherwise I really think you should—'

'I'm not going home.' Bryony rose to her feet, her eyes flashing defiantly. 'I feel awful out here but I felt even worse back home. When can you let me know about the psychiatrist?'

'Come and see me in a couple of days,' Demelza said quickly. 'Take care of yourself.'

She leaned back in her chair as Bryony went out, knowing that she could have picked up the phone and got the relevant information from the hospital. But she wanted time to discuss the case with Nick.

Her other patients that morning were all suffering from physical symptoms that could be treated with medication—coughs, colds, sore throats brought out from England but still lingering in spite of the sunshine. As the last patient left her consulting room, Demelza thought how much less complicated it was to treat the body than the mind. She felt out of her depth with Bryony.

Getting up from her chair, she looked out into the waiting room. Nobody there except Irini who was resetting the trays and trolleys they'd used that morning.

'You can go when you've finished that, Irini. Thanks very much for your help.'

The girl smiled. Demelza was pleased to have such a willing assistant. Trained at a hospital in Athens, she was proving to be a valuable asset to the clinic. Back in her room, Demelza picked up the phone, dialled the hospital number and asked for Nick.

She hung on. Hearing the babble of Greek voices in the background, it reminded her that she would have to do something about learning the language. Nick had said he would help her but—

'Nick, it's Demelza,' she said when at last she heard his voice. 'I've got a patient with a bad case of depression. I think she needs to be seen by a psychiatrist but she's out here for a long time and doesn't want to go back to the UK. Is there a psychiatrist attached to the hospital?'

'We haven't got a full-time psychiatrist. There's a semi-retired doctor who still takes patients privately but he's not cheap.'

'I don't think consultation fees would be a problem, from what I've gathered from my patient. I'll check that out and if Bryony is still willing to be treated, perhaps you could arrange it for me.'

'Certainly. But you'll need to give me a few details—not over the phone. I'm busy right now. Perhaps you could call round this evening, Demelza?'

She felt her spirits lifting. 'Yes, I'll do that, Nick. Thanks a lot.'

Putting down the phone, she dialled Bryony's room number. Her patient seemed relieved that Demelza was treating her case so quickly and assured her that money wasn't a problem. As she'd said earlier, Vinny, her ex-husband, had given her a very generous settlement and she had no one to spend it on but herself.

Arriving back at the apartment, Demelza showered and changed into her bikini. She'd contemplated an afternoon on the beach but had decided that she had too many chores to see to at the apartment. And she could intersperse the washing, ironing and sorting out the apartment with a little cautious sunbathing on her terrace.

Looking over the balustrade, she saw that Nick's apartment was quite deserted. Just as well, she thought, because she wasn't entirely secluded from downstairs and although she hadn't felt out of place in her bikini on the beach, it was a different matter at the apartment. It was true she wasn't overlooked in any direction. The hillside sloped upwards to the craggy summit and only the goats and a few sheep cropping the sparse grass would be able to see what she was up to. But outside the door to the courtyard of the villa was a street of houses where the women were definitely well covered, regardless of the temperature.

She spread the things she'd washed on an airer in

the corner of the terrace where they would get maximum sunshine. It hadn't taken long to rinse out the washing which had accumulated since she'd left England and her apartment was looking reasonably neat and tidy now. A quick swipe around with the broom she'd found in a cupboard had sorted out the ancient stone floor. She'd shaken the brightly coloured rugs, one from her living room and one from her bedroom, and repositioned them.

The easiest session of housework she'd done in a long time, she thought as she stretched out on the sunbed under the umbrella. Mmm! This was the life!

The soothing drone of the insects on the hillside, creating a continuous lullaby, coupled with the heat from the sun, was getting to her. She closed her eyes, telling herself that she wasn't going to go to sleep because that would be a waste of an afternoon and she wanted to read the book she'd started on the plane so…

It was the clang of the gate that awoke her. She jumped up, feeling completely disorientated as she peered over the balustrade down into the courtyard. Her eyes widened.

'Nick! What time is it?'

Nick seemed amused by her confusion. 'I'm home early. It's only four o'clock. I didn't mean to disturb your siesta. You look as if you've been asleep.'

She glanced down at her semi-clad figure, feeling vulnerable. Nick had seen her in a bikini on the beach but here at the apartment she wasn't sure whether it would be frowned upon to be seen like this. Maybe it was totally inappropriate in this ancient part of the village.

But Nick certainly wasn't frowning. Her new emerging self pushed the ideas firmly to one side. She had to make the most of this wonderful sunshine because it would be very cold when she returned to an English winter at the end of her Greek summer.

'Would you like a drink?' she found herself asking, boldly and totally out of character. 'I've squeezed some oranges and the juice is chilling in the fridge.'

'Great! I need to strip off and have a shower first. Be with you in a few minutes.'

His dark eyes seemed to be lingering over her bikini-clad figure. Demelza suddenly felt that she was being terribly forward and wondered how she was going to handle it. Half of her was holding back and saying that she was going too quickly towards some unknown, un-planned destination.

She turned and made for the door to her apartment. 'I'll get the juice,' she called. 'And later, when you've recovered, we could perhaps discuss my patient, the one I told you about.'

She was deliberately trying to keep their relationship on a steady footing. Inviting Nick up for a drink was merely returning the hospitality he'd shown her since she'd arrived.

Returning with a jug of chilled juice, two glasses and the olives she'd bought at the local shop on her way home, she repositioned the umbrella over the table and sat bolt upright, waiting nervously. She'd tied a black and white sarong over her bikini and felt slightly less brazen.

Nick came bounding up the stairs. He was wearing khaki shorts but his chest was completely bare. Demelza groaned inwardly at the sight of his muscular body. She tried to convince herself that it was only natural that she should feel like this after festering in the backwoods for so long. She hadn't felt the slightest desire to notice what the farmhands looked like.

'Nice sarong!' Nick said, as he leaned across the table to accept a glass of orange juice. 'You didn't buy that out here, did you?'

'I got it in Cornwall, the same time I bought my bikinis. My mother-in-law asked to see what I'd bought and you should have seen her face!'

'She didn't approve?'

Demelza laughed. 'That's an understatement! She said she hoped I wasn't going to forget that I was a widow now that I was going to start living the high life.'

He was watching her over the rim of his glass as he sipped. 'I don't think you'll ever forget you're a widow, but it doesn't mean you can't enjoy yourself.'

'That's what I've started to tell myself,' she said quickly. 'I'll never forget Simon...but it's time to move on.'

Nick leaned towards her. 'Was Simon your first love?'

She nodded. 'We met at the village school. There was never anyone but Simon for me. When I went away to London to do my nursing training we always made a point of seeing each other as often as we could. Simon was at agricultural college for a couple of years and then he went back to work for his father on the farm. But during all that time and after I was trained we were never apart for more than a few weeks at a time.'

'Sounds like a real love match. You must have been very happy together.' He paused. 'I was happy with Lydia at the beginning, but it didn't last. We had a very short, whirlwind romance and didn't really get to know each other until after we were married.'

'How long were you married to Lydia?' Demelza asked gently.

He leaned back and attempted a weary smile.

'Too long. The only thing that kept us going was Ianni who was born at the end of our first year of marriage. Soon after he was born, Lydia started having a string of affairs. She'd found out that being married to a hard-working doctor and having to look after a child wasn't very glamorous. She gets bored very easily so she worked hard at making herself attractive to other men…preferably rich ones who could take her out and give her a good time.'

'When did you find out that Lydia was being unfaithful?'

He gave a harsh laugh. 'It became pretty obvious when she insisted on having a mother's help to take care of Ianni so that she could go out more. I was so busy in the hospital at the time that for a while I shelved the problem, but I made sure that the mother's help was taking good care of Ianni when I wasn't there.'

He paused and drew in a breath. 'I was trying to ride out the storm for Ianni's sake. I didn't want the family to break up, but we couldn't have gone on much longer like that. When Lydia asked me for a divorce it was a tremendous relief. She told me she'd found someone else richer and more interesting than a doctor who was always too busy at the hospital.'

He pulled a wry face. 'Those were Lydia's exact words, actually.'

'And is your ex-wife happy with this rich, interesting man?'

He raised a dark eyebrow. 'She was for a while, until he dumped her and took off with someone else. Poor Lydia! She came running back to me, begging me to have her back, but I told her it was too late for a reconciliation.'

He broke off and gave himself a little shake. 'Can't think why I'm telling you all this. Perhaps it's to show you that it didn't do you any harm to stay on at the farm and not go out into the world until you felt you were ready. You might have fallen for the first man who took you out of yourself, had a whirlwind romance and lived to regret it, as I did.'

'Oh, I wouldn't have done that,' she said quickly, as the little voice inside her warned her that this was exactly what was happening now.

But six years down the line, wasn't she strong enough to know what she was doing? Probably not, judging by the mixed emotions that were churning up inside her.

'More juice, Nick?' She picked up the jug, anxious to diffuse the emotional atmosphere. 'It's a bit warm now. I'll put some more ice in it.'

As she stood up, the knot in her sarong unravelled and it slipped to the floor. With a jug in one hand she could hardly reach down, pick up the sarong and retie it. Carefully, she stepped over it and walked barefoot across the warm paving stones and through the open door.

Her small kitchen seemed cool and dark after the brightness and warmth of the hot sun. She bent down and opened the fridge to pull out the ice tray. It was sticking to the surrounding ice. She tugged, before resorting to grabbing a knife from the draining board and trying to prise it out.

'Ouch!' She couldn't stifle a cry as her finger caught on the sharp corner of the tin ice tray. 'Of all the stupid contraptions…!'

She became aware that Nick was bending over her. 'Here, let me do that.'

He leaned inside the fridge and dislodged the tray with apparent ease.

'Your finger's bleeding!' Nick grabbed the first cloth that came to hand and wound it round her finger. 'This cloth is decidedly unsterile, but I think you'll live.'

'Thanks!' She was still crouching in front of the fridge inwardly cursing herself for being such an idiot and feeling intensely aware that she was wearing only a flimsy bikini.

Nick was still holding onto the cloth wrapped around her finger. His eyes were unnervingly near to her own…and his mouth! She held her breath as he bent his head slowly and placed a feather-light kiss on her finger.

Immediately, his head came up and he smiled into her eyes. 'That's only what I would do if Ianni had hurt his finger.'

She swallowed hard. 'What you mean is only a child would have been as stupid as to try and dislodge the ice tray with that old knife.'

'You said it! Anyway, let's examine the wound.' Solemnly he unwrapped her hand. 'Plaster quickly, Sister. Not very big but…that'll do,' he conceded as she plundered the first-aid kit beside the sink.

'Good as new.' He drew her to her feet. 'I'll send you my bill by return of post. Talking of which—a fee, that is—I've negotiated on your behalf that you'll get paid Sister's rates pro rata whenever you help us out at the hospital.'

Demelza's eyes widened. 'Really?'

'Of course. You're a professional. I wouldn't expect you to work for nothing. I pointed out to the powers that be that having an experienced sister on the island was a valuable asset. You reserve the right to accept only the medical assignments you choose, of course. We'll only ask you to work at the hospital if you're free and if we really need you. Would you accept this arrangement?'

'Well, put like that, of course I accept. I enjoyed working in hospital when Katia had her Caesarean. It's so good to be back in the saddle again.'

'Great to have you on board, Sister,' he said quietly. And then Nick bent his head and kissed her gently on the lips.

'Haven't got the contract for you to sign yet so I thought we should seal it with something a little more enjoyable,' he whispered huskily, as he pulled away. 'Please, don't be put off by my unprofessional manner.'

'Well, after all, we are off duty, Doctor,' she said lightly.

She recognised that she was actually flirting with Nick, and it was a long time since she'd indulged in that kind of behaviour. She smiled up at him and her heart turned over as she saw his response to her lighter mood.

'You're changing by the minute, Demelza,' he said.

When his lips came down on hers again she almost gasped at her own reaction. It was so difficult not to throw caution to the winds and simply allow her treacherous body to relax against Nick and give herself up to his enthralling embrace.

She leaned against him, revelling in the feel of his

hard, muscular body against hers. His hands moved to caress her, whilst his lips teased and tantalised her.

With an effort she pulled herself away. She was reaching the point of no return, the point at which she wanted, with every fibre of her being, to make love with Nick. But she was afraid to go along with the delicious desires that were sweeping over her.

She looked up into Nick's eyes and saw only tenderness.

'I'm sorry,' she whispered. 'It's been so long since—'

'Daddy! Daddy, I'm home!'

The small excited voice shrilled up to them from the courtyard. 'Katerina said you'd come home early so she let me come straight back to you. Where are you?'

Nick gave a resigned smile. 'I'm up here at Demelza's.'

'Great! Can I come up?'

Nick laughed as he heard the pounding of Ianni's feet on the stone steps. 'Sounds like you're up!'

Wordlessly, he took hold of Demelza's hand and pressed it to his lips. She held her breath. It was such a precious gesture to make. It signified that he understood. She took a deep breath as she followed him out into the bright sunshine. Maybe Nick thought he understood her reaction and now assumed that she was never going to let down her guard.

But never was a very long time. And she would have to revise her thinking if she was to put herself out of her emotional torment.

'Demelza!' Ianni rushed towards her, his arms outstretched.

She knelt down and hugged the excited boy. Looking up, she saw that Nick was watching them with a tender expression. For an instant she allowed herself the luxury of imagining what it would be like if she were Ianni's mother and Nick was…

'Can we go to Giorgio's this evening for supper, Daddy? All three of us. You, Demelza and—'

'I'm not sure what Demelza has planned for this evening, but if she's free…'

'I haven't got any plans for this evening so I'd love to come with you.' Demelza knew she was only adding to her involvement with Nick but it felt so right. It was as if she'd suddenly been planted in the middle of a ready-made family. And the warm feeling sweeping over her put paid to her fear of moving on into a more loving relationship…for the moment.

Later, when her skin had stopped tingling from the feel of Nick's caressing hands, she would be able to reassess the situation. But for tonight…

CHAPTER FIVE

DEMELZA was in her surgery early the next morning, even earlier than Irini who usually made a point of preparing everything before she arrived. It was very rare that she couldn't sleep, but last night had seemed impossibly long and tedious. The thoughts teeming through her mind had made it impossible to do anything other than lie still and try to relax her body.

At one point, she thought of the advice she'd given to Bryony—read a book. Well, she hadn't even attempted that remedy because her mind had been so crowded that she'd known she wouldn't have been able to concentrate.

She stood at the window now, looking out over the almost deserted beach. A young couple jogged past, taking advantage of the relative cool of the morning to get some exercise before the hot sun took away their good resolutions to get fit while on holiday. Seeing Demelza at the window, the young woman waved a hand.

Demelza waved back as she recognised her as a patient from yesterday's surgery. The young woman was called Fiona and she'd called in to ask about the best time of the month to get pregnant. Apparently, she and her partner, Tim, had been trying for a baby for six months, so far without success. They'd come out to Kopelos to see if a holiday would have any better result, because they'd both been leading very busy, stressful lives. They seemed to be a happy, well-suited pair and, from what she'd seen of them, Demelza felt they would make excellent parents.

Fiona had also asked Demelza about investigating the possibility of attending a fertility clinic back in England. Demelza had advised her patient to wait a few more months and see whether natural conception was possible. Six months wasn't very long to have tried for a baby and now that Fiona was working from home and not having to travel into work as a commuter every day, she might be more relaxed and mother nature would have more of a chance.

She went back to her desk, leaning against the back of the chair as she reviewed her own situation, and her confused thoughts about Nick came tumbling back. Last night at Giorgio's taverna, they'd had another great evening together. Having Ianni with them had meant that any feelings of embarrassment they might have had about their passionate embrace earlier in the evening hadn't been allowed to surface.

She'd been introduced to Nick's aunt this time. Anna had smiled and been very pleasant with her, but Demelza had felt she'd been sizing her up. Possibly wondering what her intentions were concerning Nick?

Well, what *were* her intentions? If she could answer that thousand-dollar question she wouldn't have to stay awake all night worrying!

Although Nick had been so loving towards her when they'd embraced yesterday afternoon, he'd probably just been carried away momentarily by the close rapport that had temporarily developed between them. It could have been a combination of the sun, their relaxed off-duty situation, some natural need to caress someone... She'd thought of any number of reasons that might have made Nick so passionate towards her. But as far as a relationship went, she mustn't read anything into it because Nick had said that after Lydia he didn't want any more complications in his life.

And then she remembered how she'd welcomed Nick's advances with open arms…literally! She'd been totally shameless before she'd pulled herself away. She thought of how she'd felt as if liquid fire were coursing through her veins…

'*Kali mera*, good morning, Sister Demelza. You're early today.'

Irini breezed in, her white uniform dress crisply ironed, her long dark hair pinned up on the top of her head and her young eager face smiling at Demelza as she took hold of one of the trolleys and began to wheel it outside to be checked and reset.

'There is a lady waiting already outside. I told her you didn't start your clinic as early as this but…'

'Send her in, Irini.'

Demelza fell into her professional mode. Work always took her mind off her own personal problems.

The woman's face was worried as she came in.

'I'm Josie Donaldson, Sister.'

'Demelza Tregarron.' Demelza put out her hand and clasped the other woman's, feeling that her patient needed to be put at her ease before they could begin any kind of consultation.

The woman's face brightened slightly as she sat down on a chair beside Demelza. 'I've heard that name before. Demelza. It's Cornish, isn't it?'

Demelza smiled. 'I was born in Cornwall.'

'My grandparents lived in Cornwall and I used to spend my long school holiday with them. All a long time ago. I'm nearly thirty-five.'

'Oh, you poor old thing,' Demelza said in a jocular

voice. 'I'll be thirty-five myself in three years. So, what can I do for you, Josie?'

Josie hesitated. 'I've been very stupid...'

'We all are at times. What happened?' Demelza waited for her patient to elaborate.

The woman gave a deep sigh. 'I met a bloke last night in the bar. We had a few drinks and then went back to his room. I don't normally do these things but when you're on holiday...I haven't had a holiday for years. Been looking after my mum, but she died last month and I thought, well, time's passing me by. I'll go on holiday. Try and snap out of it...'

Someone else escaping the past. Demelza waited until Josie decided to go on with the story. If she interrupted now her patient might clam up and leave. It was obviously difficult for her to continue.

Josie ran a hand through her short blonde hair. 'At first I was flattered. I've never had time to bother with men and it was great when he told me I was attractive. I know I'm not, but what with the alcohol and...well, to cut a long story short we went to bed. It's years since I did anything like that and I wasn't prepared. Neither was he...so we had unprotected sex...'

Josie began to cry. Demelza stood up and put an arm around the heaving shoulders. When the sobs began to diminish she sat down on her chair again.

'Are you going to see this man again?' she asked quietly.

Josie raised her sad eyes, runny with tears, and her mascara-streaked cheeks. Demelza handed her a tissue and her patient began to dab ineffectively at her face.

'I hope not! He told me he was married—after we'd had sex that is, the swine!'

'The oldest trick in the book,' Demelza said, in a

sympathetic tone. 'You wouldn't believe how many patients have told me a similar story. So now…?'

'So now I want to be absolutely sure I'm not pregnant. Have you got the morning-after pill out here?'

'Yes, we have,' Demelza said guardedly. 'But are
you really sure about this? Taking emergency contraception pills, which are now widely known as the
morning-after pill, can have side effects. I'll have to
ask you a few questions about your health, Josie.
There's rather a long list of other medical problems
which would prevent me from prescribing ECP pills.'

As Demelza went through all the medical conditions
that might cause side effects if the ECP pills were
taken, she was pleased to find that Josie hadn't suffered
from any of them. She looked across and smiled at her
patient as she finished questioning her. 'Well, you seem
to be in good health, Josie.'

'I've always made a point of looking after myself,
going to the gym three times a week, swimming every
other day, whatever I could fit in when I wasn't looking
after Mum.'

Demelza had been relieved to find how well her surgery clinic was stocked when she first arrived. There
was a good supply of ECPs. This was the first morning-
after pill she'd been asked for and she was in no doubt
that it wouldn't be the last. Holiday romances were
often transitory affairs. But even with a healthy
woman, there could be side effects and it was her duty
to make Josie aware of this.

Her patient leaned forward, a pleading expression on
her face. 'Please, Sister Demelza, can you give me a
pill? And the sooner the better because I don't want to
have anything more to do with that creep and I can't
bear to think how stupid I've been and—'

'Josie, even though you appear to be healthy, you could still suffer side effects. About fifty per cent of women who take ECPs experience nausea and twenty per cent vomit. And if the patient vomits, there's a chance that her body won't absorb the pill and if a pregnancy has already started—'

'Please, Sister! I'll put up with anything so long as I'm going to do all I can to make sure I didn't get pregnant by that horrible man.'

'It's not a one hundred per cent remedy,' Demelza said.

Josie gave a big sigh. 'It's the only life line I can take…so, Sister, please…'

Demelza patted her patient's hand. 'Don't upset yourself, Josie. I had to make all these checks before I can even consider prescribing to you. I'm going to do everything I can for you.'

She stood up and went over to unlock her medical supplies cupboard to remove one of the packets. She opened it out and showed it to Josie.

'As you can see, there are two pills to take. They must be taken within seventy-two hours of unprotected sex, so we're OK on the timing. You can take the first one now.'

Demelza handed her patient a glass of water so that she could swallow it.

'You must take the second pill in exactly twelve hours so make a note of the time now and don't forget to take it.'

Josie smiled. 'Don't worry, Sister. I couldn't possibly forget.' She clutched her precious packet.

'If you suffer any side effects, come back to see me, Josie. And make sure you go to see your doctor back home in three to four weeks.'

Josie pulled a face. 'Do I have to?'

'I would strongly advise it. It's for your own good to make sure that you're still healthy. There is also the danger of sexually transmitted disease to think about.'

'I know! That's worrying me as well.'

'Go and have a check-up at a special clinic as soon as you get back to the UK. I've got a list here you can take with you. They're all very discreet and it would give you peace of mind.'

She handed over the printed list to her patient who ran her eyes over the page. 'I'll do that, Sister.'

Josie was standing up now. 'Thanks a lot. It said in the beach resort brochure that I'll have to pay for medicines at the clinic.'

Demelza gave her a slip of paper. 'Give that to Irini. She handles the finances. I hope you enjoy the rest of your holiday, Josie.'

Josie turned at the door and smiled. 'I'll try to. I won't make a fool of myself again, but it's so difficult when you're on your own and feeling lonely.'

Demelza smiled back. 'I'm sure it is,' she said sympathetically.

She leaned back in her chair after the patient had gone. Josie was going to try not to make a fool of herself again. She herself had almost cast all caution to the winds yesterday. She'd been within seconds of allowing her body to take over. Josie was right—it was hard when you were lonely. She herself wasn't lonely exactly, but she'd been on her own for so long that being with Nick had turned her head. She longed to be wanted, longed to feel his strong arms holding her against him until…

The ringing phone brought her back to the present. 'Sister Demelza here… Yes, Nick?'

She felt her pulses begin to race again and realised, with a pang, that Nick's telephone voice had the same effect on her as it did face to face. Pull yourself together, girl! You're on duty and it's probably only a professional query.

It was. Nick, in his most professional voice, was asking if she could help out at the hospital that afternoon.

'I want to do a hip replacement in Theatre this afternoon. Normally, I would send the patient to Athens or Rhodes, but it's an elderly lady who doesn't want to leave the island and if we don't do it here, she's refusing to have it done. If she doesn't have the hip replaced she'll be in a wheelchair for the rest of her life. I've had a look at your CV again and I see that you did some orthopaedic surgery during your time in London.'

Demelza smiled. 'Been checking up on me, have you?'

'Well, we really haven't got anybody else who would be so experienced here at the moment. Our orthopaedic sister is on maternity leave so if you wouldn't mind...?'

'What time?'

'Two o'clock. Ask Stavros to drive you up here.'

She grinned. 'How can I get Stavros to slow down?'

She heard the amusement in Nick's voice. 'You can't. He's genetically programmed to try and beat the sound barrier. Just fasten your seat belt and pray. That's what I do if ever I have to travel with him.'

'Thanks very much, Doctor.'

'My pleasure, Sister.'

Demelza arrived at the hospital half an hour early, needing to give herself recovery time from her whirlwind journey and time to become fully acquainted with the theatre procedure for the hip replacement operation.

The nurse in Reception showed her along to Nick's consulting room.

'Good! You're early. Do sit down, Demelza, while I fill you in on the details of the case.'

It was very much business as usual, Demelza thought as she sank down into a chair at the other side of Nick's desk. A computer whirred quietly in one corner of the small room. Medical textbooks completely lined one wall. Nick's desk was littered with case notes and papers. Demelza wondered how he could appear so efficient with such a chaotic desk.

He ran a hand through his thick dark hair. She noticed it was slightly damp, as was his creased white shirt, which had the sleeves rolled up above his elbows. He'd probably been working hard all morning and now was going to perform a hip replacement. She doubted very much if he would have taken a break.

'Have you had lunch?' she asked quickly.

He raised an eyebrow and he grinned. 'Is that an invitation?'

She blushed. 'No, no. I merely thought you looked as if you'd been working all morning and—'

'Don't worry about me. I can keep going when I have to. I've just had a sandwich and some coffee. How about you?'

'I finished my clinic at twelve so I've had time for a salad and some fruit.'

It felt strange to be discussing lunch with Nick in this stilted way. There was no doubt in her mind that he was feeling as uneasy about where their relationship was heading as she was.

'So, fill me in on the details of this afternoon's case,'

she said, unnerved by the enigmatic expression in his eyes as he looked at her across the desk.

'Our patient is called Maria and she's seventy-two years old. She's known me since I was born so she tries to keep me in my place.'

Nick smiled. 'Maria is very stubborn and none of her family can get her to see sense. They thought I might be able to have some influence over her but I haven't.'

He broke off and pulled a wry face. 'As you've probably gathered, I'm very fond of her and I only want what's best for her. Anyway, her family and I have been trying to persuade Maria to go over to Athens to have her left hip replaced. She seemed to agree for a while, so I got her on the waiting list there.'

He leaned back in his chair and sighed. 'If only it had been that simple. As the date for the operation approached she dug in her heels and said she wasn't going. Her friend had been to Athens for an operation a few years ago and she'd died under the anaesthetic. I tried to explain to Maria that her friend's case had been entirely different but she wouldn't listen. All she would say was that if I wouldn't do the operation here then she was going to put up with the wheelchair her son had bought her.'

'So when did you decide to give in to Maria?'

'I've been in touch with the orthopaedic consultant in Athens every day for a week now, ever since Maria's son brought her into the hospital and asked if I could do something to persuade her to go to Athens. She was in terrible pain and he couldn't bear to see her suffer.'

'I don't remember meeting Maria when you showed me round the hospital, Nick. She sounds like the sort of feisty patient I would have remembered.'

'The nurse said Maria was taking her afternoon nap, so we didn't disturb her.' He smiled. 'You're right. You would have remembered her. I had hoped to be able to fly her over to Athens in the air ambulance this morning. Her orthopaedic consultant asked me to do all the usual pre-operative preparations—blood for grouping and cross-matching, and haemoglobin and electrolyte estimation. The hip area had been shaved and the skin prepared, but at the last minute, Maria refused to go, so I took charge and decided to operate here. The main problem was that my orthopaedic sister is on maternity leave. But with you here…'

Demelza nodded and Nick continued. 'I contacted Athens to advise them of the situation. A Charnley hip replacement prosthesis has just been flown in and we're ready to go.'

He jumped to his feet. 'So are you quite happy with all this? As you can see, we have a strange way of doing things out here.'

Demelza smiled, partly to hide the nervousness that was creeping over her. 'Well, you said it, Nick! I can't imagine a London hospital being quite so co-operative with the patient in a case like this, can you?'

'Absolutely not! But I can't stand by and see one of my oldest friends spend the rest of her life in a wheel-chair—even if she is a stubborn old so-and-so,' he finished with a wry grin.

Demelza scrubbed up beside Nick in the small ante-theatre. She'd already checked with the nurse on the instruments they were to use. It had been a long time since she'd assisted at a hip replacement operation but she found she hadn't forgotten the procedure.

A nurse fastened the back of Demelza's sterile gown and helped her to pull on the sterile gloves. Following

Nick into Theatre, some of her earlier nervousness returned. But one glance at his steady, earnest eyes across the operating table and she felt her confidence flooding back. Her hands were steady as she handed him a scalpel to make the first incision.

As Nick exposed the head of the femur, Demelza could see that the diseased bone had almost crumbled away to nothing.

'Now you can see why I felt this operation was urgent, Sister,' he said.

She nodded. 'I can see why you're having to do a total hip replacement.'

Nick looked up briefly to speak to the two nurses assisting Demelza. 'I'm going to remove the diseased part of the bone and insert the prosthesis down into the femur.'

He then explained how he would fix the head of the prosthesis into the acetabulum in the bone of the pelvis.

Demelza found herself admiring the calm way in which Nick worked, patiently explaining what he was doing at every step of the way. Before she'd realised it the operation was finished and the patient was ready to be wheeled back to the ward.

Nick gave final instructions to the two nurses who were going to give special round-the-clock nursing care to Maria.

As she pulled off her gloves and tossed them in the bin, Demelza turned to Nick and remarked that it hadn't been very different to working in a London operating theatre.

'The air-conditioning helps,' Nick said. 'Otherwise…'

'I wasn't talking about the air-conditioning,'

Demelza said. 'I was impressed that we were able to do the operation with so few staff and so little fuss.'

Nick pulled off his theatre cap and looked down at her. Demelza noticed that his unruly hair was even more ruffled. It made him look so boyish and so…yes, dared she admit it? So desirable…

He put a finger under her chin and tilted her face so that she had to look up into his eyes. 'I'm glad you approve of the methods in our little hospital because I entirely approve of the way you handled a difficult situation. I didn't tell you before the operation, but if Maria had had to wait much longer it would have been too late for the operation to be successful.'

'I could see that by the state of her femur,' she said, wondering when Nick was going to move from this deliciously close position.

He moved his finger upwards and touched her cheek. She remained absolutely still, feeling mesmerised by the tantalisingly tender expression in his eyes. And then, as she'd hoped, he bent his head and kissed her, oh, so gently on the lips. She heard a gasp, and realised it was herself. She'd been waiting for the touch of his lips, longing for some form of physical contact with him.

The swing door flew open and Demelza jumped back.

'Dr Capodistrias…oh, sorry, sir. I didn't know you were…er, busy. I wondered if I could have a word with you about Maria.'

Demelza felt sorry for the hapless nurse who'd just barged in. Sorry and guilty that once again she'd cast aside all caution. She'd been positively angling for Nick's attentions ever since the operation had finished and been declared successful.

Nick was totally in command of the situation. 'Of course, Nurse. What's the problem?'

Demelza moved towards the door. Her brief had been to assist at the operation so she wouldn't interfere in the after-care of the patient.

'Just a moment, Sister.'

Nick's studiously professional tone brought her to a halt.

'If you'd like to wait for me I'll give you a lift back to the village. You could call Stavros if you prefer,' he added dryly.

Demelza smiled. 'Thank you very much, Dr Capodistrias. I accept your kind offer.'

She wished she was still wearing her theatre mask as she felt the annoying blush spreading over her cheeks. But if she'd been wearing a mask she wouldn't have experienced Nick's tantalising kiss.

She waited in the staff common room. It was a small room littered with medical magazines and empty coffee-cups. Typical of all the hospital common rooms she'd ever been in except that it had the most mind-blowing view of the bay. She was so entranced with the view as she stood at the window that she didn't hear Nick arrive through the open door and come up behind her.

She jumped as she felt a hand on her shoulder.

'Sorry! I didn't mean to startle you.'

'You didn't!'

She turned and felt again a mixture of embarrassment and desire as she looked up at Nick. Her lips were still tingling from the touch of his kiss and her body was in a state of heightened awareness. 'I...I was just admiring the view of the harbour.'

Nick's hand was still lightly resting on her shoulder,

a comforting, soothing, sympathetic touch. She tried to tell herself that their relationship was based purely on the mutual understanding they had of each other's problems but she failed to convince herself. She longed for more than mere sympathy from this exciting man. And from the kisses they'd exchanged she couldn't help hoping that he was beginning to feel the same way.

She looked down at the harbour, the bright blue water glistening in the late afternoon sunlight as she tried to become accustomed to the feel of Nick's hand on her shoulder. It was no good telling herself it was a friendly gesture. It was more than that—to her at least.

Down below in the harbour, the inter-island ferry was just leaving after the fascinating bustle of the loading of cargo—sheep, goats, hens and people—and the unloading of fruit and vegetables had been completed. Smartly dressed people from a cruise ship and casually dressed people from the various yachts which had tied up during the day were beginning to drift along the harbourside in search of the best taverna for an evening out.

Suddenly, the excitement of the impending evening began to get to her. She'd never been one to go out on the town—as her mother-in-law had disparagingly referred to an evening out—but she suddenly felt she wanted to do something different. And the longings that Nick was constantly stirring up in her were giving her ideas. The bright lights weren't her scene. She was more into a cosy night in with someone she felt at ease with.

She turned round, looking up into Nick's eyes. 'Would you and Ianni like to have supper at my place tonight? I'd like to cook something for all of us.'

Nick looked surprised. 'Great! How could I possibly turn down an offer like that? You're sure?'

'Just simple home cooking,' she said quickly.

'Mmm, sounds good to me. I love Greek cooking but sometimes I long for a change.'

'Shepherd's pie?' she said, planning to play safe with one of her tried and tested remedies.

Nick grinned. 'How did you guess that's one of my favourites? My English grandmother used to make that for me.'

Oh, well, if Nick's grandmother used to make it, he couldn't read anything into this evening other than a friendly invitation meant to repay some of the meals she'd enjoyed with him at the taverna.

Nick parked his Land Rover at the end of the village street that led to the villa. There was only room for a donkey to walk down the street. In the early days when motorbikes had first arrived on the island, the young men of the village had zoomed down between the ancient houses. But a petition from the villagers had convinced the mayor that motorbikes must be banned on narrow streets.

Ianni gave a whoop of excitement when he saw Nick and Demelza walking towards where he was playing outside Katerina's house with Lefteris.

'Daddy! Demelza!' The little boy flung himself against his father for a hug.

Then it was Demelza's turn. Her heart was full of happiness as she hugged the excited boy. The feeling of belonging was almost too much for her. She'd hoped for a new life when she'd come out here but hadn't dared to find herself accepted into a family.

Careful, she told herself as the three of them walked

the remaining stretch of the street to the villa. Don't take too much for granted. Don't try to take over as mother. You're simply a friend, regardless of the deep maternal instincts that Ianni is stirring up.

'I've got to stop off at the shop,' she said, pausing outside the fascinating little house crammed to the ceiling with every conceivable kind of goods, whilst fruit and vegetable boxes sprawled out into the street.

'Can I come in with you, Demelza?' Ianni asked. 'I've still got some spending money left for sweets.'

Demelza glanced at Nick. He was grinning as he nodded. 'Not too many, Ianni. We're going out for supper, remember?'

Demelza bought everything she would need for the meal—minced lamb, herbs, potatoes, onions—while Nick supervised the all-important choosing of the sweets. She'd bought the basics for her food cupboard and fridge already.

Nick was very firm with Ianni when they reached the villa and insisted that he do his homework and change out of his school uniform before they went up to Demelza's apartment for supper.

'See you both later,' she said, as she ran up the steps to her apartment.

She hadn't felt so excited about making a meal in a long time! That's all it was, a simple meal. But it meant so much more to her to know that she was going to spend the evening with Nick in a safe situation where she didn't have to worry about where their relationship was going.

CHAPTER SIX

STANDING at the cooker, stirring the mince into the fried onions, Demelza could see the relaxed evening stretching ahead of her. Nick and Ianni would be coming up to join her soon. It would be just the three of them round the table and...

Suddenly she put down her spoon at the side of the cooker and pulled the pan off the heat. What was she doing, planning to set up a cosy little family unit? Would Nick feel as if she was trying to take over his personal life? He'd told her that there were too many complications in his life already. But she wasn't planning to be a further complication. Just someone who was very close to him, mentally and physically. Whenever they were close together, she could feel a strong magnetic pull that told her they were so right for each other, so...

'Daddy's in the shower,' said a small voice.

Demelza turned and saw Ianni outlined in the doorway, with the rays of the setting sun behind him. His hair was still wet from the shower, his feet were bare and he was wearing white cotton pyjamas. He looked like a little cherub.

'Can I come in, Demelza?' he said.

'Of course you can.'

She walked across to meet him and he put his little hand in hers.

'I've got my jimjams on,' Ianni said solemnly. 'Daddy said I could wear what I liked, so I thought I'd

101

get into my jimjams so I don't have to do any more undressing and dressing. It's such a pain, isn't it?'

Demelza nodded. 'I've put this dress on because it's nice and cool for cooking in.'

'It's very pretty,' Ianni said, fingering the lime green cotton. He looked up at her. 'It sort of goes with your hair. Your hair is pretty, too. Can I touch it?'

She bent down so that Ianni could take a strand between his thumb and finger. 'What do you think, Ianni?'

'Did you have to make it this colour with some stuff from a bottle, Demelza?'

Demelza laughed. 'No, it was this colour when I was born, but I think it's faded a bit.'

'My mum's hair must have faded a lot because she has to keep putting blonde stuff on it. I asked her what colour it really was and she said she couldn't remember and I shouldn't be so nosy.'

'Does Daddy know you've come up here, Ianni?'

'Well…er…'

'No, Daddy doesn't know!' Nick bent his head to come in through the doorway, which hadn't been made for tall people. 'You scalliwag! Demelza needs a bit of peace and quiet so she can get on with the cooking.'

'That's OK,' Demelza said quickly. 'Ianni can help me.'

'Ooh, yes, please! What can I do?'

'You can mash these cooked potatoes and make them nice and soft. Here…let's put some butter on them… That's fine… Press as hard as you like. You can't spoil them…'

Demelza turned away from the table where Ianni was now crouching on a chair, bashing on the potatoes with a wide, happy smile on his face. Nick was standing close behind her, a tender expression in his eyes. Like his son's, his hair was still wet from the shower and he looked as if he'd thrown on the chinos and shirt very quickly because there was only one shirt button done up above his belt. The sight of his dark chest made her pulses race.

'I've never done any cooking before,' Ianni said, pounding away at the potatoes. 'Mum always says I get in the way in the kitchen. Anyway, she doesn't do much cooking.'

Nick's eyes flickered. 'Ianni, I had a letter from Mum today. She's decided she can come out to stay in July.'

Ianni continued to work on the potatoes, making no sign that he'd even heard his father.

But Demelza could see from the way he pursed his lips that he was weighing up the idea. She moved back towards the table.

'I think that's perfect now, Ianni,' she said. 'We'll spread the potatoes over the meat…like this…and then we'll put them in the oven…like so… Mind your fingers…'

She was trying to work out why Ianni's natural exuberance had suddenly diminished. He'd made no comment on the fact that his mother was coming out in July.

'It will be nice having Mummy here, won't it?' she asked lightly.

'Yes,' Ianni said, in a flat voice.

Demelza glanced at Nick. His expression was giving nothing away. She wouldn't try to probe. It was obvious there was some kind of problem with the mother-and-son relationship but that would probably sort itself out when they spent time together out here. Why else would Lydia be coming out except to be with her son? From what Nick had told her it had been an acrimonious divorce so she couldn't be coming to see Nick…or could she?

Was Lydia still holding a candle for her ex-husband? Demelza studiously avoided that line of thought.

'Let's all have a drink,' she said brightly. 'We can take our glasses out on the terrace and watch the sunset over the hills. There's a bottle of wine in the fridge, Nick, if you'd like to open it, and I've got lemonade for Ianni.'

They all sat out on the terrace, Ianni happily munching his way through a packet of crisps before helping Demelza and Nick to eat the olives.

'I keep meaning to find out how I can get my shower put right, Nick. Do you know who owns my apartment?'

Nick smiled. 'I most certainly do. You're looking at him.'

'Oh…I'm sorry! I'd no idea.'

'The villa belonged to my family. When my father died and my mother and I went to live in England, my grandparents looked after it. I used to come out to see them whenever I could. After they died I was totally responsible for the place even though my relatives used to keep an eye on it for me. After I'd decided to come and live out here, I got a builder in to deal with the major repairs and turn this top storey into a self-contained flat. The rent from the flat, which is paid direct to me by the travel company, helps to pay for the repairs and rebuilding. What is the problem with the shower?'

Demelza swallowed hard. Nick had been so positive when he'd talked about his father dying and he and his mother having to move back to England. But she could tell that it had been a traumatic time for him. And here she was worrying about her shower!

'It's only a simple thing,' she said quickly. 'I just can't get used to using a hand shower and—'

Nick clapped a hand to his forehead. 'I'm so sorry! That was one of the things I meant to have done before you came, but it completely slipped my mind. You're the first person in here. I'll speak to the plumber to-morrow.'

'Thanks.' She hesitated. 'It must have been a great relief for you to come back to Kopelos, having been born here.'

Ianni had already got down from his chair to play with a pile of small stones in the corner of the terrace which the builders had left behind. Nick didn't seem to be worried about the state of Ianni's pyjamas and Ianni was happy with the house he was building so it seemed a pity to stop him. There was nothing that a bit of soap and water wouldn't put right.

Nick leaned back in his chair. 'It felt like I was home at last,' he said, his voice husky with emotion. 'My father was born out here. Like my grandfather, he was a fisherman so he was, of course, an expert sailor. Which was why I couldn't believe it when I found out that Dad had drowned at sea.'

Demelza leaned forward. 'Do you know what hap-pened?' she asked softly.

Nick took a deep breath. 'A big storm blew up quickly after the fishing fleet had gone out. Normally, they have warning of bad weather approaching but that day the storm arrived before anyone was prepared. Five sailors were drowned, my father among them. At first they didn't tell me why Dad hadn't come back. But at the age of six…'

Nick glanced across at his son. 'Ianni's age. You're not stupid, especially when everybody around you is crying or… Anyway, my grandmother thought it would be better if I knew everything because she said I had to take care of my mother now that Dad was gone. Especially as my mother was expecting her second child. Mum had already told me why her tummy was getting bigger, I remember, and I was looking forward to having a playmate.'

He broke off and took a large gulp of wine. 'Anyway, Mum was homesick for England and her pregnancy wasn't going very well. We didn't have a hospital on the island in those days and my father's relatives worried about her. So Mum took me back to England and we stayed with my English grandparents. Three months later she went into hospital. The baby was stillborn and Mum died of eclampsia.'

Demelza could feel the tears pricking her eyes. Looking across at Nick, she could see that he'd come to terms with the tragedy but the deep scars were still inside him. That was the thing about suffering. You could get over it to a certain extent but it was always with you, buried deep, influencing the way you behaved and thought.

She leaned across the table and put her fingers on Nick's large hand. It was only a gesture of sympathy. He looked at her and she stood up and went round to put her hands on his shoulders. Slowly, he pulled himself to his feet and took her into his arms, holding her against him. She felt the warmth and strength of his body and it felt so right to be here in Nick's embrace.

And in that moment she knew she wanted to move things on. She wasn't going to hold back any more.

Both she and Nick had suffered, but life was too short to dwell on the past. Whatever kind of relationship developed, she was going to go for it. Nick's complicated background would make him wary of her intentions but she would make it quite clear that she didn't want to make any demands on him.

She pulled herself gently away from the circle of Nick's arms and looked across at Ianni. He was still totally absorbed in what he was doing. She smiled up at Nick.

'I think I'd better check on Ianni's grubby hands because supper's nearly ready.'

Nick reached out and touched her face, gently. 'I'll do that.'

'OK.' She moved quickly inside.

As she put the spinach in the pan she glanced out of the window. Nick was lifting Ianni up onto his shoulder, carrying him towards the door. She felt a surge of affection for both of them. Affection for Ianni, but a powerful love for Nick. Yes, she'd fallen in love, and her whole body felt alive again. The most she could hope for would be that Nick, given all the complications in his life, would be fond of her. That would do for the time being.

One day at a time. She would live for the moment.

The shepherd's pie was delicious, the spinach perfectly undercooked. She served fresh apricots as a dessert, but Ianni was already slumped against the back of his chair. Although his eyes were closing, he was still desperately trying to stay awake.

Nick got up from the table and carried him across

to the sofa, putting a couple of cushions under his head to make him comfortable.

'Let's have our coffee outside on the terrace,' Demelza whispered. 'It's cooler out there.'

He waited until she'd made the coffee in the cafetière then he carried the tray outside and placed it on the table. Demelza stacked the dishes in the sink before going out to join Nick on the terrace. In the moonlight she saw him rising from the table and coming towards her. His arms were outstretched and she moved into them as if it was the most natural thing in the world.

He held her against him, her head against his shoulder. When she raised her eyes she saw that he was looking down at her with that tender expression in his eyes that made her feel she was turning into liquid desire. He bent his head and kissed her on the mouth. She savoured the touch of his lips. She sighed as his kiss deepened and her body awakened to the touch of his caressing hands. She pressed herself against him and felt the sensual excitement as she recognised the hardening of his desire.

An unwelcome, ringing phone was making itself heard in her consciousness. Nick was cursing softly as he reached for his mobile. She moved out of the circle of his arms and sat down at the table. Reaching for the cafetière, she poured out a couple of cups, black and strong. She needed something to bring her back to earth. She could hear Nick talking in rapid Greek, and from his earnest face she deduced it was the hospital.

'I gather you're on call,' she said, as he broke the connection and sat down beside her at the table.

She handed him a coffee-cup. He took a sip before explaining.

'Technically, I'm always on call. You see, I'm in

charge of the running of the hospital as well as working as a hands-on doctor there. I've got a good staff but they know they can always call me when it's something they can't sort out themselves.'

'So what's the problem?' Demelza had come back to earth again. Her body was still vibrant from the contact with Nick but the moment had passed. She was in control of her senses again and it looked as if Nick was already planning what to do about some medical emergency.

'It's Maria, our hip replacement. She's in a distressed state and convinced the operation was a disaster. She's saying that she wants to see me to ask me what I did with her leg. The night staff say she's very confused.'

Demelza gave a wry smile. 'So you're going to go and help them out?'

He nodded. 'I think I should. As far as I can gather, there are no real post-operative complications but I'd like to see for myself what's happening. I don't know how long I'll be but—'

'Don't worry about Ianni. I'll keep him here all night. He'll be quite safe on the sofa and it would be a shame to waken him.'

'I usually take him round to Katerina's if I'm called out at night.'

Demelza shook her head. 'Leave him here, Nick. I'll send him down in the morning.'

'You're very kind.'

Kind! That was the last thing she was feeling. Frustrated was more like it! Having made the momentous decision that she wouldn't let anything stand in her way, she would now have to wait for another time to make it obvious to Nick that she wanted to make love with him.

But that was what it was like in the medical profession. Patients always came first and personal relationships had to be put on the back burner.

He kissed her lightly on the cheek and hurried away down into the courtyard. She was sipping her coffee as she heard the clang of the courtyard door. Nick's footsteps echoed eerily down the deserted street.

As Nick climbed up into his Land Rover and started the engine he was feeling uneasy—and not just about the state of his patient. If the phone hadn't rung just now, would he have been able to stop himself from making love to Demelza? He took a deep breath to calm himself as he drove away from the village and headed towards the town.

Just holding Demelza's vibrant body in his arms had driven him wild with desire. He wanted her, oh, yes, he wanted her! He shifted in his seat as his desire made itself painfully obvious. He hadn't planned to make love with her tonight but whenever he allowed himself to kiss her he felt compelled to follow his natural instincts.

And he mustn't. He banged one hand down hard on the steering-wheel. He mustn't—well, at least not just yet! Demelza seemed so scared of becoming involved with him, which was perfectly natural for someone who'd been through a bad patch and forgotten what it was like to form a new relationship. She'd only just come out of the cloistered world of demanding relatives and she was terribly vulnerable. He mustn't confuse the way she'd clung to him as being a sign that she wanted to make love. He would have to restrain himself before he took things too far, because he couldn't bear to hurt her. She was like a delicate flower which would be crushed so easily by the wrong person.

But it would be so hard to control himself when he was close to her! Just remembering her soft hair against his face as he'd kissed her, the curves of her slim figure against him…

He gave himself a shake as he drove into the hospital car park. Time to pull himself together and concentrate on his patient!

Demelza leaned back in her chair and looked up at the moon. Perhaps it's best that I didn't go overboard tonight, she told herself. She hadn't known Nick very long. Maybe she would have been rushing things to have given herself completely tonight and perhaps she would have regretted it.

She doubted it! It had been obvious that Nick had wanted to make love. His embrace had been ardent, every fibre of his body seeming to demand fulfilment. But would he have held off because he thought it was too soon?

She shivered and her body tingled as the memories flooded through her. Quickly, she put the cups on the tray and went inside. Ianni was sleeping peacefully, one arm flung behind his head, his lips in a contented curve as if he was having a happy dream.

She pulled the cotton cover over him. It was warm but it would become a little cooler in the middle of the night. Leaving a small lamp lit in the corner of the room, she went through into her bedroom. She opened the door wide so that she would hear if Ianni woke up and became confused about his surroundings. Pulling off her clothes and putting on a large, thin cotton

T-shirt, she lay down beneath the flimsy sheet and closed her eyes.

Closing her eyes, Nick's handsome face appeared in her mind's eye again and it was a long time before she dozed off into a fitful sleep.

She was awakened by Ianni jumping onto her bed.

'Where's Daddy?'

Demelza smiled. 'He had to go to the hospital last night. I think he'll be back downstairs by now but we'd better check. Would you like to have some breakfast first?'

'Oh, yes, please!'

She climbed out of bed and pulled on her cotton housecoat. Ianni waited for her before putting his little hand in hers. Together they carried the breakfast things out onto the terrace. Demelza stretched her arms in the air and took a deep breath. It was the sort of morning that made you feel good to be alive. The sun, already warm, was climbing higher over the sea down there beyond the red rooftops of the village.

It was quiet down below in Nick's apartment. She would investigate after they'd had breakfast. Either Nick was still at the hospital or else he was trying to catch up on his sleep. And she was enjoying having Ianni with her for breakfast.

She spread some butter and honey on his toast and handed it to him on a plate. He chewed noisily, showing his enjoyment.

'I love honey, Demelza,' the little boy said, between bites. 'The bees make it up there on the hillside but they don't like you watching them. Lefteris got stung once and Katerina was cross with him. I think she should have been cross with the bees, don't you? We were only having a look at them. We didn't mean to harm them. I can't think why bees can be so horrid and still make lovely honey like this. Can I have some more, please?'

Demelza smiled. 'Of course.'

She heard the door of Nick's apartment opening as she was spreading Ianni's next slice of toast. Leaning over the terrace wall, she saw him coming out, rubbing his eyes sleepily. He was barefoot, wearing only a pair of shorts and looking desirably sexy.

'Good morning, Nick.'

'Oh, hi!'

'Daddy, we're up here having breakfast. There's some scrummy honey. Come on up! Oh, you don't mind, do you, Demelza?' the little boy asked as an afterthought.

Demelza laughed. 'Of course I don't mind if Daddy would like to have breakfast with us.'

'Just coffee please,' Nick said, bounding up the stairs. He sank down at the table. 'Are you all right, Demelza? I mean, you hadn't bargained for…for everything that happened when you invited us for supper last night.'

His dark eyes held an enigmatic expression as he looked across at her. She knew he was remembering their passionate embrace, probably wondering if she was regretting it.

'I'm fine. I'm enjoying myself,' she said quietly.

'Good!' He reached and took hold of her hand. 'Because I enjoyed myself last night and I wouldn't want anything to spoil—'

'Dad, did I tell you that Lefteris got stung by a bee last week?'

Nick gave a wry grin. 'No, you didn't. What happened?'

'Well, we were just up there on the hill and there was this gate, so Lefteris untied the piece of rope round it so we could go in and look at the bees' houses—they're called beehives—and…'

Demelza got up from the table to go inside and make some more coffee. Ianni was still chattering when she returned.

'Just a minute, Ianni,' Nick said, breaking into the flow. 'I need to tell Demelza something about the patient I had to see in hospital last night.'

'Yes, I wanted to ask you how Maria was,' Demelza said.

'She's fine, as far as the operation is concerned. It's always a difficult time, as you know, in the first few post-operative days, but she was scared by being in hospital and simply wanted me to hold her hand, I think.'

Demelza knew the feeling! She was sure that Nick's bedside manner would be very much sought after by his patients.

Nick put down his coffee. 'I checked out the site of the prosthesis—the wound is clean. No problems there. The physiotherapist is coming in today to start post-operative exercises and as soon as we can we'll get Maria out of bed and moving around. That's not going to be easy because Maria thinks she's just going to lie comfortably there and her mobility will return as if by magic.'

Demelza smiled. 'I've known a few patients like that.'

Nick stood up. 'I've got to get moving, Demelza.'

'Me, too,' Demelza said, as she began to clear the

things from the table. 'Irini will probably be beavering away already, preparing for the morning surgery.'

'How do you find Irini?'

'She's excellent, thoroughly reliable.'

Nick smiled. 'Good. I handpicked her myself. She's related to Giorgio at the taverna, and so related by marriage to my father's family.'

'You seem to know everybody on the island.'

'It's a very close community which is one of the attractions of the place, at least for those of us who were born here. Katerina, who looks after Ianni when I'm not here, is my cousin. When we were very small we used to play together. She offered to look after Ianni for me and at first she wouldn't take any payment. But I persuaded her that I couldn't do my professional work without her so she ought to get paid like I did.'

'The people here are so warm-hearted. I haven't met anybody I dislike…but, then, I've only been here a few days.'

'It seems much longer,' Nick said.

'Yes.' She looked up and saw that wonderfully tender look in his eyes again.

Nick was obviously warming towards her but she doubted whether he was falling in love as she was. It was all too soon for him and maybe he wouldn't want to become too involved with someone who might prove to be a further complication in his life.

Demelza turned away and began carrying the plates and cups to the kitchen. Nick picked up the empty cafetière and followed her. She leaned over the sink and began swishing water around the plates.

'Thanks a lot…for everything,' Nick said.

She felt his hands lightly touching her shoulders but she didn't turn round.

'I enjoyed having Ianni here,' she said carefully.

She felt his hands gripping her shoulders and she turned to meet his gaze. He bent his head and kissed her lightly on the lips. She savoured the moment which ended all too quickly as he turned and strode away, as if kissing her had been the last thing on his mind.

Resuming the dishes, she wondered just how long she could contain her frustration. It was a good thing she had a busy morning ahead of her to take her mind off Nick!

CHAPTER SEVEN

DEMELZA switched off her computer as soon as she'd finished filing away the details of the patients she'd treated that morning. It had been a quiet surgery. She'd noticed that as the summer progressed the number of patients diminished. It was as if the now intense heat had cleared up all the coughs and colds, and most of the tourists wanted to get out on the beach and into the sea. Reporting minor ailments was the last thing on their minds. They were here to enjoy themselves in the sun, not worry about their health.

Looking out of the window now, she could see them all stretched out on their sunbeds, already soporific from the heat of the sun. Most of them were sensibly shaded by their umbrellas. She actually gave a short talk to each tour group as they arrived, telling them of the dangers of too much exposure to the sun's rays. Some of her instructions seemed to have sunk in. That was a relief! Back in May, her cases of sunburn had been bad enough, but now they'd reached July the sun was positively dangerous.

In her introductory talks she also stressed the importance of drinking bottled water, which seemed to have paid off, judging by the infrequency of gastric upsets.

July! Where had the weeks gone to? And why hadn't her relationship with Nick progressed any further when they spent so much time together? Apart from that first idyllic picnic on the deserted beach soon after she'd arrived here, there hadn't been anything remotely like a date together.

But the most frustrating thing was that Nick continued to take her in his arms sometimes, still looked at her with that tender expression that drove her wild with longing for him. But that was as far as it went!

She frowned as she got up and paced the room. The trouble was she was so naïve where love affairs were concerned. She didn't know the first thing about how to signal to a man that you wanted him! And Nick was an unknown quantity. He was Greek for a start—well, half-Greek—so it was more difficult to know how his mind worked. If she were to make it more obvious that she wanted to move their relationship on, would she scare him away? He'd said his life was complicated so maybe he was scared of becoming more involved with her.

She leaned against the window, staring out at the stretch of sand leading down to the brilliant blue sea as she realised that she couldn't change her nature. She'd had a sheltered upbringing with her caring but very strict, domineering parents. And she'd moved from being under their wing to committing herself entirely to Simon. So there'd never been any time when she'd experienced relationships with other men. It was incredible that at the ripe old age of thirty-two she should be so inexperienced! Incredible and frightening.

Demelza sighed heavily as she mused on the fact that all around her women were making the first move towards their men, but she wouldn't know how to begin!

Nick had made it obvious that he found her attractive. But was that as far as it went? Was he perfectly happy to go on as they were doing—meeting, sharing the occasional meal, stealing a kiss here and there, working together at the hospital sometimes and—?

Loud, excited voices coming from the waiting room broke in on her thoughts. Her door opened and Irini came in, looking anxious.

'We've got a very ill little girl, Sister. Will you have a look at her?'

'Of course. Bring her in.'

A distraught man was already coming through the door carrying a little girl of about five.

'I don't know what's wrong with my Sarah, Sister. She'd just started to eat her picnic out there under the umbrella when she started screaming that she couldn't swallow. But now she's gone all quiet and—'

'Let's get Sarah on the couch here,' Demelza said quickly. 'What was she eating when she started being ill?'

'We'd bought some bread rolls up in the village. Look, this is the one she was eating when—'

'Ah, sesame seeds!' Demelza said, taking hold of the half-eaten roll. 'Is Sarah allergic to sesame seeds?'

The man shook his head. 'Not that I know of. Well, as far as I know, she's never had any before. She's allergic to nuts and she had a bad reaction to a halva bar once. Her throat closed up and we had to take her to the hospital for treatment.'

'Halva is ground-up sesame seeds,' Demelza said, as she peered into her young patient's mouth.

She could see that the throat was swelling and closing up rapidly.

'Sarah's having an anaphylactic reaction to the sesame seeds,' she said evenly as she went over to the medicine cupboard. 'I'm going to give her a shot of adrenaline and some antihistamine medication. We'll have to watch her very carefully for the next few hours so I'm going to take her into hospital.'

Demelza was preparing the injection of adrenaline as she spoke. She glanced over her shoulder. 'Irini, will you phone the hospital and tell them I'm bringing in an emergency patient with an anaphylactic reaction to sesame seeds?'

It took only minutes to reach the hospital. On this occasion, Demelza was relieved that Stavros was the speediest driver on the island. Nick was waiting for them in the accident and emergency area.

He leaned over the little girl. 'Can you hear me, Sarah?'

The little girl moaned and opened her eyes. She gave a little cough, appearing for one anxious moment as if she was going to choke on her own saliva, and then, miraculously, she swallowed.

Demelza quickly filled Nick in on the details of the case—the state of the patient on arrival at the surgery and the adrenaline and antihistamine she'd already administered.

Nick nodded. 'The adrenaline's already had an effect. I'll just examine Sarah's throat.' He took a laryingoscope and peered down the little girl's throat.

When he straightened up he was smiling. 'Take a look, Sister.'

Demelza leaned over her young patient and the light on the laryingoscope lit up the throat.

'Excellent!' she breathed. 'What a relief! When I tried to examine Sarah's throat at the clinic, I couldn't see beyond the mouth.'

'Your daughter's going to be OK now,' Nick told

the father, whose hands were trembling nervously as he held onto little Sarah.

'Good girl!' the man whispered with relief as he stroked Sarah's soft fair hair. 'Mummy will be so relieved when I take you back.'

'I'd like to keep Sarah here for twenty-four hours,' Nick said quickly. 'Until we've made sure there are no further complications. The adrenaline and antihistamine Sister gave her have reduced the swelling but we need to do a full examination to see there are no further complications.'

The man nodded. 'Can I stay with her?'

Nick patted the worried father on the shoulder. 'Of course you can. I'll take you up to the children's ward as soon as I've checked Sarah over.'

Nick turned to look at Demelza. 'Thanks, Sister.'

There was a finality about his tone. She was being dismissed. He was anxious to get on with his work and she was no longer required.

She always experienced a sense of anticlimax when she left the hospital. This was where the action was. This was where real nursing was required and she realised that she would love to be on the permanent staff here. The beach resort clinic was on the periphery, though very necessary. But she'd been trained as a hospital nurse and at some point in the future she knew she would have to take on a more exacting role in her nursing career.

And the hospital was where Nick spent most of his time. He was totally dedicated to his patients and when she was working with him she felt the rapport growing between them. They worked well together. Neither of them ever mentioned this, but it was a growing professional bond that she valued.

It was a pity that their personal relationship seemed to be at a standstill!

Stavros was waiting for her when she went out into the hot midday sun. He smiled and opened the passenger door for her.

'Back to the beach, Sister?'

She smiled back. 'Yes, please.'

A couple of hours under a shady umbrella would help her to relax, and it would take her mind off Nick.

Demelza clambered over the rocks and found a quiet spot in the little bay around the corner from the main beach. A few couples were nearby but they weren't in the least bit interested in her. She could relax and have a restful afternoon. Stripping off to her bikini, she pulled out the bread rolls and feta cheese she'd bought in the village and ate her lunch.

Closing her eyes, she found herself drifting off to sleep...

A man's voice was speaking to her. Was she dreaming? She opened her eyes and stared in surprise.

'Nick! What are you doing here?' She sat up, rubbing her eyes as she tried to think straight.

He looked so out of place on the beach in his workday suit.

He smiled down at her. 'Stavros told me you were here. I'm supposed to be meeting Lydia but she hasn't arrived from the airport yet.'

'Lydia's coming today? You didn't tell me!'

As soon as she'd voiced her surprise and alarm, she wished she hadn't. It sounded as if she was interested in his relationship with his ex-wife, and there was nothing further from the truth!

Nick shrugged. 'Completely slipped my mind until Katerina reminded me this morning.'

Demelza stood up so that she didn't have to crane her neck to look at Nick. Grabbing her sarong, she tied it over her bikini, but not before she'd seen Nick's eyes lingering on her bare skin. She felt a surge of longing running through her. She wanted this man so much it almost hurt her to play the platonic friend.

Nick turned and pointed up the hill to where the road meandered its way down to the beach. 'I think that's the resort minibus arriving now. Will you come and meet Lydia with me?'

Demelza hesitated. 'Is that a good idea?'

Nick's eyes widened with surprise. 'Why not?'

She swallowed hard. This was another indication that she was merely a good friend. He wouldn't be introducing her to his ex-wife if they were more than friends, would he?

'Come on, Demelza. I can't stay long with her because I want to get back for Ianni.'

'In that case, I'll pack up here and you can give me a lift back, if that's OK.'

'Of course!' He picked up her bag.

'I ought to throw my clothes back on.'

'No time! The minibus is nearly here. You look great as you are. You can put your clothes on in the car.'

Demelza hurried after Nick, who was carrying everything for her. Her bare feet felt as if they were burning on the scorching hot sand. They reached the main building just as the minibus was pulling into the loading bay in front of Reception.

She felt like a peasant in her sarong and bare feet as Nick surged forward through the crowd around the bus.

He was still holding her bag so she couldn't even put her shoes on.

A tall, blonde woman was descending the steps from the minibus. She smiled and waved at Nick. Demelza followed him as he moved nearer the front of the throng.

'Lydia, this is Demelza, the sister in charge of the clinic here.'

Demelza met Lydia's cool gaze. Without her shoes she was smaller than this tall, elegant blonde. How could anybody get off a plane and still look so impeccably groomed? And the flawlessly painted long nails at the end of the outstretched hand were positively intimidating.

Lydia gave a tight little smile, revealing small white teeth, evenly spaced and looking as if they owed some of their symmetry to expensive cosmetic dentistry.

'So you work here? What was your name again?'

'Demelza.'

'What a quaint little name! Foreign, is it? Where do you come from?'

Demelza swallowed, trying to stem the surge of dislike that enveloped her as she stood next to this patronising woman.

'I was born in Cornwall.'

'Ah, the south west of England. I've never been there. Much too far from London for me. I can't stand muddy fields. And I don't suppose you've any decent shops, have you?' she said, casting her eyes disparagingly over Demelza's crumpled sarong.

Demelza stepped back, not deigning to reply to Lydia's ignorant observations. It was a relief that the odious woman was now giving her full attention to her ex-husband.

Lydia was smiling up at Nick. 'I thought you would have brought Ianni to meet me at the airport.'

'He's at school. Actually, he'll be home very shortly and I'd like to get back home for when he arrives.'

Lydia maintained her dazzling smile, spreading her lips even wider at the corners of her brightly painted mouth.

'Oh, well, then, I'll come with you. I'm dying to see my darling little boy! Has he grown since I last saw him?'

Of course he's grown! Demelza thought as she watched Nick's ex-wife simpering up to him. Nick might profess to have no feelings for his wife, but Lydia was certainly making it obvious she still fancied him. Was this visit meant to be an attempt at a reconciliation? The thought drove her spirits down into her bare feet.

'Don't you want to unpack, Lydia?' Nick asked quickly.

'I'd rather see you and Ianni. I haven't come all this way to be on my own. Will you ask that little man over there if he'll put my luggage in my room?'

Demelza was becoming more and more impatient as she watched Nick playing the dutiful husband. Surely he didn't have to be so helpful towards his ex-wife! Not when he'd told her how he couldn't stand the woman. Or had he been exaggerating when he'd described his disastrous marriage? Was the marriage completely over or...?

She deliberately tried to banish that line of thought as she looked across at Nick. He was instructing the tour guide how to handle Lydia's copious, expensive-looking luggage. The tour guide was looking highly put out by the request. Nick put his hand in his pocket and handed over some notes, which seemed to pacify the irate man.

Demelza turned away. She couldn't bear to watch Nick helping out his demanding wife any longer.

'Where's your car, Nick?' Lydia called.

'It's over there under that tree,' Nick said, as he rejoined them.

Lydia gave a tinkling little laugh. 'I'll never climb up to that passenger seat in this narrow skirt, Nick. Give me a hand, will you?'

Nick obligingly hoisted Lydia into the front seat. She was still giggling girlishly as she searched for the seat belt.

'Nick, be a darling and help me with this belt. I never can get the hang of these wretched things.'

Fuming, Demelza climbed into the back, trying to ignore the fact that Nick was now leaning across to fasten Lydia's seat belt. She couldn't bear to see the two of them in such close proximity. She was beginning to wonder if she should be here at all to witness this reunion!

Nick handed Demelza's bag over the seat, without saying a word to her. She began to put on her shoes and pull on her white cotton dress.

'Oh, how quaint!' Lydia said, turning round. 'Do you have to wear that sweet little old-fashioned uniform all the time?'

'Only when I'm on duty,' Demelza said, with steely calm. 'But I didn't bother to change before I went down to the beach. I was feeling tired and simply wanted to relax as soon as possible.'

'We'd just had an emergency,' Nick said, his eyes studiously on the winding road ahead. 'Demelza prevented a tragedy by quickly diagnosing that a small girl was suffering an anaphylactic reaction and giving her the correct treatment.'

'What exciting lives you medical people live! I sometimes wish I'd gone into the medical profession. There was a medical drama I was watching on the television the other evening and—'

'Experiencing medical drama in real life is very different to fiction,' Nick said shortly. 'I think you should stick to modelling, Lydia. How's it going?'

'Fantastic! I'm just about to sign another contract with that London fashion house I told you about. Yes, it's going exceptionally well. It was difficult for me to get away from London, actually, but I thought I simply had to come out and see the men in my life.'

Nick made no comment. He sprang out of the car as soon as he'd parked at the edge of the village, and flung open both doors for his passengers. Demelza jumped down but Lydia appeared to be having great problems with her skirt.

She giggled helplessly. 'Darling, I think you'll have to lift me down! Either that or I'll have to take my skirt off. Take your pick!'

'I think you should keep your clothes on around here, Lydia,' Nick said shortly. 'I'd better lift you down.'

Demelza turned away as Nick raised his arms up towards Lydia.

Lydia's high heels resounded on the ancient cobblestones as the three of them walked along the street towards the villa. Nick paused outside Katerina's house.

'Perhaps you should wait outside for a moment, Lydia. I forgot to tell Ianni that you were coming today and—'

Lydia stared at him. 'You forgot! But I told you ages ago that—'

'I know, but I've been busy and—'

'Daddy!'

Ianni came bounding out through the open door at the sound of Nick's voice. He flung himself against Nick before suddenly pulling away, aware that there was someone else there.

'Hello, Mum,' he said quietly. 'When did you get here?'

'Oh, my little darling! Give Mummy a kiss.' Lydia bent her head downwards but didn't crouch as Nick and Demelza were doing.

Her precious skirt would split if she tried to crouch, Demelza thought as she watched the unlikely reunion between mother and son. Ianni's little body was stiff as he accepted Lydia's kiss on his cheek. Whatever kind of relationship he had with his mother, it certainly wasn't very warm. But it was the relationship between Nick and Lydia that she was worrying about. That was far warmer than she'd been led to believe!

'Well, come on! Show me this family villa I've heard so much about,' Lydia said breezily.

She insisted on being given a guided tour of the whole house, showing special interest in Demelza's top-floor apartment.

'Oh, this is all very cosy, isn't it?' Lydia said, glancing from Nick to Demelza.

'Demelza's a super cook!' Ianni said. 'You should see the fantastic suppers she makes.'

'Well, lucky you!' Lydia said, looking up at her ex-husband. 'A cook and a babysitter on the premises. How long have you been here, Demelza?'

'A couple of months. My contract runs until the end of October.'

'And then you'll go home?'

Demelza was beginning to tire of all this questioning. She knew where it was all leading. The jealous streak in Lydia's nature was patently obvious.

'I may do,' Demelza said evenly. She couldn't help but enjoy the annoyed expression that flitted across Lydia's face. Keep the wretched woman guessing!

She saw that Nick was watching her. He cleared his throat. 'Well, now that you've met Ianni again and seen where we all live, I'll give you a lift back to the resort, Lydia. I expect you'll be wanting to settle in and—'

'I've got a serviced apartment with two bedrooms so that Ianni can come and stay with me,' Lydia announced. 'It's Saturday tomorrow so we can spend all day on the beach, Ianni. How would you like that?'

Ianni glanced up at his father. 'Will you come as well, Dad?'

Nick shook his head. 'No, I can't come. I'll have to go into hospital in the morning. It'll be just you and Mummy,' he finished off, his voice sounding apprehensive. 'You'll like that, won't you?'

Ianni was biting his lip, his eyes downcast. 'Will you come down when you've finished work tomorrow, Dad?'

'I'll come in the evening for a couple of hours when it's cooling down. We can play football or cricket on the beach. Whichever you like. I'll bring everything down with me.'

'And will you come as well, Demelza?' Ianni asked, his eyes beseeching her.

Demelza saw that Lydia was frowning and pursing her lips. She hesitated before answering as she looked up at Nick for some guidance as to what she should do.

'Of course Demelza will come, if she's free,' Nick said quickly. 'I'll take you down, Demelza.'

'OK,' Ianni said, his face brightening.

'Put some of Ianni's things in a bag, Nick,' Lydia said in a cool voice. 'Has he got pyjamas, swimming things, a sweater in case it gets cooler in the evening and—?'

'Goodbye, Lydia,' Demelza said with relief as she went back into her apartment.

She was thinking about poor Ianni as she made herself a cup of tea. It was all too obvious he didn't want to leave Nick. She hoped her favourite little boy wouldn't find the weekend too much of an ordeal. But Lydia was his mother when all was said and done. He should spend time with her. Maybe when mother and son were alone together their relationship would improve.

From what she'd seen, she doubted it, and her heart went out to the boy. He didn't deserve to have a mother like that.

The sun was sinking low in the sky when she heard Nick returning from the resort. Her heart missed a beat as she heard his footsteps on the stone stairs leading up to her terrace. She went to the door to meet him. He looked tired and sad.

'I hated leaving Ianni,' he said quietly.

She held out her arms towards him and he moved into the circle of her embrace, leaning his head down on her shoulder.

'I love that boy so much. I miss him so much when

he's away,' he said slowly. 'But he ought to get to know his mother again. Family is so important.'

She looked up into his eyes and saw the moist, give-away signs that he was hurting inside. Gently, she cupped his chin with her hands and kissed him on the mouth.

For a brief moment he stared at her in surprise and then his strong arms encircled her and he held her tightly against him.

'Demelza, Demelza,' he whispered huskily. 'Some-times I think you really want me as much as I want you, but I'm so afraid I'll frighten you away if I come on too strong.'

She snuggled against his hard chest. The desire surg-ing through her was giving her courage. She had to take the plunge now that she'd given Nick an indica-tion of how she really felt.

'Nick, I've wanted you for so long. I—'

She broke off and looked up at him to judge his reaction. She was surprised to find how easy it was to take the lead now that she'd decided to be completely honest with Nick.

'I want to make love with you, more than anything,' she whispered.

Nick groaned. 'If only I'd known. Why didn't you tell me before? I didn't dare…'

'I didn't know how to…and, anyway, there was never an opportunity. We were never alone long enough…'

'We're alone now,' Nick said, his voice husky with desire. 'And I want you so much, Demelza…'

His hands moved to caress her, slowly, tantalisingly, until she felt she could hold off no longer.

'Let's go inside,' he whispered, as he picked her up in his arms and carried her through to the bedroom.

He laid her on the bed and lay down beside her as he removed her clothes, kissing each new stretch of bare skin as it was revealed. She reached across to him and tore at his clothes, her fingers feeling as if they were all thumbs.

She pressed herself against him, his muscular body tantalising her senses, driving her wild with anticipation. His fingers and lips caressed her until she felt she couldn't contain her longing any longer. And when he entered her, she moved in rhythm with his body, feeling him sink ever deeper inside her until they were fused together in a heavenly sensation of orgasmic love. She cried out as wave after climactic wave swept over her, driving her to heights of ecstasy she hadn't known existed…

The sun was beaming in through the open window when Demelza awoke. Her whole body was tingling in the aftermath of their love. She turned to look at Nick, lying beside her. His dark hair was tousled, and he had one hand above his head in a position she'd seen little Ianni adopt when he'd fallen asleep.

As if sensing her watching him, Nick opened his eyes and gave her a languid smile.

'Come here,' he whispered huskily, as he reached out for her.

She moved into his embrace, revelling in the close feeling of oneness that still lingered from their ecstatic love-making. After their first initial, urgent consummation, they'd made love again…and again…and…

She realised that her recollection of what had happened earlier was very sketchy. It was as if she'd been transported to some heavenly place where the world had ceased to exist except for Nick and herself. They'd been cocooned in an ambience of sensual love which neither of them wanted to leave.

Nick's phone was ringing. He groaned as he scrabbled around at the side of the bed until he found it in his trouser pocket. Demelza thought how boyish he looked, with his hair falling over his face, as he tried to adopt an expression of professional concentration.

'Nick Capodistrias… Ianni! How are you?' He was smiling now as he listened to his son.

Demelza watched as the smile faded. 'Yes, but doesn't Mummy want you to stay? Oh, I see, she's still asleep. Well, don't you think you should wait until she wakes up before…? OK, OK, I'll come down now, Ianni, and sort it out. Don't worry, I'll be with you in a few minutes.'

Nick put down the phone and looked across at Demelza.

'Ianni wants to come home,' he said in a flat voice.

Demelza pulled the sheet up. 'I gathered that. Isn't he happy down there with Lydia?'

'I don't think so. I can't quite make out what the problem is but I'd better go down and sort it out.'

'I'll wait up here until you come back,' Demelza said quietly. 'When you have to go to the hospital Ianni can stay with me. He can have Lefteris round here to play if he'd like to and later we can all go to the beach.'

Nick pulled her back into his arms. 'Thank you for…for being you,' he whispered.

His kiss was gentle but as his lips closed over hers she felt desire stirring again. Quickly, she disentangled herself.

'You'd better go and get Ianni,' she said. 'Otherwise…'

'Don't go away,' he said, swinging his long athletic legs over the side of the bed.

She lay back against the pillows as she listened to him humming to himself in the shower.

He emerged, wrapped in one of her large white towels, looking boyishly handsome and infinitely desirable. She propped herself up against the pillows as she watched him trying to sort out the mound of clothes on the floor.

'Glad your errant landlord fixed the shower,' he told her with a grin. 'What did you have to do to persuade him?'

She laughed. 'Oh, it was easy really. A few bribes and he was putty in my hands.'

'The way I feel this morning, I'd like to build you a huge bathroom, with a Jacuzzi large enough for two and…'

He flung himself back onto the bed but she pushed him away playfully. 'I'm going to start the coffee, so go and get that boy.'

She went out onto the terrace to watch him going down the stairs. He turned at the courtyard door and waved goodbye. She sat for a few moments on the terrace considering what the future now held for her and Nick. They'd crossed the boundary of no return. They were lovers and they could only go forward. They couldn't go back to their comfortable, easygoing platonic relationship.

She leaned back against her chair and held her face up towards the morning sun. She was so happy that Nick had drawn her out of herself, made her feel alive again. She'd been so afraid of signalling that she wanted to move closer to him but last night he'd made it so easy for her.

So easy, and so ecstatically wonderful! She was totally and hopelessly in love with him now. He'd told her how he'd held off showing his true feelings for her because he hadn't wanted to frighten her away.

If he'd only known! She looked out towards the sparkling sea in the distance. 'Hurry back,' she whispered, realising with a pang that her life could never be the same again without Nick.

CHAPTER EIGHT

DEMELZA was humming happily to herself as she tossed the aubergines into a pan. A little oregano perhaps? She sprinkled on some of the herbs that Ianni and Lefteris had gathered with her on the hillside that morning. Stepping back from the cooker, she leaned against the window, taking in the full beauty of the gathering twilight.

She gave a sigh of contentment as she watched Ianni, out there on the terrace, drawing a picture of the impending sunset, his tongue clamped between his teeth in concentration. Before Nick had left to do his evening rounds at the hospital he'd told his son that they could spend the whole day on the beach tomorrow. And they'd had such a marvellous time this afternoon on the beach that Ianni was as thrilled as Demelza was at the prospect of another idyllic day.

She thought back over their wonderful day together. Nick had returned from the resort with a very subdued Ianni who'd refused to give them a clue as to why he didn't want to stay with his mother. All he would say was that he wanted to be with his dad up in the village. After Nick had gone to the hospital, Demelza had told Ianni to go round to Katerina's to call for Lefteris so that she could take both boys up on the hillside to gather herbs.

They'd had such fun up there, calling to the goats with their tinkling bells, patting the donkeys who'd trekked over from the other side of the hill, carrying

136

their heavy loads down to Kopelos town, and eating their midmorning picnic of biscuits still warm from the bakery. And when Nick had come up the path, telling them he'd got back early from the hospital so they could all go to the beach, she'd felt that her happiness was complete.

'I'm going to get some more coloured pencils from downstairs, Demelza,' Ianni called. 'There's a special red colour that would be brilliant for the sun, if I can find it. OK?'

'Fine! But don't be too long. Daddy will be back soon.'

She clasped a hand over her heart which seemed to be swelling with joy. This was the exact scenario she'd always dreamed of. A calm domestic situation shared with a wonderful, loving man, an adorable child who—

Her blissful thoughts vanished as a figure appeared at the top of the stairs. There was no mistaking that long, expensively styled blonde hair. Her spirits sank.

She moved quickly out through the open door.

'Hello, Lydia. You've just missed Ianni. He's gone downstairs for something. And Nick's at the hospital. He should be back soon so—'

'It's you I wanted to see,' Lydia said in a steely voice, as she sank down onto one of the chairs on the terrace. 'I was hoping to find you alone. If Nick's due back soon, I'll come straight to the point.'

Demelza moved towards the table and sat down on the opposite side from her unwanted visitor.

Lydia's eyes flickered ominously as she looked across the table. 'This is a very cosy little set-up, isn't it? How convenient for you to move in with the boss.'

Demelza bridled. 'I'll ignore that remark, but don't

waste any more of my time, Lydia. Why have you come here?'

Lydia bared her dazzling white teeth in an approximation of a sugary smile. 'I'm Ianni's mother, remember? Or had you conveniently forgotten? My only concern is for his welfare. Something that you seem to disregard entirely.'

Demelza gasped. 'How dare you? Ianni is like a son to me and—'

'Exactly!' Lydia's eyes flashed triumphantly. 'That's why I'm here. I know what your game is but it won't work. I came out here for a reconciliation with Nick. Did you know he actually invited me to come here to see if we could get back together again? He phoned me to say that Ianni was missing me and he wanted us to be a family again.'

'I find that very hard to believe,' Demelza said evenly. 'Nick has always led me to believe that it was over between you.'

Lydia gave a harsh laugh. 'Well, he would say that, wouldn't he? Nick's one of the boys. Always happy to have a bit on the side. He's a full-blooded man, for God's sake! How else could he manage without a wife if he didn't find himself a girlfriend to satisfy his insatiable lust? Oh, and he's got plenty of that, hasn't he? Don't you find he's fantastic in bed, Demelza?'

Demelza stood up, her eyes blazing with anger. 'I think you should go now, Lydia.'

Lydia remained rooted to her chair. 'Not until I've said what I came to say. When I was married to Nick I took exception to him having other girlfriends. That's why I chose to divorce him. But now I've come to realise that was a mistake. Some men...lusty, super-sexy men like Nick...need more than one woman to satisfy them. So when we get married again, as we will, I'll be prepared to overlook his philandering. But until we're back together as a family, I'm not going to tolerate any opposition.'

Demelza leaned both hands on the table and glared at Lydia. 'That wasn't what Nick told me. According to him, you were the one who was always having affairs.'

'Hah! Well, Nick would say that, wouldn't he? He's not going to admit that he was the one who always loved his little bit of extra excitement. But family is family and Nick knows where his duty lies. Very strong on family is Nick...'

Demelza drew in her breath. It was as if a cold breeze had suddenly blown over the terrace. She was trying not to believe what Lydia was telling her but the part about Nick's insistence that the family was all-important struck an unpleasant chord with her. She remembered that was a fact he'd stressed when they'd chatted together.

Lydia's relentlessly strident voice was continuing. 'Nick was reluctant to break up the family before and he's seen what splitting up has done to Ianni. That's why he wants me back. And that's why I want you to clear off and leave us to get our family life together again. Ianni needs a mother, his true birth mother. So stop pushing your nose in where you're not wanted. If you have any feelings for little Ianni, then let him have his real mother back. Nick and I made this family, not you!'

Lydia stood up quickly. Her wrought-iron chair fell backwards with a loud clanging sound. Demelza noticed how the noise echoed eerily around the silent hillside as if sounding the knell of her dreams. Had Nick really asked Lydia to come out to the island for a reconciliation? Was she herself simply just his 'little bit on the side'?

Lydia paused at the top of the stairs and turned round, narrowing her eyes as she glared at Demelza. 'Think about it before you carry on this wicked affair with Ianni's father. How would you like it if somebody was trying to break up your family?'

'But you're divorced!' Demelza flung back at her.

'All a mistake, I assure you. I should have been more tolerant with my straying husband. I've learned my lesson and when we get back together again I won't make the same mistake twice.'

Demelza found she was trembling as she watched Lydia going down the stairs. She held her breath until the courtyard door closed behind her and then she sank down onto the nearest chair and put her hands over her face.

A tiny hand touching her shoulder made her jump. 'Ianni! You're back! Did you find the crayon you wanted?'

Ianni's eyes were solemn as he nodded. 'What did Mummy want? I waited until she'd gone before I came back. I thought she'd come to take me away.'

What a sad thing for a child to say! Demelza brushed a hand over her damp eyes. Was she herself adding to Ianni's misery by confusing him as to where his loyalty should lie?

'Mummy called in to see me about something but she was in a hurry. That's why she didn't wait around to see you and Daddy.'

She heard the courtyard door opening and Nick called out, 'I'm home!'

Oh, what a welcome sound! Demelza leapt to her

feet and ran to the top of the stairs to wait for him. As he reached the top step he held out his arms and folded them around her. She went willingly into his embrace, Ianni clinging tightly to both of them.

But moments later she pulled herself away as she remembered this was exactly the sort of behaviour that was splitting up Ianni's natural family. She couldn't go on playing surrogate mother to Ianni and wife to Nick. If Nick really wanted to resurrect his marriage and she herself was simply the other woman, shouldn't she back off and allow Ianni to get to know his natural mother again?

She walked purposefully towards the open door of her apartment. 'I was cooking supper for all of us, but if you'd rather go out…'

Nick was right behind her, his arms on her shoulders. 'Of course I don't want to go out when you've cooked supper. There's nothing I like better than being here with you, just the three of us, and—'

'Nick!'

She swung herself around and looked up into his dark eyes. How she loved him! It was agony to contemplate ever living without him, but did she have the right to continue her affair with him?

'Nick, don't you think you should take Ianni down to the resort and spend some time with Lydia? After all, she's made the effort to come out here. Maybe if you took Ianni with you he would get used to his mother again. It's bound to be difficult for him when—'

'Hey! What's this all about?' Nick pulled her against him and held her so close she could hear the beating of his heart. 'Ianni wants to stay here and so do I. Unless you're fed up with us. In which case…'

She raised her eyes to his. 'I want you here with me,' she said quietly. 'But maybe you should try to patch things up with Lydia…for Ianni's sake.'

'I think we should stay here,' Nick said firmly as he sat down at the table next to his son. 'Wow! That's a beautiful picture you've done, Ianni!'

Ianni smiled. 'It's for Demelza.'

Demelza sank down at the other side of the little boy and put her hand on his shoulder. 'Thank you very much. I'll put it on the wall in my living room where everyone can see it.'

'Now, how about doing a picture for Mummy to take with you when you go down to see her on Monday?' Nick said.

'Do I have to go?' Ianni asked plaintively. 'I want to stay up here with Demelza.'

Nick turned to look at Demelza. Was it her imagination or did he look uneasy?

'I've agreed to take Ianni down to spend the morning with his mother,' he said in a careful, casual tone. 'Now that the school holidays are here he'll have more time to play and Lydia was upset that he didn't want to stay on with her this morning. So I've agreed to take him down for a few hours each day while she's here. It's important for him to get to know his mother again. Family ties are so important.'

Demelza felt her spirits plummeting. Yes, it was important for Ianni to get to know his mother again, especially if Nick and Lydia were planning a reconciliation.

'But I can come back here to sleep, can't I?' Ianni asked.

'Of course you can,' Nick said.

Demelza stood up. 'I'll go and get supper ready.'

'And afterwards we can go down to Giorgio's, join in the Saturday night fun. What do you say, Demelza?' Nick called after her.

She put on a bright smile. 'Fine!'

As Demelza listened to the haunting Greek music in Giorgio's taverna she found it impossible to recapture the excitement she'd experienced on that first evening here. Now that she'd fallen in love with Nick, the whole scenario had changed. She'd had no idea what kind of a relationship she'd been heading for. And when she'd finally overcome her fear and apprehension it had been only to discover that she was destined to be the other woman, not the main person in Nick's life.

That was, if Lydia was to be believed. Only time would tell. Nick seemed already to be taking steps to include his ex-wife back in his life.

'You haven't drunk your wine. Are you feeling OK?'

Nick's concerned voice interrupted her thoughts. She forced herself to smile up at him.

'I'm fine. A bit tired, but it's been a long day. And it's so hot. It doesn't even get much cooler in the evenings now.'

'But you're still happy out here, aren't you?'

She revelled in the tender expression in his eyes. 'I love it.'

'You don't have to go back when your contract runs out in October. We need another experienced nursing sister in the hospital. Why don't you stay on?'

The thought of remaining here indefinitely with Nick was very tempting, but not if he was planning a reconciliation with Lydia. And not if he needed to have more than one woman, as his ex-wife had insisted…and she should know!

Her dream was to have Nick all to herself and she wouldn't compromise. Until now he'd seemed the sort of man who would be totally committed to the woman he loved but, then, she'd only known him a few weeks. Was that long enough to find out his faults? Probably not. They were still in the honeymoon period. A honeymoon without any hope of a wedding!

She looked at little Ianni who had fallen asleep in Nick's arms. 'I think we should take Ianni home,' she said quietly.

'Let him sleep here for a while,' Nick said. 'Anna has finished her cooking. She loves to care for him.'

Demelza looked across the room to where Nick's kind, motherly aunt was watching them. As if sensing what they were saying, she moved between the tables to join them.

'Go and dance with Demelza, Nick,' she said, in her fascinatingly accented English, reaching down to take her great-nephew in her arms. 'Leave Ianni with me. He looks so like your father when he is asleep.'

She turned to smile at Demelza as she cradled the little boy against her. 'Nick's father, Andreas, was a handsome boy, just like little Ianni. He was five years younger than me and I used to look after him when my mother was busy in the kitchen. I would take him down to the harbour to watch the fishing boats coming in and…'

Anna broke off as her voice choked. 'Yes, I loved my little brother. And then when he grew up he was so handsome—all the girls wanted to be his girlfriend. The village girls didn't like it when he fell in love with Lucy—that was Nick's English mother. But I was happy about it, because she was a beautiful girl and she adored my Andreas so I didn't mind that she took him away from me. But when Andreas was drowned in the storm…'

Once more Anna had to pause. She pulled a tissue from the pocket of her voluminous cotton skirt and dabbed her eyes before continuing, 'When Andreas was lost at sea I thought my heart would break. But there was little Nick to remind me of my brother, and later on my little Ianni. Leave me here with him, Demelza. Nick is longing to dance with you.'

Nick leaned across. 'What are you two whispering about?'

'I was telling your lovely Demelza some of our family history,' Anna said. 'Go and dance and let me spend some time with Ianni.'

Nick held out his hand and drew Demelza to her feet before leading her away from the table.

The small three-piece group of musicians had struck up a soulfully slow dance after several loud, lively pieces. Nick pulled Demelza closely against him as they moved across the uneven flagstones that served as a dance floor. She could feel the beating of his heart against hers and the conflict inside her increased. Should she compromise and go with the flow? Should she take what little part of Nick's life he was willing to share?

For the moment the only decision she would make was to make no decision on the future! She hadn't had time to recover from Lydia's shock announcement about the possibility of a reconciliation. Maybe when she'd had more time she would be able to assess the situation without emotion creeping in to cloud her judgement. But until she knew if this reconciliation was really on the cards she must try to pretend it wasn't going to happen.

'You're looking very solemn,' Nick whispered, his lips close to her ear. 'What's the matter?'

She took a deep breath. 'I was thinking about Ianni having to go down to see his mother on Monday. How long is Lydia planning to stay out here?'

She watched in alarm as a veiled expression removed the tenderness from Nick's eyes.

He hesitated. 'I really don't know. She's planning to stay on longer than we initially anticipated.'

'But I thought she had an important modelling contract to go back to.'

'I think she's completely freelance so she can please herself,' he said in an even tone. 'When I was talking to her this morning she said she was going to stay on longer than she'd intended. Anyway, why all this concern about Lydia? I know you don't like her but that's understandable. She has that effect on most women. Something to do with the model image, I suppose. But you won't have to see much of her.'

'Will you?' she asked evenly.

He raised an eyebrow. 'Will I what?'

'Have to see much of her?'

He held her at arm's length in front of him. 'That's a funny question. I'll have to see her when I take Ianni down, of course. She's really making an effort to get to know him again, and after all she's his natural mother. So, genetically, they must have something in common. It would be nice if they could get together again.'

She swallowed hard. 'Yes, it would.'

'Now, come on, stop worrying about Lydia. Relax!' He pulled her against him once more and she weakened as the feel of his muscular body against hers sent shivers down her spine. She remembered how they'd made love together in that out-of-this-world experience which had lasted all night. How could she possibly deny herself the joys of their love-making now that she knew what it was like to lie in Nick's arms? She couldn't call a halt to this affair just because there was the possibility of a reconciliation between Lydia and Nick.

She had to fight to keep Nick! But only if it wasn't going to harm Ianni. If Ianni's place was with his real mother in his natural family unit then that changed everything.

One day at a time! She couldn't bear to look too far into the future.

They walked slowly back along the deserted village street, Ianni cradled in Nick's arms, sleeping peacefully. As they reached the courtyard, Nick stopped and looked down at Demelza.

'Will you sleep with me in my apartment tonight, Demelza?' he asked, his voice tender and husky with emotion.

She looked down at the sleeping child and shook her head. 'I wouldn't want Ianni to wake up and find me in your bed.'

'But Ianni accepts you as if you were his mother and—'

'Shh! I'm not Ianni's mother and I don't want to confuse him. He's a little boy who already has a mother, a mother who's trying to get to know him again.'

It was breaking her heart to say these things but she felt that she had to take a stance. It would be so easy now to snuggle up beside Nick, to feel his arms around her, to lie there in the morning, satiated with their love-making, pretending that she was the only person in Nick's life who counted for anything, other than Ianni. She could pretend she was Ianni's mother but deep down she would feel a terrible guilt for trying to steal Lydia's child away from her.

'Goodnight, Nick,' she said quietly.

She noticed the sadness in his eyes as he stooped to kiss her lightly on the lips. The confusion of her emotions continued as she hurried up the stairs and made her way into her own apartment. She expected to feel at peace with herself for having made the decision to back off.

But she didn't.

As the long, hot summer days continued with cloudless skies and relentless sun, Demelza found that she was having to deal with far too many cases of sunburn. In spite of her talks and discussions with the incoming tourists about the danger of over-exposure to the sun's damaging rays, there were still people who came out for a week, expecting to go back to the UK with a golden tan. She'd had to hospitalise two patients already and one of them had been so badly burned that he'd had to postpone his flight home.

It was now midway through August so there were many weeks to go before the cooler days of October would be upon them. She leaned forward to sort out the case notes on her desk. It had been a busy morning but everything was quiet now. This afternoon she would be able to relax and that was when she would start to worry again about her relationship with Nick.

Since Lydia had asked her to keep out of Nick's and

Ianni's life her emotions had been in turmoil. On the one hand her instinct was to fight, but on the other her love for little Ianni made her more cautious. If Nick really was planning to get his natural family back together again then it would be utterly wrong of her to interfere.

Nick was still as attentive and loving towards her, but she'd made a point of holding off making love with him since Lydia's revelations. She'd hoped that the situation would have been resolved one way or another by now, but she still felt that she was in a state of limbo.

Glancing out of the window towards the beach, she found herself holding her breath. As if to confuse her even further, she could see Lydia out there, walking down to the sea. Ianni was with her, holding her hand. And in the other hand he was carrying a brand-new football.

Nick had given Demelza a lift down to the beach resort this morning when he'd brought Ianni to be with his mother. She remembered how Lydia had rushed to the car park when they'd arrived, her make-up flawless, wearing a fabulous designer-looking sundress and the inevitable high-heeled strappy sandals. She'd reached up to put her arms around Nick's neck and kiss him on the cheek. And then she'd given Ianni the new football, which had made him whoop with delight.

Demelza could still hear his cries of happiness as he'd demanded to go straight to the beach.

'Come to the restaurant with me first, darling, for some breakfast,' Lydia had cooed. 'You can have ice cream if you like and…'

Demelza shivered at the disturbing recollections. Since Lydia's arrival last month, she had showered her son with presents and Ianni seemed less reluctant now to spend some of his days with her. His days, but never his nights. For some reason known only to Ianni, he refused to stay down at the expensive apartment Lydia was renting now for an indeterminate period. Nick had continued to bring Ianni down to the apartment several times a week and Demelza couldn't help but wonder how he was getting on with his ex-wife now that he was seeing so much of her.

She tried to tell herself that sooner or later she would find out just how real or false this reconciliation was going to be, but it didn't help her to contain her impatience. A couple of times she'd felt like challenging Nick, asking him to come clean about his intentions towards Lydia, but at the last minute she'd managed to restrain herself from upsetting the rapport that existed between them. She had no right to expect him to be faithful to her and therefore she should allow their relationship to drift along with no demands on either side.

It was always wonderful to be with Nick, even though she spent half the time torturing herself with thoughts that it couldn't last. For the moment she had to be content with whatever time they could spend together.

The ringing of the phone interrupted her thoughts. 'Sister Demelza here...Yes, Nick...'

She leaned back against her chair to enjoy listening to the sound of his voice. 'Yes, I've just finished,' she told him. 'I can come over to the hospital if you need me.'

It was wonderful to be needed by Nick! She could feel her toes tingling in that special way that happened whenever she was going to meet him. The fact that this was a purely professional situation didn't make any difference.

Nick was waiting for her in his office as arranged. He'd been deliberately professional over the phone and she'd gathered that he'd had a patient with him at the time. He stood up when she went in and motioned towards one of the seats at the other side of his desk.

'You know Bryony Driver, don't you?' he said, re-ferring to the patient who was sitting in the other chair.

Demelza smiled as she recognised the woman who'd come to her clinic back in May, suffering from de-pression.

'How are you, Bryony? You're looking much better than when I last saw you.'

Bryony smiled back. 'I feel great! That psychiatrist you put me on to has worked wonders.'

'Glad to hear it. It was Dr Capodistrias who found him for us. Are you still having treatment?'

Nick leaned forward across his desk. 'That's what we're here to discuss. Bryony is insisting that she doesn't want any more sessions with Dr Michaelis, but I'm suggesting to her that it's too soon to consider herself fully cured. And as Bryony is also your patient, Sister, I felt I should consult you. The problem is that Bryony hasn't even finished the first course of treat-ment and—'

'Excuse me, Dr Capodistrias,' Bryony interrupted. 'Now that Sister Demelza is here I can tell you the real reason. I wanted you both to know what was happen-ing.'

Their patient hesitated as she looked first at Nick and then at Demelza, as if to judge their reactions.

'You see, I've met a man...a wonderful man...

We're having an affair and I don't want him to find out I'm seeing a psychiatrist. I don't want him to think there's something wrong with me. Dr Michaelis wants me to continue treatment, but I don't think it's necessary any more. I feel so happy!'

'I'm glad you feel happy again, Bryony,' Demelza said gently. 'Are you still taking your tranquillisers?'

Bryony gave her a dazzling smile. 'No, that's the best part about it. I stopped taking them in June, two weeks after I met Costas, and I haven't had any since. I'm ecstatic! It's the best thing that ever happened to me.'

Nick stood up and came round to their side of the desk. He stood looking down at Bryony, his expression guarded.

'Are you talking about Costas who owns the fish restaurant, down in the harbour?'

Bryony nodded happily. 'Do you know him?'

'I've known him since we were children. We're about the same age. His wife died a couple of years ago and his mother has been helping him to look after the two children.'

'They're lovely little boys,' Bryony said, her voice warm with enthusiasm. 'I've always wanted kids of my own but my husband wasn't keen on the idea. Anyway, they've really taken to me and I think it won't be long before Costas asks me to marry him. The point is, I don't want anyone to tell him I've been seeing Dr Michaelis about my depression. I'm not depressed any more and I just want to get on with my new life.'

'I understand how you feel, Bryony, and I'm very happy for you,' Demelza said carefully. 'But are you sure that Costas feels as happy as you do about this relationship?'

'Of course he does! You should see us together! We're both very much in love. That's why I want to finish my treatment with Dr Michaelis and I don't want anybody to know I've been one of his patients.'

'I'll have a discreet chat with him,' Nick said, 'and we'll take you off his list of patients. But if ever you feel you need to see him again...'

Bryony gave him a beaming smile. 'That's wonderful. Don't worry, I won't need to see Dr Michaelis again. And you won't breathe a word to anyone, will you, Doctor?'

'Absolutely not!' Nick said solemnly.

'Thank you both for all your help.' Bryony stood up, shook hands with them and hurried out of the door, her feet in their high-heeled sandals barely touching the ground.

Demelza turned to look at Nick. He leaned forward and took hold of both her hands.

'The power of love!' he said, his voice husky with emotion.

'Magic, isn't it?' Demelza breathed. 'But do you think it will last?'

Nick shrugged. 'Who can say? Who can ever predict the future?'

Demelza felt this was all too close to home. 'This Costas, is he an honourable sort of man? I mean, he's not just stringing Bryony along, is he? She's a very vulnerable, unstable woman, and I wouldn't like to see her hurt again. She had a rotten experience because of her husband's infidelity and another disappointment could push her over the edge.'

Nick's eyes flickered. 'Costas is as honourable as any man I know. But, having said that, who am I to judge someone's character? He's never done anything dishonourable before. As far as I know, he was always faithful to his wife. But that doesn't mean he might be unfaithful in the future if he and Bryony get married. You've got to take a chance with love. There are no certainties in life, are there?'

Demelza suppressed a shiver. Was Nick trying to tell her something? She lived in fear of the day that he might tell her he was going to take Lydia back as his wife.

'Bryony will have to take one day at a time and enjoy her present happiness while it lasts,' Demelza said quietly.

'Hey, don't sound so pessimistic!' Nick said. 'It could last for ever.'

She put on the bright smile that always helped to cover up her true feelings. 'It could indeed.'

He leaned forward and pulled her gently to her feet so that he could cradle her in his arms. She felt herself relaxing against him, revelling in the feel of his strong athletic body so close to hers. If only she could be sure, if only…

'I needed to see you about something else, Demelza,' he whispered. 'I don't know what's been troubling you lately but it seems ages since we were alone together, really alone.'

'Nick, I—'

'No, listen for a moment. You've always got some excuse to make when I want you to spend some time with me. Your main concern seems to be that Ianni shouldn't find us together in a…well, an intimate situation. But tonight he's going to stay with Anna and Giorgio. They're putting on a birthday party for one of their grandchildren and they're having the Greek equivalent of a sleepover. I'd like to take you out to that new restaurant that's just opened by the harbour and then, maybe afterwards…just maybe…no promises… you would come home with me and we could be alone…really alone…'

Nick was looking down at her with that plaintive expression that little Ianni used when he was bent on getting his own way. Demelza reached up and pushed the wayward lock of hair away from his forehead so that she could fully appreciate the tender expression in his dark, searching eyes.

'I'd love to,' she whispered, deliberately ignoring the small voice of warning that constantly nagged her when she allowed herself to follow her heart's desires.

Slowly, he bent his head and kissed her on the lips, gently at first and then with an all-consuming passion that gave her a hint of what was to come later.

Pulling himself away, his eyes searched her face. 'Don't change your mind before this evening, will you, Demelza?'

She smiled. 'Why should I change my mind?'

He hesitated. 'Well, you seem so unpredictable at the moment. I don't understand you.'

'I don't understand you either,' she countered.

'We'll have to do something about that,' he said gently. 'But not here. Tonight…'

CHAPTER NINE

FROM where Demelza was sitting at their window-seat table, looking across the room and out through the open kitchen door of the harbourside taverna, she could see the succulent roast lamb cooking on the slowly turning spit. The fragrant aroma of the meat and herbs was making her feel very hungry as she waited for their meal to be served.

'Have some more olives,' Nick said, passing the plate across the table. 'You're probably starving, like me.'

Demelza smiled. 'Just realised I missed lunch. I got called out to see a patient in one of the resort rooms when I got back from the hospital. A young woman with asthma. She was gasping for breath when I got there so I gave her some oxygen while I checked on her medication. It turned out she'd just arrived that morning after a night flight and forgotten to take it. I stayed with her for a couple of hours until we got her breathing under control.'

'So you'll be able to eat your fair share of this special lamb they're serving. They like people with good appetites here, so I'm told. I've been looking forward to trying this place out but there was never an opportunity when we were both free.'

'You could have brought Lydia,' she said.

Nick raised an eyebrow. 'I don't know why you keep talking about Lydia. Tonight it's just us, remember?'

Demelza smiled. 'I hadn't forgotten.'

If only she could forget Lydia altogether! If only the wretched woman had stayed out of their lives, remained quietly divorced, out of sight and across the sea somewhere, keeping her flawlessly painted, immaculately manicured, useless hands off the man she herself loved!

She took a deep breath. Nick had said that tonight was for the two of them and she was going to go along with that. She was going to concentrate solely on this wonderful man, who was watching her with that quizzical gaze that told her he didn't know what to expect next from her.

'It's a great taverna,' she said, looking around her. 'I love the view of the harbour, with all the twinkling lights on the boats. We're so near the water I could almost reach out and dip my hand in it.'

Nick grinned. 'Why don't you? I'll hold your legs while you lean through the window.'

She laughed spontaneously at the mischievous expression on Nick's face. It was so good to be with him again and have him entirely to herself. He made her laugh, though sometimes he made her feel like crying because she loved him so much and she had to remind herself that until she knew what was really going on between Lydia and him, he was unobtainable.

She looked out across the calm water of the harbour at the little boats bobbing on the surface of the moonlit water. All around the harbour different strains of music floated out to blend with the happy voices of the evening revellers. Kopelos was such a magic place! The sort of place she'd like to live for the rest of her life…if only that were possible…

'You've got that look again,' he teased. 'Happy yet sad at the same time. What's worrying you now?'

'Nothing!' she said lightly. 'I'm only worried that I might die of starvation before the food arrives... Ah, here it is!'

They clinked their wineglasses together before beginning on the succulent lamb.

'Mmm, that's delicious!' Demelza said, as the delicate, tasty morsel seemed to melt in her mouth. 'And the beans are cooked just as I like them, slightly al dente so that they haven't lost any of their flavour.'

Nick reached across and topped up her wineglass.

'Hey, careful. I don't want you to have to carry me out to the car.'

Nick gave her a rakish grin. 'It's not very far and you don't weigh much, so don't worry.'

A couple of waiters were now dancing at one end of the taverna, explaining their intricate steps to the admiration of the tourists who were being encouraged to join in. The lively music was adding to Demelza's feeling of euphoria. She looked across the table and saw that Nick was watching her. He reached across and took hold of her hand.

'Are you happy now?'

She smiled as she nodded. 'It's good to get away...by ourselves.'

'I think so,' he said, his voice suddenly solemn.

'Nick...'

She hesitated as she realised that this wasn't the moment to spoil everything by asking him outright what his intentions were towards Lydia. What would she achieve if he were to tell her that for the sake of the natural family he was going to have another shot at marriage with Lydia? What she didn't know wouldn't harm her for this evening. And if he were to say the idea was preposterous he would still be annoyed at her for raising the subject.

'Yes?'

He was waiting for her to say something. Quickly she improvised. 'I'm glad that Ianni has family he can be with on the island. As an only child he could have been lonely, but he's got aunts, great aunts, cousins…'

She watched the expression in Nick's eyes change. 'One of my greatest wishes is that he won't be an only child. Some time in the future I hope he'll have brothers and sisters.'

She swallowed hard. Was that a strong enough reason for Nick to attempt a reconciliation with his ex-wife?

A waiter was placing a plate of oranges in the middle of their table. 'On the house!' he said, smiling down at them. 'And would you like some coffee?'

Nick ordered small cups of Greek coffee which Demelza had come to enjoy over the months she'd been on the island.

'When I first arrived, this coffee used to taste bitter to me, but now I love it,' she said, as she sipped the thick, dark liquid.

'We'll make an islander of you yet,' Nick said. 'Have you thought any more about taking a sister's post at the hospital when your contract runs out at the end of October?'

'When do I have to tell you?' she asked quickly.

'I'll need to know by mid-September, otherwise we'll have to advertise the post. There's no one here on the island who could fill it.'

'I'll let you know as soon as I've decided.'

'What is there to decide? I thought you loved the life out here?'

'I do!' She drew in her breath. 'But I have to be sure it…it would be right for me. Give me time.'

And give me some indication of what your intentions are! She looked across the table and felt her heart turning over with love for this unpredictable man. What exactly was he planning for the women in his life? As soon as she knew that, she could act, but until her position in his life became clearer she wasn't going to commit herself. There was no way she was going to stay on as the other woman!

She remained quiet as Nick drove up the hill to the village after their meal. He parked the car at the end of the village street, taking hold of her hand as they strolled along towards the villa. Once inside the courtyard he turned towards her and took her in his arms.

'You haven't changed your mind about staying with me, have you?' he whispered huskily.

She looked up into his eyes, liquid with tenderness. 'No, I haven't changed my mind,' she said softly, as the wonderful shivers of anticipation began to run down her spine.

Tonight was for the two of them. She would pretend that no one else existed in their lives.

He scooped her up into his arms as he carried her over the threshold of his apartment, setting her down only when they'd reached the bedroom. She reached for him as he made to leave her, pulling him down beside her as all her pent-up passion and frustration began to drive her wild with desire. His eyes registered surprise and then delight at her obvious longing for him.

He ran his hands lightly over her, removing her dress, gently at first and then with a great urgency that matched her own impatience to feel their naked skin pressed against each other. She tore at the buttons on his shirt, so that her breasts could feel the muscles of his chest and his pounding heart. Their clothes were scattered on the bed and the floor in their desperate demand for fulfilment.

With her naked body pressed against him, Demelza could feel the urgency of Nick's love for her. Every fibre of her being was in tune with his as he thrust himself inside her and drove her to a wild delirium of rhythmic ecstasy as he moved in that primaeval, tantalising way that turned her body into liquid fire.

And as she climaxed, she cried out with savage abandon as she assumed a completely new self, a new being without any worldly cares, living only for the present on another heavenly planet.

Later they slept, only to awaken again so that they could once more consummate their love. And as the first light of dawn crept over the window-sill, Demelza curled up against Nick, knowing without a shadow of a doubt that this was where she wanted to be for the rest of her life.

The sun was already warm on her skin when Demelza finally regained full consciousness and decided she ought to try to get back into the real world. But even as she stretched her arms above her head in an attempt to gain some kind of normality, Nick pulled her against him and began caressing her body with renewed urgency.

'Nick, I have to think about getting out of bed,' she whispered as his sensual fingers began to undermine her resolve.

'So have I,' he said, softly as he kissed her skin. 'But later…much later…'

* * *

It was the ringing of the phone that woke her. Demelza glanced at the clock as Nick answered it and was shocked to see how late it was. She grabbed her mobile and phoned Irini at the clinic. Irini wasn't in the least bit worried when Demelza explained that she would be late that morning. There was nothing that she couldn't handle by herself, the competent nurse told Demelza. She was to take her time about getting down to the clinic if she had problems.

Demelza finished her conversation just as Nick was saying goodbye to the sister who'd phoned him from the hospital.

'One of my post-operative patients is haemorrhaging,' Nick said briskly, as he leapt out of bed and began extricating his clothes from the pile on the floor. 'I've got to get over there as soon as I can. Do you think you could could collect Ianni from Anna's and take him down to the beach resort with you? Lydia's expecting him again this morning so—'

'Of course!'

She was firmly back in the everyday world. Duty was calling in every direction. There was only the tantalising tingling of her skin to remind her that she'd spent the night in an idyllic paradise with the most wonderful man in the world.

She hauled herself out of bed and grabbed the nearest garment, which happened to be Nick's towelling robe.

He bent over her as she knotted the belt. 'Very fetching! If you weren't knotting that so tightly I might…'

She gave him a whimsical smile as she looked up into his eyes. 'You'd better get a move on. Don't worry about Ianni. I'll look after him at the clinic if Lydia has other things to do this morning.'

'Thanks.' He kissed her lightly on the mouth and hurried to the door.

She listened to his footsteps in the courtyard until the clanging of the outside gate told her that he was gone. For a few moments she sat on the edge of the bed, allowing herself the simple luxury of a day-dream...a daydream where she was married to Nick, where she spent every night snuggled up next to him, making love whenever they felt like it. And in the dream there were more children besides Ianni...at least two more... A baby girl perhaps...

She gave herself a firm shake and hurried away into the shower. As the warm water cascaded over her, she felt herself returning to normality. She couldn't live in this fantasy world any longer, much as she would like to remain there for ever. Her problems wouldn't be resolved by dreaming...

Anna was delighted to see Demelza when she turned up on the doorstep of the house adjoining Giorgio's taverna.

'*Kali mera*, Demelza! Good morning.'

Demelza smiled. '*Kali mera*, Anna.'

Anna took hold of Demelza's arm. 'Come in. I've just made some coffee...yes, you've got time for cof-fee. Always in so much hurry, not good for you. This is Kopelos, not England. Ianni is still in his pyjamas upstairs. Sit down. I baked some little cakes today. Try one—this one with some of my home-made apricot jam...'

It was impossible to hurry away from Anna's house.

Demelza decided to take Irini at her word and take her time in getting down to the resort.

'No problem about your clinic,' Anna assured her. 'Giorgio will run you down to the beach resort when you finish your coffee.'

Demelza could feel Anna's eyes on her as she sipped her coffee. The older woman leaned forward in conspiratorial fashion, lowering her voice to say, 'How do you like Lydia, that ex-wife of Nick's?'

'Er…' Demelza looked across at Anna as she sought the right words. But there was no need for words as her hesitation spoke volumes.

'Exactly!' Anna said, in a triumphant tone. 'You don't have to tell me what you think about that woman because I can see it in your eyes. Why Nick ever married her I shall never know. It was a mistake right from the start. We all knew it wouldn't last. I was so happy when I heard they'd split up…not happy for little Ianni, of course, but Nick is a good father.'

Demelza swallowed the piece of cake in her mouth and took another sip of coffee. She liked this aunt of Nick's. They were united in their dislike of Lydia and their love of Nick. It would do no harm to open up her heart to this older, probably wiser woman.

'Yes, Nick is certainly a good father,' Demelza said carefully. 'But do you think it's enough for a child to have only one parent? Lydia told me that Nick had asked her for a reconciliation so that they could be a family again.'

'Never!' Anna said, banging her hand down on the table so that the cups and saucers rattled.

'My Nico would never want to be with that treacherous woman again. She's lying to you if she says Nick wants her back. She must be up to her old tricks again.

All she wanted when she married Nick was a…how do you say it in English? A meal ticket. A man to pay the bills so that she didn't need to earn any money herself.'

'I thought Lydia had a successful career as a model,' Demelza said innocently, still fishing for more information.

'Career? What career? She won a beauty competition in a small town when she was eighteen. Since then she's had one or two jobs in department stores, modelling the new clothes for a day or two, but nothing that paid any real money. She invents stories about modelling contracts but it's all lies. The only job she's ever had is shopping for the clothes that will make her look good and painting her face to try and make herself look younger.'

Demelza leaned back in her chair. 'So you don't think that Nick wants a reconciliation?'

'Absolutely not! But Lydia wants him back so she'll stop at nothing.'

'Thanks, Anna,' Demelza said, quietly. 'You've set my mind at rest. Lydia told me to back off so that I wouldn't upset Ianni's chances of family life, but now…'

'The only family life that Ianni needs is with you and Nick. I'll be honest with you, Demelza. It was my idea to ask Ianni to stay in our house last night because I thought it was time you and Nick had some…how do you say it in English? Quality time, I think. I've watched the two of you together and I know you were made for each other. Just as I knew the same thing when I watched Nick's father, my precious brother Andreas, with his beautiful English Lucy. Now, that really was a marriage made in heaven…which is where they both are now…'

Anna grabbed a tissue and dabbed at her eyes. 'Promise me you'll make my Nico happy by marrying him. I know—'

'Anna, you're jumping to conclusions,' Demelza said gently. 'Nick and I are just good friends at the moment…well, perhaps a little bit more…'

Anna was smiling. 'A lot more! You didn't get that happy-with-the-world glow that you've got this morning from having an early night in your own bed! So when Nico asks you to—'

'I need to know the truth about Nick's relationship with Lydia first.'

'The relationship is dead. Ask Nico. Go on, ask him…'

'It's not as easy as that, Anna. I don't want to force him into— Hi, Ianni!'

It was a relief for Demelza that Ianni had appeared to save her from what was fast becoming an embarrassing situation. Anna was seeing the delicate situation in black and white whereas there were many grey areas that needed sorting out.

Ianni ran into Demelza's arms and as she hugged him she raised her eyes to look at Anna.

Anna was smiling happily as she watched the two of them. 'Perfect,' she whispered to Demelza. 'You'll see, it will be perfect. But first you have to—'

'First I have to get down to the clinic,' Demelza said quickly. 'Irini is all on her own and—'

'Oh, Irini is a very capable girl! She got the top prize in the nursing school in Athens. The only reason she came back to the island is because she's betrothed to Demetrius who lives in the village. You don't need to worry about the clinic when Irini is in charge. She's clever enough to be a brain surgeon. I remember her first day at the village school. I said to her mother—'

'Did I hear you want a lift down to the resort, Demelza?' Giorgio interrupted as he came into the room.

Demelza smiled. 'Yes, please, Giorgio.' She stood up. 'Thank you so much for looking after Ianni, Anna. I've enjoyed talking to you and—'

'And you'll think about what I said and do something about it, won't you?' the older woman said, pulling herself to her feet so that she could give Demelza a hug.

Demelza gave her a wry smile. 'I'll have to think about it.'

Anna spread her arms wide. 'What is there to think about?'

'Leave the girl alone, Anna,' Giorgio said jovially. 'Whatever it is you're talking about, she'll make up her own mind. Come on, Demelza, let me get you down to the clinic.'

'Are you going to stay down at the resort with your mother, Ianni?' Giorgio said as he drove them down the winding road.

'Only during the day,' Ianni said quickly. 'I don't like staying there at night.'

'Why not?' Giorgio asked in a kindly voice.

Demelza noticed that Giorgio had reduced his speed to a leisurely pace. They were almost down at the resort and Giorgio obviously wanted to prolong the conversation.

The little boy screwed up his face as he thought of an answer. 'I'll tell you, Uncle Giorgio. And I can tell you, Demelza, but I know my daddy would be cross about it if I told him.'

'Cross about what, Ianni?' Giorgio asked.

He pulled the car to a halt at the far end of the car park and turned to smile encouragingly at his great-nephew.

All three of them were sitting on the front bench seat of the Jeep. Demelza reached across and put her hand over Ianni's. He clasped her fingers hard as he began to talk.

'Mum's got this awful boyfriend,' he said slowly.

'He swore at me. Told me to…well, go away. And when he stayed the night with Mum he…well, he sort of grunted, made funny noises I could hear through the wall, and I think he's horrid. But you mustn't tell Daddy, because he would go down and get cross with him and Mum would cry and it would be awful…just like it used to be when Mum and Dad were still married. A boyfriend came to see Mum one night when Dad was working at the hospital and then Dad came home and they all started shouting and…'

Ianni turned to Demelza as he began sobbing and she held him against her in a soothing embrace. When he'd stopped crying, she took out a tissue from her bag and gently wiped his face.

'What's the name of the boyfriend who comes to see your mum here at the resort, Ianni?' Giorgio asked, with steely calm.

Ianni pulled a face. 'Mum calls him Danny. He looks after the health club and the swimming pool during the day, but at night, when it's dark, he comes to see Mum. I think she likes him but I don't and I know he doesn't like me.'

Giorgio's face was as black as thunder as he climbed

down before reaching up to lift Ianni down on to the ground. As the little boy turned to walk away from the car, Giorgio whispered in Demelza's ear.

'Lydia's up to her old tricks again. She's man-mad. But the trouble is, she's looking for someone to support her and this Danny at the health club hasn't any money. Which is why she'd like to get back with Nick again. She doesn't stand a chance, Demelza. Can't think why she's still hanging around. This business of spending time with her son is all a pretence. If Nick did take her back, she'd soon show her true colours and stop the maternal bit once she was sure she'd hooked him.'

Demelza shivered. 'I'd better take him along to Lydia's. Thanks for the lift, Giorgio.'

'Be careful, Demelza. Lydia isn't to be trusted.'

'I know,' Demelza said. 'All I hope is that she's taking proper care of Ianni.'

'I'm going to have a word with Nick about that boyfriend of hers,' Giorgio said.

'But Ianni doesn't want him to know in case he creates a scene, as I'm sure he will.'

Giorgio shrugged. 'Someone has to tell him what Lydia's up to. The sooner she goes back to England and leaves Nick to get on with his own life, the better.'

Ianni was waiting for her at the edge of the car park. She said goodbye to Giorgio and hurried across to take the little boy by the hand. As they walked along to the beachfront suite occupied by Lydia, Ianni seemed to be dragging his feet on the sandy path.

'Do I have to spend the day with Mum?' he asked quietly.

'Mummy's looking forward to being with you,' Demelza said brightly, her heart going out to the little boy she loved so much. 'And you'll be coming home tonight.'

'And will you be there, Demelza?'

'Yes, I will,' Demelza said firmly. She'd come to a decision. It was all-or-nothing time now. She couldn't carry on, wondering what Lydia was up to. It was perfectly obvious now what her plans were. Giorgio was right. The sooner Lydia went back to England, the better!

She stopped walking outside Lydia's suite. All the curtains were closed. That was strange, in the middle of the morning—especially as she was expecting Ianni to arrive. Demelza went up to the door and knocked.

A bleary-eyed Lydia, holding a see-through chiffon robe around her, partially opened the door and peeped out.

'I've asked not to be disturbed except for room service... Oh, it's you, Demelza, and Ianni! But Anna phoned me earlier this morning to say Ianni was staying up in the village with her today. I'm not dressed, I haven't even—'

'Is that room service? About time!' A suntanned, muscular young man, wearing nothing but a pair of garishly coloured boxer shorts, appeared behind Lydia. 'Oh, it's the boy! I thought you said he wasn't coming today.'

'I didn't think he was,' Lydia said quickly.

Ianni was holding tightly to Demelza's hand as he tried to hide behind her. 'Don't leave me here, Demelza,' he whispered. 'That's the horrid man I told you about.'

'It's obvious you're busy today, Lydia,' Demelza said evenly, 'so I'll keep Ianni with me.'

She turned and quickly retraced her steps along the sandy path. Ianni was almost running now.

'Demelza, wait!' Lydia called after her in a horrified voice. 'I can explain!'

'I bet you can!' Demelza said, through gritted teeth.

'Can I really stay with you today, Demelza?' Ianni said, breaking into a full run to keep up with her. 'I can help you at the clinic. I'm going to be a doctor, you know, like Daddy. If you get a patient with a cut finger, I know how to put a plaster on. You just peel back the bits on the top till you get to the sticky bit and then you fold it round like this.'

Demelza squeezed his hand tightly. 'Of course you can stay with me, Ianni.'

They were already walking into the clinic and through to Demelza's consulting room. Going inside, she found Irini behind the curtains, leaning over a patient on the examination couch.

'Would you like to sit with Irini in Reception and draw me a picture, Ianni?' Demelza said quickly, giving him pencils and paper before he skipped back into the other room.

Behind the curtains, Irini filled her in on the details of the case before she went and sat with Ianni. The patient was a girl of nineteen called Selina who'd come out to Kopelos with her boyfriend and another couple. The other three had gone off to another island for the day. Selina had been going to go with them but she'd started to feel ill so had stayed behind.

Demelza became focussed on their patient as she leaned over her. Irini had told her that Selina was in a lot of abdominal pain.'

'Tell me exactly where it hurts most, Selina,' she

said, as she palpated the girl's abdomen, her experienced fingers working their way across the tense tissue.

Selina cried out in pain as Demelza's fingers pressed on the lower right side of her body.

'Sorry, Selina,' Demelza said gently. 'I just had to be sure where you were hurting. Just relax if you can. I'm going to give you something to ease the pain.'

She felt for the girl's pulse. It was rapid and faint. The reading on the chart also showed that her temperature was dangerously high.

'I want to take you to the hospital, Selina,' Demelza said. 'I'd like the doctor to see you, so I'm just going to give him a call.'

Demelza got through to Nick at the hospital fairly quickly and put him in the picture.

'I've got a nineteen-year-old girl with acute pain in the right iliac fossa, high temperature and rapid but faint pulse. It could be appendicitis or it could be an ectopic pregnancy. Either way, I'd like you to see her as soon as possible.'

'I'll phone Stavros and instruct him to bring you here while you prepare the patient,' Nick said quickly.

'Oh, and just one more thing, Nick. I've got Ianni with me. Lydia was…well, she didn't know he was coming today and she's…she's otherwise engaged.'

'But it was all arranged yesterday!'

'A mix-up. Anna had phoned to cancel the arrangement.'

'I can't think why she'd want to do that.'

Demelza knew exactly what Anna was up to! But there was no time to enlighten Nick now. 'Must go. See you in a few minutes.'

Ianni sat in the hospital reception, putting the finishing touches to the drawing he'd started at the clinic, whilst a couple of young nurses stayed close by to spoil him and give him anything he asked for.

In the small ante-theatre, Nick and Demelza leaned over their patient. Nick had decided to operate and Selina was now sedated.

From the answers she'd given to their questions, and taking into account all the clinical signs, it seemed likely that Selina was suffering from an ectopic pregnancy. She'd told them she hadn't had a period for two months. She was hoping she was pregnant because she and her boyfriend would like to have a baby.

Demelza looked down at her patient. It looked as if the baby that they'd hoped for had implanted itself in one of the two Fallopian tubes that led from the ovaries to the uterus. If the diagnosis was correct, the fertilised egg had implanted itself in the narrow tube. Now that it was growing bigger, it was dangerously close to bursting out through the wall of the tube.

A rupture of the Fallopian tube could be very dangerous. Demelza had seen a patient suffering from this in the past and she had nearly died from internal bleeding. So the sooner Nick operated the safer it would be.

Demelza had agreed to assist him. Having had the necessary experience, it seemed natural that she should want to be with her patient throughout the operation. The anaesthetist was preparing to administer the general anaesthetic. Now fully scrubbed and gowned, Demelza followed Nick into Theatre.

She looked across at him a short time later, under the bright lights as he located the minuscule embryo in the Fallopian tube. The tube had suffered from the trauma of being stretched to such a degree that it was now completely unviable.

'I'll have to excise the tube,' Nick said quietly. 'It can't be saved. But she still has a healthy tube on the other side which should be capable of functioning and delivering an egg into the uterus at a future date.'

Demelza nodded. 'It's never easy to explain all this to the patient afterwards.'

'I'd like you with me when we do that,' Nick said, his dark, expressive eyes above the mask looking straight at her.

'Of course,' she said.

Demelza gave Selina a few hours to recover fully from the effects of the anaesthetic before she broke the sad news that because the embryo had started growing in the wrong place it had been necessary to remove it, along with the damaged Fallopian tube, before it endangered her life.

Selina raised herself up from the pillows in the hospital bed and clung to Demelza as she cried softly.

'You've got another healthy Fallopian tube, Selina. When you feel strong enough, you can try for another baby,' Nick said, leaning over Demelza to comfort Selina.

'We hadn't intended to have a baby, me and Mark,' Selina said softly. 'But when I thought I might be pregnant, I got excited about it. And Mark wanted us to get married as soon as we got back from this holiday.'

'Mark's waiting outside,' Demelza said gently. 'Would you like to see him now?'

Selina gave a sad smile. 'Yes, please.'

Nick went outside to bring in a young man, who rushed over to Selina's bed and put his arms around her, holding her closely whilst he whispered comforting, soothing words.

Nick put his arm around Demelza's shoulders. 'Time for us to go.'

He turned to look at the night sister who'd just arrived for her turn of duty, and said something in rapid Greek.

'I've asked Sister to call me on my mobile if there are any problems,' Nick said, as he and Demelza walked out of the obstetrics ward.

Nick was carrying a sleeping Ianni in his arms. Before he'd gone into Theatre he'd suggested that Ianni might like to go to play with Lefteris at Katerina's house, but Ianni had been adamant that he wanted to stay at the hospital if that's where Demelza was working.

'I've never known Ianni to be as clingy as he was today,' Nick whispered, as he tucked up his little boy on the back seat of his car. 'Have you any idea what brought all this on?'

He settled himself in the front seat. Demelza fastened her seat belt beside him. She wanted very much to enlighten Nick, but Ianni had expressed his fear about how his father would react to the news that Lydia had another boyfriend.

'I'm not sure,' she said quietly, playing for time to consider the situation.

'Why are you being so secretive, Demelza?' Nick asked as he started up the engine and they moved forward into the darkness, away from the now silent hospital where only the muted nightlights shone out across the bay. 'You know something, don't you? I suspect it's something to do with Lydia and I've a pretty good idea what it might be. If it's affecting Ianni, please, tell me. I want to know everything that went on today before you came.'

'I'm trying to decide how much I should tell you.'
She turned to look at Nick's stern profile as he turned
the car into the deserted village street. 'I don't suppose
Giorgio has been in touch with you today?'

'Demelza, I've been in hospital all day. Tell me what
you know.'

Demelza shivered at the sound of Nick's harsh voice.
She remembered how Ianni had told them about Nick's
anger when he'd discovered Lydia's boyfriend.

'Let's get back and settle Ianni in his own bed first,'
she said firmly.

CHAPTER TEN

DEMELZA tucked the cotton sheet around the sleeping Ianni as she settled him in his bed. He stirred as she kissed his cheek but didn't wake up.

'Ianni's fast asleep,' she said, as she went back into the living room.

Nick looked across at her. 'Come here and tell me what's been worrying him today.'

She deliberately settled herself on a chair at the other side of the small drinks table from Nick. She wanted to be able to watch his reaction to the news that his ex-wife, whom he may or may not have planned to remarry, was up to her old tricks again. She hoped he wouldn't raise his voice and waken Ianni.

'Would you like a glass of wine, Demelza?' Nick said, in a polite I-am-the-host voice.

'Later, perhaps.'

In spite of the warm temperature in the apartment, Demelza felt that the atmosphere was decidedly cool. She cleared her throat as she prepared to enlighten Nick.

'When I took Ianni down to see Lydia today, she had somebody with her.'

Nick frowned. 'Not the pool boy? Tall, about twenty, longish blond hair…?'

Demelza stared at him, perplexed. 'Did you know about Lydia's boyfriend?'

He gave a resigned sigh. 'Lydia's always had boy-friends. Danny is the man of the moment, so I'm told.

Trouble is, he's got no money so he won't be any use to Lydia.'

'That's what Giorgio said. He told me that Lydia is looking for a man who can keep her financially. He was planning to tell you what she was up to but—'

'Demelza, I understand my ex-wife perfectly! I was just putting on an act while she was here for Ianni's sake. I was being as polite and civil as I could. It was a big strain, I can tell you, but I knew that it was my duty to allow Ianni to get to know his mother again. When Lydia told me she wanted to come out here to see him, I thought it was only right that she should be able to make contact with her son again. I had hoped they might have got on better than they did, but I can see that nothing has changed. That's why I've given Lydia her marching orders.'

Demelza leaned forward. 'What do you mean?'

'I've given in her notice for the expensive apartment I was paying for. While there was a glimmer of hope of a successful mother-and-son relationship developing I was prepared to pay, but as soon as I found out that Lydia was seeing boyfriends again, I put a time limit on it. She goes back to England next week.'

'But when did you find out?'

'I've suspected this might be happening from the beginning when Ianni refused to sleep down there at Lydia's apartment after the first night. I didn't want to upset Ianni by asking him outright what the problem was but I had a pretty good idea. So I asked a couple of staff members to keep an eye on Lydia for me. They soon reported back about her toy boy, and that was when I was determined to make sure Ianni only went down to see his mother during the day. Lydia usually only entertains her boyfriends at night so I thought

Ianni would be perfectly safe. If I'd thought for one moment that Ianni was going to have to cope with—'

'Lydia was under the impression that Ianni wasn't coming down this morning,' Demelza interjected quickly, as she saw how angry Nick was becoming when he realised how Ianni had suffered. 'That's why Danny was still there.' She paused.

'Lydia came to see me soon after she arrived on the island,' she went on quietly. 'She tried to convince me that she'd been a dutiful wife and that it was your infidelity that broke up the marriage.'

Nick raised an eyebrow. 'She certainly can spin a good yarn! But anyone who knows Lydia will soon realise that she's a compulsive liar. I'm sorry she imposed herself on you and I wish I'd been there to shield you from her. I know how vitriolic she can be, and I could see, right from the start, that she regarded you as her rival.'

'But did you know she was trying to get you back?'

'Of course I did! Lydia is devious but utterly transparent! All that little-girl-help-me-down stuff she put on when she first arrived. It would have been amusing if it hadn't been so painfully obvious what she was up to. She's tried so many tricks to get me back but she must realise by now that I can't stand the sight of her. She wasn't fooled by me being polite when it mattered. She knew I was only doing it to keep the peace for Ianni's sake and it was wishful thinking on her part to think that I could possibly have any feelings for her.'

His eyes were troubled as he looked at Demelza. 'So it was Danny who upset Ianni, was it?'

'Ianni told me he didn't like Danny,' Demelza said evenly. 'He said he didn't want you to know about him because you would start shouting at Lydia and she would cry and—'

'Oh, my God, how Ianni has suffered because of me…' His voice choked with emotion.

Demelza leapt to her feet and went round the table to sit beside Nick, cradling him against her. 'Ianni's OK now that he's just with you. None of this was your fault, Nick.'

Nick raised his head. 'That's why I had to divorce Lydia. I felt nothing for her when I found out what she was really like. I thought it would be better for Ianni to live without all the anger and quarrelling that occurred because of Lydia's affairs.'

'Lydia told me that the two of you were hoping for a reconciliation. Every time you were with her I thought you might be getting back together. And for a while I…' She broke off as the awful memories came flooding back.

Nick drew her into his arms. 'I wish I'd been with you when Lydia invented the preposterous idea of a reconciliation! But if I *had* been there, she wouldn't have dared to spin her lies. The only woman I want in my life is you, Demelza. I want us to be together for ever and ever. I've been longing to ask you… Dare I hope that…? What I'm trying to say is…will you marry me?'

Demelza looked up at him, her heart beating so rapidly that she felt sure he could hear it. This was what she'd longed for but had hardly dared to hope would ever happen.

'Yes, I'll marry you,' she whispered, watching his expression change to sheer joy.

He kissed her gently on the lips with such tenderness that she felt her heart would burst with happiness.

'How do you think Ianni will react when we tell him?' she asked as she drew herself away.

Nick smiled. 'You must know he'll be over the moon! You've been so wonderful with him. You're the mother he should have had.'

'Don't say that,' she said quickly. 'I didn't try to replace his mother. I simply—'

'You can't be Ianni's birth mother, but you've already replaced Lydia in his affections.'

She looked up into Nick's eyes, so full of tenderness and love as the full realisation hit her that her dream was coming true. She wasn't going to think about all the problems of marrying someone who already had an ex-wife. She could cope with whatever came along if she held first place in Nick's heart.

He bent his head and kissed her once more. As his kiss deepened, he scooped her up into his arms and carried her through to his bedroom.

'You will stay with me tonight, won't you?' he whispered, as he laid her down on the cool cotton sheet. 'Now that we're engaged to be married, it doesn't matter if Ianni wanders in tomorrow morning.'

She smiled up at him, leaning forward to tug at the buttons of his shirt. 'Of course I'll stay. I'll stay for ever…'

The rosy glow from the morning sun pouring through the open window was trying to penetrate her eyelids. Slowly Demelza opened her eyes and looked at Nick lying beside her, his hair all rumpled, his mouth curved into a smile, as if he were reliving their passionate night.

She hadn't thought it possible to be so in love that you wanted to stay awake for the whole night. It had been blissful to turn over, try to sleep for a short while and then feel Nick's hands caressing her awake once more...turning to him, feeling the hardness of his insatiable body and being completely united with him in a wild, passionate embrace that climaxed in an ecstatic heaven far away from the real world.

Nick's phone was ringing. Demelza sighed. The real world was forcing itself upon them. They couldn't stay up on cloud nine entirely.

Nick groaned as he reached out, his fingers scrabbling around on the bedside table.

'Nick Capodistrias,' he mumbled. 'Ah, Giorgio.' He launched into rapid Greek which Demelza found impossible to follow. He was laughing as he put the phone down.

'My Uncle Giorgio sends his love and he's delighted with our news.'

'You told him already about...that we're going to be married?'

Said like that, she could barely believe it was happening—but it was. She'd agreed to marry the most wonderful man in the world and...

'Of course I told him. That's why he was ringing. To tell me to get rid of Lydia and marry you at the earliest opportunity. I told him it was all taken care of. So now he's off to tell Anna who will go round the village and invite everybody to the wedding.'

'But we haven't set a date yet, Nick.'

'The sooner the better. How about September?'

She took a deep breath. 'Make it October. It won't be quite so hot and I'll have time to get used to the idea that I'm going to be Mrs Nicholas Capodistrias. We'll also have to decide on a church and a place for a reception and—'

'All taken care of already. Giorgio and Anna think we should marry at the church above the harbour where my parents were married. And they will host the reception at Giorgio's taverna. And I warn you that Greek weddings can go on for days.'

'Don't you think we should go and waken Ianni and tell him what's happening?' Demelza said happily.

Nick gave her a rakish smile as he pulled her against him. 'Not yet... This is our time, before the family wakes up. We'll have to set our priorities for when we have more children, won't we? You do want our own babies, don't you, Demelza?'

She snuggled against him and gave herself up to the desire that was sweeping over her once more. 'Oh, yes. I want lots and lots and—'

'Better make a start now,' Nick whispered.

EPILOGUE

'I STILL can't believe we've been married for a whole year,' Demelza said, as she moved a couple of anniversary presents from the living-room table into the bedroom. 'Everybody has been so kind today at our lunch party, but I thought they'd never go!'

She flung herself down onto the bed and kicked off her shoes. 'These shoes are killing me. Far too posh for a wedding anniversary, but I thought I ought to look the part. Likewise this dress! Do you think we can duck out of the evening session at Giorgio's?'

Nick climbed on the bed beside her. 'Not a chance! Wedding anniversaries are nearly as prolonged as weddings. Remember how ours went on for the best part of a week?'

Demelza laughed as she began unbuttoning the low-cut silk bodice of the dress Katerina had designed and made for her. 'This dress is utterly exquisite but far too hot, even for October.'

'Let me do that for you, darling,' Nick said, leaning over her as he finished off the final silk-covered buttons.

Demelza smiled up at him. 'A dangerous move for me to start taking my clothes off if I've got to go out again.'

Nick gave her a wolfish grin. 'We've time for a short siesta. When is Katerina bringing the children back?'

'She begged to be allowed to keep the twins at her house for a couple of hours so that her own children can get to know them. And Ianni, of course, wouldn't let them out of his sight so he's gone, too.'

Nick leaned back against the pillows and put his arm around Demelza's shoulders. 'He's so proud of his little sisters.'

'I was pleased that he found Lucy and Anna interesting when they were born in June but he's delighted now they're four months and beginning to become real individuals. The best is yet to come.'

Nick sighed. 'You can say that again! My mother would be so proud her granddaughter's her namesake.'

'And Anna is over the moon every time she holds little Anna!'

Nick rolled onto one side. Poised on one elbow, he looked down at her with that tender expression that always melted her heart.

'So, all in all, we've made a good start on our family,' he said softly. 'When you've recovered from the twins we could have one or two more, couldn't we?'

Demelza smiled up at him. 'Oh, I'm sure that could be arranged, Doctor. In fact, I've made a start already.'

Nick's eyes widened. 'You mean… Demelza, what are you saying?'

'I did a pregnancy test this morning, but I wanted the twins to have pride of place today before we announce there's another baby on the way.'

He pulled her gently into his arms and kissed her lovingly on the lips. 'You're amazing!'

She smiled. 'I had some help, didn't I? I particularly remember that the twins' conception was fun. I think it was that evening last September when we went down to our deserted beach for a swim and afterwards… Good thing nobody was counting dates when we were married.'

Nick laughed. 'Oh, I think they probably were, but who cares?' He looked earnestly into her eyes. 'Do you still have the same medical theory about pregnancy and making love?'

She gave him a languid smile. 'You mean my tried and tested theory that if the mother is healthy, making love can be beneficial, Doctor?'

Nick ran his tantalising fingers over her skin. 'Exactly that, Sister!'

She snuggled against him. 'Why don't we find out…?'

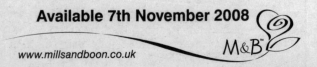

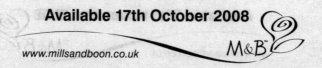

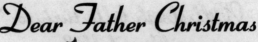

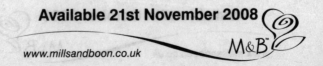

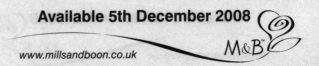

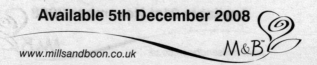

Celebrate 100 years of pure reading pleasure with Mills & Boon®

To mark our centenary, each month we're publishing a special 100th Birthday Edition. These celebratory editions are packed with extra features and include a FREE bonus story.

Plus, you have the chance to enter a fabulous monthly prize draw. See 100th Birthday Edition books for details.

Now that's worth celebrating!

September 2008

Crazy about her Spanish Boss by Rebecca Winters
Includes FREE bonus story
Rafael's Convenient Proposal

November 2008

The Rancher's Christmas Baby
by Cathy Gillen Thacker
Includes FREE bonus story *Baby's First Christmas*

December 2008

One Magical Christmas by Carol Marinelli
Includes FREE bonus story *Emergency at Bayside*

Look for Mills & Boon® 100th Birthday Editions at your favourite bookseller or visit
www.millsandboon.co.uk

0908/CENTENARY_2-IN-1